T0059317

✠A CONSPIRACY OF TRUTHS✠

ALSO BY ALEXANDRA ROWLAND

A CHOIR OF LIES

A CONSPIRACY ✠ OF TRUTHS ✠

Alexandra Rowland

SAGA PRESS

LONDON SYDNEY **NEW YORK** TORONTO NEW DELHI

SAGA PRESS

AN IMPRINT OF SIMON & SCHUSTER, INC.

1230 AVENUE OF THE AMERICAS, NEW YORK, NEW YORK 10020

This book is a work of fiction. Any references to historical events, real people, or real places are used fictitiously. Other names, characters, places, and events are products of the author's imagination, and any resemblance to actual events or places or persons, living or dead, is entirely coincidental.

Text copyright © 2018 by Alexandra Rowland

Map on pp. vii–ix by Drew Willis

All rights reserved, including the right to reproduce this book or portions thereof in any form whatsoever. For information address Saga Press Subsidiary Rights Department, 1230 Avenue of the Americas, New York, NY 10020

SAGA PRESS and colophon are trademarks of Simon & Schuster, Inc.

For information about special discounts for bulk purchases, please contact Simon & Schuster Special Sales at 1-866-506-1949 or business@simonandschuster.com.

The Simon & Schuster Speakers Bureau can bring authors to your live event. For more information or to book an event, contact the Simon & Schuster Speakers Bureau at 1-866-248-3049 or visit our website at www.simonspeakers.com.

Also available in a Saga Press hardcover edition

Book design by Nicholas Sciacca

The text for this book was set in Adobe Jenson Pro.

First Saga Press paperback edition July 2019

10 9 8 7 6 5 4 3 2 1

The Library of Congress has cataloged the hardcover edition as follows:

Names: Rowland, Alexandra, author.

Title: A conspiracy of truths / Alexandra Rowland.

Description: First edition. | New York : SAGA, an imprint of Simon & Schuster, Inc., [2018]

Identifiers: LCCN 2017047551 | ISBN 9781534412804 (hardcover) | ISBN 9781534412811 (pbk) | ISBN 9781534412828 (eBook)

Subjects: LCSH: Storytellers—Fiction.

Classification: LCC PS3618.O8767 B66 2018 | DDC 813/.6—dc23

LC record available at https://lccn.loc.gov/2017047551

For my father,

WHO KNEW A THOUSAND STORIES

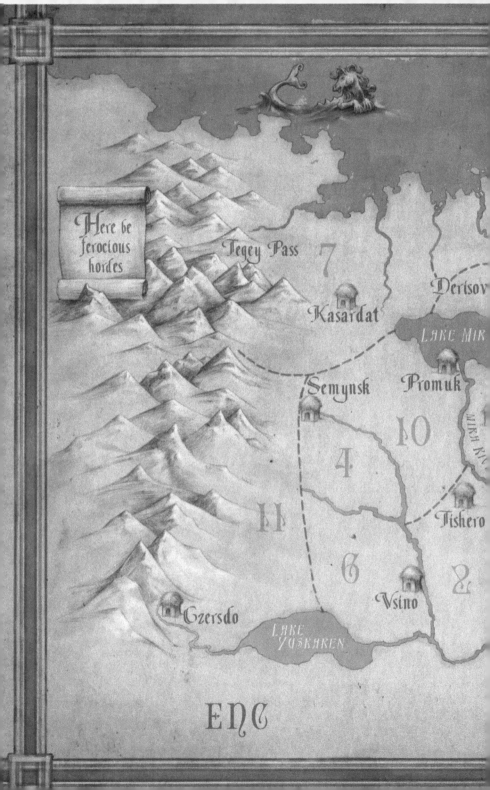

NURYEVET

Drawn in 1182 for the King of Coin Evitsen Perhotat

Zlavoi

5

Byerdor

Menova

14

GREY SEA

3

8

9

ovazska
Tova

12

Cayle

13

Uzlovaya

Vsila

1

BAY OF VSILA

OSERED RIVER

CORMERRA

The whole mess began in a courtroom in Vsila, the capital of Nuryevet, where I was being put on trial for something stupid.

"What's all this about?" I said, not for the first time.

"Charges of witchcraft," they said; at least, that was what it boiled down to.

"Utterly ridiculous," I said.

"We got some witnesses," they said.

"Your witnesses can go fuck themselves," says I, although not in so many words.

I couldn't even hear the witnesses from where I was sitting. The guards had stuffed me in an iron cage at one end of this giant fucking hall in the House of Justice, and of course it makes sense to *someone* to put the witnesses at the other damn end, as far away as possible from the man accused, like I was an afterthought of some kind.

Worst acoustics I've ever heard! I kept shouting, "What? Speak up!" and, to one of the guards near me, "Is someone speaking over there? What's happening now?" and generally making a nuisance of myself until the bored lawyer with whom they had begrudgingly supplied me turned around and shushed me.

Says she, "Can you prove you're not a blackwitch?" First thing she ever said to me. *Can you prove you're not a blackwitch?* And, of course, that was Consanza. That was how I met her. Don't like her any more now than I did then. Less, probably.

"Can you prove I am?" says I.

"The witness just now said you pointed at her cow and it died."

I rolled my eyes.

"And the one before that said she heard you talking and felt a chill up her back like the claws of a ghost. She said your familiar is haunting her house now."

"Excuse me?"

"Noises at night, something crawling across her bed."

"Tell her," I said, projecting my voice loud enough to be heard clear at the other end of the damn hall, "tell her that it sounds like some kind of vermin. A cat or a dog would take care of it."

"Hush. You're confessing? What was it, a plague of rats?" Still bored, cheeky twit!

"No," I says to her, "I'm saying that it's foolish to accuse someone of witchcraft when there are much more reasonable explanations."

She was shaking her head before I even finished my sentence. "No, she has an icon of Brevo hanging in her kitchen." Some homely little fireplace god, I suppose, or a saint. I never found out. "And the master of the public house where you were arrested testified too, and *he* said that the cask of beer he served you from went sour."

"It was sour to begin with!"

Consanza shrugged at me and turned back to face the rest of the courtroom. "Just don't make noise or they'll add 'disrespect of the court' to your charges." She did something horrible with her face for a moment, and then stuck nearly her entire hand in her mouth. "Oh, finally," she said, and spent the next ten minutes making a thorough examination of the shard of corn husk she'd extracted on one fingernail. Didn't pay a lick of attention to the proceedings. I tell you!

Still couldn't hear a damn thing, but I kept my mouth shut. Witchcraft was enough of a hassle; disrespect of the court was something they would actually have evidence for.

I'd never been in a Nuryeven court of law before. Completely dull country, Nuryevet, I'll tell you that now, not that I need to point it out. Wouldn't have even bothered passing through, but the kid wheedled me into continuing north. He was a little homesick, I think, and we hadn't seen a proper winter in years.

Don't know why I keep picking up apprentices; more trouble than they're worth, but it's part of the job, training the next one. I would have preferred another year or two in Ondor-Urt. The heat does a body good, and *they* have some basic fucking respect for their elders, once you convince them that you're hale enough (and have teeth enough) to stomach more than goat-urine soup and that vile tea. I still hold they slipped goat urine into the tea, too, even though Pashafi—my Ondoro host—swore up and down that they didn't.

Nothing but these smelly, muddy gray towns and this dull wilderness in Nuryevet. Not even interesting landscapes, even farther east from here. Just scrubland and rocks and a few halfhearted hills until you reach Vsila and the ocean, and then of course there are those uninspired mountains in the west. Hardly any decent farmland. It's astounding how superstitious they are, considering there is literally nothing around to jog their imaginations. Even their magic is scanty and twisted, and it only manifests with the blackwitches, common enough to be a problem and to dull the Nuryevens' sensitivity to the presence of magic, just as a baker's hands are dulled to heat, but rare enough that no one quite knows how to deal with them, except through rumor, hearsay, and apocrypha—and I assure you, there are rumors aplenty. Stories from the whole region, in this corner of dull, dreary land, are chock full of the creatures. It's a perverting kind of magic. There aren't any *good* blackwitches, you know.

When I was first arrested, I'd overheard some talk of just killing me outright, but I suppose that the circumstances were muddled enough and the paperwork for executions complex and tedious enough that the backcountry civil servants of the Ministry of Order preferred to pass me up the food chain rather than endure that ordeal themselves.

Nuryeven bureaucracy might have been the one key thing that saved my life, come to think of it. They didn't quite know whether I was a witch, being unable to sense the presence of foul magics, but what they did know was that paperwork could be evaded if you were clever. Put it off long enough, go to twice the effort you would have spent in the first place, and irritants like doing the paperwork eventually become a problem for other, less clever people.

My apologies. I've gotten distracted.

I reached out between the bars, as far as I could, and just managed to tap Consanza on her shoulder.

"What?" she grunted.

"I want to be able to hear what they're accusing me of, at least."

"What for? Curiosity?"

"So I can defend myself," I hissed back. My feet and knees ached from standing in that little cage for so long. There was hardly room to turn around, let alone to stretch my bones.

"Defend yourself?" She glanced back at me, eyebrows drawn together. There's really no expression that would make her face look any prettier. Her nose could fell an entire oak forest, and her eyebrows are on the unruly side, thick and black, with a trail of hair in between.

"I'm allowed to speak in my own defense, aren't I?"

She just stared at me with that idiot expression on her face.

"It's not like *you're* doing me any good," I added. "Although I suppose the court would have no choice but to be impressed with your oral hygiene."

"People accused of witchcraft have never been put on the stand. Isn't done. Well, except at the end, when you go up to receive your death sentence. Technically, you should be gagged, but the guards in the Grey Ward said you'd been very well behaved." She turned away again, her long robes swishing against the ground. "Except for being unbelievably rude."

"I haven't got a lick of magic in me!" I roared at her. "And even if I had, I'm from Kaskinen! We don't *have* blackwitches in Kaskinen. It ain't in our fucking water, woman—I'm a goddamn Chant!"

"Shut up," she snapped at me, but the court had fallen silent.

One of the five judges behind the bench sighed heavily, audible now even halfway across the hall. "Scribe, add 'blatant disrespect of the Sovereign Court in the second degree,' and 'obscene profanity in the presence of an acting court official in the first.'"

"Let's table the witchcraft charges for a moment and get the new ones out of the way," creaked the judge on the far end. "It's nearly lunchtime."

The panel made some mumbles of agreement and summoned me up before them. Well, that was one thing in my favor. The cage was opened, they clapped chains on me, and Consanza tugged me out by my sleeve, steering me ahead of her towards the bench, across miles and miles of stupid excess courtroom.

They have to have miles of stupid excess courtroom: no real schools of law. Students just sit in court and watch hearing after hearing for years. Has to be plenty of room for them. The particularly keen ones fight for seats in the front-most rows. Consanza did not strike me as one who had been particularly keen.

She gave me a bit of a shove when we made it to the bench, and I made a show of stumbling. The feeble-old-man show again, you see.

"Defendant," the senior judge said, in a tone that clearly indicated to me that he was already thinking about lunch and no longer cared much about the trial, "we hereby charge you with the following: disrespect of the Sovereign Court in the second degree, one count; obscene profanity in the presence of an acting court official in the first degree, five counts—"

"We'd better add on 'obstruction of lawful proceedings,'" said the judge on his right. She blew her nose into a lace-edged handkerchief. "One count, third degree."

"Obstruction of lawful proceedings in the third degree, one count. All in favor?"

"Aye," echoed the panel.

"Scribe, if you would." The senior judge cleared his throat. "Present evidence. Witnesses to the charge of disrespect of the Sovereign Court, please stand." Every soul in the room stood—the keen students jumped to their feet quickest of all. "Thank you, be seated. Witnesses to the charge of obscene profanity, please stand. Excellent—I think we all heard those vile words," he added with a wheezy chuckle. "But proceedings must proceed according to precedence, as it were. Be seated. Witnesses to the charge of obstruction of lawful proceedings, please stand. Thank you, be seated. I would call that fairly clear-cut, wouldn't you?" He looked around at the other judges on the panel, who nodded. "Defense?"

"Nah," said my lawyer, yawning almost theatrically. "It's almost lunchtime, after all."

Another chuckle ran through the panel. One or two of the judges gave her almost benevolent looks. I spluttered for a moment and scrambled for words. "Excuse me! I would like to defend myself!"

"Defense rests," Consanza said, and grabbed my elbow.

I tugged it away from her. "You horrible woman, if you're not going to speak in my defense, then why shouldn't I? You're dismissed."

"You can't dismiss me," she said.

"You can't dismiss her," said the chairman. "She's your court-appointed defense."

"She's shi— She's no good at her job!"

"This is highly irregular," the female judge to the chairman's right said through her handkerchief.

"Listen. I'm an old man, going deaf, eyesight not what it was"— my eyes are still as good as ever they were—"and you've shoved me in the back corner, where I can't hear or see what's happening to me, and *she* ignores me. Isn't she supposed to be defending me? I don't know how she became an advocate with this kind of attitude."

"Consanza Priyayat's credentials are not the matter of this court's present concerns," the chairman said.

"Sorry, say again?" I said loudly, just to drive home my point.

The chairman obligingly leaned forward. "We *don't care* if you think she shouldn't be an *advocate*," he said loudly.

"Well, fine, fine. You can't fault me for having an interest in my own fate, though, can you? How is it fair for me to be caged in the back, like I'm not the reason we're all here today?"

"You're not the reason we're here," said the judge with the kerchief. "It's hearing day. Happens every month."

"There are six other people whose cases are also being heard today," the chairman said, pointing around the room. There were several other cages. The prisoners in them glared at me. "You're interrupting the proceedings of justice for them as well. Hence your charge of obstruction."

My surprise was, in fact, genuine. "Well, dear me, what an embarrassing situation." Consanza, behind me, snorted. "I suppose I'd better apologize to these honorable men and women. I hope they can forgive an ignorant foreigner." They didn't look like they would. "If I'd been able to hear what was going on, or if anyone had bothered to explain, I surely wouldn't have kicked up such a fuss. Truly, I had no idea."

"The charge of obstruction will stand," the chairman announced to the court. "We will lighten it from third degree to second for your repentance."

"The charge of 'obscene profanity' ought to stand as well," said the youngest judge on the end. He still had some color to his hair. "We did all hear him say what he said."

"So we did, so we did," said the chairman. "What do we think of 'blatant disrespect,' panel?"

My no-good lawyer, primly inspecting the state of her fingernails, said, "Not that I don't *completely* agree with the charges, Your Excellencies"—I squawked at her in protest—"but he is a foreigner. And passing senile, as it seems to me."

"And deaf," I added sharply. "Mostly deaf."

Consanza gestured to me. "You see my point, Your Excellencies? He's an ignorant outlander, and unfortunately, punishment by law isn't something that can help him with that."

"Do you suggest we drop the charge of blatant disrespect, advocate?" asked the chairman, clearly dubious.

"Not drop, per se, no," said Consanza. The chit drew a handkerchief from her pocket and started cleaning the wax from under her fingernail. "I might suggest an alternate charge, however. Brazen impertinence, perhaps. Shall we say . . . third degree?"

"A charge for children!" from the sniffling judge with the handkerchief. "I once presided on a panel that found an *eight-year-old* guilty of that."

"And are ignorant foreigners any better than children? Clearly not: my client is incapable of comporting himself appropriately without supervision, thinks rude words are amusing, and would not stop scratching himself before you called us into your presence." I squawked at her again—I had done no such thing! "As stated by the philosopher Vesas the Walker, the goal of law must not be to punish or oppress those who break its tenets, but to guide them towards enlightenment, wisdom, and righteousness. I would suggest that if the court charges my client with blatant disrespect, we may be punishing him with undue harshness. What will his sentence be for blatant disrespect? Another week in Grey Ward Prison? I ask, Your Excellencies: What will he learn from that? How will it better his soul?

"Charge him instead with brazen impertinence in the third degree: With this charge in hand, the appropriate and traditional sentence is for him to state a formally structured and sincere apology, delivered immediately to the injured parties—yourselves, the students of the court, and his fellow defendants, all conveniently gathered here at once. By this method, this ignorant foreigner, no better than a child, will learn of our customs, our ways, the behavior we expect from an upright and law-revering citizen. Can you expect a child to learn good behavior by locking them in a closet? No! They must be shown the error of their ways and made to correct it, making the necessary amends. Likewise, can you expect a doltish foreigner to acclimate to our way of life without being guided towards the right path?"

I gawped at her, I'm not too proud to tell you, and then, having said her piece, I suppose, that young chit dug around in her pockets and brought out a pipe—plain wood, with a rather large bowl, an oddly crooked stem, and a silver mouthpiece. And I kept gawping at her, and she just stood there in the middle of the floor, packing leaf into the bowl and lighting it with a little flick-match.

I suppose the panel must have been discussing her argument

amongst themselves, because the next thing I heard was the senior judge saying, "All in favor of substituting a charge of brazen impertinence, third degree, for the charge of blatant disrespect of the Sovereign Court?"

There were three ayes and a nay—the nay from the creaky judge on the end, the one who had noted that it was nearly lunchtime. The chairman, it seemed, abstained.

"We hereby charge the defendant with brazen impertinence, then, amongst his other crimes," said the chairman. There was a smattering of applause amongst the students—for the advocate's argument, I supposed—but it was quelled by the chairman's hushing wave. "We'll recess for lunch and resume after the next chime. Consanza Priyayat, when we return, we will sentence your client, but as you already know we'll be demanding a formal apology. I suggest you take this time to coach him on what he will be expected to say."

The chit—my advocate—nodded, and everyone started getting up and leaving the room, except for a horde of apprentice advocates who immediately bounded up to Consanza in a flock, hounding her and fluttering around her like nervous butterflies. She pushed her way through the crowd, trailing smoke and students, and two guards came for me. Dragged me back to that little cage again! Stuffed me in it like I was some kind of decorative bird!

Didn't know if I was going to get lunch, and when my advocate had left, a big crowd of the students left with her. Others stayed behind, eating their lunch out of little boxes they'd hidden under their seats.

I watched them for a while; part of my job, you know, watching. Some of the ones who had left had marked their place by draping a handkerchief across the seat, and it seemed like others had drawn straws and left a friend or two to guard their section. A wiser choice, I thought, since I saw a few sneaks shuffle seat markers around in order to get themselves a place nearer the front, the blackguards.

I entertained myself for the next half hour by alternately taunting the guards and whining at them for a chair, citing my ancient knees. Consanza came back quite suddenly, having shaken her troop of fanatic admirers, or ass-kissers, or whatever they were.

She asked me if I was going to cooperate.

Tricky question. Loaded question. I asked her if she was going to bother to fight my case on any points besides ones she knew she could win.

"None of your business," she said. I was too appalled to reply. Of course it was my business! I was the one getting sentenced to death, jail time, and formal apologies! Then she said she brought me lunch. She held up two odd bags made of folded paper and said, "This one has a slice of bread. Warden Miloslav will get you a cup of water from the well. And *this* one has the leftovers of my lunch—half a goat pie and a baked pear. Warden Miloslav will get you a cup of water from the well, and he won't spit in it on the way back. Guess which one you get if you cooperate, and learn your apology, and promise to the gods that you'll deliver it to the court in a civilized manner." I tell you, I was so hopping mad that I couldn't find anything to say, not a thing. Just spluttered at her, something about the gall, the condescension, the utter cheek.

"It was a good pie," she said in this blank voice. Clearly didn't give an iron penny about my pride. "Going to get soggy as it cools. Not a fan of pears, so I can't speak for its quality, but that's all they had, and it came with the pie, so there we are." She shook the two bags at me, just out of reach, not that I would have tried to grab for them. Two weeks in prison and all I had left to me was my pride.

Two weeks in prison. *They* didn't bring me half-congealed pies, just salty barley porridge twice a day and a squishy, bruised apple every third day, for health.

It stings me to confess to it, but the thought of meat alone would have been enough to win my good behavior. Thrice-cursed woman! That godforsaken pear just sealed my fate for me, damn her! I had thoughts about that pear that were as lascivious as any thoughts I've had about a person, and I tell you, when I was a young man—

Hah, well, I suppose you don't need to hear about all that. Another time, perhaps.

That godforsaken pear. I'm partial to pears.

I suppose I don't have to tell you that I gave in, on the condition that I was allowed out of my cage and given a chair (*with* a cushion!) to sit on while I ate and Consanza coached me. "You've got two options," she said. "Do you have about six hundred marks on your person?"

"Pardon?"

She gave me an exceedingly patient look. "Money. Do you have any?"

"For *what*?"

"Give all the judges and the students and the witnesses a nice little gift, purely out of the goodness of your heart, to atone for your brazen impertinence. That would be a very graceful apology, and it would . . . you know. Incline them towards leniency with your other charges."

I squinted at her. "That sounds like bribery to me."

"Does it?" she said. "Mere coincidence."

"Paying everyone in the room to sway their opinion of me sounds like bribery *by coincidence*?" I said, deeply incredulous.

"It's a simple gift, merely that and no more. A gesture of regret and atonement. A mark for each of the students, two marks for each of the witnesses, twenty for each of the judges—do you have that kind of money on you?"

"What do you think?" I snapped. Mind you, I looked exactly like a man who had been wandering in the wilderness for a few weeks and then moldering in jail for a few more. I was shabby. I was smelly. I definitely didn't have six hundred marks on me.

"Some people," she said crisply, "come to court prepared."

"Well, I'm evidently not prepared at all. What's the other damn option?"

"An apology," she said dully. "A really good one." I could see she had no faith in me, none whatsoever. She didn't think I could do such a thing, not well enough to satisfy.

So she explained how. Wasn't a terribly complicated job, once she got into it; based mostly on Nuryeven philosophies of rhetoric, which were set out, oh, seven or eight hundred years ago by a dozen or so self-congratulatory morons—but then, I've never had much patience for that flavor of navel-gazing. It's not natural, not *real people*, and my business, as you know, deals in real people, sometimes too real to have actually lived.

Consanza didn't bring up the issue of bribes again, and I was too distracted and proud to mention it. A hundred marks amongst the judges to apologize for brazen impertinence and to make a pesky little witchcraft charge go away? I wondered later how much it would have taken to brush aside something worse, something I'd actually done.

Consanza fed me some quotes to use in the apology and told me the wording that would garner me at least a little more goodwill from the panel of judges. Said that if I liked, the laws of rhetoric allowed me to start with a brief anecdote to illuminate my point. "And act like you're sorry," she said.

Cheeky twit, but by that time I was nose-deep in a pear, flavored with honey and baked in a very thin sheet of flaky pastry, and I couldn't be much bothered to work up a temper again. In fact, I found myself in the first reasonable state of mind I'd had in weeks. When she was satisfied that I was adequately prepared for my sentencing, I made small talk. Not the inanities most people consider small talk, the weather and so forth, things of no consequence—small talk is a rather different animal in my profession.

There's a story in anything, if you know what to look for and how to frame it. If you can find the person who needs to hear it. That is my sacred calling—collecting stories and passing them along—but it's not just myths and tall tales. It's *people*, and the way people are.

So I talked with Consanza a little, to find out the way *she* was. She wasn't exactly forthcoming. About all I got from her was that her grandparents, all four of them, had traveled to Nuryevet from Arjuneh when they were young—there was a story there, but she gave me that blank, stone-wall look again when I tried to tweak it out of her.

From Arjuneh to Nuryevet. Thousands of miles by land or by sea, from lush, steaming jungle to bleak, stony hills and a bleak, steely sky. She has the look of that land about her, in the strong bones of her face and the rich color of her eyes, the point of her chin, the dark varnished-walnut color of her skin, and her black hair, which she wore in the style that Nuryeven advocates tend to use: tied back in a tail with a plain ribbon.

When the students started trickling back into the courtroom, Warden Miloslav locked me back in the cage—don't know why, 'cause as soon as the judges filed in and sat down, Miloslav unlocked the cage again and dragged me back out. It was the look of the thing, I guess.

There was some more chatter of formalities when they hove me back up in front of the panel, and the official sentencing—which, as we'd been told, was a demand for an immediate apology. I launched right into it.

"A very long time ago and half the world away, I met a man who had sailed through the Straits of Kel-Badur *nineteen times*—the very first to ever survive the passage with his ship intact, and he did it eighteen more times after that. An impressive number, to make an outrageous understatement, a number that earned him a near-mythic status amongst his fellow sailors in every port around the Sea of Serpents, for the straits are narrow and treacherous, with tall cliffs on either side and jagged rocks beneath the waves. It takes a sailor with an ironbound stomach to even think of attempting them, even in the calmest weather. And they say there are ghosts in the cliffs. . . .

"This man, called Xing Fe Hua, or Xing Fe the Sailor, or Xing Fe of Map Sut, whose ship was the silver-sailed *Nightingale*, whose first mate was almost as legendary as he: Faurette, golden-haired and sharp of sword. They made passage through the straits those nineteen times, escaping with their lives by the skin of their teeth and no more.

"I asked him once how he had done this when so many others had perished. It was, he said, because others had tried to defeat the straits, had approached with their own ideas of the nature of danger. They were foolish men and women who thought they could conquer the sea, who expected it to submit to their will if will enough they had. And so, for their hubris, they had been dashed upon the rocks.

"Xing Fe told me he had survived because he knew it was useless to fight against the sea, or to expect that his will could subdue its nature. He said that it was a foolish man indeed who would expect the world to behave according to his own notions.

"And that is what I have done today, Your Excellencies. I have been a foolish man—I expected you to act according to my own principles, and not only have I been met with frustration, but I have also caused frustration, strife, and at the very least, inconvenience to you, to the students of the court, to my fellow defendants—and to them I have caused real injury, too, for my foolishness is the reason their sentencing has been delayed, and it may be the reason it is further delayed. For any man who would have been set at liberty today, it is upon my head if he must spend another night in bondage.

"I attempted passage through these straits with arrogance, and it is only your mercy that has saved my ship from the rocks.

"I spent several years on Xing Fe's ship, and yet I still forgot this lesson. I profess my deepest apologies to all present, and I beg your forgiveness."

I bowed deeply to the panel in the style that Consanza had shown me. My back creaked and popped.

"When was the last time you spoke with Xing Fe the Sailor? Xing Fe Hua of the province of Phra Yala?" asked the chief judge.

I tell you now, I committed another great foolishness then— I thought my story had so taken His Honor that . . . Well. You see. I am a vain man. I tell you now, this happened exactly as I tell it, without any embellishment.

"Years ago," said I. "He sailed west towards the Ammat Archipelago from the Gulf of Dagua and was never heard from again. They say he must have been spirited away, for he disappeared entirely. No one ever saw or heard of him again. Some say he sails the waters of heaven now; some say he lives on in the waters he crossed in life, that in the moments of darkest peril, his spirit has guided ships to safety—"

"Xing Fe Hua the Sailor, of Phra Yala in Map Sut, known pirate, smuggler, spy, murderer?" said the judge.

"Ah . . . I see you have heard of some of his more controversial exploits," I replied. "If he lives still, I hope he knows how far his fame has spread. It would have delighted him, that you have heard of him so far from his homeland." So very far—Map Sut is half the world away.

"Heard of him!" the judge laughed. Something about it tickled the hairs on the back of my neck. "I was on the panel that convicted him of murderous intent towards a citizen of the realm, five counts in the third degree, one amongst a laundry list of other crimes, each more lurid and horrific than the last! That was twenty years ago! Heard of him! I was there to hear him scream when we wrapped him in those ridiculous sails and burned him!"

I tell you now, I was struck speechless. It must have been forty years since I had traveled with Xing Fe, and the width of the world and the span of time had long since separated us. It is no easy thing to be confronted with unexpected loss.

So when the judge, seeing my face, asked the nature of my relationship to Xing Fe Hua, I could only say softly, "We were friends." It had been so long, and a man like Xing Fe is a man no one ever imagines growing old, let alone succumbing to death. I had . . . I had always assumed he'd have stayed just the same, though he had been older than I back then and surely would have passed on by now one way or another.

But men like Xing Fe Hua never really die. They leave behind too much of themselves.

The judge had been speaking. I hadn't heard him, had been too busy listening to the wretched animal-cry of my heart.

The judge rapped his gavel on the table, which brought me out of it pretty well, so the first thing I heard him say was, "The court hereby passes this case to the Queen of Justice and remands him into the custody of the wardens of Order."

The courtroom burst into chaos, the students and witnesses in the galleries all shouting at once, and a guard came up on either side of me, took me by the elbows, started dragging me towards the door. I couldn't see Consanza anywhere, and whenever I tried to turn to look for her, the guards yanked on my arms to pull me forward faster—nearly wrenched my shoulders out, which didn't help with the confusion and the blur. Everything seemed to be whirling around me, and I kept flinching at the shouts on either side of the aisle, and I must have been stumbling because the guards hauled me to my feet several times before we reached the big wooden doors into the main hall of the courthouse.

They threw me into a little box, smaller than the cage I'd been in earlier and solid-sided like a coffin, and they shoved all my limbs in after me and slammed the door and locked it, and I was confined there in the dark for who knows how long until the box started moving. It was lifted onto something with wheels, and I was rolled off somewhere new, my heart pounding like a rabbit's in my chest and my breath coming short. I was almost glad of the dark, almost glad to be shut away from the noise and confusion and chaos.

But what had I done? I didn't know.

———✦———

It took two days for Consanza to come see me, or for them to let her come. I had been taken immediately from the House of Justice back to the House of Order, yanked from that tiny coffin-box, and dragged down two flights of stairs to a new cell. A more secure cell, I suppose it was, as it didn't have a window. The ceiling was low, the walls were all stony and plastered over, and the stale air was rank with the smells of filthy humans, damp, rats, piss. And no one would tell me what had happened, though I begged and wheedled and asked to simply be *told*.

At least the food wasn't any worse.

But yes, as I said, Consanza came after two days, led in by a guard, who stood by the wall a little way down the corridor and crossed his arms. He didn't look at me, and I didn't recognize him, but the light was very poor, even for my eyes. There was a little table, where sometimes a guard would sit and play solitary card games when they were watching this block—watching me. There wasn't anyone else in the other cells, unless they were bound and gagged.

Consanza entered in a billow and whirl of black robes, and I was glad enough to see someone I knew that I didn't even think to sneer at her for her dramatics. They say parting makes affections sweeter— and that hawkish unfortunate nose of hers did seem to be softened in my eyes by familiarity and, let's be honest, relief. She took a chair from the table, set it in front of the door of my cell, and sat in it backwards with her arms crossed over the backrest.

"You really got yourself into it, didn't you?" she said, and it took all I had not to cry.

"What happened? What did they sentence me with? I don't know what happened, and no one—no one will tell me what I've done."

She looked at me for a long time, expressionless except for that typical sour look. "Espionage," she said.

"Espionage!" I squawked. "Against whom? When? What evidence have they? What actions did I ever take? Espionage!"

Well, it was something having to do with my association to Xing Fe Hua, she explained, and went on in legal jargon and unnecessary detail, unknowing that each word was a punch to my heart and my gut.

"At least they've been distracted from the witchcraft for now. That's a good thing."

"A good thing! A good thing, she says! First a witch, now a spy, and they separate me from legal counsel for days. They lock me up in the dark with only one candle in the whole room! A good thing!

When I was a witch, I had light and fresh air and a guard who would speak to me!" They might not have known how to deal with black-witches, but they had *procedures* for spies.

"Be quiet," she snapped. "Just be quiet and stop running your mouth. It is a good thing. It is. If you'd been convicted of witchcraft, you'd be dead by now. They'd have burned you or buried you alive—"

"They have buried me alive!" I shrieked, and flailed my arm at the wall. "They've manhandled me down into this hole in the ground! They've buried me!"

"Hush!" she snarled. "It's not my job to hold your hand."

"Oh, not your job to hold my hand, not your job to hold my hand—what is your job, then? Hmm!" I had leaped from my bench and started pacing back and forth. Four steps to the wall and four steps to the bars. "It's your job to get me out of here, isn't it? It's your job to prove me innocent."

"That's what I came here about. It might not be my job anymore."

"Ahaha! They're burying me alive!"

"No. They can't take me off a case once it's been assigned to me." She had lowered her voice again; it was calm and level and nigh apathetic. "I might resign, though."

"You can't resign!"

"I can, and I might. I haven't decided yet."

I sat down on my narrow little bench again and rubbed my hands over my face. "Why? Why, why? You can't leave me like that," and I heard my voice come out in a pathetic creak.

"I don't really appreciate attempts to yank me around by my feelings," she said. "I *can* leave you like that if I want to. Anyone else would. A case like yours? No one would keep it for more than a day. No one would take it up after that, after a charge like yours. Ugh." She passed a hand over her forehead. "Everyone knows that other case.

Xing Fe Hua—I was barely more than a child when it happened, and even I remember it."

"But why? Why? Why!"

"Because it'd be a damn hard job! No—impossible, or nearly impossible. I'd be almost certain to lose, which would spoil my track record and put a smudge on my reputation. And you'd be dead—well, you're all but dead either way, let's face it, so that's not so much of an issue—"

"Not an issue!" I shrieked again. "Not an— Not for you, maybe, but I'm the one that'd be dead!"

"I can't talk to you when you're being this emotional." She stood up, and I thought she was leaving. My heart skipped a beat, but she was only turning the chair around, sitting in it again the right way round, and pulling her pipe and her packet of leaf out of her pockets. "I told you I haven't decided. I might not resign." She struck a flick-match and lit the pipe, puffing on it until the embers glowed just right. The stream of fragrant smoke she blew out did much to improve the air quality of the cell—it was an excellent variety of leaf, I could tell. Undoubtedly foreign, probably from Tash, if my nose was right. Besides the underlying richness of the natural leaf, it smelled of vanilla and unusual spices.

I tugged on my beard and rubbed my face again. Forced the plow of my brain into the furrow of thought. "What's the weight on the other side of the scale?"

She puffed for a long moment. "Well," she began slowly. "I might win."

"But it's a long shot."

"You got it. A very long shot." She leaned forward, just enough to tuck the packet of leaf back into its pocket. "Haven't decided. Won't decide for a little while, I think. It's a slow case, espionage."

"I'm not a spy!"

"That's neither here nor there, is it? It doesn't matter if you're a spy or not; it matters whether they find you guilty or not. It matters whether I win the case." Another long puff on that pipe. "I might win it," she added thoughtfully. "But I probably won't."

"Are there any advocates better than you?"

"None that would come within twenty ells of this case," she said in a plume of smoke. "It's me or nobody."

"So ... what, you'd take it for the gamble?" I sulked at her as hard as I could.

"Mmm. Yes. The glory, too, if I won."

"We."

"Eh?"

"If we won," I said.

She looked at me, pitying. "You're not going to be doing much of the heavy lifting, though, are you? I. If I won. If I won the case *for you*. I'm not getting paid for this, you know. I am required to advocate pro bono a number of cases per year to stay licensed. And I don't like not getting paid, but glory is close enough to coin for me. It's got a good exchange rate."

"So I can't say anything, then!" I threw my hands in the air again. "I'm just going to have to twiddle my thumbs and wait for you to decide on your own whether to hold my life in your hands or trample it under your shoes?"

"No."

"No? What generosity! You mean, kind advocate, that I get to argue my case to you before you argue it to the court?"

"Essentially." She lowered the pipe and slouched down in the chair. "It might help if you told me the truth."

"I have told you the truth!"

"You haven't told anyone your name."

I scowled at her. "My name is my own. It's a . . . religious matter. You wouldn't tell me your stars if I asked, would you?"

She snorted. "That's my grandfathers' religion. They're the ones who came from Arjuneh, not me. I'm Nuryeven through and through. I don't know my stars."

"Young people today!" I said bitterly. "Abandoning the ways of their parents. One day all this will be lost to the world, and it'll be your fault."

"Spare me the grumbling, for gods' sake. You want me to save you. I want to save you! Saving you would be a great mark for my career. It would open a lot of doors. I might even run for office later on, but probably not—too much paperwork for me, not enough glamour." She took another slow puff on the pipe. "But I have to know who I'm saving, and what the odds are. I don't like gambling. Well—certainly not on the long odds: I don't like losing. I don't like making mistakes. I'm asking you to convince me that arguing your case wouldn't be a mistake."

I took a breath. I always hesitate before going into details about what I am—makes people leery. Like telling someone you're a thief, and they start guarding all their belongings and watching you closely whenever you walk past the silver spoons. But there was nothing for it.

"I said I was a Chant," I began. "And that means a lot of things. It's not my name; it's my title, like . . . Advocate, or Doctor, or Mayor. And it marks me as a master of an order that goes back more than four thousand years."

THE FIRST TALE:
The Land That Sank Beneath the Waves

A very long time ago and half the world away, there was a
vast land in the southern reaches of the Unending Ocean,

and it was called Arthwend. In the height of its golden age, before it sank beneath the waves and into the shadows of faint legend, it was an empire that stretched from shore to shore, covering all the land from the lowest bog to the highest peak. That empire was the prize for generations of victories by one tribe over all the others, and that tribe grew and grew, and became more splendid, and built cities made of gold, full of gardens and silk and delicate arts. As they had grown, they had pressed the others back, and back, and back, and one of these tribes fled deep into the marshes, and there they took refuge. There, where no one could touch them, where no one cared to touch them.

(*"Sounds lovely," said Consanza. "So what?" I ignored her. A very rude woman, as I've pointed out already.*)

The god of that little forgotten marsh tribe was Shuggwa, a shadow god, a trickster god, a god whose gaze you should not draw. Life in the marsh was difficult, and Shuggwa took lives and caused mischief with great merriment. Family members who went out at night were lost in the dark for following spirit lights, or taken in tragic accidents and misfortunes.

They had long had their priests: the Chants—

(*"Finally, something beginning to resemble an answer," she muttered. I still ignored her. One tries to keep oneself solemn. That's what I learned from my master-Chant and what she learned from hers. Can't be shoving too much of yourself into a story that isn't yours. It requires some discipline, distance, humility—do you see?*)

—who were the keepers of their genealogies, their histories, their stories, ones who perhaps didn't draw Shuggwa's calamitous gaze in the same way as the others, ones who were perhaps the objects of his rare favor. It is said that the Chants could intervene with him, could send him messages through his servant, the bird Ksadir, and that they flouted all the mores and customs of their tribe, baring themselves to the god in an attempt to draw his attention away from the others of their tribe, who covered their heads and spoke softly. The Chants danced and sang and lit great fires at night to draw Shuggwa's Eye.

(Consanza was glaring at me at this part. I could tell she was bored. Don't know how she could be! I've always wished we knew more about the ancient Chants—but all we know is the stories we've remembered, and I suppose that's the point.)

They painted their boats bright colors, wore metal, wore jewelry, wore bells on their ankles. They laughed and shouted and danced and swore and spat, they spoke loudly and made obscene gestures and ignored all rules of politeness. They wandered naked from time to time.

Perhaps it helped—the empire that had pushed the Chants and their people into the swamps continued to grow, and as it grew, its people became arrogant. They angered their gods, and the sea came rushing across the land, drowning it in the flood. The empire sank beneath the waves. But Shuggwa deigned to warn the Chants, and they and their people climbed into their little marsh boats and floated as the waters rose, and they alone survived. They

lashed their hulls together for strength and rowed across
the wide sea, while the Chants danced day and night, sang
all the songs they knew, recited the histories of their villages
and the genealogies, and begged throughout for Shuggwa to
keep the waters calm until they reached land.

They made landfall in the Issili Islands, low and sandy.
That was four thousand years ago. And the Chants led
their people into that fertile place and they flourished. They
flourished so they forgot their god's power—he had little of
it there. He faded away and evolved over time until Shuggwa
was only Skukua, in the people's tales a foolish trickster, a
fox-god, a bumbler and yet still a clever bumbler, who could
get himself out of trouble as well as he could get himself into
it, though not always in a way that pleased other people.

The Chants faded with him. Once priests, the keepers
of all knowledge, the protectors, the sacred storytellers,
as the centuries passed and their services were made
redundant by writing, by new gods and new priests, they
became wanderers, mendicants. Ones who still ceremonially
sink their homeland beneath the waves and walk the earth,
remembering. There are things that will never die because
the Chants remember them. Your grandfather's stars, we
remember. The heroes of the cold reaches of the north,
we remember. From master to apprentice, we pass on the
knowledge of what once was, and it lives, and Arthwend
never will be truly lost to us.

Consanza had been puffing away all through the story and finally
lowered the pipe when I finished. "Look, I didn't ask for the history
of the world here."

She'd be more grateful for that knowledge if she knew how few people know it these days. Or she wouldn't. She's an ungrateful twit. "Well, now you understand what I do."

"No, I understand what you're allegedly supposed to do. I understand what men and women four thousand years ago did. You told me nothing about yourself, as usual, and as usual I'm still not convinced I should advocate for you."

"Fine!" I burst out. "Fine! What do you want from me? I can't tell you my name without breaking the vows of my order. Do you want to know what homeland I threw into the sea? Kaskinen. How long I've been doing this? I was thirteen when I began. I'm seventy-something now, haven't really been keeping track. Do you want to know where I was before this? Cormerra. And before that? Echaree. And before that was Johe, and Tash, and Xereccio, and Ondor-Urt, and Zobuo, and N'gaka, and before that we were sailing the Sea of Serpents with a merchant vessel from Birrabar. What? What else do you want to know?"

"We? Who is we?"

"My apprentice and I."

"And where is your apprentice now?"

"We were at an inn in some little town—Syemna, that was the name—when I was arrested on those trumped-up witchcraft charges. He saw me arrested. I don't know where he is." Now, she already knew all that, but here's what really happened: Ylfing and I had been minding our own business, see, and I was trading a story for a meal (it was "The Twelve Tasks of Tyrran"—not one of my favorites, but it gets a good reception), and out of nowhere, a couple city policemen swooped down like giant gray bats out of the maw of Qarrsi the Ravenous, and I was dragged off to the capital and thrown in jail. You see now why I was so mightily surprised about the witchcraft thing?

Anyway, Consanza asked, "Is he safe?"

"How should I know?" says I. "He's a naive little thing, thinks everyone's fundamentally kind and good. Not much street smarts; he just traipses along with his arms and his heart open to the world. Zero sense of self-preservation. He'll be out on the streets by now—we don't usually carry money, and I wouldn't let him handle it anyway. Lads his age fritter it away to their friends betting on which pig will fart first. He knows a bit about surviving in the wilderness, seeing as we've been stomping through it all the time he's been apprenticed to me." And he's Hrefni besides; he knows a bit about living close to the land. I stood up and began pacing again.

"What do you teach him?"

"The trade; are you dull-witted? Knowledge. How to get more knowledge. But he keeps wanting to write things down. He thinks it would be better that way. Laziness, that's what I call it."

"And this knowledge he knows, it's things that have been lost?"

I tugged at my hair. "Not just that, it's—stories, *people*. It's the way people are in one place or another. I can't say I much like the way people are here."

"What does that mean, the way people are?"

"Customs! Manners! Languages! The ten thousand gods of ten thousand nations! The tales they tell their children when they wake from nightmares, the tales they tell their sons and daughters when they send them off to war, the tales a midwife tells a laboring mother, the tales old men tell each other in the twilight of their lives."

"So you *are* a spy—sort of."

"No! I don't know secrets, I don't look for—well, all right, sometimes I do look for secrets, but not useful secrets, not anything that could be used badly!"

"You're a spy."

"No!"

"What kind of secrets do you know, then?"

"The mysteries of the Faiss peoples, that whole unfortunate business with the former princess's dowry in Avaris, the secret words of the dragon cults in Xereccio, the location of four hidden temples in Girenthal—"

"So . . . spy things."

"Those aren't spy things! They're part of history! They're treasures that could be lost to time—all right, except the princess, but that's just gossip! It's not really a secret."

She puffed silently on her pipe. Clearly she had made up her mind.

"No, look, those are the least of what I know. I know the twelve runes of luck that the Hrefni ward a house with. I know sixteen languages! I know the charms that the Umakh sing when they shoe a milk-white horse. I know how to travel across the great desert, the Sea of Sun, without disturbing the beasts beneath the ground. I know—I know the stars of your grandfathers and I've seen the colossal temple wagons rolling through the streets in Arjuneh, all hung with tinsel and wind chimes and silk banners and garlands of flowers."

"Ignoring the witchcraft, then—"

"It's not witchcraft! It's folk custom!"

"Ignoring the witchcraft, you know Umakha husbandry secrets. You know how to travel undisturbed."

"You're twisting my words," I said. I felt a black wave of despair about to break over me. "I only know what others have told me when I asked. It's not—it's not practical knowledge."

"Crossing the Sea of Sun undisturbed by the beasts in the ground sounds practical to me. My grandfather went by ship along the coast when he came from Arjuneh. He says only the tribes in the walking huts can cross the desert safely." She puffed on her pipe. "Have you seen the beasts?"

I was startled that she asked—I really hadn't expected her to take an interest in anything I said, and I confess that a tiny part of me was a little pleased. A very tiny part. I thought then that perhaps she wasn't *completely* terrible. "Yes, once."

"What do they look like?"

I shook my head to clear out some of the black fog. "Like . . . half wolf, half panther, but larger, and longer, with feet like paddles for digging in the sand, and luminous eyes, and long muzzles. They have fur, but it's mangy, and their skin is scaly, and it's said they drink wells and oases dry to lure their prey deeper into the desert. It is said they can hear your heartbeat through the soles of your feet, so they can find you even if you're standing as still as stone."

"Can they really dig up under you without being noticed? And snatch you into the sand?"

"You'd hardly even have time to scream. It's like seeing a child fall into a deep river. One moment they're there, and the next—just ripples. Just the sand, disturbed."

We shared a little shiver of delicious almost-fear, the kind all humans share, the kind that makes children beg to hear a terrifying story over and over, though they know it'll keep them wide awake and flinching at every noise. "So how do the desert people cross?"

Yes, she wasn't completely terrible. "They never let their skin touch the sand. If they must walk, they wear sandals like—like snowshoes, you have snowshoes here, I suppose?" She nodded. "Wide, made of layered leather, but as thick as four fingers, and padded on the top and bottom with goat felt. Makes walking arduous. They only use those in the case of direst need. They mostly ride in their huts, which—as your grandfather rightly told you—walk. They look like delicate wooden beetles, and they go scuttling across the dunes in packs, from one oasis to another."

"How? Magic?"

"Wind and sails, girl! Not all strange things are the source of magic."

"Here they are," she said. "In Nuryevet." And that seemed to be the end of that. She sat back and put her pipe back in her mouth. "See, that is practical knowledge. Do you know how to build any of those walking houses?"

"No. I'm not a craftsman. Why? Is Nuryevet planning to invade Ondor-Urt?" I sneered. Impossible endeavor, even if they cared to— they'd have to go through a minimum of five countries first, not to mention some very thick wilderness, or else cross the mountains and fight their way over the steppe.

"No, but we have merchants. The more knowledge a man has, the less he has to pay for it from other people. But you, with your knowledge—there are people who might pay for that. Then you would have money, and we might be able to begin doing something efficient about your charges."

"So that thing the other day wasn't just *coincidentally* bribery," I snapped. "I'm innocent! Why should I bribe anyone when I haven't done anything they've accused me of?"

"For one thing, because it might save your neck," she said flatly. "I'll be the first to admit to my pride, but I'm not stupid. I don't throw away an advantage just because I find it distasteful."

"Is this normal?" I said. "Honestly, is it?"

She shrugged. "I guess you could say that."

"And you don't care at all? You, an advocate, someone who apparently believes in the rule of law enough to make a career of it—you'll suggest that your clients bribe the judges as casually as you'll discuss the weather?"

"I beg your pardon, but whatever gave you the idea that you had leave to be condescending to me?"

"I'm trying to understand how you sleep at night."

"I sleep content in the knowledge that I've done my best to work within an imperfect system to give help to the people who ask for it."

"Oh, don't you sound noble and righteous," I simpered. "And I suppose you *never* take bribes, then."

"No," she said sharply. "Most of the time I don't."

"*Most* of the time."

She smoked at me in glowering silence. "This part of the conversation is over. You've made yourself clear; I won't bring up that particular solution again."

"Good. It's useless. Haven't paid for anything in ages, knowledge or not. Don't like carrying coin."

"Surely you don't buy your supper with songs and stories?" she said flatly from around the stem of her pipe.

I sniffed at her. These Nuryevens have no imagination whatsoever—the story of the sand beasts of Ondor-Urt seemed to have held her interest for a moment, but perhaps that was just the last faint heritage of Arjuneh in her. The Arjuni are *flush* with stories, may the gods smile upon them. I used to marvel at the vibrancy of that place, the colors, the warmth, the *life*—I see now that they're just balancing out these fucking Nuryevens. "It's a complicated trade, advocate."

"So is advocacy." She paused, then smirked at me. "It's only about telling the right story in the right way, isn't it?"

I should have given her more credit. It's my favorite mistake, one I should have stopped making when I was a young man, but it has only gotten worse as I get older. She'd surprised me with that observation, too, if I'm being completely honest—and I'm always completely honest, which you know if you know me at all. Well, mostly. "Are you going to keep my case, then?"

She sighed. "I'm not convinced you're not a spy, but I'm not convinced that you *are* a spy either. This will be a slow one, though, so there's time still for me to abandon ship if it seems to be turning sour." She turned her pipe upside down and tapped the ashes out onto the floor, stepping on them to extinguish any remaining embers. Then she began packing it away into the pockets of her robe. "I'll keep it for the moment, until I get a better feeling about whether I should stay on or look for greener pastures."

"That isn't very fair," I said sharply. "If you were a really good advocate, you'd take it. You'd win it."

"Maybe anywhere else, old man," she said in a low voice. "Not in these parts. They've already made up their mind about you. I'm not arguing to neutral minds, I'm arguing against ones that have already decided you're guilty. It's an uphill battle."

"Uphill, and you haven't decided yourself if I'm innocent."

"Not my job. I haven't decided if I can talk everyone else into deciding you are."

"So you might just leave me to the wolves."

"I might. We'll see how many more wolves you whistle for when you run your mouth to the Queen of Justice. You'll talk yourself right into a noose on the gallows. So if she comes, maybe just don't talk until I get here."

"Comes? What about a court? Witnesses? A trial?"

"There's a room upstairs they use for things like this. Spies have friends, and friends help break people out of jail."

Friends! I only had Ylfing. Probably starving in the streets by now, or dead. Murdered, maybe, killed in a back alley by thugs. Like I told Consanza, he hasn't got a whit of self-preservation when it comes to people, but it's not often that a young man or woman feels like sinking their homeland beneath the waves and taking off to see the world. They all talk like they would do it in a heartbeat, but give them the actual opportunity and . . . Well, Ylfing took it. Grabbed it with both hands. It was possibly a youthful lack of foresight on his part rather than any kind of truly steel-keen thirst to see the world.

I didn't miss him, mind you. Of course I didn't. Why would I? He's the bane of my old age! Let me tell you, we have never once walked past a smelly shepherd boy who didn't instantly turn Ylfing's head. Every single damn time. Not only that—he once composed a poem about a boy he glimpsed across a street. It doesn't even matter if they're cute or not—he'll glance at these boys and find something completely wonderful and unique about each of them, and then guess who has to listen to him blush and burble about it for the rest of the day? Me. I have to. I'm the one who suffers. Mind you, he does that with every person we meet, but with boys it's a *compulsion* and insufferable. So no, I didn't miss him at all, not even a tiny bit. In fact, I was enjoying the vacation.

"Would it be possible for me to send a letter?" I asked, as Consanza turned away.

"Eh?" she said, turning back. "To whom?"

"My apprentice."

She shook her head immediately. "No, I'm afraid not. They'd just snap him up for being an accomplice, and I'm not taking on two cases this troublesome."

"Could you go to the inn we were—"

"Not a chance. They'd just snap me *and* him up for being accomplices, and unlike some people of my acquaintance, I have no interest in initiating an intimate relationship with a length of sisal rope."

"But could you ask? Could I ask?"

"You can ask all you want. Petition the Queen of Justice when you see her, if you want. I'm not going to argue for it, though."

"He's like family! Aren't prisoners allowed to contact their families?"

"Prisoners generally are. Spies, generally not. It's a sensible policy if you think about it."

"When will she come? The Queen."

"I haven't been informed about when your hearing will be. When I find out, I'll let you know."

And finally, as she turned away once more: "Will you come back and talk to me?"

"If I have time. You're not my only client."

And then she left, her robes billowing behind her, and the cell was cold and cramped again, though the smell of her pipe leaf lingered for an hour or two after.

———◆———

The Queen of Justice came without warning a day or two later. If Consanza had sent any word of the hearing, it hadn't reached me. The guards came to unlock my cell, wordlessly, and took me in shackles to the main level of the prison, where I was put in a cage much like the one I had stood in at the courthouse. The Queen of Justice was shown in without fanfare. Not an actual Queen, mind you—the Nuryevens got rid of them long ago, but they kept the titles. The Primes of the realm, their so-called Kings and Queens, are people just like any other citizen, elected to their offices by simple majority.

The Queen of Justice was Zorya Bozimiros Miroslavat Bartostok, a woman ancient by anyone's standards. She was dressed in deceptively simple and severely cut clothes, but the fabric was rich and fine, the forest-colored cloak over her shoulders lined in thick dark fur, the hem of her skirt densely embroidered with wool yarn nearly the same green-black color as her dress, and glinting here and there with black glass beads. The only jewel she wore was a golden locket on a chain around her throat, and a long string of tiny beads upon which were hooked a pair of half-moon spectacles with gold rims. She was so well-dressed in comparison to all the other people in this country. I remember noticing that. It didn't really strike me as excessively strange then—she was a Queen, after all, even if she had been elected, and Queens are almost always well turned out, just as peasants almost always look like peasants—I'd seen plenty of *those* in the backwaters of this backwater. Miserable, the lot of them. Miserable, suspicious, afraid, angry. I'd thought nothing of it at the time, and even standing in front of Zorya Miroslavat, I still thought nothing of it.

Behind her was another woman of middle age who held the door for her, pulled her chair out, took her cloak, and set a bundle of papers bound between two flat boards before her on the table. All in silence. I assumed at the time that she was an aide; I found out later that she was Yunia Antalos Yllonat Csavargo, the Duchess of Justice, Zorya's second in command.

Zorya Miroslavat was one of those women who seem like they must have shrunk with age. Her fingers were curved and knobbly with arthritis as she pulled loose the knot and set aside the top board of the bundle. She licked her fingertips to page through the first few sheets of the file, and when she finally looked up at me, her eyes were bright and glittering. "So, a spy, are you? And possibly a blackwitch," she said, her voice surprisingly loud. Annoying habit.

"Not that I know of, madam. Might I know where my advocate is?"

She unhooked her spectacles and shakily slid them onto her nose, looking me over with those sharp little eyes for, I assumed, signs of witchcraft. She seemed in no hurry to reply, and she skimmed through another page of the file before she answered. "I don't think your advocate will be coming today."

"That seems . . . unusual. She said she would be here."

"Hard to be somewhere if you don't know you're supposed to be there, isn't it?"

"Advocate Consanza said that I should keep my mouth shut and let her"—*do all the talking* sounded suspicious—"state my case for me."

"I don't think that will be necessary," Zorya Miroslavat said with a small smile over the rim of her glasses. "This isn't a truly formal hearing for you."

"Even so, I'd rather not speak without my advocate present to advise me. I don't know anything about your laws or customs."

"What was her name again?" Zorya Miroslavat asked absently.

"Consanza. Advocate Consanza Priyayat."

"Mm, yes, I think I've heard of her. Bit of a celebrity in the lower courts, isn't she?" Zorya Miroslavat addressed this to Yunia Antalos, who stood at her shoulder.

"I believe so, ma'am. She's never lost a case, but I haven't heard that she takes particularly risky cases either."

"Heh." Zorya Miroslavat tapped her finger against the table several times. "She must be a smart one, then. Tactical."

"The judges seem fond of her," Yunia said. "I hear she has a certain . . . flair."

"The students like her too," I added. "Had a whole flock of them following her around at the trial. You should meet her. Perhaps we could send for her now."

"If things go well for you, I'm sure my path will cross hers at some point." Zorya Miroslavat drew herself up. "But back to business. You say you don't know anything of our laws and customs."

"Nothing, I'm afraid, but what I've seen firsthand."

"Have you ever visited any part of Nuryevet before?"

"No."

"Not even the fringes? One of the outlying villages, perhaps? Passed through the mountains?"

"No, I've never even been within a hundred miles of this place. I would prefer not to answer any more questions without my advocate."

"These aren't questions. We're just getting to know each other a little better." Her voice was silky. *We're just chatting*, it said. *Nothing to fear*. It set my teeth on edge. "Now, I'm told you go by the name . . . Chant?"

"A title, not a name."

"I see."

"Advocate Consanza said that when I met with you, I might petition you to allow me to send a letter."

Zorya Miroslavat looked up from the paperwork. "To whom, Master Chant?"

"My . . . apprentice. He's like a nephew to me."

"I see. And why would you be writing to an apprentice?"

"He's on his own and I haven't seen him since I was arrested—I only want to tell him what's happened to me."

She broke her gaze and returned to shuffling the papers. "No, I can't allow that at the present time."

"I understand, given the circumstances and the crimes that I have been accused of, that you may be reluctant to allow me contact with the outside world, particularly anyone who may be on my side. Is there any situation in which you could find it acceptable? Even the shortest message would be—"

"No," she said briskly.

"Not even, 'Apprentice, I have been charged by the Nuryeven courts and I am awaiting trial'?"

"Not even that." Zorya Miroslavat folded her hands on the papers. "If we find you guilty and sentence you, we will send a notification to any family members—and that includes your nephew or apprentice or whatever he is, if that's who you'd like it sent to. If we find you innocent, well—you'd be free to go and you can tell him yourself. Now. You confessed in court to having a close association with the famous spy Xing Fe Hua, also known as Xing Fe the Sailor, is that right?"

I crossed my arms. "I'd rather not answer any more questions without my advocate's counsel."

"Well, you don't have to answer, but it's a matter of record already, so that's fine."

"As long as I have you here, madam, perhaps you could discuss the quality of your prisons—all the cells seem to have a terrible draft, and the blanket they gave me is full of fleas."

"Not my problem," she murmured, examining another sheet of parchment.

"I—I beg your pardon! The keeping of prisons isn't your problem?"

"No," she said coolly. "It is not. It is, in fact, in the jurisdiction of my colleague, the Queen of Order. But I will be sure to pass along the fact that there is a man charged with espionage who feels that he has the right to critique her maintenance staff. Now, the witchcraft charge—whatever were you doing to get arrested for that?"

"I would strongly, strongly prefer to answer your questions with counsel from my advocate."

"Certainly you would. By the way, what brought you to Nuryevet?"

"I would strongly," I repeated, "prefer to answer in the presence of my advocate."

There was a sharp knock on the door. Yunia Antalos stepped quickly towards it and yanked it open. There was a young woman on the other side, dressed in a navy-blue three-quarter-length coat and black trousers, both of which had the cut of a uniform. Her face was swathed in a charcoal scarf that covered her nose and mouth, and there was nothing shiny or reflective anywhere on her. Even the slight shine of her fingernails had been buffed off. She pulled the scarf away from her mouth and made a small bow to the aide. "Duchess Yunia Antalos, greetings. I'm a messenger from Her Majesty, Anfisa Vasilos Zofiyat Lisitsin—"

"Yes, we know," Zorya Miroslavat said. "You're wearing her colors. Do you think we're blind?"

"—Queen of Pattern," the messenger finished. "And I have a writ demanding the release of the accused spy Chant into our custody, citing the right for the Prime of Pattern to question all suspects accused of treason or espionage without obstruction or veto from any source, in accordance with section five of the Nineteenth Modification." The messenger held out a rolled-up piece of parchment.

Yunia Antalos snatched it out of the messenger's hand, broke the seal, and skimmed it. "It's in order, madam," she said darkly.

The messenger smiled.

"Of course it is," Zorya Miroslavat snapped. "Anfisa doesn't cut corners." Then, to the messenger: "Did you bring guards?"

"I did," she said. "They're in the hall."

"Yunia, clean this up," Zorya Miroslavat snapped, gesturing at the file of papers, and hauled herself, creaking, to her feet. "Fine," she said to the messenger. "Take him, then. Vihra Kylliat has already signed him over to you?"

"Indeed, madam."

"Take me where?" I asked. None of them answered me, Yunia Antalos being too busy shuffling the papers into order and securing them into their bundle again with a swift knot. The messenger stepped out of the way as Yunia Antalos and Zorya Miroslavat stalked past her, and then she leaned out and beckoned to someone down the hall. "Take me where?" I repeated.

"Somewhere more comfortable than here, I daresay," the messenger said with a wry smile. "The House of Order doesn't allow much in the way of creature comforts, does it?"

"No," I said slowly. "It doesn't. Who are you?"

"Captain of the Pattern Guard, Vladana Anatoliyos Lyubiyat Ostakolin. Captain Ostakolin to you."

"And the Queen of Pattern is . . . ?"

"Someone who has an interest in talking to accused spies." Two women—a pair of Order guards in red-and-white uniforms—came into the room, unlocked my cage, and removed the shackles from my wrists. Captain Ostakolin replaced them with new ones, locked with a key from her own pocket. There were four more blue-and-black-uniformed guards standing just outside the door now. "She'll make it worth your while if you cooperate," the Captain said in a low voice. "She may be able to help you, even, if you make yourself helpful in return." She smiled at the Order guards and gave them a little salute with one hand, pulling the scarf back over her nose and mouth with the other. "Always a pleasure, ladies."

The escort seemed far less strict than the ones I had enjoyed on the way to and from the courthouse—I wasn't thrown into any coffins, nor manhandled. Captain Ostakolin led me gently by the elbow, the four guards flanking us before and behind as we navigated the long, twisting hallways, all nearly identical and built of the same dull gray stone as every other building in this damn country. We even left by the main entrance, the ceremonial entrance, rather than the loading dock where they drag prisoners in and out. There was an incongruously well-appointed carriage, lacquered in matte black, with three interlocking crescents painted in dark blue on the side, and two perfectly matched black horses, and wispy fountains of black feathers towering on each corner of the carriage and from the horses' bridles—another show of wealth and luxury that simply didn't *fit* in the Nuryeven landscape. Two of the guards entered the carriage, and Captain Ostakolin handed me in after them. I liked her. She was the pinnacle of graciousness and chivalry. She followed me in after, and the other two guards climbed up, I suppose, to the driver's seat and the footman's stand. The inside of the carriage was just as elegant as the outside, with navy-blue velvet cushions on the seat and swirling carving across all the wood trim—it was possibly the most lavish thing I had seen in all of Nuryevet, quite surprising for such an austere and severe people, and I was completely baffled as to why the Captain of the Pattern Guard would be using such a carriage to simply fetch a prisoner.

The Captain was given one bench to herself. I was squeezed in between the two guards, and, bracketed like that, I could feel evidence of several weapons hidden under their coats. Daggers, it felt like. If they had those, they probably had other weapons too.

Captain Ostakolin rapped on the roof of the carriage and it jerked forward. She gave me a beatific smile. "You look confused, Master Chant."

"I'm just an old man," I quavered at her. "It's been so chaotic...."

"Of course it has," and she fairly brimmed over with sympathy. "The Queen of Order's a penny-pincher, amongst other things. Well, she has to be; her term of office is only eleven years. And the office of Order doesn't tend to draw the sort of person who ... enjoys the little luxuries in life. Military background, most of them, and Vihra Kylliat is no different. Is she, Lupsek?" Above her scarf, her eyes glittered with merriment at the guard on my left.

"Like a rock wall in winter, Captain."

"Who is the Queen of Pattern, please?" The frail-old-man play seemed to be gaining an audience. "And where am I going?"

"Queen of Pattern, Queen of Secrets, Shadow Queen—you've never heard of her? You *must* be foreign—well. We know you're foreign. *Really* foreign, I meant."

"From half the world away," I agreed.

"Oh? You speak the language rather well—we thought you were from Enc at first, with that accent."

"I speak a lot of languages."

Captain Ostakolin smiled. "I'm sure Her Excellency will be interested to know which ones."

———◆◆◆———

The carriage came at length to a Tower—a single Tower, perfectly round and rising one or two hundred feet in the air, dotted with arrow slits lower down and glazed windows higher up. There was a single door, so narrow that only one person could pass through it at a time, and on the inside there were slots to hold wooden bars three times as thick as the door itself. When we passed inside, one by one, I saw that there was a tight spiral staircase in the very middle of the Tower, leading both straight up and straight down.

"We have to take you up," said the Captain. "All the way up. It's a lot of stairs, even for a strong young lad like Lupsek, but we are to keep you comfortable, so we'll go at your own pace. Eh, grandfather?"

"Aye, Captain," I said. I should have seen what they were doing at the time, buttering me up like that, treating me gently so that I would lower my guard. But I was tired, exhausted from being cooped up in the cell, and exhausted from the stony silence from the Ministries of Order and Justice. I remember being simply relieved that I had finally found at least one person with more than a nominal respect for their elders. Completely fell for the lines they were feeding me, ate up the story they handed me without questioning it.

She was right—it was a lot of stairs. We stopped frequently on the way up, and neither the Captain nor her men made the slightest complaint or show of impatience, so I took the opportunity to get a good look at the Tower. The lower floors were open to the stairwell, with no walls between them—they were mostly desks of clerks, it looked like. As we went higher, the stairwell was ringed by a narrow landing and a wall with a number of doors in it. "Training rooms," Captain Ostakolin said, or, "Confidential storage," or "Plain confidential." I was thoroughly winded by the time we reached the top, even with regular and judicious breaks. The final floor was a circular landing with six doors. When the Captain unlocked one of them with a key from the ring on her belt, I saw it was doubled: a thick wooden door on the outside, swinging out, and a barred door behind it, swinging in.

It was, to put it mildly, a great improvement over the cell in the House of Order. It was wedge-shaped, like a piece of pie with a bite or two taken from its point, and it took up an entire sixth of the Tower. There was no stove or brazier, but there were enough people in the Tower, and enough stoves lower down, that the heat rose and made it comfortable enough. And a window! Yes, it was barred, and upon later inspection I found out that it did not open, but the presence of natural light was a blessing. The furnishings were sparse but serviceable, but even so, it was difficult not to be an improvement over my previous lodgings. A bed! A mattress directly on the floor, but a pillow! And no smell of rat shit or mildew; truly the gods had smiled upon me. "Her Excellency will be up soon to speak to you. Make yourself comfortable. Did they feed you lunch at the House of Order?"

"Not today, nor any other day—a stale biscuit at breakfast and a bowl of slop at dinner."

Her mouth twitched with the slightest sneer. "I'll ask the steward to send something up before Her Excellency arrives."

"I thirst, more than anything," I said, doing my frail voice again.

She gestured to a small urn by the window. "There should be water in the pitcher."

Truly I felt the gods had smiled upon me.

———◆———

S oft brown bread, soft white cheese, half a potato and two carrots from a stew, and a bruised apple: a feast fit for kings, as far as I was concerned—no, truly! It was! I scarfed it down so fast I almost choked twice, and a good thing I was so quick, too, for I was mopping up the last of the stew juice with the final morsel of bread when I felt a strange chill come over me. The air felt suddenly dank and foul, though I could smell nothing strange. The little hairs all over my body stood on end, and all my base instincts flinched to awareness and caution, but none of my senses presented evidence for the sudden feeling of dread and danger. Then it faded, and the doors opened, and a woman walked in—a woman who could only be the Queen of Pattern, Anfisa Vasilos Zofiyat Lisitsin. I scrambled to my feet and bowed as well as I knew how—it was a style more traditional in Echaree, which is south of Nuryevet's southern neighbor, Cormerra. It was close enough, I thought, for a prisoner accused of espionage.

She wasn't young, but nor was she old, and she clearly had a family inheritance of persistent youth in her face. I can tell you all the details about what she looked like (dark hair, dark almond-shaped eyes; a cat-shaped face, broad in the cheeks and narrow in the chin), but I can't describe the way she carried herself, the set of her shoulders, the way she filled up the entire room, the way she walked as silent as a shadow, without even the rustle of clothing.

"Chilly in here, isn't it?" she said to me. "Captain, have a brazier brought up and set in the corridor. If you don't mind"—to me again—"we'll leave the outer door open and you'll get a bit more warmth in here. You can shut it again easily if you'd like privacy." She smiled, then—dimpled at me, and I was set off balance.

"Thank you, Your Excellency."

"And a couple chairs, Captain, if you'd be so good." To me again: "You may call me Anfisa Zofiyat. I daresay that's formal enough for just the two of us. Please, sit down again if you were comfortable."

"I'm very confused, madam," I said. "No one has really explained anything."

"There's nothing much to explain, Master Chant. Did you get enough food? I know that Vihra Kylliat is not the best representative of Nuryeven hospitality." Not that there are any good representatives of it in this damn country.

"Yes, thank you, madam. I was told you . . . wanted information?"

"Oh, there's no rush," she said, dimpling again. "You just rest for today. We've sent for a clean set of clothes, and the steward will bring up some warm water for you to wash with later tonight."

"You're very kind, madam," I murmured, bowing my head.

"Not at all, Master Chant, I was merely raised more gently than . . . others of my rank. I have instructed the guards and the Tower staff to treat you as if you were a guest in their homes." I didn't have high hopes for this, but then, low expectations are very difficult to disappoint. "I don't mean to linger long. I only came up to introduce myself and to offer you a formal welcome while you're under my roof."

"Thank you, Anfisa Zofiyat. Um. If I am truly a guest with you, I . . . Might I be allowed to send a letter?"

She put her head slightly to one side and considered. "Well, you are still a prisoner of Order, formally accused by Justice, and I only managed to wrangle you away from them on a technicality, so ..." She got an impish twinkle in her eyes. "I'd be bending the rules a little bit. But then, my whole Ministry is one founded on a little bit of rule bending here and there. Shall we make a deal? You may send a letter if I have your honorable word as a gentleman that you will agree to be pleasant and cooperative. I've heard stories about your hearing day, you know."

I nodded solemnly. Winced a little that she knew about that already. "A time locked up underground has worn off some of my sharper edges, madam."

"Ooh," she said, knotting her eyebrows. "They put you in one of those little burrow cells? I'm surprised you haven't started growing mushrooms from your hair."

I laughed, surprised. "So am I."

"Well, I'll leave you to rest. We'll get this room warm for you—if there's anything you need for comfort, there'll be guards nearby somewhere. Just call out for them. Reasonable requests," she stressed with a smile. "Let's not get carried away—a guest has a duty to behave well, just as the host does, don't they?"

———◆———

I was given a bucket of piping-hot water, as promised, and a cloth, and a little dish of soft soap, and I scrubbed all over. So much dirt came off me that the water was almost as dark as my own skin by the end. The soap was nothing fancy, the simple kind that the working class uses, but it was another blessed luxury to add to the piles that Anfisa Zofiyat had already heaped upon me—a proper dinner, meat and vegetables and more of that soft brown bread, as warm as it could be after being hauled up dozens of flights of stairs. I asked for a comb and one was given to me, and I cleaned the elflocks out of my hair and beard until they fluffed out in a coarse woolly cloud around my head. And then: a soft bed, clean sheets, a clean blanket, a second pillow. A *second* one! I have known deprivation before in my life— comes with the territory, you know, sleeping on the ground, taking shelter from the rain under trees or in caves, or not being able to find shelter at all and walking for miles in a cold drizzle. Yes, those times I was deprived, but I was free. Now I felt positively decadent, but I still was not free—there were bars on the windows and the door, and once I had gotten a good meal or two in me and slept as hard as ever I have, I started thinking a little more clearly.

So when Anfisa Zofiyat came to see me the next morning, I asked for my advocate.

"Oh, no," she said—this was the one time she denied me anything outright, without preamble or negotiation. "No, that's one thing we can't have."

"Ah. Why, if I may ask?"

"I don't know her."

"You don't . . . know her. Is that the only reason?"

"I know everyone who works in this Tower," she said. The soft-eyed smiling expression had flickered away. Her eyes were steelier now, set solidly against me. "No one comes into this Tower and no *thing* comes in without my knowledge and permission. Never. I can't be having that."

"I would like to communicate with my advocate—and send a letter to my apprentice, but we already spoke of that."

"Strangers don't come in here. Zorya Miroslavat and Vihra Kylliat can afford to allow such things, but they're not Queens of Pattern. It's different here. No. No strangers."

"I'm a stranger, though."

"You're imprisoned," she said sharply. "There's guards in the hall, and we've taken precautions. You're not a threat."

I found myself taken aback. "Well. No, I'm not. You're the first one who's agreed with me there," I said with a faint laugh. "They all keep telling me I'm a witch, which is honestly news to me."

"You're not a witch," she said, as if she were a doctor giving a diagnosis with a very poor bedside manner. As if she were . . . reassuring me, somehow.

"Yes, *I* knew that," I said, "but how did *you*?"

She shrugged one shoulder. "We tested you. We have ways of recognizing blackwitches, even if they're new or unusually subtle."

I'd dreaded that the Nuryevens would try to test me for it. I'd had waking nightmares of being tortured as they tried to make me confess or show magic to save myself. I'd thought of hot pokers, or horrific instruments. . . . But why go to such trouble? The most terrifying imaginings were of a simple, solitary barrel of cold, dark water. "I beg your pardon, you tested me? When?"

"When you arrived, naturally."

I didn't know what to make of that.

She rose and paced—towards the window and back again, once. "Never mind this, it's none of your concern. I hear you know languages?"

"Yes, madam, several," I said; I tried to keep up with the conversation. I had to be pleasant, no matter how frustrated I was about being cut off from Consanza, no matter how shaken I was about the *test* that I had somehow passed.

"How many is several?"

"Seventeen fluently, eight well enough to insult someone's mother, a handful more well enough to buy an inn room and supper."

"Enca? Cormerran? Echareese?"

"About as well as I speak Nuryeven."

"Umakha?"

"Fluently."

"Xerecci?"

"Well enough to get by. There's this odd thing they do with the nouns. I've never been able to get my head around it."

"Fine. What else?"

"What other languages? Several dialects of Ondoro and Urtish, both fluently. Arjuni, Sharingolish, Dveccen, moderately. Hrefni, fluently—"

"We don't care about the Hrefni. They're practically on the other side of the world."

"Ah, I'm . . . surprised you knew about them at all."

"I have *very* good intelligence." Her soft-eyed mask had not slipped back down entirely. She paced back to the window and stared out of it. "Were you in Cormerra?"

"Some months ago, my apprentice and I passed through. On our way here."

"What did you see there?" Her voice was tight, and a thread of iron ran through it.

"Farms, mostly. Sheep. Forest. We didn't come anywhere near the cities. Just ugly little mud villages." I paused. "Primitive things, not like what you have here."

"Certainly not." She rolled her shoulders. "Sheep, how many sheep?"

"I didn't count them."

"Cormerra is the closest to home and the hardest to read," she murmured. "They know us on sight. They're looking for us. They keep patrols on the borders. I get news from sources inside the cities, but I don't trust them." She asked me details about my trip through Cormerra, and when that proved mostly fruitless, she said, "Tell me about the Umakh." Habits, seasonal movements, the significance of eagles . . . Things she knew about, things she had been told but didn't understand, had no context for. I had to tell the truth about all that, of course—I couldn't afford to lie. It could have been another test.

At length, we fell silent. I had answered all the questions that I could.

"What does a Queen of Pattern do?" I asked.

She was quiet for a moment. "I was elected to this office to safeguard the secrets of the realm. To hold them in trust. To know everything that's going on. To be an all-seeing eye, and to use my knowledge for our protection and defense. To see the pattern in the tapestry of fate before anyone else, to advise the other Kings and Queens on matters of state so that we might work together. I protect us from insidious enemies at home and abroad."

"A powerful place to be," I said.

"Yes. And no. Secret power—like water. Not immediate power, like Order."

"You seem to have considered your peers carefully." There was something here that I thought I could dig up, something interesting to know about her if I could brush away the dirt quietly enough that she didn't notice me looking for it.

"Part of the job description."

"Yes—part of the pattern, I suppose." I tugged my beard. "How do you hear so much?"

"I listen," she said. She turned away from the window, brushed off her dress, and left without another word.

———◆———

nfisa Zofiyat came every day to see me, clothed in deep dusky blue, to ask me questions, and every day she began calm and soft-eyed and smiling, and ended fidgety and brisk. On the third day, she allowed me to write a letter to Ylfing. Brought me a little desk and a fine feather quill and midnight-blue ink. Don't remember exactly what I wrote, but it took me a good while and a couple sheets of paper. I think I ended with an explanation—that I'd been arrested, imprisoned, charged, put on trial, charged with something else, imprisoned again. . . . Anfisa took the letter herself and tucked it into a pocket of her jacket, promising to send it by her personal messenger to Ylfing, if they could find him.

She began asking me about her peers—what had I heard about them? What had they said about her? What were they planning?

She brought us back to that several times over the course of those few hours we spent together every day—what were they planning? What were they planning? She was sure they must be planning something.

I found out that she would hold her office for life. The other royals were elected for terms of varying length, but Anfisa's term would last until she chose to retire or, more likely, until she died.

"Is it really more likely that you'll die before you retire?" I asked thoughtlessly. "How many of the other Kings and Queens of Pattern have died in office?"

She left suddenly at that question.

Belatedly, I began to think. It's something I never seem to have gotten the knack of.

I asked the guards if I might have some books or reading material to keep myself occupied, particularly histories. They were reasonably accommodating, bringing me stacks of books and taking them away again as I looked for the information—slow going, as reading

Nuryeven is much more difficult for me than speaking it, and their printing presses seemed of rather poor quality. Nothing wrong with my eyes, of course, they're as good as ever they were, but what am I supposed to do if the printers don't keep their type sharp?

I should have known to stick to tried-and-true methods: I spoke to the guards. I suppose I was turning out to be a prisoner of some significance, as there was always a guard strolling around and around that circular landing outside the door or sitting on a chair, or tending the brazier. I nudged the outer door open and pulled up my own chair.

"What's your name?" I asked the man there. He was short and stocky, with a thick black beard, not yet touched with silver.

"Steward Ilya Svetozaros," he answered, not unfriendly. He wore the typical blue coat and charcoal trousers of the Pattern Guard, but the coat he had unbuttoned, due to the cozy warmth of the brazier not ten feet away.

"I'm bored to tears, Steward Ilya Svetozaros," says I to him.

"And I as well," says he. "You're not a very exciting prisoner."

"Dealt with many exciting prisoners in your time, have you?"

"Some," he said—these Nuryevens hate communicating new information, don't they? "I thought you'd at least break the glass and try to squirm out the bars on a rope made from your blankets by now."

"It's a hundred feet to the ground! I am a very old man!"

"It's what I'd try."

"Have much experience breaking out of cells?"

"Mmm," he said, and I thought that was going to be all I got from him, but he really must have been as bored as he claimed. "Actually, yes. Part of, ah . . . ongoing training. For the elite guard, you know. The Weavers."

"I don't know, in fact. Are you to be promoted?"

"Maybe one day. Hard to say at this point."

"How did you come to work for Pattern?"

"I applied when I filed my paperwork for adulthood. Started out with the patrol, promoted to the stewards two years ago."

"And what does a steward in Pattern do?"

"Administration. Guards the Tower. Helps on city work sometimes, if the patrols are short staffed."

"Doesn't Order patrol the city?"

"The streets, sure. Pattern keeps an eye on . . . big-picture concerns." He smirked. "Any fool can arrest a street thief or a murderer. Takes a sharper eye to find evidence against embezzlers, spies, foreign agents."

"And the elite guard?"

"Away work."

"What do you mean?"

"You know, the country. Abroad. Going places, looking at things, sending letters back. Taking care of inconvenient problems for Her Excellency. Delicate matters."

"Examining the pattern," I mused.

"Aye."

"Is that what you'd like to do one day? Be part of the elite?"

"Well . . . The pay is the best anywhere. But you're away from home a lot, and obviously it's quite dangerous—and I'm thinking of marrying a couple friends of mine, see."

I had to pause for a moment there. "Plural friends?"

"Yeah. Good business match, it'd be. We've been close since we were kids."

"Perhaps my Nuryeven isn't as good as I thought. When you say marry, you mean . . . joining your households together and producing heirs, yes?" It wasn't that the concept was alien to me. It's just that I hadn't expected such an arrangement to be commonplace in

Nuryevet—well, no, I'll be honest. It's that I hadn't spent even a blink of time thinking about their practices, and if you'd asked me at that time, I probably would have told you that all Nuryevens lumber along like they're made of stone, not a drop of hot blood in their bodies and no interest whatsoever in romance, and that they acquire children by filing paperwork in quintuplicate and being assigned one by an advocate.

My new friend Ilya said, "Aye, that's right. Though I don't think Anya and Mikket will care to manage it themselves. Heirs are cheap, though, you can scrape together half a dozen of 'em right off the street, so long's you got flexible standards."

I shook my head. "Is this a common thing in these parts?"

"Eh? Oh, aye, common enough. I've seen marriages with more partners than that." He pulled his chair to face me fully. "The Umakh only ever have two-partner marriages, did you know that? And it's not about business. They don't even seem to care about their assets at all."

"Well, no, the Umakh marry for love and sex—"

"Is that right? That seems messy—lots of feelings involved if you combine sex and business."

Ilya had certain opinions, shall we say, which may not have been representative of the general Nuryeven philosophy. Marriage here is a great amalgamation of every kind of legal partnership: they get married when they're going into business together, they get married when they want to own property jointly, they get married when they're in love. . . . Some of these arrangements do involve a physical element or the biological production of heirs, as they do elsewhere; some, as Ilya mentioned before, simply involve formally adopting half a dozen heirs off the street; some are a mere legal formality. Like many things in Nuryevet, you can do as you please so long as you've got your paperwork in order. I didn't quite understand all this at the time—it took a while for me to glean the intricacies of it. Or, rather, the lack of intricacy.

At the time, I only asked Ilya if he had a separate lover.

"Not right now," he said. "I hire a private contractor for that."

"A prostitute, you mean?"

"No, a contractor. Prostitutes are—well, you're foreign, you wouldn't know. We don't have those here. Prostitutes just stand on the street and don't have a license or pay taxes, right? They just have sex with whoever in an alley?"

"Ah . . . Some of them. In some places. In other places, they're . . ." I waved vaguely. "Higher status."

"Meaning what?"

"Meaning they're more expensive; they do things besides the act. In some places, they're priests and priestesses. In some places, they're popular society figures with property and businesses, patrons of the arts and so forth."

"Here, you hire one of them like you'd hire a doctor or a tailor or someone to build a house for you—and you wouldn't grab just anybody off the street for *that*, would you? They show you their license, and you sign a contract together, and so on. It's a good system."

"What about people who don't have a license?"

"Arrested, of course, just like a doctor practicing without a license would be, or a . . ." He waved his hand, gesturing at me. "What *is* your trade, anyhow?"

"I travel. I look at things. I remember what I've seen. I tell stories about it."

"Ah, like one of the Weavers."

"I don't know what the Weavers do, exactly, but I have a feeling it's wildly different." It is.

"It's what you're doing for Anfisa Zofiyat—telling her about things so she can plan accordingly."

"Spies, then. The Weavers are spies?"

"Well . . . That's a nasty word, 'spies.' Sounds sneaky."

"Do they sneak? You mentioned being disappointed I didn't try to escape out my window."

"Well, sure they sneak; they sneak everywhere, but they ain't *sneaky*, if you know what I mean. It's different. They can come up behind you quiet as anything, probably kill you if they feel like it, or pick your pocket, or find out anything about you that they want, but that's not *sneakiness*. That's just . . . Weaver stuff."

"That's not what I do. I'm more like a teacher. I tell stories."

"Aye, then, teach me something."

Nothing brings me so much joy as a captive audience willing to have their boredom eased, but I was on a mission for information. "Perhaps we could trade stories. An even trade. Nothing comes free," I said, thinking this would appeal to Nuryeven sensibilities.

"If you like," he said.

"What are you interested in learning?"

He thought about it, leaning his head back against the wall and looking at the ceiling. "Something strange. Something no one's seen or heard of before."

"If no one's seen or heard of it, then I probably haven't either."

"No, not like that—just something most people would never see in their lives, something rare. Something that if you saw it, you'd know you'd been lucky. You ever seen anything like that? Traveling all over like you do?"

I leaned back in my own chair and stroked my beard. "Have you ever been to sea?"

"Nah, not me. Riverboats, that's about it, and even then I don't like the tossing."

THE SECOND TALE:

An Ocean of Peculiar Things

In the middle of the Unending Ocean (*I said, improvising something from a ragbag of memories and story fragments, not all of them exclusively mine*), waters unknown and uncharted by all but the most adventurous sailors, the waves at night rise in placid and inexorable rolls like great monsters of the deep, their edges limned by the soft light of the strange creatures who glow with their own light, moving like little moons beneath the surface of the sea. The strangeness of the creatures here reflects the strangeness of the whole ocean—there are bizarre currents that run through these waters, places where the water is as warm as a garden pool in summer, and regions where the sea is as still and smooth as glass. It is an ocean of peculiar things.

(*"Like what?" said the guard, which was annoying, because I was about to tell him.*)

    The farther in you sail, the more the water becomes somehow *more* than water, flowing around the ship like dark oil, and the air becomes more than air. . . . It is a sensation, almost, a strangeness in the air. Sailors call this the *ufstora*, the touch of the gods, and none of them that I have ever met will consent to go in search of it. There are places, though, where it can be found, in the most remote places of the ocean, as far away from land as it is possible to get anywhere in the world.

    But even without the *ufstora*, the night sky above this sea is extraordinary—a velvet of such richness as I have seen nowhere else in this world, and so deep that it seems like you're looking into the reflection of the deepest reaches of the ocean. The stars shine above like jewels, glowing with divine light in an infinite cosmos.

(Mind you . . . It's a sky. A pretty sky, to be sure, but I was fluffing it up a little for him; you know how it goes. Ilya nodded along the whole time and said things like, "Goodness," and "You don't say.")

One of the many exceptional phenomena of the sea is something the sailors have no name for. *(This part is absolutely true.)* When I first encountered it, I called it *ufstora* too, but the crew was quick to correct me—this was not a supernatural thing. You see, there is something in the atmosphere here, a mist or a miasma that appears in the sky over certain areas, as unpredictable as the wind or the clouds or the northern lights, and when this mist comes overhead, there is no visible warning—and suddenly the stars explode into brilliant splendor all across the sky, their light scattering and multiplying into ten thousand shards and splinters of fire and color, and the sky behind them appears in an amazing array of hues, arranged in dazzling clouds and streaks, filled with the light from stars never before seen—even the dimmest star becomes as big and bright as a candle flame held at arm's length. It lasts but a few moments, no longer than it takes for a cloud to pass over the moon. I can call it dazzling, but that is as close to the truth as a sigh is to a hurricane.

But encounters with the nameless brightness or the *ufstora* are rare. Some have seen them many times. Many

die without seeing them once. There are other things here,
in this place that is not a place: The odd creatures that swim
up from the unknowable depths. The stormfire that comes
during a tempest and blazes on the ends of the bowsprits,
as steady as anything even while the boat is being tossed to
pieces.

*(He shuddered at this, and I don't think he was faking the faintly sickened
expression that came across his face.)*

Once, many years ago, I crossed the sea in a rowboat
tethered to its ship by a long rope.

*(He looked further sickened at this. By the way, this was a lie: it wasn't
me who did this, but my own master-Chant, well before I ever became her
apprentice. She had a great love of the ocean.)*

I wished to study what I could of those eerie maritime
occurrences, and riding in the rowboat put the noises of
the ship at a distance so I could focus. I would pass the
nights half sitting, half lying against the stern, with my feet
propped up on the thwart and my right hand hanging over
the gunwale, trailing my fingers in the thick, rich water. I
remember one night when we were passing through the
doldrums, when all the waves stop and the sea goes as still
as glass, all soft and sweet, and the smallest ripples of waves
just lapping at the hull of my little boat were the only thing
that broke the perfect silence. Both moons were shining
that night, and the stars, and the only other light was from
the Captain's lamp as she stood at the wheel and whispered

wind charms into the sails, just enough to keep them billowing. In those days, they used silk sails when they were doing a Great Crossing, which is the name for the course that takes a ship directly across the middle of the sea. That night I wasn't sleeping, but I had my head propped up and I watched a pair of moonfish following my little boat, twirling around each other as they swam. Moonfish are small, for ocean fish—their silver bodies are the length of a man's forearm, and they have delicate trailing fins that glow with a pale green light. You never see them alone. Always and only in pairs. It is said that they mate for life, and that it is bad luck to catch one and not the other.

(That is exactly as my master-Chant told it to me. I myself have never seen moonfish, and I'm too old now to be crossing the ocean in a rowboat anyway.)

I went on in that vein for a little while, but those were the interesting parts. He was an attentive audience, nodded along with everything I said, interested but not pushy. When I finished, I said, "Now it's your turn."

"Aye. And what would you like to learn about?"

My heart beat a little faster in my chest, and I hemmed and hawed to cover my nervousness, feigning indecision. "Well," I said slowly, at long last, "I suppose I'd like to know more about Nuryevet. And you—you seem like a patriot, being a public servant and all, so you're a good person to tell me about it."

"I guess," he said, frowning a little. "And what is it that you want to know about, specifically?"

"Well. Hmm. I suppose I'm most curious about things that are going to affect me personally, to be honest with you—how trials work, how long I can expect to be imprisoned. . . ." I could have gotten that information from Consanza before, if I'd thought to ask. This was all camouflage for the things I really wanted. "Or—well, I suppose I don't even understand your system of government at all. There are so many Primes," I quavered, a feeble old man, "I just can't keep them straight." All lies, of course. "Maybe you could tell me about them . . . or what their Ministries are concerned with and how they came to be. . . ."

What I actually wanted was gossip and blackmail material, or at least enough of a personal sketch of each of the Queens that I could deduce things about them. I had spoken to two Queens already at that point, and knowing anything about who they were as people would have given me a foothold into turning my fortunes around. If I could give Anfisa Zofiyat what she wanted, then she would begin to like me, and I could use that as leverage.

Ilya shrugged. "All right. It's not as complicated as all that."

THE THIRD TALE:
An Introduction to Nuryeven Social Science
About three hundred years ago, there was only one King.
His name was Chadvar Chadvaros, and he was awful.
He taxed the common folk to poverty and starvation and
spent all the money bribing foreign merchants, and he very
nearly sold us out to Enc and Cormerra. Long story short,
everyone decided that hereditary monarchy was a stupid
idea, and they killed him.
    "I have an idea," said someone. "What if we all just
pick someone who we think would be good at looking
after things around here, and after a while we have the

opportunity to pick someone else if the first person starts
being terrible?" That sounded like a good idea, so they
elected someone smart and tough, Timea Dorotayat. She
was the first elected Prime, so they called her the People's
Queen. A bunch of stuff happened, and as it turned out,
not every Prime was good at every aspect of ruling—some
sole-ruling Primes were great with money, but crap at war.
So they started splitting the government into branches so
they could pick people who were right for each individual
job. First they divided it into Hearth and Field. Hearth
concerned everything to do with things inside Nuryevet:
law and taxes and so forth; while Field concerned
everything outside: diplomacy and war and foreign trade.

Eventually, after a few more splits, they ended up
with the current system: Law, Justice, Order, Pattern,
and Commerce—or Coin, as you'll more often hear. Law
obviously makes the laws, Order enforces the law, and
Justice interprets it. Coin is pretty self-explanatory, and
Pattern is there to see the big picture, to offer wisdom and
guidance, and to provide a sense of long-term continuity.

("Surely Zorya Miroslavat has more life experience? More wisdom? Why
would they elect someone as young as Anfisa Zofiyat to Pattern, if it is
about those things?" I said. I was bored of all this dull, useless stuff. I
wanted some specifics. Something contemporary, something practical.)

Anfisa Zofiyat is as shrewd as they come! (He was quick
to assure me.) She has worked in Pattern since she became
an adult; there is no one more qualified, no one more
discreet.

("Oh," I said. "It's just that Zorya Miroslavat seemed dismissive of her talents and abilities.")

Well, she has a grudge against Anfisa Zofiyat and the Ministry of Pattern. We know she's up to all kinds of tiny crimes, and we keep finding them and making her look bad. If we wanted, we could blacken her name at the next Justice election and put her out of a job, and she knows it.

(It was at this point that I began using Ilya's own tactic: "Goodness," I said, and "You don't say," and little meaningless questions to tweak more information out of him.)

Zorya Miroslavat's got her favorites, you know. Everyone does. She's given promotions to a lot of people who shouldn't have gotten them. She's taken a few bribes. A few times she's told her judges what verdict they should give on a case. . . . She words it as a suggestion, and all her correspondence makes it sound like she's just debating the merits of one hypothetical interpretation of the law or another, but that's what she's doing. She really ought to keep her nose out of their work. The judges need to be able to make their own decisions, but she hangs over them, as anxious and fussy as a mother watching her child learn to cut onions.

This is common knowledge if you know the right people, by the way. This isn't a huge secret. I don't mind telling you, because I want you to know about the good work Pattern is doing.

Oh, and Zorya got Vihra Kylliat elected as Queen

of Order, too. Vihra's also engaged in a little harmless nepotism in her time. She and Zorya are very close. It makes things difficult for us, whenever the Primes meet for anything, because—well, Vihra and Zorya double up together, and the King of Law dodders along, taking no notice of anything, because he's nearly too old to even hold his own head up, and the Queen of Coin is equally useless. She's definitely embezzling funds from the treasury, but we've got our eye on her. She hates us too.

There's other things too, but I can't tell you about those.

We're not doing anything wrong, of course. We're just trying to keep everyone in line so the Pattern stays straight and even. We're part of the balance of things, and we have to be smart about it. A lot of folk get angry with Pattern because they don't understand. They think things are bad, but we know that's just how things are. When you think about it, it's not as bad as it could be—here, we get to choose who is in charge, we get to choose people to make mistakes on our behalf. Lots of places, they don't do that. You have to endure whatever you're given by the fates. King goes mad? You keep him. Queen dies of a cold? I guess you're out of luck.

When you look at it that way, we're lucky to live here.

All in all, it was a reasonably productive conversation with Ilya.

———◆———

Anfisa Zofiyat came every day for at least an hour and asked me everything I knew, and I tried my best to cooperate with her as much as possible. She said that her messenger was out looking for Ylfing, that the journey out took at least a day, and that's assuming that he hadn't left the town where we'd parted and traveled elsewhere.

I wrote another letter and sent that one out as well, just in case.

"I'm not a spy," I assured her over and over again, whenever she asked for information I didn't have—secrets, blackmail, hidden information, knowledge of the neighboring countries' weaknesses.

Once, early on, she came to me and was . . . strange. Exceptionally strange. She stood close to me and sniffed me, checked my eyes and under my tongue as if I were a horse she was looking to buy. She watched me eat. She snapped her fingers, and there was an enormous din in the hallway, guards clattering metal on metal and banging things against the stone walls. It startled me out of my wits, and then she and I sat there staring at each other: she, expectant; I, deeply confused. She dropped a colorfully painted wooden ball in my lap, the sort a child might play with.

Another test, I know now. Double-checking whether I was a blackwitch.

I found out, through more story-trades with Ilya, that Anfisa slept in the Tower, rather than going home to her own house. She occupied a locked room in the deepest basement, four levels underground and walled with stone two feet thick. I found out that she served herself from the same food the head steward served everyone, that she washed her own dishes and kept them locked in her room when she wasn't using them, that she drank from a water barrel that even the newest patrolman used, and that she never touched wine, tobacco, or anything else that had been made especially for her.

I found out, too, that her predecessors, six of them over the course of not quite eighty years, had all been assassinated. Seven rulers before her, one King of Pattern had managed to die of natural causes (or what seemed to be natural causes, at least). Three more rulers before him had been assassinated too.

It didn't seem to be a very cushy job, to say the least.

Then, one day, after I had been in the Tower for nearly a week, I was looking out my little window and I saw a small squad of red-uniformed guards approaching the Tower door. Order had sent her emissaries.

To fetch me, it turned out. Anfisa had used up her allotted time to question me. She wouldn't allow the Order guards inside the Tower, of course, but she came up to see me, tense and pale, and she spoke quickly to me, entreating me to remember her kindness, promising that she would send one of her most trusted aides to continue speaking to me, that she might in fact come herself if the situation demanded. Then Captain Ostakolin brought me downstairs and signed me over into the tender mercies of Order.

The days were getting shorter, and though it was already mid-morning, the sun was just then beginning to rise.

———✦———

On the upside, the new cell I was given was not so deep underground. There was, I think, a window somewhere down the hall, because there was a faint glow of natural light from around a corner. I was put in the cell and left to myself.

Consanza arrived within the hour, wrapped up in thick wool now that the weather had begun to turn. She pulled off her gloves—fine leather, I noticed—and stuck her pipe in her mouth before she even said hello.

"So you had a vacation at the Tower of Pattern, eh?" she mumbled from around the stem as she lit her pipe-leaf. "Apparently Anfisa Zofiyat is saying you're not a blackwitch; I don't know how you convinced her of that, but let me be the first to offer my most hearty congratulations. Did you know she submitted a memo that suggests the witchcraft charge might be a waste of time? So you have that, at least. Well done. I think we can put that out of our minds for now; no one's going to pursue that unless they get really desperate. From start to finish, this Pattern business has been an interesting development."

"Has it?" I asked. I was overcome with despair, regardless of Consanza's news—back to a cold, cramped cell, back to a hard bench to sleep on and a ratty blanket, back to stale bread and slop for my meals. I was already missing the Tower. As Anfisa had asked, I remembered her fondly, though the news that she officially didn't believe I was a witch only frustrated me—how enraging it is when people announce something obvious as if it were a breakthrough! "I met the Queen of Justice before the Pattern Guard arrived to take me."

Consanza crossed her arms and blew out a stream of smoke. "Did you? A social call, was it?"

I shook my head. "She and the Duchess of Justice came. I was taken to a room, they asked me questions, I refused to answer without you—"

"Good."

"—they refused to send for you. I asked to send a letter. They said no. Anfisa Zofiyat let me, though."

"So you met her in person, then? Hmm."

"She came to talk to me every day." I curled up on my bench and tried to cover up my ankles and my shoulders at the same time.

"And here I assumed she would delegate that task to someone she wanted to punish," Consanza said dryly. "What did you talk about?"

"She wanted to know—you know, the same things everyone else wants to know." I was tired, and suddenly it came over me in a wave. "Just get out," I snapped. "I'm tired of being shuffled around like a pawn in a chess game, and I'm tired of being interrogated all the time. Come back tomorrow, unless you can get me a proper blanket and a messenger to carry another letter to my apprentice."

"Can't come tomorrow, I have a hearing—with one of my paying clients, you know. You were only supposed to be a tedious little witch-craft trial, and now this. And just so you know? Anfisa saying that you're not a blackwitch doesn't mean that you're out of danger with that espionage charge, so don't get your hopes up."

She left.

I thought fondly of the Tower of Pattern.

———————————————

I asked the guard who brought me my next meal if I could send a letter and was, as I expected, conclusively shut down.

Consanza came again two days later, with a bundle stuffed under her arm. "Here. I asked around about secondhand stores and went all the way up to Bent Street to get this. Smelly, but it should do you." She unfurled the bundle as she spoke and flung it between the bars. It was an old horse blanket, and it *was* smelly—stale horse sweat and stale hay—but it wasn't any worse than the cell itself, so I wrapped it around my shoulders and was grateful for it. "You ready to talk today?"

I nodded silently.

"The Queen of Pattern spoke with you every day, you said?"

"Yes. Wanted to know . . . everything I knew about anything. Intelligence. I didn't have much. I'm not a Weaver."

"Did you answer her questions?"

"Well, yes."

Consanza sighed heavily. "Did you ask to see me?"

"Obviously. I'm not stupid. She wouldn't let you in. Too much of a security risk—funny, 'cause all I saw of their security at the Tower was a wooden door and a lot of stairs."

"Mm, yes. All you *saw* of their security. All *you* saw." Consanza waved that away. "But you cooperated with her and ran your mouth—again—without my counsel? I'd be dubious about keeping you on, at this point, but . . . Well, finish telling me about what happened."

I told her about the comfortable room, the hot meals, the warm bed, the brazier in the hall.

"And in exchange for your cooperation, she sent your letters out with her messengers?"

"But it's been days—more than a week—and I don't know where he is now, or if they even found him to give him the letters—"

Consanza snorted. "You're pretty naive when it comes to that kid, aren't you?"

"I could be your grandfather, woman! Don't you disrespect me! I just want to—hmph! I just want him to know where I am, that's all."

"She probably didn't even send the messages out."

I scowled at her as fiercely as I could manage, bundled up on the bench in a smelly horse blanket. "She liked me," I said. "She said she'd help me if I helped her, and I did my best, so why wouldn't she do the same?"

She rolled her eyes massively—it wasn't a good look for her. "Oh, I don't know, because she's a Queen of spies, one of the most cunning women in the country, with dirt on everyone and no qualms about using it, and in the year or so since she was elected has become a famous paranoid who barely leaves the Tower except under heavy guard by her most trusted Weavers and stewards? She probably kept those damn letters and has someone tearing them apart to find a code. You didn't write anything in code, did you?"

"Of course I didn't! What have I to say in code? I have nothing to hide! I said, 'Ylfing, I have been charged with crimes I have not committed, and I am being kept in prison in Vsila until my trials are over. Be very careful of how you talk to people; they're a very suspicious bunch, and terribly rude to strangers.'"

"And that's all?"

"I think so. They were short letters."

"None of them even left the Tower. I would bet money on it, and you know I don't gamble on the long odds. Your apprentice is still wholly ignorant of your fate. But back to your case. This is getting a little bit interesting for me."

I narrowed my eyes. "Interesting? How so?"

"The Queens seem to be having a bit of a spat over who gets to sink her claws into you." Consanza tapped her fingers on the arm of her chair. "I did some digging and found out what was happening with them during your time in the Tower. First Anfisa Zofiyat pulled that stunt with her Nineteenth Modification right to question traitors and spies—*suspected* traitors and spies," she corrected herself, seeing me about to object. "Then the Queen of Justice, Zorya Miroslavat, basically threw a giant fit—that's the legal term for it, don't you know—anyway, she threw a fit about Anfisa Zofiyat getting to keep you locked up in the Tower where no one could get to you, and she filed what I think we can technically refer to as an *epic fuckload* of injunctions and objections and, well, all the legal paperwork tantrums she and her clerks could think of. But the law is the law, and Casimir Vanyos—that's the King of Law—said that there wasn't any way to get around it, but then Vihra Kylliat came in on Zorya Miroslavat's side, *obviously*, because Order and Justice have always been like this"— she crossed two fingers to show me—"no matter who the Primes are, and Vihra Kylliat and Zorya Miroslavat have been even more like that. They're like mother and daughter, practically." This all lined up with what Ilya had told me, and my head spun just imagining the mental acrobatics I would have had to do to follow all this without his explanations. "Anyway, once Vihra Kylliat got involved, Casimir Vanyos had to take it to a formal vote among the Primes, and since Taishineya Tarmos abstains most of the time because she doesn't give a shit, and the Prime of Law is required to always abstain except in the case of a tie, it was just Pattern against Justice and Order, and Anfisa Zofiyat couldn't provide enough evidence to show that her questioning of you was turning up information crucial to the safety and prosperity of the nation, so she had to give you up. And that's that, and here you are."

"Here I am," I said, dazed. "Who was the last one you mentioned, the one who abstains by choice?"

"Ah—Taishineya Tarmos Elyat Chechetni." It took a moment for me to wrap my brain around how all those names could belong to one person. The Nuryevens love bureaucracy, you see, and they're not terribly creative, so every person's name goes by the exact same formula—a use name, a patronymic, a matronymic, and a family name. Makes it easier for the advocates to alphabetize their filing cabinets or something, probably. "The Queen of Commerce—you'll more commonly hear her called Queen of Coin, though. Or the Queen of Gold, Penny Queen, Dragon Queen, Trader Queen. The Thief Queen, too, during tax season. Better than what they call Zorya Miroslavat, worse than what they call Casimir Vanyos."

"Dare I ask?"

"Casimir's the Loophole King," she said, with a slight wry smile. "Or the King of Convenient Precedent. And Zorya is the Rope Queen or Gallows Queen."

I felt a little sick. "Why does Taishineya Tarmos abstain?"

"Personal preference. Likes to keep her options of allies open, I suppose. Prefers smiling over talking, prefers no one to know where she stands on any given subject. I don't think you'd like her."

"How would you know who I'd like?"

"Just a hunch."

"And all this is interesting to you?"

"Oh, fascinating," Consanza said calmly. "Imagine the opportunity to argue a case in front of a panel of all five of them. And if the fighting between Pattern and Justice keeps going on like this, and if Order keeps supporting Justice, then it'll have to go to a panel. There won't be any choice." Consanza leaned back in the chair and folded her hands across her stomach. "At this point, it's looking like I could lose this case horrifically and still walk away covered in roses."

"I wish you'd be more serious about this," I snarled. "It's my life on the line. My freedom, at the very least. I have a *religious duty* to attend to."

"So attend to it in prison. Everyone has stories, right?"

She was right. I didn't care to admit it. "So you're going to stick around because it'll be good for your career."

"Oh, sorry; I was perhaps unclear. No. Your case itself is going to be shit for my career, in all probability. But having a few months of being in the same room as the Primes of the realm, having a few months to kiss ass like I've never kissed ass before—if I play my cards right, I could end up with some nice cushy administrative position in Law or Justice and spend the rest of my days peacefully raking in the cash. Probably wouldn't go for Order; Vihra Kylliat's a known hard-ass. Coin's risky—the term of office for the Prime is only five years, so there's a lot of jumbling up every time someone new comes in. And Pattern's creepy and impossible to get into, and the Pattern Primes always end up going crazy or getting killed, so their so-called life term is really more like eight years or so, maximum, *if* they're lucky. Too much excitement, not enough cush. It'll be Law or Justice for me—good long terms of office for those Primes: twenty and fifteen, respectively. Nice and sedate. Stable. Not immediately, though—I've got another seven or ten years of trial court dramatics in me, but I'm not as young as I used to be, and I'm getting sick of these fucking students following me everywhere, wanting to be mentored or something."

"Haven't you ever heard of integrity? In some places, it's thought to be honorable to advance yourself through your skills and personal honor, rather than this . . . kissing ass, as you so eloquently put it."

"I'm not interested in doing things the hard way. I've never had to do it that way before, and I'm not about to start now." Lucky for her that she ever had a choice about doing things the hard way or not. "Look on the bright side. I'm probably not going to heave you overboard at this point. Probably—as long as the Primes are this interested in you." She tapped a finger against her cheek, deep in thought. "Casimir Vanyos is going to stay interested—he has to—as long as those three are at each other's throats, but Taishineya Tarmos . . . I wonder if we could get her to come down on our side. Are you sure you don't have anything to bribe her with, if it came to that?"

"Only what's in here." I jabbed a finger at my forehead. "It doesn't seem to be valuable to anyone but me."

"Hah, so said Vanya the Smith."

"Who?"

"Vanya the Smith. Vanya Skyforger?"

I shook my head. "Folk hero?"

"Sort of. Aren't you supposed to know all the stories there are?"

"I never claimed that. I only know a lot of them," I grumbled. "Only as many as I've heard in my whole life, or that my master heard in hers." I wrapped the horse blanket tighter around my shoulders. "I'd like to hear it. I was starting to think you people didn't have any stories."

THE FOURTH TALE:
Vanya the Smith and the Thirty Iron Swans

Right. So. Vanya the Smith was working in his shop one day. Slow day. Slow week. It was the middle of winter, and there wasn't anyone who wanted to trek all the way through the drifts to get their things repaired or to buy tools. So there's Vanya, right, amusing himself by practicing some tricky smith things—I don't know the names of them, I'm not a smith—making little toys out of iron and steel, making pretty weapons and such. He had to keep his forge hot, you see. I think that's important. Maybe it was a magic forge.

Anyway, so he starts making these animals out of wrought iron. He makes an iron mouse, but it's not right, so he melts it down and starts over. Makes an iron cat, but it's not right either. Melts it. Makes an iron dog, melts that, too. He keeps going. Persistent guy, Vanya.

So then he makes an iron swan—a big one, a swan-size one. And when he's finished, it comes alive and starts flapping, right into his rain barrel, and he jumps back and there it is, floating on the top of the water. Every time it flutters its wings, they chime, because each feather is made of metal.

Well, Vanya thinks this is amazing, so he makes another, and another—I guess he must have had a lot of iron lying around—and basically he fills up his whole yard with these iron swans. Well, what good is an iron swan?

thinks Vanya. Not much use to anyone, but he likes them real well, and they're quiet except for that metally chiming noise they make. He's a smith, he likes metal, he thinks it's a nice sound. Anyway, they're alive and he feels bad about trying to grab one and get it melted down.

So they stick around his smithy for a while—they wander down to the pond and swim around, they make nests out of scrap metal on his roof and stuff, but they don't cause any trouble, and he goes about his own business.

So eventually there's a little warm spell, and everyone who needs something from Vanya comes up to see him, and they're all astonished to see these iron swans sitting around all over the place. "Vanya," they say, "what are all these swans?"

And Vanya says, "Oh, just things I made. I think they're pretty."

So a young man thinks one would be a nice gift for his spouses, and he tries to find out how much Vanya wants for them, but Vanya refuses to sell them, and he insists that they're of no use to anyone but him. Gods know why. Doesn't make any sense to make a thing and not sell it to someone who wants to buy it, but that's how the story is.

So everyone goes away, and they tell all their friends about the iron swans at Vanya's place, and when the next warm spell comes, an even bigger crowd goes over there, and some people want to buy the swans, but Vanya says no, and all those people go home and complain about it.

Then the Earl of Order in the village hears about the swans, and he doesn't even wait for the blizzards to stop— he treks out there in the snow and the wind and knocks on

Vanya's door, wants to give him all this coin for one of the swans. Vanya says no, says they're not worth anything to anyone but him.

So the Earl of Order goes home and he gets all his patrolmen, and they go back out and beat Vanya up and take all the swans.

"Is that it?" I asked, when she was done.

"What do you mean, is that it? Of course that's it. It's a good story."

I put my head in my hands. "Your grandfathers and their fathers and their fathers would be ashamed to know that their descendant had fallen so far." It occurred to me that Consanza must have grown up very comfortably, considering the vague, dismissive way she'd talked about Vanya's smithing. Anyone less fortunate would have *seen* a blacksmith working at some point, but I got the feeling that Consanza never had.

"Well, if you don't like it, you can just say so. There's no call to be insulting."

"Two and a half thousand years of myth and storytelling tradition in Arjuneh and this errant daughter just ran off some little fable like it was town gossip," I groaned.

Consanza took out her pipe and chomped on the end of it. "That's just the way it was told to me. You're being very rude."

"It's a story about a man who was too much of an idiot to see that other people valued what he had for some quality that he didn't even know about."

"At least you *get* it."

"It's hard not to get it," I muttered, "when you all but bashed me in the face with the moral of it. Poor Vanya."

"Well, I can't just go around changing it to be different or better based on what *you* think, can I?"

"Are there other stories about Vanya?"

"I suppose so."

"What's his pattern? What's he always do in stories?"

"Makes interesting new stuff, doesn't think it's any good, doesn't let anyone else do anything with it but look. Magical things, things that come alive. He once made a plow, but it turned out to be evil—or he thought it was evil, anyway."

"And then what?"

"And then someone comes along and says something or does something that should prove to him that he made a good thing, but he's never convinced."

"There's a story like that your grandfather's father would have told in Arjuneh. 'Priya, Majnun, and the Wondrous Blue Panther.'"

"Well, you can keep it to yourself," she sniffed. "I don't find myself much in the mood to listen to you right now."

"Fine. Did you find out about me sending a letter to my apprentice?"

"I didn't," she said. "Maybe I'll do it if I can figure out a better way to ask about it."

"Look, it wasn't—" I stopped. Huffed. She was taking it far too personally, and it wasn't even her story. Not one she'd come up with. What call did she have to get so offended? "Fine. Listen—the purpose of that story was to prove a point to me, yes? To show that maybe I have something the Primes want even if I think that everything I have on offer is worthless to them. You made that point. I got the point. I could teach you how to make the point better, but if that's the way Nuryevens tell stories, then that's the way Nuryevens tell stories, and even if it goes against everything I consider best practice, I still don't have any right to make a judgment call on it. I was . . ." I harrumphed. "It was unfamiliar and it made me miss familiar things."

"I'm leaving," Consanza said.

"Will you come again tomorrow?"

"I'll come again for your next hearing."

The room was colder after she left, and I was quietly grateful for the horse blanket. The cold seemed like it had made my joints into rocks.

A glimmer of regret dawned in me—I had been too harsh with her after all, and the story really hadn't been as bad as all that. I had held her to Chant standards, not layman's standards, because she'd understood about telling stories. Because . . .

She has this way about her, the same gift as Ylfing but backwards. Ylfing looks at anyone and sees the best thing about them, sees their kindness, their loves, whatever little whisper of divine grace they have within them. Consanza sees . . . not the worst thing, I don't think, but the wretched parts, the petty parts, the little jealousies and grudges. She's more like me than Ylfing is—more like me than I would admit to just anyone. I think that's why we clash as we do. We see a mirror of ourselves in each other, and neither of us can come up with a story about ourselves to disguise it. It's uncomfortable and upsetting to have yourself stripped naked down to the bedrock of your soul with one hard glance from someone as unsympathetic as yourself.

Ylfing embraces the whole world, loves unreservedly, gives his entire heart away with the blind faith that he'll get something equal in return. Consanza and I give nothing of ourselves away, and yet . . . as much as I annoy her, and as much as she annoys me, neither of us has quite concluded that there's nothing in humanity worth redeeming. She's an advocate, after all. It's right there in the title: she speaks for people who cannot speak for themselves. She tells their stories to save their necks, or their souls, or however you want to look at it.

And so do I.

I know exactly why I can't bring myself to be kind to her. I have no illusions about that: to find her likable, I'd have to find myself likable, and I know I'm not, and I don't care to make myself so.

That's that.

As it happened, Consanza came again before the hearing. To tell me, in fact, that she didn't know when the hearing would be.

"Order and Justice are pushing to try you as soon as possible, but Anfisa Zofiyat is claiming previous engagements, and Casimir Vanyos isn't always available. It's quite hard to get all five Primes together in one room at the same time. It's rare that they need the whole panel in person for something like this. But there you are," she said. "It just keeps getting more and more interesting, doesn't it?"

"If I even live that long!" My teeth were chattering that day. The dull chill of autumn had dipped into the first bite of winter the night before. "Can't you do something about this?"

"No," she said flatly. "What do you expect me to do?"

"Anything! More blankets, a fire. Do they want me to die here?"

"Oh please, it's not that bad."

Our breath clouded faintly in the air between us. I glared at her. *She* had a cloak and her woolen robes.

"They'll light fires when it gets properly cold," she said.

"In Pattern they gave me a fire! Can't you have me sent back there?"

"I'm not going to intentionally ruin my chances with Justice by doing something so foolish!"

"Then take a message to Anfisa Zofiyat. Ask her to come see me, and tell her I've thought of something she must know, and when she's here, I'll ask her to do something about—"

"I'll do nothing of the sort. Do you want to see me arrested for illegal collusion? Please!"

Needless to say, that visit didn't go well. Consanza stormed out again not too much longer after that.

They would have heated the cell blocks a little, eventually, just enough to keep it above freezing, but the Nuryevens have a higher tolerance for cold than I do, and I thought I might die of exposure even before they thought about putting on their mittens.

I wrapped the blanket around me as well as I could and forced my aching bones to work and move me around my little cell until the blood started pumping. I devised, finally, a cunning plan. It wasn't quite witchcraft, but it was as close as I had available to me.

Eventually, the guard walked past. I had seen him earlier when he came on shift. He had a tendency to keep moving through his patrol and to make rude comments to me whenever he looked into my cell.

Sure enough, he walked by, looked in, and saw me shivering in the middle of the cell with my blanket around my shoulders.

"You freeze to death yet, grandfather?" he said.

I leaped forward, thrust my arms between the bars, and seized him by the front of his tunic. I began in a snarl: "A very long time ago and half the world away—"

THE FIFTH TALE:
Death Under a Blue Heaven

—I was walking through a familiar market in the smallest hours of the night when Death came upon me.

I had met Death before. She and I were old friends, and I had been fleeing her ever since. I spoke to her that night, and she told me six secrets, holding me close just as I am holding you now, staring into my soul with her frost-rimed eyes, her breath rattling in her chest. These secrets bound me into silence until I completed a task for her, and I knew there is only one task Death ever asks for.

But all she commanded me to do was to warn my friend that she was going to come for him in his home in three days, that she would come for him when he walked next under a blue heaven, and that she would come in the form of something long and brown and slithery.

She released me. I ran from her. I fled like a child. I went to my friend's house as she had ordered me. I told my friend everything that had happened. The front of my tunic was stained and smudged with grave dirt, and when I breathed, I felt a rattling in my chest just the same as hers.

My friend went pale. His hands shook, his knees knocked. He asked for my advice. I told him three things: that he must never travel by daylight, for if the heavens were not blue, then she could not come to him. I told him to wear thick boots, to protect against snakes. And that he should leave the city immediately, for if he wasn't at home, then her prophecy would come to naught.

My friend left that very night, vowing to travel only in darkness.

And yet he died three days later—he had gone to the house of his father, where he had grown up, his first home. He had worn thick, new, heavy boots that weighed him down, made him slow. He had left the house in the twilight to visit a wine merchant, and on his way home, he took a shortcut through an alley and passed under a blue awning, where a pair of thieves set upon him and throttled him with a hempen rope.

I ask you: Did I kill my friend?

————— ◆ —————

ow, the only reason I got all that out was because the guard
froze in terror at the first words I spoke, and I could see, *Oh
gods, a blackwitch*, in his eyes, as clear as words on a page. He'd
probably never had a prisoner attack him like this before, and I talked
quick before he could figure out what to do, and by that point I'd
gotten him all tangled up in it. As soon as I finished, he squirmed free
and scrambled out of reach, wide-eyed. He made a gesture of warding
at me. I retreated a step too and looked coolly at him.

"You saw *Death?*" he asked.

Blackwitch, I saw in his eyes again. "No," I said, innocent. "It was
just a story. Did you like it?"

"Gods, no." He shook himself and straightened his clothing. "I
should have you beaten for assaulting me."

"I just wanted to get your attention. You guards won't speak to
me when I ask you questions. Didn't do any harm, now, did I?" A little
smarmy, perhaps, but he was a thoroughly smarmed lad himself, so he
should be able to take it as well as give it.

"I'm going to report this to the warden," he said, pointing at me
for emphasis. "You'll be punished."

"I seem to have frightened you."

"I'm not frightened!"

"Eerie stories aren't to everyone's taste, I suppose."

"I'm not afraid."

"Do you know any?"

"No."

"Oh," I said, feigning great disappointment. "Well, of course,
since they're not to your taste, why would you remember any? What
about other ones? Do you know any about Vanya the Smith? My

advocate told me a rather good one about some iron swans."

"No," he said again, more firmly.

I sat down on my bench and huddled into my horse blanket. "I'm sorry for startling you," I said, with the greatest of all possible sincerity. "It'd be a lot of paperwork for you, probably, to report such a silly thing I did. I was bored, is all. I won't do it again if you accept my apology."

The mention of paperwork set his resolve off balance. "Fine," he muttered. "It's fine. But *don't* do it again."

"Actually, I was wondering . . . What's your job like? I see you walking around the halls, and I thought it must be very boring for you, same as it is for me."

"It's a job."

"Not a very exciting one, though, eh?"

He shifted from foot to foot. "No."

"Hmm. Shame. It's not exactly a thrill to sit in here in the cold by myself all day either. I'm an old man, you know. How do you keep yourself entertained? Besides shooting terribly clever verbal jabs at elderly prisoners, that is," I added with a wry smile.

"Why do you want to know?" he asked.

I sighed. "Just making conversation. I like getting to know the people around me. When I was at the Tower of Pattern, I was guarded by—by none other than a Weaver."

Aha, there—*that* got him. You can always see it. It's in the way they suddenly seem to take *notice* of you even if they were already looking right at you. "No, you weren't."

"I was," I assured him. "And whatever you've heard about them . . . That's not even half of it."

"What do you mean?"

"Well . . . If you really want to know . . . Do you really want to know?"

Yes, said his face, and *Absolutely not*.

"If you bring me a cloak or another blanket, I'll tell you anything you want to know about them."

His face clouded with anger. "No," he snapped. "I'm not allowed to give you anything, even if I wanted to." He stomped off.

After fifteen minutes or so had passed, he returned with a bundle in his arms. "You really have things to say about the Weavers in Pattern?"

"I do, lad." I eyed the fabric—dull, dusty, faded stripes of burnt orange and red. He shook it out and wedged it through the bars, tossing it into my lap. I huddled into it. I licked my lips. I looked shiftily up and down the corridor, and I gestured him to step closer. "Do you know, they're all marked?"

"The tattoo? Yes, I know. Everyone does." His face pinched. "If you don't have anything useful to say, you'll have to give it back."

I hadn't noticed tattoos on any of the guards, but they'd kept themselves covered to the wrist, to the ears, to the toes. "No, besides that—a hidden mark. I saw it with my own eyes." He wrapped his hands around the bars, and I pitched my voice even quieter. "A ring of runes—magical protection against evil and a charm for invisibility. That's how they move so quietly."

He nodded slowly. "And the beast shapes? Did you see any of those?"

The what now? "I saw . . . a few animals around the Tower. I thought nothing of them. Were they . . . ?"

"Weavers," he whispered. "They can change into cats and birds."

I shivered dramatically. "A raven perched on my windowsill the entire time—they must have been spying on me. Thank goodness Order came to take me away."

"Yeah, yeah, whatever. Give the blanket back. I told them you wouldn't have anything useful to say." He reached through the bars, trying to catch the corner of the fabric between his fingers, but I pulled away.

"That's not all!" I cried. "I have more!" I could feel my blood thawing a little, and I knew it'd feel even colder if he took the blanket back now. "It's worse than—than rings and shape-changers. It's so much worse than that. There's . . ." I dropped my voice down to the barest whisper. "There's a blackwitch in the Tower of Pattern. Right at the very top, where no one goes but the Queen of Pattern. You know she's odd?"

He was pressed bodily up against the bars now, holding on to them with both hands. His eyes had gone wide. My little fishhooks had pulled him as close as he could get without coming into the cell itself. "A blackwitch?" he whispered. "In *Pattern?*"

"That's why she's odd. Because she keeps him prisoner. I heard him sobbing in the night—his cell was right above mine."

"What is she keeping it *for?*"

"Hidden secrets. Charms against poison or violent death. I heard one of the Pattern stewards say that she makes him scry for her, that he can see you wherever you are, hear whatever you're saying . . . even listen in on your thoughts. She's got him all bound up in iron chains, but the evil magic seeps out, like water under a door. Soaks into your skin, like, and gives you nightmares and dark thoughts—that's why Anfisa Zofiyat has gone so odd in the last year. That's when she started visiting the blackwitch in the Tower. They have all sorts of magical protections around the Tower too. If one hundred Order guards approached with the intent to attack, a field of fire would spring up under their feet and burn them where they stood. Burn them to ash. Boil the air right out of their lungs. You'd be dead before you hit the ground, but your body would keep screaming—that's what it'd sound like to anyone watching. But it'd just be the white-hot air rushing out of your dead mouth." I leaned in. "Remember this. Don't attack the Tower unless you feel like dying that day."

There are times to run your mouth and make up anything that flits into your fool head, and there are times to use some judgment and prudence. Saying the words "a blackwitch in Pattern" was a deeply unfortunate move on my part, as it turned out.

"Who else have you told this to?" he hissed.

"No one! I told you, child, I've been trying to get the guards to pay attention to me. You're the first one who let me speak long enough to get to the warning. The story was just to catch your attention, see? To tell you that I've faced down Death herself." I emphasized the *her*. "To warn you, to save you if I can. To be honest," I lied, "I really am so thankful that Order came to collect me when they did. That woman would have started torturing me in a few days." I let my eyes fill with tears. "Thank you, lad. Thank the others for me, the ones who were there especially. You saved me from a fate worse than death. Praise be to Order and the noble men and women who uphold it."

"Long live the Queen," he breathed.

"Long live the Queen," I echoed. I kept my blanket.

The guard gave me a significant look the first time he passed me the next day. The second time he passed, he paused, then stepped up to the bars and gestured to me. "Is there anything else you could tell me about what's in the Tower of Pattern?" he whispered.

"Ohh," I said. "I . . . maybe." I shivered theatrically. "It depends. What do you want to know?"

"We know that woman is up to something," he hissed, glancing around. "Yesterday my supervisor sent me back with the blanket to see if you really did have anything to say. And then she passed on what you said to her supervisor, and they passed it on to theirs. And . . . and so on. And now some very important people want to know what you know."

I smelled an opportunity to win myself a few more creature comforts. "Lad. Lad, listen to me. It's terribly important. I can't remember all that happened to me when I was in that . . . that horrible place. I think the blackwitch enchanted me—but please, I know that if I could just get warm, I could work up the energy to fight it off. It comes over me like a sickness. . . ." I paused and gasped for breath. "It squeezes its shadowy fingers around my heart . . . I can feel it coming now. Ach, save yourself, child, save yourself. Or else bring me a fire, or some soup. . . . I fear the sickness may spread!" I clutched at my throat and wheezed for dramatic effect.

The guard looked conflicted. I could see the war happening in his face—he knew I was probably hamming it up for personal gain, but his superstition was nearly as strong. . . . If I *was* telling the truth about the blackwitch, it was entirely possible—nay, probable—that I had been tainted by dark magic, and it was therefore probable—nay, likely!—that I was suffering for it.

"Fine," he mumbled, gesturing away the evil, almost unconsciously. "Will you die before I get back?"

"I can hold it off that long," I wheezed. "If you hurry."

I ended up with a brazier set just out of arm's reach, piled with wood—not slabs or logs, but pathetic skinny sticks and straggly, twisted, dried bushes. It wasn't a slight at me; Nuryevet is notoriously poor in wood, and so they conserve every bit of it they do have for building and toolmaking, and to keep warm they burn sticks and twigs, scrub and bushes, grass or straw twisted tight into hard little logs, or dried dung. Or coal, if there is enough ventilation. It had been no different in Pattern.

The young guard brought me another blanket as well, a decent one. I pulled the bench closer to the radiant heat of the fire and folded the horse blanket to use as a seat cushion. I tucked yesterday's blanket over and around my legs, and hugged the newer one around my shoulders. Proper warmth, what relief!

"Ahhh, yes, I can feel the shadow balking already. I'll be able to fight it off today, I think. As long as I have a fire."

"Sure, good," said the guard, clearly uncomfortable. "But you'd better give me something really good about Pattern—the Captain wasn't too pleased at all this extravagance for one prisoner."

I was, at this point, prepared to burble anything they wanted. "Lad, I can give you dozens of things. Let me think—I must sift through my memories, unlock the ones that were locked away to me. . . . I heard too many secrets in that dreadful place, child. Too many secrets. Bloody ones. It'd turn your stomach inside out to hear them, scorch your ears right off. . . . All the Pattern Guards are ensorcelled into absolute loyalty to Anfisa Zofiyat, so there's no way to get them to betray her unless you find the way to break the spell. The blackwitch, you know. And if anyone gets past that ring of fire to attack the Tower, a huge thicket of briars will spring up from the ground, briars with thorns a foot long and as sharp as daggers, growing all around the Tower as tall as two men standing one atop the other's shoulders."

The guard nodded. "What about—what about other things? Things about the other Primes?"

"Ohh," I moaned, clutching my head. "It pains me to think about it—I must have heard something *dreadful* that that woman and her blackwitch don't want me to remember. Aaarghh . . ."

"What? What is it?"

"It's about . . . What do I see?" I grasped at the empty air before me, my eyes shut tight. "A book of some kind . . . There's something written in it. . . ."

"Yes? Go on."

"I—It's—! No, I can't. It's vanished for now. It was something terribly important. Whatever it is, I know it will shock you. I will fight for it, lad, I promise you that."

He settled back on his heels, clearly a little disappointed. "Well, I'll tell them about the other things you said."

"Good, yes. Do that, lad. Warn them . . ."

"The Queen of Order will appreciate your cooperation."

"And I appreciate the help in fighting off the cold shadow that foul sorcerer cast upon me." I nodded towards the brazier. "Long live the Queen."

"Long live the Queen," he said, and I saw a slight smile quirk the corner of his mouth.

That night I got a small roll of bread with my slop.

———————◆————————

The young guard had a new assignment. His patrol had been shortened, I suppose—he now walked up and down just one corridor. I think they brought in another prisoner or two, because the smell got worse and I heard noises of protest down the hall.

I didn't think much of them. I was coming up with stories to tell the guard about what had happened in the Tower.

I told him a little more that day—something offhand about how I thought Anfisa Zofiyat might have some kind of protective charm that she wore about her person, something about her paranoia against poison and assassination.

"Have they all been like that?" I asked the guard. "The Primes of

Pattern. I ask because . . . well, who knows how long that blackwitch has been imprisoned there."

"As long as I can remember. They're not always as odd as Anfisa Zofiyat. Most of them just go a bit strange in the head, but usually it takes years."

"Mmm. That's what comes of knowing too many secrets," I grumbled. "And of locking up a blackwitch, of course."

"You're making a good impression on the Queen of Order, all this information," the guard whispered. "We both are—we could really . . . help each other out, if you think about it."

"Oh . . . Could we?" I said guilelessly. "How d'you reckon that?" It had occurred to me at some point that I could win a few considerations more significant than blankets, bread, and braziers. In the dark moments of the night when despair came upon me, I thought to myself, *What's Consanza really going to do to help you?* I thought, *Help comes to the man who helps himself.* I don't remember exactly when I decided to set my sights higher; I think it must have been a gradual thing, like the turning of the tide.

He edged closer to the bars. "I know you're keeping something big back from me. Maybe you haven't remembered it yet, maybe you're just drawing all this out. . . . I know you have something important, though. There might be other guards asking about it, especially tomorrow. I won't be here tomorrow."

"Day off?"

He nodded. "So if you remember anything . . . don't tell the others. Actually, if . . ." He took a deep breath. "If you tell them I'm the only one you'll talk to, I'll bring you . . . another blanket?"

"Oh, I don't know. . . . Sometimes I just burst out with things. You must have heard about my behavior when I was in court a few weeks ago. . . ."

"Another blanket and . . . and I'll bring you some of the food they feed me and the other guards. Bread, meat. Nothing fancy—it's just horsemeat, leaner than leather, but it's better than the trash they serve you prisoners."

I considered it. "Cheese? Fruit? Cleaner water?"

He winced. "Sure, I can try."

"I suppose I can *try* not to talk to the other guards. It'll be difficult, though, seeing as how I'm such an old man and my eyes are so weak, and seeing how all you young pups look the same in those garish uniforms. . . ."

"Fine. I *promise* I will bring you food."

"And a blanket."

"And a blanket, yes."

"And . . . is there any way you could send a letter for me?"

At that, he looked troubled. "That I don't think I can do."

"Why?"

"We leave our uniforms here when our shifts end, and we're patted down by the other shift before we go out. Anything—*anything* we have in our pockets is looked at."

"Couldn't you say it's a letter from your sweetheart?"

"Everyone knows I don't have a sweetheart. I've never been interested in . . . any of that." He made a face. "Men or women. Not for me. Everyone knows that."

"What if I gave you a short message and you wrote it down later, after you've left?"

"Can't write or read."

"What? Were you raised in the country? You don't have a country accent."

"No, here in Vsila. Born and raised."

"Aren't there schools in the city?" I thought back to the astonishing amount of seemingly at least semi-educated people I'd seen or heard alluded to while I was here: the students in the courtroom, everyone who had to carry a license to practice their craft, the amount of bureaucracy and paperwork in every aspect of their lives. . . .

"There are schools everywhere. It's the law," said the guard. I hadn't seen any during the few brief weeks of liberty I'd had in Nuryevet; I thought perhaps I had simply overlooked them. "But a blackwitch cursed me cross-eyed when I was a baby. So I can't read."

"What do you mean?"

"When I look at something written down, the letters get all mixed up and it's hard to focus on them. Sometimes they sort of squirm around. My parents tried all sorts of cures."

"And you think it's because a witch cursed you?"

"What else could it be? Anyway, it doesn't bother me any. Must bother you right now, though."

I sighed. "Could you memorize a message and have someone else write it down?"

"I'm not getting someone else involved in this!" he hissed.

I gave up. There was no way to make this avenue work. "What's your name, anyway?"

"Vasili Ansonsos Lienityat Negutesco."

"And what do I call you?"

"Vasili Lienityat. Or . . . just Vasili, I guess. You only have the one name?"

"These days, yes."

"You used to have more?"

I nodded, closing my eyes and leaning back against the wall.

"Did a blackwitch take them?" Vasili asked, very serious.

"No, I gave them away."

"Why?"

"As a sign of devotion to my calling. A sacrifice." I thought of something. "A question I've been wondering about, child: The Queen of Coin—Taishineya Tarmos, isn't it?"

"Yes."

"She uses her patronymic instead of her matronymic—but the other Queens use their matronymics, and so do you, and the King of Law uses his patronymic. Isn't that right?" In most places, there's some kind of system, but the Nuryevens seemed entirely random.

"Yes."

"So why does she do that?"

"Her father was more well-known than her mother, I guess. Or she likes the sound better."

These Nuryevens. No sense of drama.

———◆◆◆———

For my hearing, I was transported to the House of Law in one of those small coffin boxes. I was beginning to develop an almost sickening aversion to them, and I spent the ride with my hands and eyes clenched tight, breathing carefully to keep from gagging and panicking in the close, confined space.

I heard us pass through a noisy crowd of people, heard the two huge doors groan open. The clamor of the crowd surged forward, but there were guards yelling at them to stay back, and then the doors swung closed again and silence fell.

When the guards opened my box, I stumbled out and found myself caught in Consanza's arms. "You stink," she said, blunt as ever.

"Trim your nose hair," I gasped, trying not to heave up the meager breakfast I'd eaten.

She just scowled at me and led me forward.

It was the same cavernous courtroom we'd used before—or one

similar enough that I couldn't tell the difference, which wouldn't be surprising. They don't care to make their buildings terribly distinctive here. The only thing different was that it was almost completely empty: just us, the Primes, and a small flock of attendants, assistants, and scribes.

Rather than sitting in a row behind the table on the dais, the Primes had taken chairs on the same level of the floor as I now stood, in the middle of the wide-open space in the center of the room, surrounded on three sides by benches where the students and witnesses had been sitting the last time I was here. The tall windows behind the dais streamed watery, wintry light into the room—in other places, there might have been tapestries hung on the walls, or murals painted on the high, vaulted ceiling. Here, there was almost nothing. Long green woolen curtains, the color of Justice, framed the windows, and the wooden doors were carved in a simple repeating pattern and fitted with shiny brass bands.

Anfisa Zofiyat was off to one side of the semicircle, flanked by no fewer than six of her guards. I recognized Zorya Miroslavat sitting opposite her, with the Duchess of Justice, Yunia Antalos, standing behind her.

Next to Zorya was a woman I had not seen before, but who could only be Vihra Kylliat, Queen of Order. She was a large woman; not fat, not at all, but large with strength. She had wide shoulders, thick arms—or arm, rather, as I saw that her left was amputated just above the elbow, as was her left leg, just below the knee, yet she wore cunningly made prosthetics of some pale-colored metal, undecorated and unadorned, and she had an equally plain walking stick leaned up against the armrest of her chair. She was somewhere in her late forties or early fifties, at my best guess—besides the white scar across her right cheek, she had lines on her face that suggested tension or anger, and she had touches of gray to her dark hair, which was cropped quite close to her head. A saber hung from her belt, and her right hand was gloved in white; her short coat and trousers were of a deep burgundy red, several shades darker than the crisp scarlet-and-white uniforms of Order. She sat quite still, without any attendants, without speaking, without moving. The red of Order stands out in any room, and on any street—the Nuryevens favor duller, drabber colors for superstition's sake: blackwitches can't tolerate the sight or touch of color. It's Order's little show of bravado, you see: *Look how brave we are. We have nothing to fear.*

The King of Law, Casimir Vanyos, sat in the center of the curve, midway between Anfisa and her opponents. He was a very elderly man, slow moving, and he had two young clerks with him who each held a stack of books and files. Casimir Vanyos himself wore ceremonial robes of dusty sky blue trimmed with bands of gold braid, which would have been very imposing on anyone else. On his gaunt, hunched frame, the fabric hung like a potato sack on a scarecrow and made him look small and, frankly, ridiculous.

Finally, separated from all the rest and seated on the far left, was the last Queen, Taishineya Tarmos, bedecked from head to toe in vivid purples and sparkling gems, a display of wealth that struck me as entirely alien in this country—hell, her finery would have been remarkable even in the noble courts of the Araşti merchant-princes or the guildhalls of Edness. Her sleek black hair was curled upon her shoulders (artificially, I presumed, for the Nuryevens tend towards silky, straight dark hair), and jewels hung glittering at her ears, around her throat and wrists, and across her forehead, and glimmered from hidden folds of her gown, which was embroidered all over with a quatrefoil pattern and tiny seed pearls. She was the only one looking at me, and she was looking with undisguised curiosity.

It took a few moments for the court to get settled—Casimir Vanyos needed a table for the files in front of him, and Consanza saw to it that both she and I got a chair apiece and a table to share for ourselves. In all this last-minute shuffling, the Queen of Coin, Taishineya Tarmos, rose from her seat and floated over to us. She moved as if she were as light as air, though I imagine, considering the amount of heavy fabric and rocks hanging on her, that the weight she carried was *substantial*.

She was quite young—younger than I had expected for a Prime, compared to the others; even Anfisa Zofiyat, the next youngest, was on the ambiguous side of early middle age. Taishineya Tarmos had a deliberate, affected tilt to her head and the arrangement of her hands, and there was the distinct air that she was mimicking something stylish. "Good morning, Master Chant," she said to me. "What a pleasure to meet you. I must say, I've already heard all about you."

"At your service, madam," I said, with a short bow—as much as I could manage with my cold-cramped joints, my brain rattled out of my skull by the movements of the wagon on the cobblestones when it transported me, and my stomach half turned inside out. "I hope that my name will be cleared so I can get out of your hair forever."

"Oh, not at all! Even if we do clear you, you mustn't go running off right away, never to be seen again! No, no—everyone is terribly fascinated with you right now, you know," she said with a secretive, impish grin, as if letting me in on some scandalous secret. "We just can't stop talking about you."

"I profess myself flattered, madam."

The Queen of Order rapped her walking stick on the floor, once, and the sound rang out through the room like a firework blast. "Taishineya, are you quite finished *chatting* with the accused?"

Taishineya Tarmos smiled sweetly at her. "I suppose you all want to get along with your silly old trial. Dear me, I seem to have gotten in the way again." She retreated to her chair, her silk brocade skirts swishing along the floor. Her clothes were flavored in the Echareese style, and I fancied that perhaps she had an Echareese tailor with opinions on how to cut the Nuryeven fashions with a little more style and flair.

The King of Law held a page at arm's length and peered at it, then at me. Consanza ushered me to the chair next to her, and as I sat, she rose. She cleared her throat and smiled sweetly at the panel of the Primes.

"Your Excellencies, it is my honor to appear before you as the advocate for the accused, Master Chant of Kaskinen. Before we get started, I just wanted to take a moment to say what a great privilege it is that I should be here today. You see, ever since I was a little girl . . ."

I could feel already that it was going to be a very long day.

The next day Consanza swept up to my cell in a billow of robes and gestured sharply for me to pay attention. "I've had an idea," she announced as I extricated myself from my nest of blankets and put down the book I was reading—Vasili's latest gift for the services and information I provided him.

"Wasn't expecting to see *you* so soon," I muttered.

"What's all this?" Consanza waved at the blankets, the brazier, the book.

"You haven't done anything to make my life any easier, so I . . ." I stretched, luxuriating in the heat from the fire. "I took some initiative."

"Huh. Well done. How?"

"Vanya the Smith."

"You found you had something of value?"

"I found I could *create* things of value," I corrected. "Please, have a seat. Would you like a blanket?"

"No, thank you. I've had an idea."

"Is that right?" I asked flatly. "Regale me."

"Have you met Taishineya Tarmos yet? Besides yesterday, I mean. She hasn't come to visit you, has she?"

"No, she hasn't. Neither have those other two—Casimir Vanyos and Vihra Kylliat."

"We can change that," she muttered.

"Change? Are you trying to get Taishineya Tarmos to come see me?" I shook my head, laughing. "Ladies like her don't come to prisons."

"Ladies like her get their hands dirty if there's a good reason to, and we're going to come up with a good reason for her to."

"And that's going to help send a letter to my apprentice?"

Consanza huffed. "I wish you'd look at the big picture. Anfisa Zofiyat likes you, right? That's what it sounded like."

"Sure, I suppose she might. She thinks I could be useful, anyway. And now so does—"

But she interrupted. "And Taishineya Tarmos came to talk to you at the hearing—she was interested in you. She thinks you're fashionable." Consanza crossed her arms and paced back and forth in front of my cell. "I thought it was strange. I've been asking around—everyone knows about your trial, of course. But Tarmos's circle is *agog*. They love drama and scandals, and you're . . . hah! You're an infinite well of those, aren't you?"

I did not dignify this with a response.

"I have an idea," Consanza said. "But it's not a very good one. It involves you being charming and cooperative, so obviously I feel like it's a long shot, but . . . I think you could do that if you saw that it was in your best interest, don't you?"

I did not respond to this, either. I primly smoothed my blanket over my legs and folded my hands in my lap and waited for Consanza to reveal her great plan, or not, as it suited her. I didn't want her to know that I cared even a whit.

I could lie to her, but I can't lie to you: I cared very much.

"Have you found out anything about Taishineya Tarmos yet?" she asked casually.

"No. Why?"

Consanza nodded and sat herself down on the chair. She packed and lit her pipe and puffed a few times to get the embers going. The silence stretched and stretched.

At last she sat back, lowered her pipe. Smoke trickled out of her mouth as she spoke and a fragrant, spicy scent, different from before, filled the space. "Taishineya Tarmos Elyat Chechetni. Born to Tarmo Yuliat and Elya Borisos, the former a merchant, the latter an actress in her youth and, later, a particularly shrewd investor. Taishineya grew up surrounded by luxury and the cream of society. She ran for the office of Coin during the last election on, I am told, a dare from a friend. I am not sure if this is true—no one knows which friend it was. There don't seem to be any primary sources. So that's probably apocryphal. Regardless, she doesn't take the office seriously—she thinks it's an excuse to throw fancy parties and wear pretty dresses and have people kissing her ass and telling her how important she is. Which, mind you, isn't irregular for a Prime of Coin. It's practically required, at this point." She sighed heavily and paused for another puff. "And," she continued darkly, "we all see the results, come tax season."

"Not surprised. Earrings like those don't pay for themselves."

Consanza pointed her pipe at me. "Exactly." She gave me a rather funny look then. "You like knowing things about places, and why they are the way they are."

"Yes."

"What do you think of Nuryevet so far?" she asked conversationally, as if I were some visitor on a jaunt through for my own amusement.

"Is that supposed to be a joke?"

She shrugged, blew smoke. "Yes and no."

"Let's put it this way. Out of all the places I've ever been, I'd rather go back to the day that I was dying of thirst, wandering in the dunes of the Sea of Sun, than spend another day here. I'd rather camp for a month in the Ebbshore swamp. I'd rather—"

"I get it," she said.

"—be obliged to accept a dinner invitation to the Mouse and Millstone Tavern in Llanrwsteg—"

"I *get* it."

"—even though I swore I'd cut off my own hand if I ever again came within a mile of it. In short, it's a miserable wretch of a place, and I can't believe anyone actually *likes* living here."

"It takes money to leave," Consanza said, and I remembered that her grandparents had done just that, had left Arjuneh. "And it's not so bad. As long as you work with the system, you can use it to your advantage."

"Until tax season," I said. "When they scrape a bit here and a bit there until they've scraped every bit of meat off your bones. And you're implying that's why Nuryevet is this way? With this sulking desolation as far as the eye can see?" I wasn't unconvinced, but she wasn't going out of her way to persuade me one way or another. I suppose that was too much like advocacy. Too much like real work, and I've told you before how much Consanza abhorred *that*.

"Everything, all of it—it's all tangled up together. A few generations ago, having many spouses wasn't so common—people would have one or two, occasionally three. But taxes kept going up, and it makes more sense to bring in a fourth source of income, or a fifth, to share the burden. But people are poor even so. Taishineya Tarmos's sort never stop making pretty promises and offering beautiful misty dreams, so they keep getting elected. And every election cycle, everybody sinks a little deeper into the mire." She blew a long stream of smoke. "Do you know how many lawyers there are per capita in Nuryevet? One in twenty. Five percent of the population. Because we have this—this fear. In our bones, we have fear. Fear of not having quite enough to get by, fear of having that little bit taken from us. By the tax collectors, by the raiders who come over the mountains every spring, by the Enca and the Cormerrans. And when people are afraid . . ."

"They want to protect themselves," I said, and a glimmer of understanding began to dawn. "So—courts, and lawyers." And laws against witchcraft, and a wild suspicion of foreigners.

"Mm."

I studied her. "Do you think you're lucky to live here?"

"I beg your fucking pardon?"

"Do you?" That steward in Pattern had thought so.

She shrugged. "At least we get to choose." That's what he had said too. "I don't know if that's luck. We all complain, and every tax season there's always a bit of fuss, always a few people who decide they can't stand it anymore. Keeps me and my colleagues busy for a month or two."

I snorted. "Goodness, people upset around tax season. I've sure never heard *that* one before."

She gestured at me with her pipe again. "See? Exactly. It's normal."

"And this has something to do with your brilliant idea?"

"In a way. Sometimes you need to understand a place before

you can understand a person, don't you? Before you can understand where they fit."

I nodded. "Context. Yes."

"Our jobs really are surprisingly similar." Consanza sat back. "Taishineya Tarmos! She wants to be important, and so she's probably fairly easy to lead. She already thinks you're fashionable, so if we can get the two of you alone for a little while, you can convince her that you're not just fashionable, you're an *investment*. She wants power? Give it to her. Tell her a story. And get yourself a promise that in return she'll support having you exonerated and released. If we can count on her and on Anfisa Zofiyat . . ." Consanza gave me a significant look over the stem of her pipe.

Then there'd be a tie. Coin and Pattern against Order and Justice. Then it'd come down to the King of Law and his vote.

"Do you know as much about Casimir Vanyos?"

"I *am* an advocate," Consanza said, smoke pluming and curling around her. "But it may interest you to know that I happened to work in the Law offices when I was a student. Reporting to the Prime and the Second—Casimir Vanyos and Rostik Palos."

"You've met him—Casimir Vanyos?"

"Many times."

"You know him?"

She shrugged artfully, but I could tell how pleased she was to reveal this by the way she hid a smile with another puff from her pipe. "He's always seemed fond of me."

I let out my breath. A glimmer of hope, though it was a tiny, distant glimmer, a single candle on a windowsill miles away, across a river on a cold, dark night. "I can do it," I said.

"You think so?"

I dropped my eyes so I wouldn't accidentally glare at her—even if it was an unlikely plan, I didn't want to discourage her from, perhaps, coming up with other, better plans in the future. "And the letters to my apprentice?"

"Does it matter so much if I'm going to get you out?"

"Don't jinx it!" I said sharply. So much for my efforts to be polite to her. I'm not even that superstitious, but—bah. This is what comes of being around everyone else's superstitions for so many decades.

Consanza scowled at me. "Look, just focus on the task at hand, would you? She's the *Queen of Commerce*, Chant. Do you know what *commerce* means?"

"Of course I do," I snapped. "Merchants! Shops, ships, sailors. Trade."

"Yes, yes. *And* the royal mint, and the *post office*."

"Ah." My building irritation was quenched, as surely as a red-hot steel swan dipped into a bucket of oil.

"And as a Prime, she can wander in and out of prisons whenever she wants without subjecting herself to needless searches."

"Do *you* get searched?"

"Of course. I could be smuggling weapons to you."

"Why can't you just memorize a message for me and send it?"

She gave me a look, half-pitying, half-irritated. "I'm not going to be complicit in anything illegal," she said crisply. "I'll scheme with you about how to curry favor and win your case, but that's my limit. Do you know what would happen if I got caught sneaking messages out for you?" She narrowed her eyes at me. "That said, they don't mind me bringing in ink and parchment to take notes on your case," she added, and drew the items out of her pockets. "These don't come free."

I rolled my eyes. "Of course not. What do you want for them?"

"You're going to do me a favor sometime. Before you leave, after I get you out." Apparently she didn't care about jinxes. I remember thinking that I wasn't even sure whether she truly cared about black-witches. "Don't make that face. I have a good feeling."

She was smiling now, her eyes glittering with the twinkle of her plot—it did help her. She looked much nicer now than when I had first met her, and perhaps that was because her expression was more pleasant, and perhaps it was because she wasn't quite as con-temptible as she had been. "Fine," I said. "I'll owe you a favor when you get me out."

She handed the parchment and ink through the bars, and I hid them under the fold of a blanket. She gave me a metal dip pen too—they have no shortage of metal in Nuryevet. "It's a shame, but I don't think we have a hope of making headway with Vihra Kylliat. She's not likely to fall for any games."

"I'll handle her," I said. "I've got my own swans in the fire." She gave me one of those long, cool looks that said she clearly didn't think I was competent enough to buckle my own belt, let alone execute some complicated maneuvers such as these. I sniffed at her. "You handle Coin, I'll see what I can do with Order. Come back in two days, and I'll tell you if I've done it. If I fail, you have leave to smirk all you like at me."

"If you say so," she muttered from around the stem of her pipe. "But remember what I said—don't play games with Vihra Kylliat. She won't take it well." She paused. "Well, none of them would take it well, but I doubt you have anything Kylliat wants, so . . . Mind your tongue."

"Mind your own tongue, young lady!" She snorted and left, with a final slow, appraising look at the blankets and the brazier. Vasili wasn't on duty tonight, but the other guards had been instructed about the special considerations I was to receive, and while they didn't bother me, neither did they bring me lumps of the hard, nutty orange cheese that Vasili seemed partial to, or handfuls of dried fruit, or an extra piece of bread with my dinner.

I scrambled out of the blankets and gestured Vasili over as soon as I saw him the next morning, and I set into motion the first grand misstep of the path that eventually brought me to you. "Is Vihra Kylliat here?" says I.

"In—in the building?" says young Vasili.

"Yes, in the building."

"Well, this is the House of Order. . . . Her offices are in another wing, though."

"I need to speak to her."

"Excuse me?"

"I need to speak to the Queen of Order!"

"About what?" he demanded.

"Vasili, child, listen to me. I've remembered something that happened to me in the Tower—or most of it. And the Queen of Order must know immediately—she's responsible for the guards, right?"

"Well . . . yes."

"And the army?"

"What is this about?" Vasili's eyes were getting wider.

I seized him by the forearm. "Please. Go fetch her, ask her to come here or to have me brought to her."

"Fine, fine." He eyed the pile of blankets on the bench in the corner. "Can you at least neaten that up? She hates mess, and I don't know whether she's going to come down here or have you brought to her."

"Tell her . . ." I paused. "Tell her I wouldn't want to inconvenience her—tell her I see it must be difficult for her to get around. You know, with her *leg*."

"I am *not* telling her that."

"You're not telling her anything you said, you're only telling her what I said."

"She'll come all the way down here just to punch you in the face," Vasili whispered between the bars. "You've never seen her move. She was a general, you know! She trained in seventy different kinds of weapons. She even traveled to Xereccio to learn from their masters."

"She lost her arm and leg in battle?"

"Arm, yes. Leg was an accident—injured and took fever or something while she was abroad." Bless little Vasili for being so easily incited to running his mouth. "Look, you don't understand. Everyone thinks that her leg slows her down—at first. I've heard stories from the other guards. Every couple years someone new does something like open a door for her, thinking he was being nice, right? And she walks him right outside and makes him spar with her until he's collapsed on the ground, shaking and throwing up and pissing himself. She's *terrifying*, and I'm *not* telling her you said anything about her leg. You're just a prisoner. She can have you flogged, you know, that's her right, just like it was Anfisa Zofiyat's right to take you for private questioning. Do you want to be flogged? A man your age, you'll probably die, and none of the Primes will care at all, and neither will your advocate. And whoever you wanted to send a letter to will never see you again."

I ground my teeth. "Fine."

"There's just things you shouldn't say to people," Vasili added. Beating a dead horse.

"You're wasting time, kid, get out of here! Go tell her I want an audience with her."

Vasili gave me one final reproachful look and loped down the corridor.

I shook out my blankets and folded them up as neatly as I could, hid the ink and parchment in a new place, and waited.

After fifteen minutes, I heard footsteps, one set of which was almost certainly Vihra Kylliat's—every other step was a metallic ring of her artificed leg against the stone.

She came suddenly around the corner and stopped just out of arm's reach of my cell. "Vasili Lienityat said you begged an audience. Said you'd be happy to walk up to my offices, but I don't think it's wise to let spies out of their cages for flippant little reasons whenever they ask."

"Thank you for coming down," I said, rising and bowing slightly.

"Vasili says you've been cooperating with his questioning. You've provided us with a lot of interesting information already."

Ah, good, I thought. *Everything I've said has reached her. Good!* "He said . . ." *What would make little Vasili look good?* I wondered. "He convinced me it'd be in my best interests to be honest."

"A generally wise course of action," Vihra Kylliat said dryly. "And what is this great new epiphany you've had about the Tower?"

"Actually, Your Excellency, it's not about the Tower specifically." I paused—builds tension. "Not directly. It's about some of the guards and soldiers who answer to you."

"Go on," she said, nearly expressionless. I couldn't read her. She was a rock wall and I was patting around in the dark to find a chink, taking gambles. But I was not without clues. . . . Anfisa Zofiyat had given me some, Consanza and Vasili had given me others, and I'd seen some with my own eyes during the trial. I'd seen the cold, steady glare Vihra leveled at Anfisa.

The Queen of Pattern, Consanza had told me, had dirt on *everyone.* And everyone, as I know myself from my years of wandering, everyone has something to hide. Either Anfisa had Vihra's secret in the palm of her hand or she didn't. Either way, what Vihra had was fear. I can use fear, mold it like clay, direct its course like a river bound in dams and dikes.

I just needed to find an angle. Spies, then. Spies, and witches.

"I saw a ledger," I said, taking a guess. "When I was in the Tower—lists of wardens of Order who are taking bribes from Pattern. People who are betraying you for real. Actual traitors, not just this unfortunate misunderstanding I've gotten myself caught up in."

"Have you any proof?" she growled. Not a moment of hesitation.

"Well . . . only my word." Which wasn't that valuable in and of itself, and Vihra Kylliat didn't think so either.

"The word of a prisoner."

"A prisoner who has seen some of what the Weavers do in there. Some of them are traveling to other lands, to find texts of magic that they can use to strengthen Pattern even further against the other Primes." I took a deep breath and another guess. "You know Anfisa Zofiyat thirsts for power. She's taken up one of the most powerful Ministries. Spies. Weavers. Assassins. Assassins with a blackwitch to back them. Do you think she's going to stop at being just *one* of the Primes, if she has the tools available to her to further the reach of her power? If she has an army hidden in darkness, spelled to be unwaveringly loyal to her? If she has *your* army in her pocket?"

"And you tell us this because . . . ?"

"Because I just want to go *home*." I let my voice crack a little. "Because I'm innocent and I want to go home. Because people are going to die if she moves before you can oust the traitors from your ranks and take essential pawns away from her."

She narrowed her eyes at me. "I don't believe you. I don't believe anything about you. I don't believe you are who you say you are, or that you do what you say you do. You're a fraud, an imposter, and I don't know what your game is. I don't think you'll ever let on what it really is."

Somehow, the gods smiled upon me and allowed me to hold my tongue. I was playing games with her, and as Consanza had predicted, she was having none of it.

Vihra Kylliat pulled up the chair that Consanza always used and sat down. Her metal limb clinked as she crossed her legs. "They say you're a storyteller, amongst a laundry list of much more ridiculous and unlikely professions. Is that what you are?"

"And a scholar, sort of," I said.

"What do you study?"

"I go to places and I talk to people, and they tell me about the great deeds of their ancestors. Their heroes, ones who fell in battle for honor, for glory. They tell me how they lived, how they ruled, how they died."

"I suppose a historian is a variety of storyteller," she said. Her tones were still flat and unimpressed.

"Yes," I said. "And history is cyclical, you know. Which is why I was so alarmed to find these things out about Anfisa Zofiyat—it's because I've *seen it before*."

"Is that right," says she. Patting around in the dark for a chink in the wall, I thought I felt a breeze on my fingertips and narrowed my focus entirely to that. I didn't know what it was, but all my instincts said *follow that*.

"Yes," says I. "I study these things, and then I tell the stories to other people, so that maybe we can learn from the mistakes of those who went before us. And, ah, this situation, this whole situation, it's familiar. You're like characters in a play and you don't even know it. You don't even know that you're following your lines as if you'd learned them by heart." She was quite still, and she made no move to respond, so I continued. "Anfisa Zofiyat, well, she's the Grand Dowager Duchess Banh Seu. Zorya Miroslavat is almost the Empress-Mother Sen Hai Soh, the Flower in the River. And you—you're the Honorable Lady Ger Zha, the General of Jade and Iron. You're *exactly* her."

"These names are unfamiliar to me." But she had that look in her eyes, you know, the same as Vasili. She'd been looking right at me, and then she'd *noticed* me.

I stifled a smile and leaned forward.

THE SIXTH TALE:
The General of Jade and Iron

A long time ago and half the world away, Jou Xi (the King of the World, Earthly Son of the Glorious Sun-Tiger, Reflected Brilliance of the Mirror of Heaven and, the most mundane and relevant of his titles, the Emperor of Genzhu) died of river-fever in the heat of summer and well before his time, and the land fell into chaos. This is part of the natural life cycle of an empire, and we should never be surprised by it. There were three primary factions in the struggle that followed.

The Flowers: those who were loyal to the throne and who backed Jou Xi's son, the Eminent Prince Te Suon Csi. The Eminent Prince was nine, so support for his rule was understood to be support for a regency by his mother, Sen Hai Soh, the Flower in the River. This faction consisted of a number of the less powerful nobles and almost all of the army (led by the General of Jade and Iron herself, the Honorable Lady Ger Zha). The Flowers represented dynastic continuity, stability, tradition. These are always popular concepts. At least, they're popular with the people who've already gotten most of what they want out of life.

(Vihra snorted here and half-smiled, and nodded very slightly.)

Most of the resistance against the Flowers originated with a fundamental prejudice against Sen Hai Soh herself, and an outrage at the idea that someone such as she would wield power and influence for so long—ten years until the Eminent Prince attained his majority. You see, she was not a native daughter of Genzhu, but had been born and raised in the courts of Map Sut, just downriver. She was a close relation of the former ruling family of that nation, whose dynasty had been broken by Genzhu's expansion and conquest two generations previously, and she had been married to Jou Xi in a vain attempt to strengthen the ties between the empire and its most troublesome province, inconveniently located immediately south on the Ganmu, their shared river and Genzhu's only easy route to a warm-water port.

And so there was a certain irreverence for the foreigner-Empress, a certain outright disdain. Map Sut was generally regarded as less civilized, less cultured, less educated, simply *less* in general. Comments like "all shit flows downstream" were so prevalent as to be proverbs.

Thus, the opposition:

First, the Tiger's-Claws, headed by the Grand Dowager Duchess Banh Seu, Jou Xi's younger sister, a legitimate claimant to the imperial throne. She made no secret of the fact that she wanted power, and she was fully prepared to use whatever means necessary to secure the throne for herself, including sorcery. Now, fortunately for the world as we know it, Genzhun magic is difficult, intricate, and not terribly powerful. It is practiced by court magicians, scholar-priests of a sort, whose primary duties are the calculation of the movement of the heavens in order to determine which dates and directions are particularly auspicious. However . . . Some of them, the very great ones, have the power to summon demons. Banh Seu was popular amongst the more powerful nobles in the court, and she had the support of nearly all the court magicians, not to mention that of the general populace, who rankled at the idea of being ruled by the foreigner-Empress and her half-breed son.

And finally, the Iron Knives, a faction of merchants and their mercenaries, supported by an underground web of peasantry, interested more in using the chaos as an opportunity to claw their way up from their current positions than any more specific ambitions. They had a few powerful names in their group, men and women who could have stood a chance of taking the throne for themselves if they'd wanted to, but none of them seemed truly fixed on it, and none was personable or charismatic enough to draw the sole support of the faction. History remembers them as a force for chaos more than anything else, an unpredictable element. The whole affair could have been ended without a sea of blood if it hadn't been for the Iron Knives.

That bright, humid summer was a dark and difficult time for Genzhu. It was a time of dishonor, broken loyalties, shattered promises. And wading through this mess was Ger Zha, the General of Jade and Iron. She was a woman of irreproachable honor and courage, a tiger on the battlefield and a gracious and upstanding diplomat at court. She backed the Flowers because she was loyal to the *empire* above all else, and because the Empress-Mother and the Eminent Prince *were* the empire. She could have supported Banh Seu—the Grand Dowager Duchess may well have been the better choice of ruler, when compared with a nine-year-old boy and his mother, both unfamiliar in the arts of war and nearly ignorant in matters of statecraft. But *they*, not the Dowager Duchess, were the empire, and Ger Zha had sworn herself to its service.

I don't think there was ever a question of who she would fight for. I don't believe she would have had even a moment's hesitation. And when her opponents were, first, a bloodthirsty woman who would have the Black Hand Demon summoned to eat the hearts of the Iron Knives' children, or the Yellow Tongue Demon to lick gruesome disease into any unwarded Flower, and second, a cadre of self-interested, greedy, grasping merchants—no, there was never a question of it. She had been laying down her life for the empire for forty years at that point, and the only reason she failed in the end was because she thought that the Tiger's-Claws and the Iron Knives would see sense, would . . . I don't know, brush the debris from their minds and hearts and find an essential core of honor they'd forgotten they'd had. I think she believed everyone was essentially capable of honor.

That's why she died, and that's why the Eminent Prince was murdered, and the Empress-Mother tied with silk ropes to heavy stones and thrown into the river alive.

The Grand Dowager Duchess Banh Seu won the day,
in the end. Such are the ways of empires.

Vihra Kylliat watched me as I spoke, a lioness lying stone-still in
the grass. I think it was the bit about the demons, to be honest. The
suggestion of magic as political warfare.

Now, what I had heard of blackwitches at that time was mostly
foolish stuff. You know, ascribing to them responsibility for all sorts
of little inconveniences, like Vasili's odd experience with reading, or
a keg of beer going sour, or a house plagued with vermin. And more
magical but still foolish things—blackwitches stealing the color from
your eyes, or your name from the world. . . .

But there are other stories. I hesitate to tell them now, and if
that makes me no better than the Nuryevens, so be it. These folk are
loath to speak of the blackwitches' specific evils too often, for fear of
calling down those misfortunes on their heads, just as the people my
ancestor-Chants protected were loath to draw the Eye of the trickster
god Shuggwa.

Found out later how much this little snip of story had worked
on her. They're like boots, stories. Some fit you just right, some keep
your toes warm in the winter, and some of 'em rub at you until you're
sore and blistered. I'd tucked a burr into her shirt with that one, and
it itched and rubbed at her until she was raw.

———◆◆◆———

Consanza came early the next morning. "Right, grandfather, I
left it to you—did you manage it?"

"Yes. I told her Anfisa Zofiyat is paying off some of the
wardens of Order."

She went very still. "Chant. Is that true?"

I shrugged. "No idea."

"Chant!" she cried. "If Anfisa Zofiyat finds out you said something like that, you can say good-bye to her support in the trial!" She looked like she would have strangled me herself if the cell bars hadn't been in the way.

"Please," I scoffed. "She won't find out. It's all just jabber, it's nothing they'll talk about specifically. Order just wants an excuse to give Pattern some trouble. I've seen it all before," I said airily. "Vihra Kylliat wants to put Anfisa Zofiyat in her place. She'd do that whether or not I was here. You don't get it, Consanza, she was *hungry* for it. It's not just professional irritation, it's deeper than that. Personal. So what if I told her that there's bribes being passed around? When in the history of the world *haven't* bribes happened?"

Consanza pinched the bridge of her nose for a moment. "What's done is done," she said. "It might be true. I suppose she'll need to find only one traitor to be convinced."

"See? Exactly as I thought. Have you handled Taishineya Tarmos?"

"I sent her a letter this morning. As you say, it was just jabber, but I didn't put my neck on the line with egregious, provable lies. Now we sit quiet and see if she comes through."

"She likes fashionable things, doesn't she? What's fashionable now, besides me?"

"Fucked if I know," said Consanza, which didn't surprise me in the slightest.

"I don't know anything about Nuryeven fashion," I grumbled. I could have told her all about fashion in Kaskinen, if she didn't mind the information being sixty years out of date. And I could have gone on for *days* about Map Sut and their astounding hats. Lovely place, Map Sut. Best pair of shoes I ever owned were given to me there.

They were a comfy pair of turn-toe boots, made just for me, made for walking and tromping all over this world. Would have lasted me ten, twenty years, those boots, but they were stolen by some urchins not two weeks later. I have long held the loss of those boots close to my heart, and in their memory I have complained about the urchins at any possible opportunity. It's not often that you come across a pair of boots that good. They were perfect, and they had looked rather dapper as well, with that saucy little pointed toe turned up. And *watertight!* It was a shame, that's all it was.

"I honestly pay no heed to such things," Consanza said. "My household is very practical. If any of my daughters were going to make a career for herself out of knowing everyone in the city and giggling like a tinkling bell ... Well, I guess I wouldn't stop her, but I'd wish only that she'd go about it better than Taishineya Tarmos. The thing can be done without being an obnoxious twit, you know?"

"If she's so obnoxious, is she really worth all this trouble? With the headway I've made with Vihra Kylliat ..."

"I don't like gambling," Consanza snapped. "Take every advantage you can. And don't underestimate Tarmos. She's not incompetent, she's just selfish and irritating. She wraps herself up in silly ribbons and jewels and scandalous gowns, but she's just as calculating as the rest of them."

I say a lot of things about Consanza, it is true, but whatever she said to the Queen of Coin was effective: Taishineya Tarmos, quaintly, sent along a calling card the day before she stopped by. By the time it got to my cell, it had been handled by fifteen or twenty different wardens, and it had a sad thumbprint of grime on one corner of the beautiful, thick, wood-pulp paper (very expensive in these parts, even without the narrow line of gold leaf running about the edges).

Her footmen arrived before she did, laying out a small knee-high table, a rug, a cushioned stool, and for some reason a silver dish full of water. They heaped more fuel onto my brazier, set a kettle on the fire, and laid out a modest tea service alongside a porcelain dish of honeyed apricots stuffed with spiced chopped nuts.

It was a simple picnic for a Queen, but to my eyes it looked like the grandest feast I had seen in years. My mouth watered to look at those glistening, honeyed apricots.

The footmen, in frustration and disgust, also swept the room and sprayed thick perfume up and down the hall in an attempt to dampen the unpleasant smells of the ward. By the time Taishineya Tarmos came and settled herself on her stool, with some kind of tiny fluffy animal lapping out of the water dish by her feet, I couldn't smell anything at all, let alone differentiate between the perfume she was wearing and the one that had been so liberally splashed around. I will probably never escape that smell. It will haunt me to the end of my days.

"Good afternoon, Master Chant," she said. She plucked a juicy piece of candied apricot off the plate and ate it in one bite. "Your advocate sent me a letter, all about you and your tragic situation. I really had no idea. She's rather clever for what she is, isn't she?"

"You mean for an advocate?"

Taishineya giggled. "Oh, you. You remind me of my own grandfather."

"I apologize, madam, I truly didn't understand what you meant."

"Oh—for a foreigner, of course!" She giggled again.

"My impression is that her father and mother were born and raised here, as was she."

The Queen ducked her head and smiled. "Well, of course, you're a foreigner too. I suppose I shouldn't expect you to understand what I mean." She ate another apricot. Didn't offer me any. I decided then that I didn't like her.

The fluffy animal at her feet was staring hard at me. I ignored it.

"Anyway," Taishineya Tarmos said, "goodness me, I've heard so much about you. I seem to hear new things every day! Your advocate told me quite a lot. It seems I've been rather left out of the loop!"

"The loop?"

"Well, when your advocate wrote to me, I wasn't feeling particularly inspired to vote one way or another—espionage charges are exciting to hear about, but the trials are *so* boring to listen to. Most of politics is boring," she added in a confidential whisper.

"Is it? Then certainly you would have had matters more interesting to attend to besides running for office."

"No, indeed! Because now everyone carries a little handful of my portraits in their pockets! *Such* a thrill." She fished out a heavily embroidered and beaded velvet purse from a pocket in her skirt and tipped out a few gold and silver coins. She held one up close enough for me to see. "It's a rather good likeness, wouldn't you say?" Her lacquered fingernails shone like jewels.

"Yes, it seems to be."

"But you must look at it properly. Let me turn in profile for you so you can see what a really good likeness it is." And she did just that, glancing at me expectantly out of the corner of her eye.

"Being imprinted in gold could not possibly increase your beauty," I said obligingly. She had a rather weak chin, I thought, and if she kept eating candied apricots at that rate, she might have a second one before too long.

But she was clearly delighted with the compliment, and she poured her riches back into her purse and vanished it amongst her skirts again—all shades of lavender, with an oddly styled vest or doublet in rich royal purple, as heavily beaded as her coin purse had been. "So . . . I'm not the only one who has been sneaking in to see you, am I?" she said, scrunching up her nose in a way that I expect she thought was endearing. I didn't like it. And I didn't trust her. There was something about this giggling doll that didn't ring quite true.

"I've only spoken to my advocate. . . . I don't think anyone's snuck in to see me. I don't get visitors."

She laughed. It was clearly practiced and perhaps intended to sound like tinkling bells. It sounded like a five-year-old. "No, the other Primes. Apparently I'm late to the party." And, mercurial, the tinkling laughter shifted into a little moue. "Unfashionably late."

Her expression set me on edge. If she was revealing that tiny amount of displeasure, it meant there was a hundred times more of it lurking beneath the surface. "I wouldn't say that, madam. Casimir Vanyos hasn't been to see me yet."

"Oh, old Casimir." She waved that off with an airy gesture. "He just sits in the House of Law with his books and his little clerks. He's an old grump, takes no notice of society."

"And the other Queens do?"

"They should." She smoothed her skirts over her knees and folded her hands primly. "It's important to know what the people want."

"Do you spend much time socializing with the people?"

"Of course! All the time!"

"Where?"

"Oh, parties. I get invited to *all* of them now I'm Queen. It keeps me quite busy!" She bestowed another glimmering smile on me. "I canceled a lunch date to come see you, you know."

"I'm flattered," I muttered.

"Oh, shy man!" She popped another apricot into her mouth, and then picked up a second and offered it to the little fluffy thing. The fluffy thing scarfed it down. I clenched my jaw.

"Just parties, then?"

"Oh, no, of course not. Also lunches, suppers, picnics, hunts, carriage rides, holidays in the country . . ."

"What about everyone else? The people who aren't invited?"

"The *poor*, you mean?" Another tinkling laugh. "I don't think they have enough time to care about politics. I understand that—I barely have enough time for it myself! But never mind all this. There's something that I have been *dying* to ask you."

"Oh?"

She scooted her stool closer and leaned forward, her face a little more serious. "Am I going to win the election next year?"

"What election?"

"The Commerce election!"

"How should I know?"

"Because you're a fortune-teller or a prophet of some kind! Aren't you? Weren't you up for witchcraft charges before they went after you for treason?"

I was completely speechless.

"Here, do you need to read my palm?" She drew back her cuff and began extending her hand, but paused and glanced at my own hands, which were filthy and calloused, the nails chewed short. "Or something else to scry with, maybe?"

"I don't read the future."

"Whyever not?"

"Because I'm not a blackwitch." That wasn't the only reason—as I said before, I don't have a lick of magic in me.

She furrowed her brows at me. "What does that have to do with anything? They've been saying you know things, and what I want to know is whether I'm going to win." She put her hands back in her lap, clenched into fists.

"Who's been saying that? What do they think I know?"

"Oh, everyone. It's practically common knowledge at this point. You know how news spreads. Someone talks about the blackwitch on trial; someone argues that you're not a blackwitch; someone else points out that blackwitch or no, you seem to know a lot of things, so you certainly must be a spy. Someone else gets huffy that there's no crime in knowing things. Then it turns into a jolly argument about whether you're a spy or an oracle, and I've decided to come find out for myself." She twinkled at me. "So. Which is it?"

"But I don't have the gift for it," I blurted before I could think better of it. Then I heard what I said. I had no doubt that someone would take that as me confessing to espionage—do you see? Offered the choice between being a spy or an oracle, I deny the latter, so therefore . . .

Iron swans, whispered a desperate voice in my head. Taishineya's expression had turned frosty.

I scrambled to regain my footing. "I mean—not for just foreseeing the future willy-nilly whenever I choose to. It's more difficult than that. It requires . . . persuading the spirits to help me." Her expression eased slightly, and I seized upon an opportunity. "And it requires assistance."

"What kind of assistance?" she asked, suspicious.

"Well, my apprentice knows what to do. . . . If he were here, if we had the materials, I could certainly try to peer through the veil. I'm certain I could foresee what you need to do to win."

"Then let's summon him here now!"

"Well, that's the problem. I don't know where he is. When I was arrested for that silly witchcraft charge, I was dragged off before I could speak to him or communicate where we should meet. I may have lost him forever. . . ."

"Couldn't you have asked Anfisa Zofiyat to look for him?"

I gave her a wry look. "I did, madam. I wrote letters, but she kept them for herself. She thought they had a code in them. She's one of the people who has decided I'm a spy, not an oracle."

"Hmph. She's crazy," Taishineya Tarmos said sharply. There was a hint of an edge behind the giggling doll after all. "Someone's going to kill her one of these days—she's the worst of them. She thinks she knows things about—about people. Everyone." She was nervous—more nervous than Vihra, and less well-equipped to handle it.

"She certainly seems like she's been swept away by paranoia."

"Swept away . . . What a delightful way to put it." She picked up the fluffy animal—was it a dog? It looked more like a round puff of golden cotton than a dog. She set it on her lap and stroked it. Fed it an apricot, put another in her own mouth. "She's not the only one who has people."

"People like the Weavers, you mean?"

"The Weavers ought to be shut down, the whole institution. And they should all be called home and executed. They're interfering little *pests*," she hissed. "They stick their noses in where they're not wanted, at home and abroad, and they . . . make things difficult for me."

"Difficulties that must be unwelcome, if you're looking to get reelected next year."

"To say the least." She smiled again, but it was strained. "But I have men and women who are used to travel—give me a message and write down the last place you saw your apprentice, and what he looks like, and the most likely places he would have gone, and his name, and I'll have my scribes copy it out. I'll send five people looking for him. And when he comes, you'll tell me how to—" She jolted to a stop. There was a vicious light in her eyes, and I was sure that if she'd continued, she would have said something like *you'll tell me how to destroy the others.*

"I'll tell you the path to take towards victory, I promise," I said, trying to sound soothing. I pulled out a folded, unsealed piece of parchment from under my blankets. "As for the letter, I've already written one, if you wouldn't mind taking it today."

"Oh! How cunning of you. And the directions?"

"If you give me a moment . . ."

She nodded, waved airily. Her invisible mask was back in place, her persona as firmly affixed as Nerissineya's birthmark. She turned to devote her full attention to the candied apricots, and I pulled back the blankets and found another scrap of parchment, the ink, and the pen, and I lowered myself slowly and creakingly to the floor—there was no desk, so it was the only thing to write on. Seeing this, Taishineya dropped the folded parchment I had handed her and wiped her hand hurriedly on her skirts.

I narrated aloud as I wrote the directions, though I imagined that she probably wouldn't remember or care. "His name is Ylfing. He's a youth, in his seventeenth or eighteenth year, as near as I can guess. He's of the Hrefni people, who live far to the west off the coast of Genzhu's north flank, past four mountain ranges and the Amariyani Sea. He's tall and strong—I make him carry all our things. Middly brown hair, like dead grass. Very pale skin, the Hrefni have, much paler than I am, but not so pale as—well, have you ever seen a Norlander or a Vint? Most of them have skin the color of white shelf mushrooms, the ones that grow on trees in the summer. The Hrefni are a little browner, but not much—like very milky tea. And he has blue eyes, the color of shadowed snow. He's going to stand out in a crowd, is the point I'm trying to make here." I wrote all this down as I said it. "I last saw him outside the house of a man who had given us lodging for the last few days—I don't remember his name, but this was near . . . Uzlovaya, I think, was the name of the big town. The village was Cayie. I was down the road from the man's house when I was arrested—I was only telling stories to some people in exchange for bread. We were going to move along in the next day or two, because Ylfing had been paying for our lodging with chores, but the man was running out of things he needed done and wanted money instead. We hardly ever use money. I guess he would have had to leave, unless the man has let him stay on." I folded up the description and directions and held it out to her. She looked at it with open distaste and took it from me by pinching one corner between two fingernails. One of the footmen whisked it away instantly.

"And in return, you promise you'll scry?"

"I can promise to *try*," I said, and that was true. I knew a score of different techniques for telling the future. Some of them even worked—sort of, and for other people. Kaskinen doesn't have that magic. I didn't know if Ylfing had it either, but I didn't think so—if he were any good at that, he would have told me. It's the Hrefni way.

"I don't know that I should do you a service in exchange for the *possibility* of payment. Perhaps that works wherever you're from, but it's not how things are done here."

I rubbed my hands over my face and combed out my beard with my fingers. "Then I can give you advice now, as a down payment, and scry later."

"I've had advice from dozens of people. I hired people to give me advice." There was that petulant little moue again, but I saw another glimpse of that edge of steel behind it.

"I will wager you haven't had this advice before."

Another airy wave. "All right, go on."

"What story are you telling?"

She tilted her head. "What?"

I repeated myself.

"I'm not telling any story." It was fascinating, what she was like when she forgot to perform her little act. Her voice dropped to a more natural register; her posture shifted so, so slightly, transforming her from a lovely, delicate flower to a *person* with strength in her spine and a beating heart.

"Of course you are. You're in the public eye—your actions tell a story about you. They tell a story about a woman who is concerned with appearances. With *seeming*, I think, rather than *being*."

"There's no difference." She laughed, the false tinkling laugh from before. "This is rather funny advice so far."

"A very long time ago, and half the world away . . ."

THE SEVENTH TALE:
The Glass-Merchant's Wares

. . . there was a woman who owned a little shop where she sold glassware. Beautiful, fine work by the best artisans in all the city, little fantasies of crystal. She also had some poorer work, which she kept for people who weren't quite high enough in society to be able to afford the very best, but who were clawing their way up as fiercely as they could, who wanted to *seem* like they were doing a better job than they were. It was a rather boring trade for the woman—she had inherited the business from her father, and she had not much use for or interest in glass, except for the money that it brought in and the reputation it granted her, but the shop was known throughout the city for its exquisite wares.

One day a lord of the city came in. He needed to buy

an entire new suite of wineglasses, for a clumsy servant, dusting the shelf, had knocked it loose and the whole glittering collection had fallen and shattered into the smallest fragments.

(*I paused for the faintest moment here to see if Taishineya would have a reaction—a bark of laughter, perhaps, or the declaration that she hoped the lord had dismissed the servant immediately, but she just sat there and looked . . . innocently blank. At the time, I thought she looked like she was obviously feigning inquisitiveness, but in hindsight she might have been feigning the feigning of inquisitiveness.*)

The lord was hosting a great banquet that very night to celebrate the engagement of his eldest son to a young woman of much renown—he needed to go home with the glasses that very afternoon.

The glass merchant nodded calmly, but her heart had gone still in her chest. She simply did not have that many wineglasses in stock, certainly not of the quality that this lord was looking for. But she had a clever idea, and she had a lot of poorly made wineglasses, enough to supply the lord twice over.

"Well, my lord . . . Usually I wouldn't suggest something like this, but since your whole collection has been destroyed . . . It just seems like true serendipity that this would happen to you, today of all days," she said.

"Why?" said the lord.

The glass merchant shooed her assistant out of the shop, locked the front door, and beckoned the lord close. "I've just received a shipment of wares so rare that only a very few people in this entire city have ever seen them before."

The lord's interest was piqued. "Show me these wares."

"I shall have to go into the storeroom and count the glasses to make sure I have enough . . . but I think I might. It will be very close." The lord nodded eagerly, and the merchant vanished into her back room, where she counted the wineglasses, ran a dust cloth over them, and composed herself. She brought back one, covered in a piece of fine white silk, and she set it on a velvet cloth on the counter, peering out behind the lord at the street, as if to make sure no one was looking in. "I don't display them, my lord," she said, "for fear of thieves. These are rare indeed. Made by the blind monks from the abbey of Silverbed Lake, on the top of the mountain Eibe in far-off Vilarac."

"Goodness," said the lord, marveling, "if they're blind, how do they blow glass?"

("Yes," said Taishineya Tarmos, her head a little on one side.)

"My lord has cleverly spotted the source of their rarity," said the merchant, with great pride. "I expected nothing less. It is said that the gods guide their hands, my lord, although they may have some small assistance from novices who still have their sight. They use an ancient method, handed down in secret from generation to generation, which no one outside the abbey has ever learned or been able to replicate. Owning these glasses is like owning a relic from a thousand years ago. They are, to make a gross understatement, *priceless*. I had planned to sell them one by one to some of the best collectors of fine glassware in the city—" and she named several of the lord's peers and superiors, all of whom were noted for their good taste. "I didn't think the opportunity would come along to be able to preserve the set in its perfect entirety. It would have been a right shame to sell it in bits and pieces—like separating members of a family and shipping them off alone to each of the corners of the world."

The lord urged her to show him the glass, and so she whirled the silk cloth off it with a flourish and let her breath catch in her throat, as if she were overcome.

"Behold, my lord: Vilarac Unseen glass."

The glass was thick and heavy, and the bowl was set just *slightly* off center on the stem, but she had polished it clean and put it in a patch of sunshine, where it reflected light into the lord's eyes and dazzled him so that he could not quite see it clearly. And then she whirled the cloth back over it, looking with great concern out of the shop window behind him. "Pardon, my lord, I thought I saw an urchin peering in."

"Never mind the urchin. Did you say you had enough of those?"

"My lord, I have merely one more than you asked for," she said solemnly.

"And what price are you putting on these priceless glasses?" The merchant named a number, and the lord paled slightly and adjusted his neckcloth. "Perhaps," said he, "we might look at a few others that you have on offer?"

"Certainly, my lord, I would be happy to show

you. I understand that perhaps the Unseen glasses
may be too much for you. . . . I see now they could be
considered rather ostentatious for something like an
engagement."

She led the lord to a shelf holding one of her finest
pieces, a tall flute with a stem shaped like a seahorse,
decorated with rubies for eyes. "But surely you wouldn't
want something this gaudy and garish."

"Surely," the lord said, uncertain. She nodded and tossed
the glass over her shoulder, and it shattered.

(*Taishineya blinked.*)

"And surely you wouldn't want anything this shoddily
made," she said, picking up a simple cup of glass as thin as
gossamer, through which the light broke into rainbows.
"It's trash, really. I never should have bought it from that
charlatan, that reprobate." And with that, not waiting for
his reply, she smashed it on the ground also. "Not to worry,
my lord, we shall find you something that perfectly suits
your needs. Not this one, though, I've sold this to thirty
families in town," and she smashed yet another glass. "And
my lord surely doesn't want glassware that simply *everyone*
has, do you?"

"Perhaps I'll take another look at the Unseen glasses," he
said nervously.

"Ah, certainly," she said, without missing a beat. And he
saw by the delicate, careful way she handled them that this
was the real treasure. He bought all of them, even the extra,
and the glass merchant immediately packed up and left
town, with enough money to comfortably retire on.

But she needn't have done so—the lord spoke grandly

to all his guests of the history and quality of the pieces, and they were all terribly jealous. So everyone lived happily ever after.

Then I said, "Madam, what was the difference between the shoddy glass and the fine glass?"

"Quality of craftsmanship. The lord should have known she was swindling him."

"Then why didn't he?"

"He was a fool," she said with a delicate shrug.

"Who is permitted to vote in this country?"

"Any adult citizen."

"And how many of them do you suppose are fools?"

There was a long pause between us. "*Oh*," she said at last.

"The quality of craftsmanship wasn't the important distinction. The difference was that the Unseen glasses had a *history*. They had a *story*. And humans value stories above all else, whether they know it or not. I travel through a land gripped in famine, where *food* should be the most valuable thing, correct? But I can stand up in front of a starving crowd and sing for them, and whisk them away from their hunger for a moment, and I'll have at least a crust of bread when I'm done. Enough to get by on.

"Another story, a shorter one: There was once a king who hated the neighboring kingdom. They had a dispute over which of them owned a mountain on their shared border—a mountain filled with silver. So the king told a story to his people that taught them that they were the ones the gods truly favored. He made their suffering noble. He made their little successes into heroic victories. And then they followed him into war and obliterated themselves and most of the opposing army. For a story someone once told them."

Taishineya Tarmos nodded and pushed the small animal off her lap. Smoothed her skirts again. "I have a lot to think about," she said. Her voice was clearer than it had been the entire time before. I hadn't realized how much of a falsetto she'd been adopting.

"Will you have my message carried?"

After a few heartbeats, she nodded. "You sang for your crust of bread. It was good advice. I will see that it is done."

———

Days later Vasili walked up to my cell and unlocked the door before I could even put down my book. "You have a visitor."

"Who?"

"Young man by the name of Ill-thing or something."

"Ylfing!"

"Right, that's it."

"He's here!"

"In the visiting room, apparently. Get up and follow me. You carrying anything that could get us in trouble?" he hissed. I had continued feeding him little scraps of information about the Tower of Pattern, but I was trying to wean him off of it now. Consanza's rebuke had adequately spooked me, and considering how many things Taishineya Tarmos had heard about me . . . Well. Anfisa had much more elegant intelligence systems. I could only cringe at my poor judgment and hope that perhaps the worst parts might slip through the cracks.

"I have nothing! Is he all right?" I scrambled up. Vasili gripped my upper arm and pulled me out of the cell and down the corridor.

"Who?"

"Ylfing!"

"Looks like he's in one piece."

I didn't miss him, mind you. Not at all. I was just rather pleased to know he wasn't dead—it's not every boy or girl who wants to run off and become a Chant, to unname themselves and to disavow their homeland, to sink it beneath the waves. I haven't let Ylfing do it yet; that's why he still has his name. He has time to back out of it, if he's going to.

My heart was behaving rather oddly—felt all light, like a soap bubble. Not because I was happy to see Ylfing. I was probably having a heart attack at that moment, that's all.

Vasili took me to a small room, like the one where Zorya Miroslavat had brought me for my first so-called hearing for the stupid espionage business. Right before the door opened, Vasili instructed me that I was not to come within eight feet of Ylfing, that he had been patted down just as I had, and that we would both be searched again when our visit was over. "I don't think you'd do something like that," Vasili admitted. "But I have to say it just for formalities."

"Yes, yes, yes, all right," I said, and he opened the door, and it was all I could do not to hobble across that room and catch that stupid boy up in my arms, even if he is half a cubit taller than I am.

He looked . . . not as well as he could, but well enough under the circumstances. A little thinner than when I'd left him. And he had—on his neck—! "What is *that?*" I demanded, jabbing a finger at it.

I swear it to any god listening: that terrible child turned purple, clapped his hand to his neck, started stammering.

"Is that a *bite mark?*" says I.

"No?" he said, trying all he could to make puppy eyes.

"*You'd given up on me?*"

"Chant! By all the gods, no!"

"Don't lie to me! You were lolling about in some haystack with one of those smelly shepherd boys you like so much."

"He's not a shepherd boy!" Ylfing shrieked, hand still clamped to his neck. "And he's not smelly!"

"Instead of looking for me! You were—you were *canoodling*. *Canoodling*. While I was languishing in *prison*, you were *canoodling*."

"It wasn't canoodling!"

"Even if he wasn't a shepherd boy, he was one of these horrible Nuryevens." I switched over into Hrefni. I'd had enough of this goddamn country, and having no one with whom I could bad-mouth it. Hrefni is a comfortable language, and it was a great relief. "It was some rich city idiot who kept you in silks and fed you peeled grapes, wasn't it? *Wasn't it?* While I was *in prison.*"

"There weren't grapes!" he squeaked. "Not a single grape! And no silks! And he's not rich! I looked for you all I could, I asked everyone in Cayie where you would have been taken, and I came straight here when they said that's where you'd be!"

"And then you get here and—" I stopped, gasped. Clapped my hand to my mouth. "*Prostitutes?*"

"I didn't go to any prostitutes!"

"What have I told you about those places? You have to be careful! Did you use a sheath? I hear there's paperwork involved here—you read everything *carefully* before you signed anything, right?"

"I am *not* talking to you about this, Chant. I am *not*. Talking to *you*. About *this*."

"You're talking to the gods and everybody about it, my boy, with that bruise blazoned there for all the world to see."

"It was just once, a few days ago! I met him at the House of Law when I was trying to find out where they'd taken you—when I was *looking for you.*"

"You're fucking an *advocate?*" I shrieked.

"I am not *fucking* anyone!" he shrieked back. "I spent the night, past tense, *one time*, with a *scribe* of the courts. Is that acceptable to you? At least it's not a shepherd or an advocate!"

I turned away and folded my arms, glaring at the wall. Had to think about that. I supposed I didn't have any grudges against the court scribes. None of *them* had screwed me over, not yet.

Ylfing should really learn to restrain his sarcasm. No respect for his elders, none at all. He bullies me, you know. It's a terrible thing.

"They wouldn't even tell me if they had you at first," my errant apprentice went on. "And then—they kept moving you around, didn't they? First you're in the House of Order, then Order doesn't have you and won't tell me where you are, then I hear a rumor that you're in the Tower of Pattern, then after that, all they tell me is that you've been transferred out of Pattern again. . . . I tried to come to your hearing the other day, but there was a huge crowd and they wouldn't let anyone in." He huffed, then added, "That's when I met Ivo, by the way. He's got beautiful handwriting. Much better than mine."

"I wish you two the greatest happiness together after I am *dead*," I sniffed.

"Dead? Wait, what have they really charged you with? Everyone keeps telling me something different—first it was witchcraft, then they said it wasn't witchcraft, that you'd been convicted of something odd like 'heinous behavior in the twelfth degree'—"

"Brazen impertinence," I muttered.

"Yes, that's the one—can't say I was surprised about it—but then they said it was espionage!"

I turned around again and sat down at the table with a great sigh. Ylfing backed up—good of him, I'd forgotten that we weren't to come within eight feet of each other. We both glanced at Vasili, standing at the door, who shrugged.

"What did you do, Chant? Did you do something bad?"

"I didn't do anything but what you saw me doing in Cayie! I was doing my job, and they came up and arrested me!"

"Maybe it was because you rubbed herbs all over that woman's goat's udder even though she asked you not to."

"It was inflamed. I was healing it for her."

"I think she probably thought you were cursing it."

"I wasn't cursing it, obviously. She should have known."

"I just think that it's not very polite to touch other people's goats when they don't want you to."

"I was helping!"

"I know, I know," he said, holding his hands up all defensive. "At home it wouldn't have been a problem. She would have listened if you said you were good at healing goats."

"You should stop calling it that. Home. One day you're going to have to—"

"Sink it beneath the waves, yeah, I know. Unless you run me off before I become a master-Chant," he chirped. "Then I will go to my home, and I will probably be the best at many things, and I'll know more stories than anyone in all the villages. I'll probably get taken to every Jarlsmoot."

"And I'll be dead and all the things I have left to teach you, lost. All the things my master taught me before she died, the secrets she told me on her deathbed . . ."

"Not all the things. You've had other apprentices." And yet I was pleased to see him look at least a little unsettled.

"You want me to die, I suppose, so you can sleep around with court scribes and shepherds."

"I don't want you to die at all!"

I sniffed and abandoned this line of argument. He isn't very satisfying to snipe with, not like Consanza is. That woman loves an argument like she loves her own breath. Ylfing just protests and wobbles his lower lip. I turned to a new subject: "Do you have any powers of prophecy?"

"What, so I can tell you how the trial will go?"

"No, I had to make a deal to get that message to you."

Ylfing slapped his hand to his forehead. Disrespectful child. "Did you promise someone I'd read their future?"

"I promised the *Queen of Commerce* that *we* would *attempt* to scry to see if she will be reelected next year."

The disrespectful child groaned. I glanced at Vasili—fortunately, we were still speaking Hrefni, which has no relationship to Nuryeven whatsoever. He didn't seem to mind that we were speaking a different language, but I supposed that we didn't look much like two people who were plotting anything suspicious, like how to break one of them out of prison or how to convince the Queen of Coin that we were really reading her future. "Stop that whining, Ylfing, we have to think of something. Can you scry or not?"

"No! I don't think so, anyway. Although one time, I had a dream that my friend Bjorn went to the Jarlsmoot with his father and proved himself the best at fishing of all the children, and then he *did* go."

"Did he win at fishing?"

"Well, no, but he did catch a few good ones. Not the best, not the worst. That's a nice place to be." He blushed and ducked his head. "You know, Ivo taught me a little of scribing the other day. I wanted to know how to write beautifully like him—do you think he might be the best scribe? He can't be, he's only a year or two older than I am, but he must have practiced for a long time. I bet he's the best out of all the other scribes our age." He plopped himself down into the other chair. "Did you know they don't teach the foundations of an art here? If you want to learn scribing, you just learn scribing, you don't have to learn ink making or paper making or how to whittle pens or make nibs. He says he knows *sort of* how to cut a quill pen, but they mostly don't use quills, unless you're some sort of official person writing something fancy, and even then Ivo says you'd only use a quill from some exotic southern bird and everyone would know you were trying to brag about how much money you have. They're rather odd here, don't you think? They think having money is a skill, and that if you have lots of it, then you must be the best out of everyone, like a jarl, but if you don't have any, then you should be ashamed. Seems like most everyone here feels that way most of the time, but why would you be ashamed of not having a money skill? Nobody in Hrefnesholt has money; should we all be ashamed? The Umakh didn't either, not really."

"The Umakh have a lot to recommend them," I agreed, as soon as I could get a word in edgewise. "They didn't imprison me, for example."

"Yeah. They're odd in their own way, though—that sour milk they drink all the time, ugh! And Syrenen didn't notice that I wanted him to show me how to shoot a short bow from horseback." He looked terribly crestfallen. He'd been crestfallen back then, too.

"It's a good thing he didn't notice. You noticed they were a little dubious about men together—'women own the men and the horses,' as they say."

Ylfing shrugged. "I just wanted to learn. I didn't like him that way." Which, if that was true, gives poor Syrenen the dubious distinction of being the only young man in the entire world Ylfing *hasn't* mooned over.

I sighed. "Well, O young man of so many skills, how are we going to persuade the Queen of Coin?"

"What's she like?"

"Flighty. Smart, though, smarter than she wants anyone to notice.

Much concerned with *seeming*. I told her about the glass merchant's wares; she appeared to take it to heart. She's bored with politics, but she wants to be reelected. Pure vanity."

"Then just *tell her* she'll be reelected!"

"We're not in the business of telling lies!" I snapped.

"What are you talking about? You lie literally *all the time!*"

"Little white lies to ease the way, nothing that hurts anyone," I scoffed. "Nothing that they'll ever find out wasn't true."

"Then tell her you don't know. Or tell her she should either do something that makes her happy or try harder to be good at politics."

"Brilliant idea, genius apprentice, and after telling her that, I'll go ahead and tie my own noose, lay my own pyre. Perhaps you can invite that Ivo to watch the spectacle! I can't speak as to how romantic it will be, but I'll do my best to come up with some kind of tragic monologue, if they even let me have my last words. All this knowledge, gone! You might never find another Chant to teach you, and even if you did, they might not apprentice you. Then you'll never be the best Chant."

Ylfing rubbed his hands over his face in a gesture I recognized that he had stolen or inherited from me. "Then tell her something so vague that she won't be able to tell whether or not she'll win."

"Do you think I haven't already thought of all this? Do you think you're coming up with new ideas? She's not going to buy it if it's vague; she'll know we're swindling her."

Ylfing ruffled his hair with his fingers in frustration, a gesture that was all his own. "What if you gave her a conditional, then? She'll win the election if she does such and such—if she slays the dragon, goes on the quest, finds the lost relic, kisses the forest queen. Something like that."

"I don't know what conditions the election would hinge on! And

I can't find out—I'm stuck in here! There's only one guard who will speak to me, and he's standing there at the door, and I don't even know if I can trust him to give me good information! So I can't find out!"

"I'll find out for you! Obviously!"

"You're the *worst* at being polite," I snarled.

"Being polite isn't a skill," he countered, "but if it were, it is better to be bad at something than to be good at it, because it is pleasanter to anticipate the journey than to nurse your blisters."

"It's a wonder your people bother to learn anything at all, then!"

"Learning is how you live prosperously," he said, disgustingly earnest. "It's a duty of honor to your family and to your village. No one ever fed themselves by looking at the water and waiting for the fish to catch themselves."

"Fine. Go find out, then; find out *every possible thing* about Nuryeven elections, and do it all before they manage to throw me to the executioners for spying."

"But if you haven't done anything, surely they can't convict you without evidence."

"You remember all those stories I told you about Xing Fe the Sailor?" He nodded. "He ended up here, apparently. Made some mistakes. Got convicted. I . . . may have mentioned in court that we were friends. I didn't know they knew him. It was part of my apology— had to apologize as my sentence for brazen impertinence."

"Gods, that's it? That's all they have on you?"

"So far—and anything else I've accidentally told them."

Ylfing nodded, somber. "You do lecture a lot. At anything that stands still long enough, I used to think. You've probably told them a lot of things."

"You're one to talk! You're the one who should be convicted of brazen impertinence! And I so appreciate the vote of confidence. Where would I be without that?"

"Who is your advocate?"

"Consanza Priyayat—I don't know her last name, just the matronymic." The naming system is complicated but consistent, and I'd overheard enough names by that point to have slowly gleaned the structure of 'em.

"Oh! Oh, I didn't realize—in the crowd, at your hearing, everyone was talking about her. She's amazing, apparently; she's won all these cases. I think someone said she's never lost one? And Ivo said she's one of the very best at arguing. How lucky you are! You got one of the very best ones!"

"Ivo can *shove it up his ass*. He doesn't know what the fuck he's talking about. She's awful. She doesn't care about this case. It was just assigned to her as a requirement to keep her license. Well, okay, she does care about it a little bit now that the Primes are involved, because she wants to, as she put it, kiss ass like she's never kissed ass before. She wants to have a cushy desk job waiting for her in ten years when she's ready to retire from idiotic courtroom theatrics. Lazy twit. We don't get on."

"I bet I'll like her," Ylfing said, all sunshine. "You just don't like people with strong personalities. I bet you're just clashing horns with her. I'll go see her and introduce myself. I bet if we put our heads together, we can come up with a way to get you out of this."

"Optimism is the surest sign of a fool."

———

The very next morning I was rudely awakened at a truly obscene hour. "Chant!" someone hissed. "Chant, wake up!"

"Fuck off," I muttered, pulling the blanket up to my chin.

"I have food. Fried dough with sugar on it, they were selling it outside the courthouse! They're called monk's-puffs! I bought a lot—Ivo lent me some money, I saw him again last night, so there, now don't make a fuss about it—and when I came here, I gave half of them to the guards and they let me bring in the rest to you! And look, open your eyes, Consanza is here too!"

"What time is it?" I cracked one eye open. "It's still dark."

"Don't know, but it's getting towards winter now so . . . It's just like home! So dark and cold! And I saw the northern lights last night, just a whisper." He sighed with great nostalgia, only half joyful. "Look, the monk's puffs are still warm, wake up and eat. Consanza said they only feed you slop, and you looked so thin when I was here yesterday. Get up! Get up or I shall throw them at you, and they'll get all over the floor, and I know how much you dislike eating off the floor."

I pushed myself upright. The blankets didn't help much with the discomfort of sleeping on a bench, and it was so narrow that it wasn't easy for me to turn over or change positions in the night, so I always woke up cramped and stiff and achy. Consanza, already smoking, was poking a crumpled-up piece of paper into the brazier, which had burned low overnight. When it caught a little lick of flame, she piled small logs of twisted straw on top of it.

"They keep it too cold in here," Ylfing said to her. "He could get sick, he could die—that wouldn't be fair, would it? Him dying before they've even convicted him of anything. It's negligent."

She shrugged. "Take it up with Vihra Kylliat."

"Maybe I shall," Ylfing said with all the loftiness of youth.

"I don't recommend it."

"But you just told me to."

It was bitterly cold, and it would be until the fire was going again. I wrapped a blanket around my shoulders and shuffled up to the bars.

Ylfing handed me a piece of those sweets he'd brought—it was as soft and warm as he'd promised, even in the bitter cold. He must have kept it well wrapped.

"Isn't it good? Consanza said the guards love little treats."

"Your accent is atrocious," I said, sitting back down on my bench and nibbling the thing slowly. "What are these called again?"

"Monk's-puffs, generally," Consanza replied. "Some people call them other things."

"How did you get him in here? I had to go to the other room last time."

My advocate shrugged. "Told them he was *my* apprentice."

"Chant, Chant, Chant, listen," Ylfing said, breathless. "I started talking to people about the Queen of Coin, and Ivo helped me, he told me all about how elections work—"

"You saw him again?"

"I already told you I saw him again."

I eyed my apprentice. He had a very convenient scarf wrapped around his neck, but so did Consanza, and Ylfing was still wearing mittens, even. "Where'd you get the new clothes?"

"Borrowed them from Ivo. I already told you about that, listen—"

"Consanza, do you know this Ivo fellow?"

"Can't say I've met him," she said, scratching her chin and adding another few straw logs to the brazier. "There's dozens of court scribes, and advocates don't usually have any reason to interact with them. But," she said, sucking pensively on that damn pipe, "from what I've heard from Ylfing since he came to my offices yesterday, I feel like I already know him."

"I haven't talked about him that much," Ylfing muttered into his monk's-puff.

"I think I could recognize Ivo simply by looking at his

handwriting," Consanza added to me. "It is, or so I hear, *beautiful.*"

"Ivo says," Ylfing began loudly, his cheeks all pink like a maiden's, "that Taishineya Tarmos only won Commerce by three percent. Ivo also says that Commerce is elected every five years, making it the shortest term of all the Primes. Ivo *also* says that most people don't think she's doing a very good job. He doesn't think she's embezzling from the treasury, but she did throw a silly party with Commerce funds, under the guise of wining and dining some merchant speculators from Cormerra. And he doesn't like her, nobody likes her. He says she's raised taxes a lot in the last four years. A *lot.*" Consanza nodded grimly at this in the background. Ylfing continued, lofty, "Ivo also says that my handwriting is getting much better."

Consanza snorted and blew smoke. "Ylfing, you'd better tell Chant about that dear thing Ivo said to you this morning. What was it? Something about—"

"My hair, he said he liked my hair. Except he didn't just say it as, 'I like your hair, Ylfing,' he said it like . . .'" My twit of an apprentice dropped his voice lower and hooded his eyes and, I think, attempted to purr: "*I like your hair, Ylfing.* Do you hear the difference? *I like your hair, Ylfing.* It just sounded so full of *meaning.* And he kept curling a little piece of it around his finger when he was telling me things about the election, and it was really distracting, but so sweet, right? It made my heart all fluttery. Don't you think he sounds nice?"

"Ivo should take up *poetry,*" said Consanza. She winked at me, and I felt more camaraderie with her in that moment than I ever had before. It took all I had not to laugh.

"Oh, oh, I agree!" And then Ylfing wittered on for several minutes about various other allegedly adorable things that Ivo had done; Ivo this and Ivo that, which I will not inflict upon you—it was all how much he knew about everything, and how much he *cared* about things, and how he sent money home to his family in the country, and so on. Meanwhile, I finished off the rest of the monk's-puffs and Consanza and I just looked at each other in silence (she, at least, seemed incredibly amused) while Ylfing talked himself out. It's a good skill for a Chant to have, the ability to talk at great and elaborate length, but Ylfing has yet to learn how to sift out the most interesting parts of a story and discard the dull ones. For example, he waxed poetic for almost a full minute about how handsome Ivo's hands were, and how attractive to see his fingertips stained with ink, and isn't it beautiful to see someone's craft upon their skin—and if you think that a minute isn't a long time to talk about hands, then I recommend you try it for yourself. I couldn't very well tell Ylfing to stop chattering, for every few sentences he'd remember some other useful piece of information that Ivo had provided him and then off he'd go on another wild tangent, and Consanza stood over the brazier the whole time, just smirking with an odd kind of fondness at Ylfing and occasionally dropping a comment—which only encouraged the boy, and I tried to signal to her that she should stop.

At long last, when Ylfing paused to gasp for breath, Consanza slipped in, "They've scheduled another hearing for you."

"Ah," I said. "Wonderful."

"Wonderful is what you might think, yes. You'll need to finish up securing Taishineya Tarmos's support before that. What else have you to bribe her with?"

"Not much money," Ylfing said, dejected. "I don't think she'd want our pennies anyway."

"Secrets," I said. "That's all I have. Secrets and stories."

Consanza nodded. "Sure. What secrets you got?"

"Not many of those either." I scowled. "I'm not a spy, you know. My knowledge is a cross section of things most people know. What have *you* been doing, anyway? Haven't you been working on any kind of defense for me in case this grand plan doesn't work?"

"There's a lot of paperwork to do," she said absently. "I think Anfisa Zofiyat might try to file for having you serve another stint in the Tower."

"Better there than here," I grumbled.

"Seriously? *Seriously?* After telling everyone who would listen that she has a blackwitch in the Tower? Say good-bye to your head if she gets custody of you again!"

Ylfing looked at me with huge eyes. "Chant! That's not a *little white lie*! That's something someone could check!"

"She can't know I was the one who said it," I scoffed. "Surely it's not that wild of a theory. All this spookish stuff about Weavers!"

"Who else could it be?" Consanza said. "No one else has come out of the Tower recently, and Vihra Kylliat is threatening to file an appeal to the other Primes to possibly enter the Tower with patrolmen and search it top to bottom."

I fidgeted. "Well, yes, I expected she might do that. All she needed was an excuse—but she won't find any blackwitches, so it's not a problem! If she finds something else, something illegal, well." I folded my hands. "I certainly didn't put it there, so I can hardly be blamed. And if Anfisa has nothing to hide, then she won't be more than a little irritated at the inconvenience. If she's upset when I go back to Pattern, I'll just talk her out of it." I don't know why I thought that I could do that—I was feeling quite sure of myself, probably overconfident from how deftly I fancied that I'd handled Taishineya. "I know what I'm doing. It's not like Vihra Kylliat is *expecting* to find an actual blackwitch." I hadn't thought Vihra Kylliat to be the type to swallow a story whole. I'd just meant to shake her up a bit, fan the banked embers of her superstition and paranoia.

"You think Anfisa Zofiyat will be *a little irritated* when Order seizes anything that looks like it might be valuable to them, under the auspices of *investigating?*" Consanza demanded. "Justice will, of course, back up Vihra Kylliat's petition if she chooses to submit it. Anfisa Zofiyat is fighting tooth and nail, and I'm sure she's started playing some of her dearer cards—even the famously upstanding Vihra Kylliat has some stains on her petticoats. And you! You're just digging your grave deeper every time you open your mouth."

"They'll keep me alive as long as I have information. That was the point you were making with Vanya's swans, wasn't it?"

"They'll keep you alive as long as you're still a useful pawn," Consanza snapped. "So we can kiss Pattern's support good-bye, unless she plans to have you released so she can kidnap and torture you at leisure." She tapped the mouthpiece of her pipe against her chin, looking speculative. "I suppose that would be fine. It wouldn't be my problem then." I squawked in protest, but she continued heedlessly. "I wonder if we should have been courting Law instead of Coin. But Casimir Vanyos is so reticent, so neutral, and he wouldn't want to get in between Pattern and Order and Justice except in an official capacity. It's a difficult situation. But let's discuss your defense. They're going to keep asking you about your relationship to Xing Fe Hua—"

"What did he do, exactly?" Ylfing asked.

"Tried to blow up the House of Law while the Primes were in session together—*with* the Seconds in attendance. The Dukes and Duchesses, that is."

"Is that what he actually tried to do, or is that what they convicted him of?" I asked.

"Hard to say. I'm trying to get the records unsealed." She sighed. "These things take time."

"How do you get them unsealed?" Ylfing asked.

"You fill out a lot of forms. Then you fill out some different forms. Then you hire a new assistant for this case only, because the forms have to be filled out in quintuplicate and filed with the office of each Prime, separately, and one simply does not have enough hours in the day. Then you go home very tired to your family, having eaten dinner at your desk again, and you fall straight into bed without enough energy to do more than kiss the children and your spouses good night. And the next morning you get up and you fill out more forms, and you visit the clerks to see if anyone has read your requests, and they say no. And you do this once a day for a week or so, and if you've filled out all the paperwork *perfectly*, then you flip a coin to determine whether or not they unseal the records for you."

"Gosh," Ylfing said, eyes wide. "That sounds like a lot of work. Why'd you decide to become an advocate?"

"The glamor and the personal glory, of course," Consanza said. "I thought that was self-evident."

Consanza's mention of kidnapping and torture had overcome me with a sudden black feeling. The lingering sweetness of the monk's-puffs turned bitter in my mouth. "Ylfing, I need you to stay here for the rest of the day."

"Eh? Of course I will. But what for? I was going to go out and learn more. Ivo's invited me to meet some of his friends."

"No. Stay. It is necessary to prepare for an unpleasant eventuality."

"Oh, gods above and below, you're going to throw a tantrum about paperwork?" Consanza shook her head.

"No," I said. "I'm going to teach my apprentice all I can, because in a few weeks I might be dead."

"There's no way to know for certain yet," Ylfing was quick to say. "Consanza will think of something. Won't you?"

She shrugged. "I did hire an assistant for your case, Chant. I'm doing what I can. But as I said, what happens to you when you get out is a fate of your own making."

"Ylfing, lad. We have to get to work. There's things I haven't even begun to teach you yet. There's things I won't be able to teach you—"

"Consanza, do you have paper with you?" Ylfing asked. Rude child. He didn't understand how serious it was. "I have to practice my handwriting anyway. I'll write everything you say down—"

"You can't just write things down! You have to learn them! Memorize them! Remember them! What good are bits of paper? You can lose them, they can get burnt or stolen! If they get wet, the ink runs!"

"Yes, that's true. But if they're just in your head, then if you die, they're lost. If you get old and senile, they're lost."

"That's why you tell them to other people. If lots of people remember them, they can't ever be lost."

We bickered while Consanza unpacked some blank paper for Ylfing and left, and I abruptly tired of the argument. It was an old one, and we'd had it many times before. Once we settled into the work, I was surprised to find what a comfort it was. Hours passed, and I could see that Ylfing was getting tired. He stopped writing several times to shake the cramps out of his hand, but . . . I couldn't stop talking. I couldn't let him leave. I hungered for the work in a way that I hadn't hungered for it in years.

Brought me right back to my youth, you know. I was just about Ylfing's age, or a little younger, when my own master-Chant tumbled into my life. I don't often think about those earliest days, and I never think about my life before I met her. Not that there was anything particularly terrible there, but why would I spend even a second dwelling on what I left behind, when what I gained that instant I first laid eyes on my Chant was so much more, immeasurably more?

There's moments in your life when something suddenly clicks into place in the clockwork of fate. Sometimes it's a moment that seizes you, that thunders within you, unheard by anyone else, and makes you think, *Ah! Yes, this, this, here it is!* And sometimes it's a moment, like when I met my Chant, when the noise fate makes as its mechanisms engage is no louder than that of a single grain of sand dropped onto a sheet of copper, and in the moment you pause and think, *Hm?* and then forget about it. And it's only days or weeks or months or years or decades afterwards that you look back and say, *Oh, now I see. That was the moment it all changed, the moment the river of my life diverted its course: it was when I first heard your name spoken aloud.*

I've never regretted my river's diversion for a moment, even when I was lying in a filthy cell waiting to be either sentenced to death or released and assassinated.

And so I talked and talked until my voice cracked, and then I talked some more, until both of us were trembling with exhaustion and hunger, and Ylfing could not even muster the strength to grip the pen anymore.

He left for the night, and when the guards brought my evening slop, it was accompanied by a familiar gold-edged calling card.

———◆———

We had determined that pyromancy would be the best course of action—we had the brazier already there, and there's something romantic and primal about fire, something that makes people in big cities and thick-walled stone houses remember that there is a wilderness out there, dark forests, hungry beasts.

The other part of it was that there are interesting things you can do with fire that require no magic whatsoever, fortunately for Ylfing and me. He brought in a little bag of arcanum duplicatum, bless him, all ground up into a rough white powder the texture of salt. There was a fresh pile of sticks to add to the brazier, and another bag of an odd variety of incense, which Ylfing had found in a dusty back-alley shop, staffed by an ancient man of Arjuni descent, like our Consanza.

The sun was setting so early those days that it was already twilight when Taishineya Tarmos arrived in the middle of the afternoon, resplendent in rich plum silk. She had brought a smaller retinue this time, no lunch or dish of candied apricots, and no sign of that odd fluffy creature from her first visit.

"Master Chant!" she cried, as if we were old friends reunited for the first time in years. "Delighted to see you again, dear, just delighted. So pleased we were able to find your apprentice, too—is this him? Charmed, young man—and what is your name?"

"Ylfing, my lady," he said, and bowed a little awkwardly. I made a note of that; the Hrefni don't bow to each other, and we hadn't had much truck with persons of authority in the time since he'd begun traveling with me. Just one of the thousands of things I'd have to teach him before they killed me.

"Ill—how did you say it? Elfin?"

"Ylfing."

"Ill-thing!" There was that tinkling-bell laughter. "What a funny name. I've never heard it before." She settled herself on the cushioned stool and folded her hands. "Shall we begin?"

"If you wish." I nodded to Ylfing, who began to build up the fire. I sat cross-legged on the floor, with the horse blanket folded under me for a cushion. "Would you like to send your guards out of the corridor? It is uncertain what knowledge the spirits will impart, but it often has . . . private significance."

"No, no, it's fine, just get to it."

"Are you sure?" I dropped my voice. "I don't wish to alarm you, madam, but you never know who you can trust. You never know who might be . . . taking your portraits from someone else's hand, if you understand me. Some people can get their ears into the oddest places."

She ended up sending her guards away after all—far enough down the hall that they could hear her if she called, too far away to hear us speaking in normal tones.

"Now focus on your question with all your will." I nodded to Ylfing, and he threw a handful of incense on the fire and heaped twigs atop it. The thin smoke took on a heady, dark perfume. I let my eyes drift half-closed and stared into the fire. Ylfing added more sticks until the flames were licking high and the heat on our faces became uncomfortable, though my back was still tense with cold.

I groaned suddenly, throwing my head back. Ylfing, right on cue, scattered the bag of arcanum duplicatum over the flames. They turned a ghostly violet, and Taishineya Tarmos gasped.

In a rough fisherman's dialect of the language of my homeland, in a gravelly rumble, I intoned: "These are just random words. Sunflowers. Mountain. Turquoise. Seventeen. You think they sound very mystical. You're a bigoted twit who would rather believe gossip than get the facts straight for yourself. I hate the way you laugh and I think it's ridiculous that you don't know how vapid it makes you sound. Fire. Brazier. Prison. Thirty-eight. Awkwardly. Maritime. I have no respect for people who pretend to be stupid. Uphill. To dance. Fish knife. Complaint. Ambitious. Quickly. Shuggwa's Eye is watching you." Then, in Nuryeven, "The future is in flux. There is still time to decide your fate. A day will come when the people will choose a great leader, and that leader will bring the nation into a time of prosperity and fortune the like of which has never been seen in this realm before. That is a certainty. It is carved in the stone tablets of destiny. There is a blank space to carve that leader's name. Pick up the chisel. Pick up the chisel. To win the election, you must *pick up the chisel.*"

I fell backward, sprawled across the floor, and I stared at the ceiling and twitched slightly, muttering, "Sandwiches, sandwiches, sandwiches," in that same dialect of Kaskeen.

The violet flames gradually faded back into their usual yellows and oranges and slowly died down. "Is he all right?" Taishineya Tarmos whispered.

"I hope so," Ylfing said. "It's very hard on him, reading the future. He's not as young as he used to be."

I made a mental note to scold him about that later.

"Shouldn't you get him something?"

"I can't help him when he's locked up in there. He's not twitching too badly, so he'll probably be okay as long as he doesn't swallow his tongue." I heard him shuffling around. "Did you see the flames go purple? That's a good omen."

"Is it?"

"Purple's your color, isn't it? Your dress."

"It's just the color of my office," she said absently. "All the Primes wear the colors of their offices. What did he mean, pick up the chisel?"

"Oh . . . I'm just an apprentice, I don't know all the ways of interpreting the visions. He said there was a blank space on the stone tablets of destiny—you have to carve it yourself."

"But it was a *chisel,*" she said. "Specifically a chisel. And stone tablets. Why is destiny recorded on stone instead of on paper? Stones and chisels . . ." I heard her stand up. "It's odd. I think it means something."

"Good! Keep it in your mind. Many times the spirits speak through us in ways that we speakers don't quite understand. Sometimes it's only the asker, like yourself, who can truly understand the symbols the spirits use in their answers, because those images are only meaningful to you personally. It's quite usual. If stones and chisels are ringing a bell for you, pursue it." Ylfing managed to say this with great earnestness—because he actually believed it was true, I supposed, even if the prophecy itself was made up.

"I will." There was a soft jingling. "Here. This is for you—or your master."

"Thank you, madam!"

"I suppose I will see you at the hearing in a few days."

"If they will allow me in the courtroom, certainly."

"Good day."

"Good day!" I waited until the rustling of her skirts had disappeared down the corridor and then I cracked one eye open. Ylfing was sitting by the brazier, poking through a palmful of coins. He looked at me when I sat up. "A generous tip from the Queen of Commerce," he said, all smiles. "I'll be able to pay Ivo back."

"I'm sure he'll be delighted." I pulled myself up off the floor and got comfortable on the bench. "Is there water or food?"

He winced. "I brought some, but not enough—the guards took all of it."

"Never mind." I leaned back against the wall. "So, you like Ivo."

He blushed immediately. "Oh, you know . . . Sort of."

"And," I said quietly, "you know that if I'm set free, we're leaving immediately. We're running far, and fast, and we're not stopping to say good-bye."

"I know," he whispered, not meeting my eyes. "I'm prepared for it."

"Are you sure?"

"Yes." He nodded. Then, with more confidence, "Yes. I like him very much, and his handwriting *is* beautiful, but I wouldn't give this up. For anything. For anyone. This is what I was meant to do."

I was probably having a heart attack again, and it was the smoke from the fire that was making my eyes sting and water.

———◆———

I went to the hearing. The details don't matter, and I didn't pay very much attention anyway. They didn't let in any of the crowd except Ylfing and some young man accompanying him, whom I assumed was Ivo of the much-revered handwriting. They came in with Consanza—I suppose she said they were her assistants. Her real assistant was with them too, a harried-looking woman of Consanza's age or slightly older.

Consanza did her best, I suppose, making arguments about how association was no proof of malicious intent, but Justice was just as set on their accusations as ever they had been, and chillingly, Anfisa Zofiyat's tide had turned against me too. She asked me several sharp questions—don't remember what they were in reference to, and she gave nothing away in her expression or her tone, but I knew . . . I knew. Something was happening, something was in flux, and it was my fault. The scales had been tipped out of their delicate balance, and I was no longer a useful tool, but an outright enemy.

Well, they voted on my guilt. The ballots were secret but the results were easy enough to read: Law, in compliance with tradition, publicly abstained; Pattern and Justice called for my head; Commerce recommended mercy. There was another abstention, which could only be Order.

I was to be executed in one month's time.

Ylfing did me proud. Didn't cry, didn't interrupt, just sat there with Ivo, still and pale.

The three of them—Ylfing and Ivo and Consanza—came to the House of Order that evening after I was safely locked up again. The guards were a little more lax about the things they could bring me, now that I'd been sentenced—or maybe they'd just pulled together enough of a bribe to have the guards look the other way. Consanza had a basket with a pot of tender stewed goat, a whole roast chicken, crispy with salt and rosemary, seven or eight steaming potatoes baked in their skins, and a mincemeat pie for each of us. Ylfing had another basket, this with three sweet fruit pies, still molten hot in the middle, a paper bag of monk's-puffs, two bottles of a surprisingly fine white wine (only Echareese, rather than Vintish, but it made no difference to me), and four sets of cups and plates. The treasure of the feast, however, was a few tablespoons of fragrant, fresh-ground coffee in a little silver pot, ready for brewing. I couldn't imagine how expensive it must have been to buy it this far north—it would have had to come all the way from Tash or Zebida, at the very least.

For a meal like that, I wouldn't mind being sentenced to death every day.

"Coffee or wine?" Consanza said while Ivo carved the chicken and Ylfing served up a little bit of everything onto each plate. The lad—Ivo, that is—had been openly agog as they unpacked the baskets. I couldn't blame him—I too have rarely seen so much food in one place. The only really surprising things in the basket were the wine and the coffee (and I now suspect Ivo had never tasted the latter before in his life), but it was all good, hearty food of quality that any moderately well-to-do family would have been unashamed to put on their table.

"Coffee later," I answered. A treat that fine should be saved for the end. "Wine now. After today, I need the fortification. Don't you have a family or something?"

"Sure do," she said. "My two wives, one husband, all our children."

"How many?"

"Four. Fifth on the way, coming in late winter or very early spring."

"To their health," I said, taking a draft of the wine. "Why aren't you with them tonight?"

She pulled up a chair next to the brazier and took a plate from Ylfing. "Don't much feel like going home yet," she said, after a long pause.

"Why?"

"I've never lost a case before. Well—there's still time for an appeal or two, so technically I haven't lost it yet. Haven't lost it until you're . . . you know. But that's not proper talk for dinner. I'm not going home yet because I don't know how to tell them."

"What are you worried about?"

"Wouldn't say I'm worried," she said, picking at a piece of chicken. "Helena's going to come up to me when I get home, and she'll kiss me and say, 'Did you win all your cases today, darling?' like she does every day, except today I'll have to say that I didn't. And I'm not quite ready to do that yet. It's none of your business, anyway."

"You sound like you're very fond of her. Helena."

"Very fond of all of them," she muttered around a mouthful of food. Her Arjuni skin was so dark that I couldn't tell if she was blushing, but there seemed to be a bit of blush in her voice. "Particularly fond of her, though."

"Tell me about them. All of them."

"Miriana and Velizar were married first—primarily a business match, but they get on famously. Always taking each other's side, always plotting something. They go everywhere together. The three of us are all the same age—I knew them when I was just a student, and they married me a few years after I received my license." She smiled a little wryly. "They thought it'd save them some money to have a live-in advocate. And then I met Helena six or seven years ago and brought her home, and we've been married for five. That was purely a love match. Turned out she wasn't too bad of a business match either. She's a schoolteacher."

"And the children?"

"The oldest is fourteen, the youngest is two. Two girls, two boys, and I guess we'll be breaking the tie one way or another with the baby. Radacek, Inga, Nedyalka, Andrei."

"All Velizar's?"

"Radacek, Nedyalka, and the new one definitely are. Inga is from one of my former lovers—before I met Helena, that is—and Miriana isn't sure about Andrei."

"You don't differentiate between legitimate children and bastards?" Ylfing asked.

"Inga and Andrei aren't bastards," Consanza said, blinking at him. "They were born within wedlock."

"But they're not Velizar's?"

"No, why?"

"Oh, I just thought that was interesting. Where I'm from, you wouldn't have children with anyone but the person you're married to. But we only have love matches. People don't get married for business like you do here. People don't have other lovers, generally, and when they do, everyone's angry about it."

"What a backwards way to live," Consanza said, then laughed. "Sorry, no insult intended. You probably think we're backwards too."

Ylfing shrugged. "People are the same everywhere."

"What!" I squawked. "I drag you across this godforsaken earth for three long years while you hang off my sleeve or the sleeve of some smelly shepherd boy, and *that's* the big conclusion that you come to? 'People are the same everywhere'?"

"Well, they are," Ylfing protested. "Even in somewhere like Map

Sut, where love matches are almost unheard of, they still understand love *stories*. Everyone does. And everyone understands stories like the ones about Sappo."

"Who's Sappo?" Ivo asked.

"A man with two very stupid older brothers," said Ylfing. "They're greedy and rude, and always getting into trouble, and Sappo always comes up with a clever way to get them out of it."

"Ah. Yes," said Ivo with great satisfaction. "I have two older brothers."

"See!" Ylfing said to me. "People are the same everywhere. That's why we have a job."

"We have a job because people are *different* everywhere."

"But that's not the story we tell them! We tell them about one another so they know: 'Ah yes, on the other side of the world, people live just the same as we do.'"

I put my head in my hands. "I can't die yet," I groaned.

"Ivo," Consanza said suddenly, "this is shaping up to be a long argument if we let them go at it. Ylfing keeps talking about how fine your handwriting is; would you mind scribbling a bit?"

"You've been talking about me?" Ivo asked him. Ylfing turned bright red and muttered something I didn't quite catch, and Ivo grinned. "Sure I will, advocate. Do you have paper?"

"Chant does. Chant, stop groaning and get out your paper for Ivo."

As it turned out, the lad did have a very nice hand, a clean, round one with neatly sloped slants and delicate, spindly ascenders.

The admiration of Ivo's admittedly lovely handwriting effectively distracted Ylfing from arguing with me, and the conversation turned to other things for a time, though the weight of my sentence hung heavy over us.

Consanza eventually packed up the dishes into one of the baskets, while Ylfing put all the leftover food into the second basket and left it right next to the bars of my cell. She nodded to me as she prepared to leave. "I'll file an appeal tomorrow."

"And if it fails?"

"If it fails, then you die in one month."

"How?"

"That won't be determined for a little while yet. Could be anything." She shrugged. "If two appeals fail, I can always file one to demand a more merciful death. Poison, if you like, or the ax. Something gentle or something quick."

"You're simply brimming with generosity."

"Wish me luck with my family tonight," she said with a heavy sigh, hauling up the basket of dishes.

"Good luck winning the appeals," I said dryly. "I don't want you to have to tell them either."

Ivo and Ylfing lingered for a while after that. I hounded Ivo to tell me about himself, his life. He'd grown up in the far western edge of the country, he said, near the mountains. "My parents were coal miners, all of them," he said. "I would be too, but I was lucky—we had a school."

"Lucky? I was under the impression that there was some kind of law about it."

Ivo snorted. "Oh, there is. Fat load of good that does."

"Why is that?"

"Because they're paid for out of the treasury, which is run by Coin. And every year the Coin Prime makes a big fuss about what a terrible state the schools are in, and isn't it a shame, those are our children, our future. Then they say they're raising taxes so they can do something about it. But somehow, *amazingly*, nothing ever changes. They open five new schools in the cities, and close fifteen old ones in the country. So yes, I *was* lucky—I had a school right down the street from my house. Some of my friends had to walk twenty, thirty, forty miles, and people would let them sleep on their hearths, or in the barns. I was lucky." He took a breath then, as if he were going to continue, but then he shook his head.

"Why did you come to Vsila?"

"Same reason everyone does," he said in a flat voice. "I wanted to live. There's no living out there, just surviving. Scraping what you can from the land and giving most of it up anyway. It's better in the city. Sort of." Ylfing was looking back and forth between the two of us, puzzled. "It's better as long as you keep your head down and your mouth shut."

"Well," I said, "you're young and you have a good job—"

He barked a laugh. "I'm a civil servant. A *scribe*."

"It puts you in a good tactical position," I said. "You meet people, don't you? Lots of people. And you learn as much as the law students do. You could be an advocate yourself in a few years, or all manner of other things. And then you could start trying to—"

"If you're going to say 'change things,'" he began sharply, but Ylfing made a startled noise and Ivo paused before he spoke again, and continued more mildly. "If you were planning on saying that, please don't."

"All right," I said. I think I was as startled as Ylfing was. "It just sounded like that was something that mattered to you."

"It does matter to him," Ylfing piped up. "Don't mind Chant, Ivo, he always thinks he knows best and that nobody else gets good ideas before he does."

"Hmph!" I said.

Ylfing smiled brilliantly at me. "Ivo has good ideas too, you know. I said he ought to run for office someday, but *he* told me about—"

"I'm sure Chant doesn't want to hear about all that," Ivo said suddenly. "It's getting late, isn't it? We should go. It's been a long day, and I'm tired."

"Oh," Ylfing said. "I'll tell you about it another time, Chant," he said, while Ivo pulled him to his feet and started piling layers of clothing onto both of them—things from Ivo's own wardrobe, I assumed. They were well-worn; not ragged, but clearly years from new. We said our good-byes and good nights, and Ylfing hesitated just before they turned away.

"Am I really wrong, Chant?" he asked. "About . . . what we were talking about. About people being the same everywhere."

"You really are, my boy," I said. "What's so great about sameness? Difference is what makes the world interesting. If people were really the same everywhere, we wouldn't have a job. We could just stay in one place, knowing people are the same everywhere. We wouldn't have any stories to tell, because people in the stories would all be the same. And," I added, "no one would ever come up with any new ideas—no new ways to farm, or to make war or music or love, no new way to design a ship or a hammer or a boot."

"Is it possible that you're both right?" Ivo asked; he wasn't bothering to hide how impatient he was to leave.

"Maybe," Ylfing said, at the same moment I said, "No."

"Listen," I said. "Saying that everyone universally understands a love story is all well and good, but you can't just leave it at that. It doesn't matter that they all understand it, because the important part, the part that matters, is the details of their experience of it: *how* they understand it, and what it means to them when you tell it to them." Ylfing didn't look convinced. I went on: "Any fool in the world can tell you, 'Yes, that's a love story, everyone knows *that*,' but what *matters* is whether they think that story is a tragedy, or a cautionary tale, or— here. I've told you about Hariq and Amina, haven't I?"

"Yes," said Ylfing, and then, turning to Ivo, "Typical star-crossed lovers, their families forbid them from seeing each other, but they disobey and run off in the night and get married, and they come to a tragic end. It's very sad." Ivo nodded.

"Congratulations on sucking all the feeling and soul out of that story, Ylfing." I looked at the ceiling and prayed to the gods that they would keep me from death while this half-trained idiot was loose in the world. "But all right, we'll take it. You're illustrating my point for me. You tell that story to an idiot from Hrefnesholt and he remarks on how sad it is. You go to Map Sut and they snort and say, 'They got what was coming to them, they shouldn't have betrayed their families like that.' Why is that? Why would they say that? If you ask them whether it's a love story, they'll certainly say yes, and they'll understand why Hariq and Amina came to no good end. But in Hrefnesholt, they sympathize with the lovers, and in Map Sut, they sympathize with the families of the lovers. People are not the same everywhere. They are astoundingly, elaborately, *gloriously* different."

Ylfing nodded begrudgingly and glanced at Ivo out of the corner of his eye. "So . . . Do you want to hear it?" he asked, adorably shy.

Ivo looked down at himself, already gloved and cloaked and scarfed and behatted, and he looked at me, and when Ylfing entirely failed to notice his hesitation, he said, "Yes, all right." I made Ylfing tell it; he needed the practice.

THE EIGHTH TALE:
The Tragedy of Hariq aj-Niher and Amina aj-Mehmeren

A very long time ago and half the world away, there was a city made of golden stone, high on a plateau that overlooked the desert. At the city's feet lay a great lake of sweet fresh water, the Glass Sea, and at its back stood a tall mountain. These people were worshippers of the sun and the moons, and they called them the Bright One, the White One, and the Stately One.

(This was all fine, but his delivery was a little flat and over-rehearsed.)

There were three temples in the city, each of which received the patronage of a great noble family. Twice a year, at midsummer and midwinter, the three families would send a child of their house to sit in vigil by the treasure of each temple: the eternal fire of the Bright One, the great silver disk of the White One, and the black celestial stone of the Stately One.

(He hesitated a little over the last two, likely trying to remember which went with which, but I don't think Ivo noticed.)

The doors of the three temples faced one another across a triangular courtyard, and a child of each patron house would sit on the steps twice a year, often all by themselves, and they would guard the temples vigilantly from dusk until dawn. The three houses were all competing with one another, and so the temples were too.

One of the daughters of House Mehmeren was named Amina, and she was sent to sit vigil at the temple one midwinter night. There was a great feast beforehand, and celebrations all through the city, and Amina was washed and combed and groomed to within an inch of her life, and put in the grand regalia of her house and temple: the white-

and-silver cloak of the White One, soft white leather shoes
and gloves, and a diadem of silver and diamonds, laced
through with fresh jasmine so that wherever she walked,
sweet scents followed her.

(Ylfing loves unnecessary detail. Can't resist it. The only thing that mat-
ters is the cloak. He added in the rest.)

She was put on a snow-white horse, and in a great
parade of all her family and her family's friends and the
common folk who lived within their district, she was taken
to the temple and put on the steps. There were musicians
playing all around her, and girls casting rose petals and
jasmine in the air until the pavement was thick with them.
(See what I mean?)

As she mounted the temple steps and looked across the
court, she saw the heirs of the other houses taking their
places as well—the Bright One's heir in gold and the Stately
One's heir in black and gray. At any other time of the year,
great crowds from each house gathering like that would
have turned into a rioting mob, but just twice a year, the
families managed to studiously ignore one another for the
sake of their worship.

As the sun sank, the crowds dispersed, and Amina
made herself comfortable on the steps. She wandered in
and out of the temple to keep herself warm, to do her duty
by checking on the silver disk of the White One, a thirty-
foot-wide circle of hammered silver, suspended from the
ceiling of the temple by two thick chains. The night grew
colder, and she bundled her cloak around her and drank

the coffee that her family had smuggled behind the temple door, so that she'd be able to stay awake the whole night. She did so surreptitiously, just as her older cousins had firmly instructed—it would not have done for the other heirs to see that she needed *help* to keep her vigil.

(He has a tendency to linger rather, drawing a story out—which is no bad thing, I suppose. Refinement will come with time, and Ivo was clearly sufficiently taken with Ylfing that he was willing to listen no matter how unpolished and undisciplined Ylfing was. So it didn't matter.)

Around midnight, the White One was at her zenith and the Stately One had just risen above the rooftops in the east. Amina was struck with an odd whimsy, and she descended the marble steps of her temple and crossed the court to the fountain in the middle. She thought about approaching one of the other temples but hesitated. If she went to the Bright One first, then the Stately One would surely take offense and there would be trouble between their families tomorrow. And if she went to the Stately One first, then the Bright One would do just the same thing.

(Now, if I had been telling this, I would have left all that out. One doesn't need to explain it. Feuding families are not so uncommon that one has to spell it out for one's audience.)

Instead she sat on the edge of the fountain, facing the other two temples, and waved at them. They were both watching her—the Stately One's heir had been pacing back and forth across the black granite steps, and the Bright

One's heir had been huddled up close to the braziers that burned on either side of the tall golden doors.

The Stately One's heir started forward first. When the Bright One's heir saw this, he was quick to follow after. They both arrived by the fountain at the same moment, eying each other and Amina with suspicion.

"Happy Midwinter," Amina said to them politely.

"Happy Midwinter," they echoed. The Stately One's heir, dressed rather severely in a high-collared black robe edged in fur and a solid band of iron for a crown, crossed his arms and glanced again at the Bright One's heir. The Bright One was the source of fire and warmth and life, and so it seemed that his heir was, apparently, supposed to have no need of clothing appropriate to the season. The Bright One's heir wore the same costume for Midsummer or Midwinter—a knee-length, sleeveless toga made of cloth of gold, sandals, and a golden crown hung with tinkling bells.

The Bright One's heir hugged himself and rubbed his arms briskly.

"What are your names?" Amina asked.

"Hariq aj-Niher," said the heir of the Stately One.

"Piras aj-Behet," said the heir of the Bright One, his teeth beginning to chatter.

"Don't they give you warm clothes?" Amina asked.

"The Bright One's warmth touches us all," Piras replied. His lips were beginning to turn blue.

"Would you like to borrow my cloak for a minute? I'm warm enough—I'm wearing two pairs of trousers under this big skirt." She lifted up her hem a little to show them. "And three pairs of socks."

"I'm fine," said Piras.

"Perhaps you might invite us over to the temple of the Bright One so we might all be touched by its warmth," Hariq said. "I didn't have quite the foresight to wear multiple pairs of trousers, or more than one pair of socks."

"I don't know you," Piras snapped. "And I'm supposed to be guarding the eternal flame. If it goes out—if *you* put it out—then I'll be in trouble."

"But surely the Bright One would see that I was the one to do it and he'd curse me, wouldn't he? Or give a sign so everyone would know that I was at fault and you were innocent? And anyway, why would I want to put out the only fire on a cold night in the first place?"

"If Piras takes my cloak and we all sit by the fire, we'll all be the same amount of warm," Amina added. "That's fair, isn't it?"

"It is Midwinter, after all," Hariq added. "We're all at peace today."

"Fine," Piras said. "Give me your cloak, you. You didn't say your name, either."

"Amina aj-Mehmeren," she said, undoing the round silver clasp and swinging the cloak off her shoulders and around Piras's.

He pulled it around him immediately. "Oh Bright One, it's warm."

"Um," said Amina, "If we're sharing the fire . . . I have some coffee."

"Coffee!" Hariq said, lighting up. "Go fetch it! I have some cakes."

"I don't have anything," Piras grumbled, turning around

and walking back to the Bright One's temple.

Amina and Hariq scuttled off and a few minutes later, they were all huddled around one of the braziers on the front porch of the Bright One's temple, passing around Amina's carafe of coffee and Hariq's sticky honey-cakes, all folded up in a bundled napkin.

"Why'd you wave us down?" Hariq asked, once they were sufficiently fed and coffee'd.

"I was bored. There are still hours left of the night to go."

Hariq nodded. "Midsummer is easier. It's a comfortable temperature, and the night is shorter then, of course. I just brought a book along last time."

(*That's the other thing Ylfing does—he thinks about people a lot, and he's always trying to sneak extra crumbs here and there into characters to make them more relatably human. It simply doesn't occur to him to wonder whether his audience cares about how Hariq entertains himself on vigils, because of course Ylfing cares. Remind me to tell you about the time he made up a story about Nerelen, the Bramandese god of wine and a famous cad, falling in love with—you guessed it—a beautiful shepherd boy. I swear it, I was too confounded to know whether I should be outraged or proud.*)

"I wouldn't know," said Amina. "This is the first time I've stood vigil."

"I've been volunteering to do Midsummer the last few years—thought it was time I should try out Midwinter. Is it your first time too, Piras? I've never spoken to the Bright One's heir before, and usually it's too dark and too far across the court to see who is sitting vigil."

"I did Midsummer once, a few years ago. Certainly wouldn't have volunteered to do Midwinter."

"Why'd you get sent? In my family, it's always a volunteer."

"Got in trouble," Piras muttered. "Dad thought I should do penance or something. To build discipline."

"Well, it certainly takes discipline to sit vigil, particularly on a midwinter's night for the Bright One, it seems," Hariq said agreeably. "And Amina? Did you volunteer, or is this punishment?"

"Neither. My family always sends someone different to the White One every Midwinter, someone who's never done it before—we try to, anyway. For Midsummer, we don't mind repeats. I heard that the Midwinter before I was born, all my cousins were sick except one, and he was only two years old. He stood vigil officially, but of course my aunt, his mother, had to stay with him."

"How can you stand doing it?" Piras asked. "Over and over again? It's so dull."

(Much like Ylfing's interminable dialogue! Of course I wasn't going to interrupt and shame him in front of Ivo, but I was grinding my teeth by this point and wishing he'd get on with it.)

"I don't mind it," Hariq answered. "I can't get to sleep at night anyway, most nights, and I like being by myself and thinking. And the city looks so much different in the dark. And I like feeling close to the Stately One."

They sat there talking all night long, and Amina found herself quite struck by how cordial and mannerly Hariq was, and how intelligently he spoke, and the line of his jaw, and the color of his eyes. . . .

Well before dawn, Piras gave Amina back her cloak, and she and Hariq gathered up their things and scampered back across the court to their respective temples, settling themselves in wait to be collected by their families. There would be more festivities in the morning, but Amina's eyes were growing heavy and tired, and she fancied the idea of going to bed. Before she sat down, she looked into the temple at the White One's disc. As expected, it hadn't moved anywhere.

Months passed, and Midsummer came about, and Amina was again dressed in the richly embroidered robes of white and silver, but this time they felt heavy and burdensome. She was uncomfortably warm, but she remembered that Hariq had said he liked to volunteer to sit vigil for Midsummer. She rather looked forward to seeing him again. It would have been utterly forbidden to exchange even a glance with him at any other time—it would have sent both their families into an uproar.

So there was another feast and another parade to take her out to the temple, and pretty much as soon as the sun had set and the last of the revelers had left the court, she and Hariq were both running down the steps to the fountain, chattering almost as soon as they'd gotten within earshot of each other.

(Here Ivo said, "Aww," and couldn't hold back a smile. He'd already for-gotten we'd told him it was a tragedy, already forgotten Ylfing had spoiled the end and how badly he'd wanted to leave a few moments ago. I could see *a bit then why Ylfing liked him—for all my apprentice is a genuine idiot, I'll allow he can spot a soft heart from a mile off. Or perhaps it's just that hearts soften after he spots them.)*

And then they went up to the temple of the Bright One, but Piras wasn't there. It was some older member of the house, and he just sat there and glared at the two of them. So they sat on the base of the fountain for a while and talked, and they walked back and forth across the square so they could be sure to keep an eye on the relics. Amina had seen the heaven stone from a distance before, because even if the Stately One was Hariq's house's temple, the Stately One was everyone's god, just as the Bright One and the White One were. Hariq brought her inside the temple and showed her around—the heaven stone was the color of blackened iron, and it was the size of a wheelbarrow, all lumpy and odd-looking.

They talked all night, and it being just the two of them, with a fountain and the stars and the moonlight—things got a little *romantic*. By the end of the night, they had agreed that they had to find a way to keep talking, no matter what. Hariq showed Amina a loose stone on the side of the Stately One's temple, and they devised a plan to leave notes hidden there for each other. At Midsummer's dawn, Amina kissed him and ran across the square to the White One's temple, just before the processions arrived.

Need I describe the months of delicious subterfuge?

(I thought to myself, "Oh gods, please don't." But he didn't.)

The cunning excuses they found to pass by the loose stone in the temple wall? The close calls that each of them risked, Amina trembling like a leaf when she was almost caught with a letter, or Hariq with his heart in his throat?

By the next Midwinter, they were in love and out of hope. Hariq was to be wed. He had persuaded his family to let him sit vigil once more, and he begged Amina to find a way to do the same. She made honey-cakes, sweet and sticky, and she mixed in a measure of a certain herb she knew that would make a person very ill. Not dangerously ill, but ill enough they wouldn't want to move too far from the chamber pot. She made platters and platters of the sweets, and when her whole family gathered together to dress her cousin up in the robes and send him off to the temple, she made sure that her cousin ate several of the cakes, and that all her other cousins who hadn't sat vigil ate them too. By the end of the party, more than half the family was lying about in agony, and the other half was panicking for the doctors.

(He got dangerously close to calling attention to a key flaw in the story, which is: How did she make sure all the cousins ate the tainted sweets, and how did she escape suspicion? But we must not inquire too closely into the internal logic of stories like this. It needs to happen so that Amina can sit vigil again, and so it does.)

Amina helped her cousin take the heavy robes off, since he was already sweating buckets and clutching his stomach. "What shall we do?" her aunt cried. "Have we angered the White One?"

"You must stay here and take care of everyone. I'm

feeling fine, so I'll go to the temple. I'll pray all night!"
Amina said. Her aunt nodded. Amina was the only
unmarried one who wasn't ill; she was the obvious choice.

Amina didn't even look across the square to see who was
sitting vigil at the Bright One's temple when she arrived.
She flew up the steps of the Stately One's temple and into
Hariq's arms by the heaven stone. They wept together for
a time, and Amina declared she couldn't live to see Hariq
marry anyone else.

———◆———

And here Ylfing broke off and frowned.

We all stared at him for a time, waiting. "Go on," says I at
last. I'd bitten my tongue so much during that story that I'd
almost gnawed it right off. "Finish it. You're doing fine."

"Um," says he. "I've forgotten the last bit."

"Forgotten the last bit!" says I. "Forgotten! How could a person
forget?" How *could* a person forget? I ask you now. But, "Forgotten!"
I says.

"Not the whole of it," he protested. He could see I was spluttering. "I know they die in the end, and—"

"Oh, well done," says I. "Now you've gone and ruined it for Ivo
twice over."

But Ylfing had gone and forgotten the bit that linked their
declarations and their death. I couldn't roll my eyes hard enough.
What a time to sputter out! Right at the climactic moment. So I had
to take over, but it wasn't the *same*. You can't start a story from the
end; it just don't work. Didn't have any time to get rolling, you know,
to work myself into it. They're like hot baths, stories. Gotta ease into
'em slow. I made a muss of it, I'm not too proud to admit, but it's

Ylfing's fault anyway. It was a mere summary at best, like this:

They run away. Piras, once again on vigil at the Bright One's temple, sees them and raises the alarm (that was the bit Ylfing forgot). Their families come after them. Amina's family thinks Hariq seduced or bewitched her. Hariq's family thinks *Amina* seduced or bewitched *him*. They flee on horseback from the two mobs, and, cornered where the plateau drops steeply down into desert, and overcome with despair and desperation, they fling themselves off the cliff to their deaths. When their families climb down, they find the bodies too broken and bloodied to identify, but still clutching each other. The end.

You see? How can you forget all that?

"I'm sorry for making a mess of the ending," Ylfing said to Ivo.

"It's all right," Ivo replied immediately. Ylfing had been making puppy eyes at him again, and I defy any boy to hold out in the face of that. Ylfing will be an excellent Chant one day if he can learn how to make that face on purpose. "But we'd really better go."

"Oh, right!" Ylfing fussed with his scarf and cloak and pushed the basket of leftover food closer to my cell. "Ivo's taking me to meet his friends, since I missed it before." He reached through the bars and patted my knee with his hand, thickly mittened. "Don't mope about today, all right? Consanza will think of something."

Ylfing came again early the next morning, with another paper parcel of monk's-puffs. He poked them at me through the bars and spread his cloak—or Ivo's cloak, it probably was—on the ground. Had a bag with him too, with a wad of paper and a thin sheet of slate that he balanced across his knees.

"How was your night out?" I asked, once he'd gotten settled in. I spoke in Hrefni; it was cozier than Nuryeven.

"What?"

"Meeting Ivo's friends."

"Oh. Yes. It was fine, I think." He seemed distracted.

I frowned. "You *think* it was fine?"

"Mhm." He didn't meet my eyes. "Do you want to get started on today's work? You can tell me about . . . something."

He'll be an excellent Chant one day if he can learn how to lie. "Actually, why don't you tell me about something."

"Hmm?" He fidgeted with his cloak a little, fussed with the brazier. "I don't have anything." He brightened. "This morning I heard some sailors from Tash singing a sea shanty I'd never heard before—"

"Why don't you tell me about how the rest of your night went?"

He twitched. "Oh, you don't want to hear about all that."

I made a mental note to teach him better evasion and redirection techniques. There are times Chants have to keep things to themselves. "Actually, young apprentice, with every moment my interest grows."

"It was boring."

"You said it was fine. And I've never once seen you bored with a new acquaintance."

"I—I meant the people were fine, but the things we did were boring, that's all."

I pinned him to his chair with my eyes. "So you did some things."

"No," he said quickly. "That's why it was boring. The lack of things! Really dull."

"So you and Ivo's friends sat in stillness and silence."

"Yes," he said.

"Lying." And if I hadn't been sure of it before, the blush that lit his cheeks would have done it. I leaned forward, narrowing my eyes, peering hard at him. "You've got shadows under your eyes, so you were up late, but you don't have any new hickeys, so I seriously doubt that you were alone with Ivo very much. What were you up to, staying up so late if the company was so boring?"

"Just—just talking."

"About what?"

"Nothing!"

"Sure doesn't seem like nothing."

"Chant," he said weakly. "Please don't ask me. I can't tell you."

"You *can't* tell me? Well! That certainly puts me right at ease!" I'd been curious before, but ... something about his face ...

"I'm fine, I promise. It was just talk. You don't have to worry."

"Talk that you can't talk about."

He bit his lip. "I said I wouldn't."

I squinted at him again. "Did they make you promise not to tell anyone about this so-called *talk*?"

He said a phrase in Hrefni, *hwæn weo*, which I can only translate as, "Well, you know," but it has more layers to it than that.

"Ylfing," I said. "My lad. I want to make something clear—if you truly, truly cannot speak about the conversation you had with Ivo's friends last night, if you are confident in the necessity of your vow of silence, then tell me now and we'll forget all this." I paused for a heartbeat or two, just long enough for him to squirm. "But if, as I suspect, you're *not* certain, if you have an instinct about it, then trust your gut. You're my apprentice; you're allowed to ask for guidance if you need it, and I can keep a secret as well as anybody. You know that."

He looked wretched. "I want to tell you."

"Then do so. I'm your master-Chant. My *job* is to guide you."

"But they said I shouldn't tell you. Specifically."

"Why?"

He swallowed hard. "Ivo said—and his friends said—that the Queens might try to drag information out of you, if they thought you knew something." His voice lowered to a whisper, though I doubt there was another Hrefni speaker within a thousand miles. "He said they might hurt you for it."

"Torture? They haven't tried it yet."

Ylfing tilted his head back and forth, which is the gestural equivalent of *hwæn weo*.

"Don't you think I could come up with a more enticing story to tell them, if they did try that? Stories always make more sense than reality."

"Ivo cares so much," Ylfing said, quiet and sudden. "About so many things. The minute I saw him, I knew he was a person who really, really *cared* about something. I could see it in his eyes." He looked into the fire. "I'm . . . confused."

"About Ivo?"

"No. No, gods, no. I'm more confused about . . . myself, I guess." He took a deep breath. "Have you ever—do you notice—" Another breath. "What do you do when someone tells you something, and another person tells you something else, and they both sound like they're certain of the truth, but it'd be impossible for both things to be true at the same time?"

I couldn't help but beam at him. "My boy!" I cried, so full of pride I could have wriggled with it. "You're asking very Chantly questions these days." But I saw how helpless and lost he looked, and I got myself under control. Goodness, though. I'm pleased to bits even remembering it. Think how proud you were every time one of your oath-nieces came home from her first successful hunt, with a fat bustard or an egret hanging from her pommel. That's how proud a master-Chant is when their apprentice starts asking such questions. "You've stumbled upon something very fiddly and *very* important, lad. You want to know what to do? When you start noticing discrepancies, then you close your mouth, and you watch. Carefully. You sharpen your eyes and you examine every word they say to you."

"But ... Ivo wouldn't lie to me. Would he?" He was nearly wringing his hands, and his brow was knotted up all fretful.

"Not on purpose, lad," I said, as soothingly as I could. "Ivo is telling you *a* truth. He can't tell you *the* truth, because he doesn't know what it is, and that's not his fault. You look at Ivo's truth, and then you look at the truth you're hearing from other people, and you pick it apart, and at the end, perhaps you find a truth somewhere in the middle."

"And that's the real one?"

I sighed. He's still got a ways to go yet, even if he is starting to trip into Chantly questions by himself. "No, that's just Ylfing's truth, separate from Ivo's."

"Oh."

"It's messy, lad, it's all messy." I waved my hand airily. "You just question everything that anyone tells you and assume they don't really know what they're talking about, even when they sound like they do, and you remember that everybody has a reason for telling you something in the way that they do and that most reasons are selfish. It will be second nature to you by the time you're a master-Chant, not to worry. But what's the thing Ivo is telling you that's different from what you've heard elsewhere?"

His voice was faint and a little dazed: "He says Nuryevet is a bad place."

That didn't bring me up short like it should have, didn't give me pause at all. "That's because it *is* a bad place," I said.

"Consanza doesn't think so."

I bit my tongue hard on my response to *that*, let me tell you. "Never mind her," I said. "Focus on Ivo." Looking back on it, I can't believe I actually had to encourage him to tell me about Ivo. May wonders never cease.

Ylfing took another, final deep breath. "Ivo and his friends meet every so often to talk about how bad it is here. He told you what it was like growing up here."

I nodded. "The schools, yes."

"He says that it hurts people, living like this. He says people starve, or die, and that no one's allowed to say anything about it. He says people get angry about the taxes, and they try to argue about it, and they get arrested. That happened to some of their friends, so now they meet in different places, secretly, and—"

I sat up very suddenly. "They're revolutionaries!" Hrefni doesn't have a word for that, so I had to cobble one together, but Ylfing seemed to get my point, because he looked hunted.

"No," he said firmly. "Not like that. They just talk. Like I said before, just talk."

"Except for the ones who got arrested. Go on, then, what do they talk about?"

"How to make things better, that's all." He squirmed. "I did promise not to say anything. I shouldn't have mentioned it."

I eyed my apprentice and wondered which of the two of them, him or Ivo, had the other wrapped around his little finger. Ylfing was terribly, terribly taken with Ivo, obviously, but Ivo . . . Well. There was potential there. Not that I could trust Ylfing to manage things delicately. "I'd like to talk to Ivo sometime," I said. "If he wants to."

Ylfing squirmed again. "I'd have to tell him that I told you. . . ."

"Were you planning on keeping that a secret?"

"Yes! I was!"

"All right. Well, if you happen to change your mind, then." Or, more likely, if he ended up being unable to manage the ticklish matter of finagling Ivo for information. He's so bad at lying. "You might as well find out as much as you can from that boy, either way. You can tell me all about it if we manage to get away from this horrible place. Now. To work?"

We had a bit of a squabble, again, about whether he was going to write down everything I had to tell him or not, and it ended up that he won simply by moving out of my reach and refusing to put aside the lap desk and his supplies. I was too distracted to argue with him anyway. The cold had set in during the night, and even though Ylfing heaped twigs on the brazier, I couldn't shake the chill out of my joints. Terrible thing, getting old. Bits of you that used to work start breaking. You start noticing parts of your body you never had reason to notice before.

"We only have a month," Ylfing said. "We can't go all wild and frantic like yesterday. It's a waste of time. So we'll make a list of all the important things you have to tell me, and then you can tell me about each one and I'll write it down."

"However you want," I said. The monk's-puffs Ylfing had brought lay in my hands. They'd gone cold during my interrogation about Ivo, and now they were nowhere near as appealing. The twist of brown paper they were wrapped in crinkled a little, and I set it aside.

"Well, there's definitely no time for languages, and I can learn those myself wherever I go. So we'd better start with things I can't learn myself, or things that are hard to learn, things that take a lot of time."

"If that's how you want to do it."

"So we'll go alphabetically. By . . . by the name of the place, I guess."

"The Ammat Archipelago."

Ylfing nodded and bent over his lap desk. The pen nib scratched. He was a very painstaking scribe. "The . . . Ammat . . . Archipelago," he mumbled. "Okay. Go."

"You're going to be giving away everything you own while you're

there, so don't get attached to objects, and leave anything you particularly care about on your ship, or in a safe place with a friend
somewhere else. When you meet someone, they're going to give you
a gift, and you *have* to take it, and you *have* to have something to give
back to them—"

"Wait, wait, hold on!" my stupid apprentice cried. "Everything . . .
you . . . own . . . Give me just a minute to catch up."

"Ylfing," I said, "we don't have time now to write it down." It was
a great struggle not to shout at him, but we didn't have time for that,
either. Gods, though, the more I thought about Ivo's little band of
revolutionaries, the more frustrated I got that I couldn't go out and
handle them myself. "Why don't you listen closely and then write it
down later?"

"But I might forget—"

"Ylfing. We don't have *time*. You know it. I know it." My chest
was getting all tight again, probably just another heart attack or
something, nothing to worry about. "I'll tell you a secret that only
master-Chants know: all Chants forget things. You can't transpose
one person's knowledge into another person without parts of it getting muddled or lost. It's all right to forget some of it. You just need to
learn to recognize what's important and remember that. Or remember how to remember. It's not a science, my boy, it's an art. And art is
messy. And that's okay."

He took a breath, and then I noticed that he was trembling. At
first I thought it was from the cold. I've never claimed that I wasn't
a fool. "Ivo says . . . Ivo says he's going to help Consanza with your
appeal."

"Don't cry," I said immediately. I don't know what I would have
done if he cried. I've never been very good at it when strangers do
it, let alone people I know, even if it is just my lovesick fool of an

apprentice. I'm not *afraid* of it, mind you. It's just very awkward for everyone. It wasn't like I could do anything but reach through the bars and sort of pat him on the shoulder anyway.

"I'm not crying," he said, but his voice was all thick. Made my heart stop in my chest, I tell you.

So: "Don't do it," says I.

"I'm *not*," he said, and he seemed to have gotten it under control a little more that time.

"The Ammat Archipelago," I said quickly. "Tens of thousands of islands, hundreds of thousands of tribes. Live in little huts by the water. I've told you pieces about them before, I think." Drilling facts, yes, that's what he needed. "See what you can remember—magic?"

"Shamans," Ylfing said. He swiped his sleeve over his face and sat up straighter.

"Go on."

"They—they have a bond with a spirit, and they can't cross water."

"Can't they?"

"Uh . . ." He sniffed loudly. "Well, *they* can, the shamans can, if they really had to, but it'd break the spirit bond and they'd have to start over. They'd lose all their ability and start from the very beginning, because it's the spirit that does the actual work for them."

"And is it learnable, or blood-bound?"

"The magic? I . . . I don't know."

"No one does. Not everyone can be a shaman. It's rare. And not enough foreigners stick around with them long enough to find out."

Ylfing nodded and glanced at his paper.

I shook my head. "Ask questions. They'll help you remember."

"Yes. Uh. Who—who becomes a shaman? Is there a pattern?"

"They say it has to do with souls. For example, an old soul in a new body, or someone whose soul doesn't fit right in their body, or a body with more than one soul in it, or half a soul. Or they have a full soul, but it's a particularly bright one. But who knows what any of that means? This is what I was told."

We continued in that vein for several hours. Ylfing got some practice at asking the right questions, I got a good lecture into him about things he ought to know. Not too many real facts, after we'd finished discussing the Ammatan. It wasn't just about collecting bits of information about people—it was about telling it. Matching the person to the right story—you remember what I said before? The right story fits like a familiar shoe.

Towards noon, Ylfing went out to get us a bit of lunch and himself some fresh air. Thank goodness—I don't know how long it would have taken us to hear the news otherwise. He came back in all aflutter with it. Anfisa Zofiyat, Queen of Pattern, had been arrested by a team of Order guards on suspicion of harboring a fugitive, accessory to witchcraft, and, confusingly, treasonous espionage.

Ylfing scribbled off a message to Consanza and loped out again to find someone to run it across town to her office, against my advice. Didn't see why he thought it was necessary to tell her about this or ask to talk to her—I suppose it was a significant event, but *I* was already sentenced. This would only distract her from working on my appeal.

It took another precious hour of the day to settle Ylfing down enough for us to return to work. Boys his age are jittery, flighty, *not* prone to great sweeps of concentration, unless it's on the contents of their trousers.

I allowed him to write for this one—told him a great list of all the places he could go that knew about the Chants, places where we were welcomed, places where he should exercise great caution. I finished that list with, "Of course, remember never to get arrested for witchcraft in Nuryevet. You'll regret it to the end of your days." It was supposed to get a bit of a giggle out of him, but it just made his nose go red and his eyes well up again while I flapped my hands and squawked at him to get himself under control. Chants can't go around flinging their emotions about willy-nilly.

He sobered soon after that, and asked how he should . . . Gods great and small, he asked how he should sink his homeland beneath the waves, if the month should pass without much luck.

"Can't," said I. "You'd do that at the end of your apprenticeship."

"I know, but you said I'd never find another Chant again, probably."

Crossed my arms at him. "No, you probably never will."

"Even if I went to Kaskinen?"

"Even then! What do you think we have, universities? Perhaps a secret conclave, a coffeehouse where we all meet up? The Chants haven't been *from* Kaskinen for thousands of years. They belong to everywhere now. And everyone."

He fidgeted and shrugged a bit. "Surely there's people somewhere who know where the other Chants are, then."

"Only in the vaguest of terms. 'Oh yes, one of them went east from Mangar-Khagra a month ago.' Good luck with that. Have you gotten a sense of how big the world is, child? And how small we are? You'd be lucky to run across a second Chant, and luckier still if he or she didn't have an apprentice along already."

"Just give me directions! I'll follow them to the letter. I'll learn everything I can—please."

"Directions?" I snapped. "Directions for the next seven years of your life? And leave you to wander this world on your own with perhaps a tenth of the knowledge you need to be a proper Chant? We haven't even touched on any of the rites—"

"I've never seen you do rites. What are they?"

"All right, they're not rites so much as . . . tenets. Laws. Reasons for . . . for why."

"I don't need a why."

"Stupid child, of course you need a why. You need a why for yourself, but you probably already have that one. Wouldn't have left Hrefnesholt if you didn't have your personal why. There's other whys. A personal why can change. The others don't."

"You mean for why Chants exist? I know that. You tell me that all the time."

I flapped my hand to wave off his words. "I could tell you there's a clearing in the woods, and a lake in the middle of the clearing, and an island in the lake, and a tree on the island—and you could see it in your mind's eye, but I haven't told you why the tree is important, or the taste of the fruit that grows on it, or the kind of beetle that dimples the surface of the water at the edge of the shore, or the smell of the breeze at the very cusp of spring. I might have told you a very shallow why before, but it's not the really important part."

"What is, then?"

"I can't tell you—it's not something that can be *told* in words, boy, otherwise any fool could be a Chant. It's . . . a story, and the only way to truly know a story is to *hear* the story, and this is a very, very long one. It's something that has to be learned. Uncovered slowly. Savored. Like someone beautiful lying beneath a sheet and smiling at you."

"But I *want* to be a Chant. I don't want to go home. I don't want home, I don't need it."

I think I must have been getting pneumonia or something from being in that dank cell so long. There was an uncomfortable lump in my throat. I poured myself a cup of water and swallowed it down. "I'll teach you all I can in the time that we have. And . . . and the appeal might go well."

"What if . . . Well, what if it doesn't?" he said, with a wretched look. "What if I just kept . . . going? Without you?"

I shrugged. "That's on you, boy. People do."

"But I wouldn't be a Chant."

"I suppose you could call yourself a Chant if you couldn't bear to do otherwise."

"But I wouldn't *be* a Chant. I wouldn't be the best Chant."

"No such thing as the best Chant, boy." He wrapped his arms around himself. I heard footsteps down the hall. "That might be the guard. Don't make a fuss if they've come to throw you out for the day." It wasn't, thank goodness—Ylfing wasn't in a state to go wandering the streets by himself. He could have gotten mugged or something. (Like when those damn urchins took my turn-toe boots off me in Map Sut, may they have all died early and gruesome deaths.)

"So," I said to him. "You need to explore the *whys*. Why can we ply our trade wherever we can speak the language? Why do people feed *us* when there's a famine, even when the other beggars on the street starve?" Ylfing opened his mouth, but I held up a hand. "It's a question for you to think about. Not for today, not for the next week. This is a question Chants ask themselves their whole lives: Why can we do what we do?" He nodded. I gestured for his paper and ink. "Hand those to me and I'll show you something." I drew a large square with a gap in one side, and I picked up a few bits of debris from the ground—a chip of stone, a short piece of twig, a leaf that someone had tracked in, that kind of thing. I placed them on the piece of paper and said to Ylfing, "Watch."

I didn't really pay attention to what I was doing, I just sort of poked the things around randomly, made them crash into one another, made them go through the gap and around the square I'd drawn. . . . Carried this on for thirty or forty seconds while Ylfing watched intently. Then I used one of the twigs to flick the leaf off the paper onto the floor. "There. What did you see?"

He took a breath. "The big man who owns the house, he was bullying his children, and then one girl went outside to see if anyone was coming, and she and the boy looked around for something, and then they went back inside and saw the man intimidating the other girl, and then they all killed him and got rid of the body."

I nodded thoughtfully. "That wasn't what you saw."

"Yes, it was!"

"No, you saw me playing with a piece of paper and some bits of trash. You saw me moving them around as the whimsy took me. You didn't see a big man, or a house, or three children. You saw paper, and a leaf, twigs, a pebble. So where'd these characters come from? Where'd the story come from?"

"Don't pretend I'm stupid, Chant, you made it up. It's like puppets, isn't it?"

"I didn't make up shit, lad. Didn't even make up this game. Chants made it up generations and generations ago, showing their stupid apprentices what people are like. What did you see?"

"Twigs and a pebble and a leaf and a square drawn on a piece of paper," he said sullenly, still not convinced.

"And your little human brain grabbed onto them and tried to make sense of them. Entirely random events, and you forced a story onto them."

"It just happened, I couldn't help it—"

"Quiet, boy, it's not a bad thing. Would you listen to me? I'm trying to make a point."

"Fine. Fine, what's the point?"

"The point is that I want you to take this paper and—are you seeing Ivo tonight?" His blush was answer enough. "Show this to Ivo.

You can use coins or a saltpot instead, or bits of bread and cheese. Whatever you like. Clear your mind, and just toy with the damn things. Just move them around, and then ask him what he saw."

"Fine."

"You can try it on Consanza, too, if you like, but I daresay she'll just say she saw bread and crumbs and paper." I snorted. "Useless woman. No respect for illusions."

Ylfing shook off the twigs and pebbles and rolled up the paper. "Is this something to think about for years too?"

"Obviously. You can show it to anyone—drunks in a tavern, farmer's daughters, nobles and peasants and merchants, women soldiers you meet on the road, smelly shepherd boys. . . . Just don't bother explaining to them what it means. Don't point out to them that they didn't see whatever it is they see. Most people don't take well to being told the story in their head is wrong. And you can learn something about people from what they see in random movements like this. It's like reading tea leaves or looking for constellations."

"Can I explain it to Ivo if he asks?"

I shrugged. "You can tell anyone you like, it's just not always a good idea. Especially kings and folk like that, people who can have you killed or . . . you know, thrown in jail for witchcraft. Just say it's a story someone once showed you and you thought it was an interesting little piece of whimsy. And *listen* to what they tell you about it." I took a breath. "It's not going to be easy, if you choose to go it alone. You're young, you haven't learned the things that make people *people*."

"I know some things," he grumbled.

Well, he was Hrefni, after all. They have this way about them, always assessing their own skill levels and those of the people around them. Very realistic about it too; only children bother with vanity in Hrefnesholt. So I shifted my viewpoint and spoke to Ylfing as one

Hrefni would to another: "You're not the best and you're not the worst," I said, and he relaxed. Amazing what speaking the same language will do for two people trying to have a conversation.

"Yes, that's true. Do you think I could do it? By myself?"

"I don't know. If I knew, you wouldn't be my apprentice anymore—I'd have let you go if I knew you couldn't do it at all. I'd have had you sink your homeland beneath the waves and sent you off as a journeyman if I knew you could. I don't know either way. That's why you're still here." He nodded and dropped his head. I pulled my horse blanket around my shoulders. "Would you like to keep working, or do you think that's enough twisting of your brain for the day?"

"Both," he whispered.

"Go take a walk. Buy some more monk's-puffs. Splash some cold water on your face; it'll do you good."

———◆———

Well, that was the night that everything changed. I even heard some of it, distantly: a great commotion off somewhere else in the prison, shouting and doors slamming and running feet. It sounded noisier than it usually did when new prisoners came in—some of them screamed, but it was mostly quiet except for the creak of cell doors echoing down the long, bare stone chambers, the clash as they slammed closed. People calling out, weeping sometimes.

But this much disquiet and fuss in the night? I'd been there long enough to know that wasn't usual. It was days and days before I knew what was going on, but for your sake I'll describe it as it happened.

As I said: a great commotion in the night, and then Ylfing wasn't allowed in to see me—not that I knew about that, either. He just . . . didn't turn up. And didn't turn up. And didn't turn up. I thought for a few days that he'd been sidetracked or that he'd fallen on misfortune and then that he'd decided he didn't want to be a Chant after all. I had some wishful fantasy that he'd set up with that Ivo; at least then he'd have an ally at his back. In barbarian countries like these, you need all the allies you can get your hands on—no pun intended.

But Consanza didn't show up either, and that was odd too.

So all I heard was what I could glean from Vasili, my little friend amongst the guards, who brought me my two meals per day, my allotted basket of pathetic sticks and twisted-straw logs for my fire, and a relatively fresh bucket. Vasili was tense. More than usual, I mean, all the guards were—more sullen and stoic than usual too. I kept asking and asking for someone to send word to my advocate, or to my apprentice, and it was only when I began asking to speak to Vihra Kylliat or to send a letter to Taishineya Tarmos that I started getting any idea that something bigger might be afoot. It was the look in their eyes, a sudden startled twitch when I spoke the names of the Primes. It was the sudden disinterest Vasili had in hearing anything I had to say. It was the distracted air, the efficient way they shoved food at me and left instead of lingering for a verbal jab or a cold, wary glance. I wasn't worth their breath anymore. I was slated for execution still—both dead and alive, in some sense, stuck in this little iron box underground.

I started hearing people screaming down the hall. I saw people being dragged past, too, and the whole cell block got a little more lively. I began hearing whispers between the cells—unfair arrests of common citizens, of civil servants, of suspicious-looking foreigners. . . . This is always the way when a country begins to gnaw at its own flesh. It is a sign of sickness, a sign that things may be about to get much worse than they are.

Someone, down the corridor, screamed that they were innocent, that they had nothing to do with it, that it was all *her*, that they'd testify however they were told to testify. Two guards walked by a few minutes later, having silenced the screaming one way or another.

And then, at last, I got a little solid information. One of the guards muttered to the other as they passed, and the part that I caught was, "A Prime hasn't been arrested in fifty years, y'know."

"Arrested? A Prime?" I said, springing to the bars of my cell. "Who? Why?"

And then, for some reason, they told me.

"Anfisa Zofiyat," said one of the guards. I don't know their names, so we'll call them Ana and Mila to save on confusion. "Treason, harboring a fugitive, and witchcraft."

We all know how a Nuryeven witchcraft trial goes. I was . . . unsettled, to say the least. "Aha," I said.

"Order's arrested several of her blackwitches," Ana said. Innocents, I assumed, the same as me. Normal people, minding their own business, who got caught in the middle of things because someone thought they looked suspicious. I suppose I ought to have felt sorry for those poor accused souls, ought to have felt a kinship with them. Maybe part of me did feel that way: I didn't *want* anyone innocent to be found guilty, of course, but . . . I'm only human, and in my ugly parts, I thought it served them right. "You were the one who told Vihra Kylliat that they were there, right?" She gave me a grudging nod of appreciaton. "I'm sure she'll be grateful."

"As soon as she's got a moment to spare a thought," Mila agreed.

I couldn't even be relieved at that. I was already slated to die. What good would it do me either way? "A moment?" I said. "Well, I suppose she must be very busy with the, ah . . . situation."

They both gave me a hard look. "Watch your tongue," Mila said.

"What did I say?"

"I don't know; what *did* you say?" Ana said, stepping forward. I retreated from the bars, out of her reach. "It sounded like disrespect."

"I'd have to know what was going on to be disrespectful of it! I'm ignorant—what is she so busy with, if not a *situation?*"

"She's been arrested, idiot," Ana said, as if I were supposed to be a fully informed citizen instead of a man moldering to death in a jail cell.

But arrested! Vihra Kylliat! "How?"

Ana leaned against the bars, crossed her arms. She looked at me for a long time; Mila hung back. "I guess," she said after an age of silence, "that you wouldn't have heard from anyone."

"I could hear from you, if you'd tell me," I said.

"Vihra Kylliat was arrested by the Coin enforcers." See, I'd thought Order was the only one who could arrest people, which is . . . *mostly* true. But supposing Order starts misbehaving—who arrests them?

Order handles the vast majority of criminal arrests, but Pattern has its Weavers, and Commerce has a small force of its own too. The reasoning is that Commerce-related offenses are rather more delicate, require a certain amount of expertise to investigate, and can often be resolved without throwing someone in prison to await a lengthy, boring trial. It takes a trained eye to identify forgeries, for example, or to ensure that the city bakers are adhering to mandated quality standards. The Commerce enforcers track down debtors, tax evaders, and merchants operating without licenses, and when they've found an offender, they simply . . . balance the books. If they can't, *then* the criminal is turned over to Order and Justice.

"Arrested on what charges?" I said.

"Stupid ones," Mila answered.

Ana added, "Suspicion of embezzlement and accepting bribes, criminal nepotism, and brazen impertinence."

"Those are stupid ones," I agreed, as quick as I could—best to agree in situations like this. "What does Taishineya Tarmos think she's doing?"

"She thought she was next," Ana said, again as if I were an imbecile.

"But why?"

"Because of what happened last time."

"Oh, I see." I looked back and forth between the two of them. "What happened last time?"

THE NINTH TALE:
What Happened Last Time

About fifty years ago, things were really screwed up. The King of Order wanted to go conquer Enc, but he needed a lot of money to do it, so he bribed the King of Coin to approve his budget in return for, uh . . . land rights or something.

("Canal tariffs?" Mila said uncertainly.

"Coin would have had those anyway." Ana turned her attention away from me, away from the story.

"They would have had the land whatsits too."

"Yeah . . . Anyway, it was something like that," Ana said. "It was something that was supposed to go to that King of Coin individually, not to the office or the Ministry."

"Right.")

Anyway, all that isn't important. They were colluding together on shady dealings for personal profit, is the thing, and they were going to drive Nuryevet into ruin in a war that would have bankrupted the country for a stalemate. And even if we had won it, we wouldn't have had the resources left to manage what we'd gained. Everybody knew it was a stupid plan, and nobody wanted to go to war with Enc on that scale—we've been picking at each other's borders for a thousand years.

So the Queen of Law tried to pass some legislation that would have upset the balance of power, so that she'd be able to overrule Order and Coin and stop the mess. Order accused her of treason and arrested her. The Queen of Justice knew that was a spurious accusation and arrested the King of Order. The King of Coin then arrested the Queen of Justice for tax fraud, on the grounds that the advocate who prepared her paperwork had listed his name without his patronymic. Then the Queen of Pattern stepped in and put a stop to all of it, and that was that.

I was silent and expectant. "That's it?"

"Yeah," said Ana.

Thrice-curse these people! "What about the ending?"

"Eh?"

"How did the Queen of Pattern stop them?"

"Oh. They were impeached, all four of them." She said it casually, offhanded.

"What!" I squawked. "For what? All those silly charges?"

She blinked at me. "For being criminals." Mila was frowning at me too; she clearly couldn't understand why I couldn't understand.

"What sort of criminals were they?" I asked, careful not to snap at them.

Ana sighed. I could tell she didn't have much patience left. "Do I look like a history scholar? I don't remember all the details; ask someone who cares."

"I know Justice was harboring a blackwitch," Mila said suddenly. "I remember that from school."

Of course she was, I thought to myself.

Ana nodded in agreement. "And in all the trials, it came out that the King of Coin had some very unsavory sex-related offenses that he hadn't kept quiet enough, so he ended up getting kicked out of office too."

"Doesn't matter how quiet your scandals are, though, because Pattern always hears about them," Mila grumbled.

"So witches and sex scandals," I said.

"And bribes and things," Ana said in that same careless tone. "You know, the usual sort."

"Is it? Usual, I mean? Common?"

Ana and Mila shrugged in unison. "They're politicians," Mila said. "They've all got their plots and such, haven't they? Except Vihra Kylliat."

"Yeah. She doesn't like games. If she did, maybe she wouldn't have gotten arrested," Ana mumbled. Mila gave her an inscrutable look.

"Fine, fine, but what happens next?" What happens to *me*, that's what I meant.

"Well, with the three of them locked up—"

"Three? Who else? You've only mentioned Pattern and Order."

"Oh. Tarmos."

"Her too?" I shrieked.

They gave me a long, cool look. "You don't seem happy about it," Ana said. "Are you working with her?"

"She did come to see him a while ago," Mila muttered to her. "We'd better mention that to the Duke's office." The Duke of Order, they meant—Ardan Balintos, Vihra Kylliat's second in command.

"I'm on trial, that's all!" I hurried to assure them. "She came to discuss that with me, nothing more. But who arrested *her*?"

Mila leaned in and whispered something into Ana's ear; Ana

nodded sharply in reply, and they both turned on their heels and off they went down the hallway, leaving me alone with dozens more questions than I started with and only one or two more answers.

— • —

I had to piece together the rest in scraps like a quilt of rags. Taishineya had panicked, I guess—arresting Vihra Kylliat was a severe miscalculation on her part. But it was a panic mixed with overconfidence: fear that she was on the cusp of losing everything; confidence that she could protect it with all her powers and expect no consequences in return. And perhaps it would have been different if the dice had fallen otherwise. I daresay no one would have batted an eye if she'd gone for Anfisa Zofiyat's throat, but Vihra . . .

Well. Order and Justice had always been cozy with each other, hadn't they? That's what Consanza said. Taishineya should have known she couldn't touch Vihra Kylliat without retribution from Zorya Miroslavat.

I suspect that part of the miscalculation was rooted in what I'd told her in our little meeting—I certainly hadn't given her the impression that she had anything to be particularly wary of. Or perhaps at that point she felt that "pick up the chisel," as I'd told her, meant "start playing their games, get involved." But she'd tried to play *her* game, not theirs, and hers was about social circles and knowing people and reputations. She wasn't playing the political game, which is a game with teeth.

Vsila did not quite fall into chaos. People don't really *need* a fully functioning government; it's just a very helpful thing to have. Business went on as usual, for the most part, but it was strained, labored. All this I heard from Ylfing later, so if you want specifics, you should ask him—though I daresay he missed a few significant sections too. He would have been very absorbed in sticking his tongue down Ivo's throat.

Vihra Kylliat, Taishineya Tarmos, Anfisa Zofiyat. Three Queens arrested in two days. Those two days, that was when the first tremors started, though the cracks wouldn't show for a little while yet.

I expect you're thinking that I seem awfully indifferent about this, and you wouldn't be wrong. I'd been in a murky, sluggish mood since I'd been found guilty and sentenced to death—you know the sort of mood I mean? That kind of mood always makes me feel like a blunt knife. Everything becomes dull and cottony, and I stop feeling hungry. Sometimes I'll put food in my mouth and move my jaw, but my tongue doesn't wet and it's a struggle even to rationalize why I ought to waste the effort on swallowing. Most times, I don't even notice it coming upon me; I don't even notice it until there's a cup of water in my hand and I'm having a serious debate with myself whether it's worth raising it to my lips—it was that sort of mood that had crept over me, locked in the cold, damp little cell, huddled in my threadbare blankets next to the brazier that I nursed like an orphaned puppy with a supply of twigs that had become, more often than not, too miserly to noticeably improve the conditions.

My fate was to bide and to trust my neck to Consanza. There were still the appeals. The whole mess with the Queens had bought me a little time. And as I sat in that cell, I thought to myself that if it all settled down and it turned out they were angry at me for lying about the blackwitch in Pattern, or for putting ideas into Taishineya's head, well, what were they going to do about it? Kill me?

It dawned on me that I had nothing else to lose. Perhaps I was going to die. And perhaps, before I did, I could give someone else the power to avenge me.

I hoped and hoped that Ylfing would be as bad at lying as he usually was. I hoped he would bring Ivo to me again.

You know, they weren't telling me the truth about things, Consanza and that steward in Pattern. They swore up and down that Nuryevet was no different from any other place, that it was normal. They had gone out of their way, both of them, to tell me how lucky they were—how lucky that they got to *choose* the person who exploited the office for gain, how lucky to have money wrung from them like they were dishrags. There were other choices available, lots of others, but such a thing had never occurred to them—they knew in their bones that they were lucky with what they had.

Yes, Nuryevet was already sickly when I arrived. Consider how the Pattern Primes kept abruptly dying in office. Consider the very existence of Taishineya Tarmos as a viable choice of elected official. Consider how offhandedly Mila and Ana talked about political corruption and bribes—people aren't bored with things like that unless they are obnoxiously common. Consider what Ivo had said about the country schools and what Ylfing had told me about Ivo's friends.

But I'll be honest: I hadn't been in Nuryevet long enough to really get my hands into it, to uncover the depth of the rot for myself. I arrived and was snatched up and thrown in jail within a week or two; there was no time for me to be out amongst the people, taking the pulse of the country, listening for the rattle in its lungs, looking for sores on the back of its throat. What little time I did have in freedom was out in the country, the villages and farmland.

So you'll just have to take my word for it, I suppose: Nuryevet was already sick when I arrived. Perhaps, without me, it would have staggered forward on its own momentum for another generation, perhaps two. But sometime, eventually, it would have broken down. That, at least, is a certainty. So when I tell you what I had to do to escape, to save my own neck . . . Just remember that much. Nuryevet was dying.

Perhaps I hastened its death, yes, but isn't a swift death arguably preferable to a long, slow, lingering one? There's no way to know how many deaths I caused, but there's no way to know how many lives I saved—from slow starvation, from sickness, from despair, from a bloody civil war. That's got to be worth something, hasn't it? There was nothing in Nuryevet worth saving, and everyone knew it, even if they refused to say so aloud. They only wanted better for themselves and their families, and then to be left alone.

I should clarify. When I say "Nuryevet" here . . . How do I describe this? Nuryevet wasn't a real thing—it was a story that people told one another. An idea they constructed in fantasy and then in stone and mortar, in lines of ink in labyrinthine law books, in cities and roads. It was a map, if you will, drawn on a one-to-one scale and laid out over the whole landscape like so much smothering cloth. So when I say there was nothing in Nuryevet worth saving, that's what I mean: the story wasn't worth saving, and none of its monstrous whelps were either—the government, their methods, the idea that they could feed their poor to the story like cattle to a sea monster so the wealthy could eat its leavings. And not only the wealthy. Even the well-to-do like Consanza and her family, who could afford coffee, good foreign wine—hell, *meat*. That came about because of people like Ivo and his family paying taxes for schools they never saw built and roads they only saw maintained for the good of the tax caravans. You'd never see someone like Consanza thinking to change anything. She'd told me outright that she wanted a cushy desk job in Law or Justice; she wanted to do the bare minimum she needed to get by, and of course that left no room to care about anyone but herself.

Perhaps it is unfair of me to lay any blame at her individual feet—it's not as if every aspect of her life was the result of simple good fortune. I bring her up only as an avatar, an example, a symptom of Nuryevet's sickness. She, like many other people, was in a position to do something; she had the means, the education, the social standing. And yet her highest concern was to avoid as much *real work* as possible, and to protect and advance herself. To kiss ass like never before, and to win herself comfort, ease, and security. She had even balked at helping me in any way that might hurt her chances, and I was her *job*.

The Queens' trials dragged on interminably, and the first snow of winter fell around the same time that the riots started in the streets.

It was colder than hell in the prison, and I almost caught my blankets on fire more than once, huddling up to my brazier. Outside, there were people dying. Ylfing told me that there was a whole week or so when you couldn't buy a loaf of bread for love or money anywhere in the city.

I ate my usual gruel. My usual apple every three days. I wondered if everyone had really abandoned me. I thought that was the low point, that it couldn't get any worse, and I remained vaguely grateful to be alive, though the cold sank into my bones and made me ache and ache.

And then Casimir Vanyos died—he'd been ancient and decrepit anyway, and he'd probably been fading out for months or weeks, but to die now in the midst of all this . . . I heard there were some suspicious circumstances, but it may have been pure speculation and rumor. An equal number of people attributed it to stress.

In any case, it was Zorya Miroslavat's next move in the wake of that that clinched things for the speculators. She declared martial law and appointed herself interim Queen of All until the judiciary proceedings could be carried out and Casimir Vanyos's sudden demise investigated. At which point Ardan Balintos, the Duke of Order and Vihra Kylliat's second, promptly arrested Zorya Miroslavat on suspicion of the murder of Casimir Vanyos in an attempt to grab total control of the government.

I sound like a historian instead of a storyteller, don't I? I apologize—it's difficult to tell a story this fresh and raw when I wasn't actually involved in any part of it, when I was shut away from the action while all the excitement happened to other people. And this, I suppose, *was* history, and it was happening before our eyes. In any case, I commend your patience with me. I'm nearly finished—I wasn't shut away from *all* the action, just the first half of it.

I'll make it quick: Ardan Balintos patched things together. He got trade moving in the city again, got people fed and warm. It took nearly a month, but Vihra Kylliat was cleared of all charges. Criminal nepotism had been a frivolous charge, something that was on the books but never actually brought up in court. Apparently, the so-called nepotism she'd been accused of was a personal tendency to play favorites amongst her junior officers and some kind of sex scandal from twenty years ago.

Ardan Balintos and Yunia Antalos, the Duchess of Justice, were most likely sleeping together, which brought up a whole host of ethical concerns, but together they cobbled together a solution: for Vihra Kylliat's trial, Yunia presided on the panel, supported by the four youngest judges there were in Nuryevet at the time—ones whom Zorya Miroslavat herself had appointed, and recently. Ones who would rule in favor of Zorya's other protégée—Vihra Kylliat's accusers didn't stand a goddamn chance. It was criminal nepotism being used to brush off a charge of criminal nepotism. You can't make this stuff up.

Vihra Kylliat was released from prison and, as the highest-ranking free member of the government and using Zorya Miroslavat's decree of martial law as leverage, seized sole control of the government. Ardan Balintos and Yunia Antalos put up no objection. I thought that was an unexpected act of loyalty and honor, considering, but Consanza explained later: while some little bit of honor may have been in play, it was mostly a show. Ardan Balintos was young, and mostly unknown; he had no military glory to rely on in a political campaign—he'd been in the quartermasters' corps for his entire career with Order, and had been sent on only two brief, mediocre wars with Cormerra. But he wanted to run for King of Order one day, so he needed at the very least to be known as an orderly, rule-of-law kind of person. In short, releasing Vihra and reinstating her power made him look good.

She wasn't a merciful Queen—she enforced a curfew, sent troops of guards to patrol the city, and expanded the situations in which the use of force was authorized. My time in jail got markedly less lonely quite soon after that as the cells filled further. The prisoners whispered through the bars to one another while the guards were elsewhere, and it was then that I heard the parts that I had been missing.

Gyorgy Imros, the Duke of Coin, was implicated during Taishineya's trial, and Vihra promptly had him arrested on charges of unlawful arrest of a citizen and the making of fraudulent accusations; the embezzlement, bribery, and general corruption charges, which had come to light in court, were tacked on as more of an afterthought than anything else. Gyorgy Imros was sentenced to a year's imprisonment and stripped of his title. This in particular was a terrible idea on Vihra's part, because it meant that no one was captaining the ship of Commerce, and it contributed to the mess that followed later. I'm sure she felt very pleased with herself at the time, having defanged Coin like that.

Vihra Kylliat came to me the night that she sentenced Gyorgy Imros. The guards had spent the day moving prisoners farther away from me, crowding them into another wing of the prison: Vihra Kylliat and I were alone in the room. I heard the clanking rhythm of her step several moments before she appeared in front of my cell. She drew up a chair, and I noticed that she too sat close to the brazier. She wore a thick red woolen half-cloak with white trim— she wasn't fine enough to spring for fur lining, or perhaps she didn't want to seem like she was showing weakness by needing the warmth. Or perhaps she was merely accustomed to the cold.

"Pretty necklace," I said, nodding to an oddly shaped pendant of twisted metal hanging from a long chain around her neck. I hadn't seen her wear jewelry before.

"It's not a necklace," she snapped, and stuffed it beneath her tunic. "You used witchcraft in the service of Taishineya Tarmos, I hear."

"What? When?"

"You read her future for her."

"Oh. Does that count as witchcraft?" I muttered. "I don't know that I really believe in such things...."

She waved her hand. "It doesn't matter to me one whit whether or not you actually told her future. She believes that you did, and her staff believes that you did. I've just had them questioned. Anyone can make up things and sound like an oracle. Be vague enough, and anything you say can be somehow interpreted to fit the circumstances that actually happen. Is she paying you?" she asked suddenly.

"Paying me?"

"For information. You're a bit of a slut with your mouth, aren't you?" She snorted at me. "You'll blab information to the highest bidder."

"Only to save my life," I said dryly. "As I don't owe loyalty to anyone but my personal beliefs and my life's work."

"And your apprentice."

"Sure, the kid's all right. Don't want to see him hurt. He's like a nephew to me."

"Certainly. I'm no barbarian, Master Chant. I don't hurt children to get information from their parents. Or parental figures," she added. "Why tear out his fingernails when you have ten perfectly good ones?"

I swallowed. "Fortunately, ma'am, I'm fairly fond of my fingernails where they are, and I'm willing to be a . . . how did you put it? A slut with my information, in order to keep them. How can I help?"

"I never said I wanted your help."

"No? My mistake." She wasn't making me *nervous* or anything, mind you. She—well, she was an intimidating woman, that's all.

"You're known as a person who knows things."

"Depends on the things you want to know." I swallowed again. "I know a few things, maybe. And, like many people who have lived as long as I have, I have a good bit of experience in worldly matters. Are you sure I can't help? What is it you want of me?"

She sat in silence.

"Perhaps I can make a guess, then, Your Majesty," I said, inching closer to the bars. "You're a strong woman, and you've inherited a bad situation. You're the only Prime at liberty now, and that's a *tricky* position to be in. Delicate. That said, Coin's not an issue anymore, and the Duchess of Justice and the Duke of Law aren't causing you any trouble. Thing is, maybe you've noticed you have . . . you have a wealth of opportunities available to you. Maybe you want someone to help you choose the right path. Maybe you want to know what would happen if you were the only Queen. Maybe you—"

"I'm no traitor to my kingdom," she snarled. "I won't be the only Prime."

"Oh," I said. That surprised me—if it had been me . . . I take what opportunities are handed to me, you know? But perhaps she was even more like the General of Jade and Iron than I'd expected. I took the opportunity to stop running my mouth. "So . . . to what do I owe the honor of this visit, then?"

She tapped the fingers of her hand against her knee.

There was a long silence.

"Things are falling apart," she said at last. "They've been falling apart for a while. I want to fix them."

"Perhaps the system is broken." Like I said before, Nuryevet was already sick when I arrived.

"The system is *fine*. I won't go making wild changes, especially not while I'm in this position. I have to be careful. If Casimir Vanyos hadn't died . . ."

"I got the feeling he wasn't much respected amongst his peers."

Her jaw tightened. "He was a good man. He worked for the realm for decades, he knew more about the law than anyone else alive today, and he had principles and ethics. More than I do."

"Taishineya Tarmos seemed to think he was weak."

"As water is weak, perhaps. But water flows downhill—it will get around barriers, it will wear through stone, it will quench fire, it will rise through the air and rain down on dry fields. He was careful, precise, and deliberate, and his understanding of his Ministry was second to none. We are lesser without him."

"And his second? The Duke?"

She shrugged. "We'll see, I suppose. He will take over until Casimir Vanyos's term of office ends in four years, and if he does a good job, he may be elected in his own right. That remains to be seen. I've never felt that he was a particularly forceful personality, but I suppose Casimir Vanyos didn't give that impression until you got to know him either."

"So what will you do? You want something from me, otherwise you wouldn't be here."

"Casimir Vanyos was wise," she said, as if she hadn't heard me. "In some ways, you remind me of him. I don't actually think you're wise in and of yourself, but you say wise things sometimes, and . . . as I said, you are known as a man who knows things. The higher you go in society, the colder it gets, you know. Queen of Order is a wintry place to be indeed. The Queen of All, even more so."

I pounced on that spark: I laughed softly. She raised an eyebrow at me. "Sorry, Majesty. It's just . . . I know what you mean."

"How could you?" She flicked her eyes over me. "You're a pauper."

"I am a friend of queens and princes, madam. I have sworn by my blood to be a brother to chieftains and lords."

"And yet you say you hold loyalty to no one. You have no honor, have you?"

"I swore to them as men and women, not to their titles. I owe their titles no loyalty, no. I owe them the loyalty due only to a friend."

"And so you think you know how I feel?"

"I'm more familiar than you think I am. I spoke to you once about the General of Jade and Iron. . . . But you probably don't want to hear me yammer about her anymore."

"Genzhu was a powerful empire. Still is, in its way," she murmured. "I would have dreaded to go up against its armies, in my youth. Before I was retired from service and put out to pasture." She smacked the palm of her hand on her knee above the prosthetic.

I nodded. "General Ger Zha was a great tactician. They used to call her the Sword of Heaven. For fifteen years, she was the empire's worst-kept secret, but that was a century ago. She was fading from memory when you were just beginning your career. But in her day, she gave new meaning to the word 'glory,' and she did it without taking the slightest scuff to her honor."

Vihra Kylliat grunted, pretending not to care, but she said nothing, and so I took a gamble.

THE TENTH TALE:
The Sergeant of Yew and Silk

A long time ago and half the world away, a young woman named Ger Zha joined the army and swore to serve, to be steadfast, to advance the glory of the Queen of the World, Earthly Daughter of the Glorious Sun-Tiger, Reflected Brilliance of the Mirror of Heaven, the Empress of Genzhu, En Bai. She was given a war bow, and the first thing she learned was how to care for it—to push her knee into the belly of the bow when stringing it, to unstring it when it was idle or at the first sign of damp, to fletch her own arrows, to never pluck the string without an arrow nocked to it, to whittle a draw-ring from antler or bone, and to draw to her cheekbone, always her cheekbone, in perfect unison with the rest of her company: Nock, draw, fire. Nock, draw, fire. She learned the singing twang of the silk bowstring, the hiss of arrows flying past her ears—the offbeat volley from the second line, behind her. She learned the painful snap of the string against her inner wrist when it rolled off her draw-ring instead of releasing smoothly, the lashing sting of it that she could feel even through her leather vambrace.

Ger Zha learned to march in formation, to shoot from horseback. By the time she saw any real action, she'd loosed more arrows than she could possibly count and worn through a dozen draw-rings. The blisters on her hands had risen, healed, risen again, healed again, and formed at long last into the particular calluses that distinguish all Genzhun archers from any others.

Genzhu sent her west, across the river valley and into the mountains, and she was glad to go—with each arrow loosed from her bow, she expanded the reach of the empire and redoubled its glory.

It should have been a fairly simple campaign, and likely it would have been in the hands of a younger commanding officer, a more energetic one who was still excited about their studies of tactical treatises. And indeed, in his youth, General Hei Ano had been known as the Ravening Bear. But just as the year turns and the bear, having gorged itself, trundles into a cave to sleep through the winter, so too had time overtaken General Ano. It was a shame he had amassed so much glory, because when his mind started to go, no one was brave enough to suggest it might be time for him to be put out to pasture. He made a series of stupid decisions on that campaign, from trouble with the supply chain, to working the horses lame, to an unfortunate mismanagement of a cholera outbreak amongst the troops. By the time they reached the mountains, their glorious force had been reduced by a quarter, and every soldier was tired, hungry, and footsore.

General Ano not excluded, of course, and if we are feeling charitable, we might attribute what happened next to the sheer frustration and weariness of a cranky, tired man much too old to be playing at being a young man still.

We'll just go straight through and have done with this

damn fool thing, he said, which turned out to be exactly the wrong thing to do.

Ger Zha, in the meantime, had already been elevated to the rank of corporal and then, technically, was the most senior corporal present amongst her particular archer company—the cholera, you see, had taken out a good number of the others. Two had been seized by river monsters one night in camp, and the last had been sent home with more than several broken bones when his horse, struggling up a hill, slipped on the rocks and fell atop him.

So. General Ano said to go straight through the mountains, and they did so. And they were promptly obliterated by tiny bands of mountain people harrying their fringes to nothing, like minnows nibbling at an elk's carcass in the river until it vanishes.

Ger Zha was one of only twelve soldiers who survived. Of the other eleven, ten were archers from her company, and one was General Ano, with two broken legs and a concussion. As the story goes, the ten archers pointed out to one another that Ano was already 90 percent dead, and the thing to do would be to dispatch him the last 10 percent, sneak out of the mountains, and make their way home. And why not? He had caused the death of a good two and a half thousand Genzhun soldiers, not to mention the camp followers, horses, oxen. . . . If you added in the material cost of the equipment lost—food, cookpots, boots, wagons, carts, chariots, maps, armor, swords, sabers, daggers, spears, javelins, tower shields, round shields, short bows, longbows, quivers, more arrows than the mind could possibly fathom, abacuses, nail files, shoelaces, et cetera . . .

Surely even a great and venerable man deserved at least 10 percent of a death for this outrage?

Ger Zha disagreed most strongly—her argument was that honor was honor, and as long as General Ano breathed, they had an obligation to protect him and see him safely delivered to the capital at any cost. There was no room for compromise, and the last eleven archers of the glorious Genzhun army came to no agreement that night.

Corporal Ger Zha slept with her arms around the unconscious and feverish general so that the others could not kill him in the night, and when she awoke, she found that they were completely alone. The other ten had deserted her, had taken every scrap of food, every weapon, every arrow. They left her only the clothes she wore and the contents of the pack she'd used to pillow her head: a spare uniform, a small folding knife, a tinderbox, and some letters. She was alone in the wilderness with only these, and the boots on her feet, and an aged, sickly man to whom she owed her solemn fealty.

The ten archers made it back to the capital within the month, tattered and grimy and footsore and sullen, and they told the story of how the army had been wiped out. They were given long robes from Empress En Bai to honor their sacrifice and bravery, and they were named the Ten Noble Heroes, and each of them was awarded an arrow with a shaft of silver, a golden head, and peacock-tail fletchings. A dozen solemn banquets were given to honor the perished general and the glorious army's tragic stand against the mountain barbarians, and the Ten Noble Heroes attended each one, as solemn and haunted as any soldier would be.

At the stroke of midnight during the twelfth banquet, just as the dancing boys were winding up their long veils and collecting their tambourines, when all the guests were stuffed like roasted geese and swaying with the vapors of rice-wine, of barley-wine, of tamarind-wine, the great doors to the feast hall opened, and a woman in an army uniform stood in the doorway, lit by the torches and candles. The Ten Noble Heroes froze when her eyes caught theirs from across the room and glittered like thin black ice crusting a deep river. She was bloodstained and mud-stained, but her tunic was cinched neatly at her waist. Her boots were scuffed and water-marked and worn through, her leggings torn, her hair cropped short and sloppy.

And she bore a war bow of a strange, snow-white wood, strung with braided red silk.

And she bore a red quiver, with red-shafted arrows fletched in feathers of every bird of the forest.

And she bore, shining on her breast and on each shoulder, battered lieutenant's pins of a style older than she was that had nevertheless been polished to shine like flames and glittered no less brightly than her eyes.

And behind her, palace servants, nervous and wary.

"Who is this?" the Empress asked. She stood, great and terrifying, with her child swaddled and sleeping at her breast—the crown prince, Jou Xi, who would one day die of river fever well before his time.

"No one," blurted one of the Ten Noble Heroes, and it was at that moment that their fate was sealed.

"My name is Lieutenant Ger Zha of the Third Camellia Company, and I am a survivor of the campaign to Hashelon."

This was a little unsettling, of course. There was an elegance to how the Ten Noble Heroes had presented themselves at the gates of the city. It was an easy story to tell—this brave group of loyal comrades fighting their way out of hostile enemy territory, surviving against all odds, and sticking together all the way home. The heralds had proclaimed it all through the city, and the troubadours had begun composing songs about it.

And Ger Zha merely appearing out of nowhere struck a blow against all that. But then she spoke, and the empire learned the treachery of their celebrated Ten Noble Heroes.

Ger Zha had carried General Ano on her back out of the mountains, traveling only at night to avoid the mountain tribes. She had foraged for food, which she fed him now and then when his fevers allowed him to wake up, and she trickled water into his mouth, and she—

Vihra stopped me. "What's the purpose of this?" She had been surprisingly quiet until then.

"Of telling you about it?"

"Yes."

I was rather taken aback. "You didn't like it?" That was interesting—the first tale about Ger Zha had held her rapt, but this one she scraped off her boots like mud without a second thought beyond impatience.

"Is this all you do? Come up with stories?"

"I don't *come up* with them. This one happens to be true." I sniffed. "I thought it would be helpful."

"How? How is a syrupy story about someone else's problems 'a long time ago and half the world away' supposed to be helpful?"

213

I shrugged. "Maybe it isn't. Maybe it's useless. Maybe you wouldn't have seen your problems reflected in the mirror of the general's problems. I just thought you might be interested, that having a little of her in your head might help you."

"I don't have time to listen to all this right now," Vihra snapped. She pushed herself to her feet. "I don't care about her steady adherence to ethics and honor, as if that's supposed to make her special. That's the bare minimum required of a decent person, and she deserves no adulation for it. And I? I'll do the right thing. There was never any question about that."

"What's the right thing?"

"Abide by the law. Use the system we have in place. There will be proper trials."

"Even for Zorya Miroslavat?"

"Yes," she said, without hesitation. "Of course."

"Even though her second got you acquitted?"

"Even so. That was their decision; this is mine. They should have known this is what it would be. She was arrested, so she will have a fair trial. I have no doubt that she is innocent, but that must be proven lawfully, or there's no point at all and it'll plague both of us for the rest of our lives. And, moreover, they arrested *me* for criminal nepotism, and I won't go proving them right."

"May the gods smile on all your endeavors, then."

She left, in a swirl of wool and a clank of more metal than her artificial limbs—I heard the separate ring of at least two daggers on her. You learn to hear these things after a while, and I wasn't surprised that she'd come armed. When a woman like Vihra Kylliat has a convicted spy and an accused blackwitch in her custody, she takes no chances.

In accordance with Vihra Kylliat's declaration to me, Anfisa Zofiyat was investigated for the charges that had been laid against her. An inquisitorial team was sent into the Tower of Pattern, where—not to my surprise—everyone claimed to know nothing about any blackwitches and insisted most staunchly that all who had been arrested on those charges were completely innocent, upstanding members of society and loyal civil servants. I don't know what hard evidence the inquisitors were expecting to find. Vihra Kylliat was not pleased with me.

"You lied, didn't you? You made it all up," she hissed through my bars. "You've made me look a fool. I should have you killed tonight."

"You'd be wasting a resource," I said quickly. "I can help you, I swear it."

"From a cell? Bound and gagged, so you can't spout any more lies and turn my guards' brains to clay for you to mold?"

"Keep looking," I insisted. "She's got *something* to hide, surely, and if she doesn't, she'll just try something as soon as you let her out. The blackwitch was just a rumor—maybe they were trying to frighten me into compliance! It was psychological torture, is what it was." I had already lost the argument, though. That would have been it for me, but . . . well, I'd been having terrible luck for weeks, and I was due for a favorable roll of the dice. We both heard a commotion elsewhere in the prison—there were screams. Vihra Kylliat vanished at speed, and I sat back to twiddle my thumbs and wait. As I had been waiting for weeks. I thought about resources—which ones I could offer to Vihra Kylliat, which ones I had available to get me out of this mess.

The greatest resource one can have in times like that is a friend. I thought of all the people I knew, all the people who could have helped me if they weren't half the world away, who had helped me in the past— Pashafi, who found me thirsting to death in the desert and pulled me up from the sand onto his walking hut, shaded me with his own shawls, shared his water with me. Ciossa, sensible woman, who taught me to play draughts and never once lost, who always saw through me like I was made of glass and yet was kinder than I ever expected I'd deserve. Heba and Azar in Xereccio, whose love was like something from stories, who opened their home and their hearth to me, who whiled away long, starry summer evenings with me, laughing and joking, all of us plying one another with wine, trading stories as they looked at each other and held hands like they were still in the first wondering flush of young love. Ylfing, sweet child, who always thinks the best of everyone, who gives his whole heart to the world. Ivo, with his anger, with his dream of something better for his country, with *his* friends.

And you. I thought of you. I thought how, by this time of year, you must have made your way to the foot of the mountains with your horses and all your kin. I thought how perhaps at this moment you were sitting by a fire as other clans arrived and built the vast tent city to shelter for the winter. I thought of you trading your smoked meats and your furs, and of your wizards humming songs of strength and warmth as they pitched the tents and picketed the horses. You, of anyone in the world, you were the closest. Two weeks' ride away, that was all. Less, perhaps, if the weather was favorable and the horse bold-hearted.

So close. I had fantasies of sending for you, how you might come over the mountains with your horse-tail banners and parlay for me, or ride in like thunder and snatch me away, out of the jaws of death.

If only, if only.

My thoughts were interrupted.

The first thing I noticed was *foulness*. It was familiar—I'd sensed it before, right before I met Anfisa Zofiyat. It prickled over me like flies walking across my eyeballs and filled my mouth and nose with a scentless miasma of death, and it grew stronger with every heartbeat.

I didn't hear the footsteps, of course. When the four figures appeared in front of my cell, I knew two things immediately—that they were Weavers, and that they were here to kill me. I would have known without their blue-and-charcoal uniforms. They had scarves over their mouths, and their skin had been grayed with ash, all the better to keep any kind of light from shining off them. Even with the faint light from the banked embers, I could barely see them.

I was frozen in terror.

Now, there's no need to fret, is there? You see me sitting before you, clearly not gutted or drowned in the bay. I would not have lived to see you again if it hadn't been for two small pieces of luck. First, something I did not know at the time: Weavers rarely work in groups. They are trained as lone wolves. Second: the lock on my cell door, ancient and rusty, stubborn on the best days.

One of the Weavers dropped to their knees to try to pick the lock. Tense moments passed; I was crammed against the back wall of my cell, unable to even scream. The foulness pressed against me like a physical force—the Weavers didn't seem to notice it at all, and I thought to myself, *Magic*. The Nuryevens have magic in their earth and water. They were immune; they couldn't feel it.

Three of the Weavers carried crossbows, including the one failing to pick the lock; the fourth was unarmed. One of them was breathing like a dying man, a long, slow rasp.

"It's jammed. Rusted." A man's voice. That's all I could tell. He rose from his knees and raised his crossbow as if to smash the lock, but the fourth Weaver stepped forward silently.

They raised their hand and brushed the lock with their fingertips. I felt a sudden pulse of the foulness. The lock creaked. Rust spread across it, ate away at the metal like a hundred years of neglect had set upon it all at once. It crumbled to pieces and fell, and the Weaver breathed with an awful, death's-rattle in their chest.

Blackwitch, screamed the animal parts of my brain. *Get away, get away.*

There was nowhere to run.

A clatter at the end of the corridor; one of the Weavers shouted and fired their crossbow, and I heard the thunk of quarrel hitting flesh, the gurgling cry of pain. The others' attention was wrenched from me, and then chaos descended.

Three of the Order guards went down with quarrels in their necks as soon as they turned the corner, and the Weavers drew long, wickedly curved daggers and flung themselves at the others. They moved like water in the dark, swift and deadly, but they had been trained to fight individually, assuming that each would be defending themselves alone. The Order guards trained in squads and teams, and they had the advantage of knowing their own territory.

The Weavers' daggers rang against the small bucklers the guards carried. A Weaver went down, and two more guards, and the tide would have turned against Order if reinforcements hadn't arrived from the other end of the corridor. The Weavers were summarily butchered in front of my cell. They died in silence. None of them begged for mercy. None of them looked at me. The guards slit all the Weavers' throats, even the dead ones, just to be absolutely sure.

"B-blackwitch," I stammered, pointing. "That one. Blackwitch." The guards froze and stared at me for a moment.

They fell upon the body of the blackwitch. Hacked it to pieces. Dumped its head in my brazier.

There was a scream from another part of the prison. "They're going for the Queen," one of them shouted, and they clattered off back down the hall in a great rush.

I sat there and looked at all the corpses for three or four hours. The blood pooled all across the floor—*you've* seen things like that, you know how much blood is in one person's body, and there were eight or nine in here.

As soon as I could move again without feeling like I was going to throw up, I piled all my spare twigs and grass logs onto my brazier. I tried not to look at the head, though as the flames rose, I had no choice but to smell it—first, the sharp acrid bite of the hair burning, then the flesh after. Better that than the alternative.

The alternative was to sit in the dark with all those dead bodies and wonder why it was so important to dismember a blackwitch, even when you were sure it was dead.

I closed my eyes tight to fan up the flames as high as they could go and tried not to think about any of it.

———◆———

They barely spoke to me when they eventually came to drag the bodies away, but a younger Order soldier, assigned to cleaning duties, came with buckets of water and rags, and he let me have one of his cloths to wipe off the blood that had spattered across my face and hands. "They were coming to take me," I said to the kid. "They were going to kill me, I know it."

"Not just you," he grunted, scrubbing the stone floor. "Anfisa Zofiyat. She was in the central wing, max security, and up a floor."

"Oh," I said. The guards had said that, hadn't they? The Queen, they'd said. I thought they meant Vihra Kylliat. "Did they . . ." I swallowed. "Did they get her out?"

He shook his head. I saw that his hands were shaking, and he kept swallowing hard. Not the strongest stomach, perhaps, or just not used to mopping up an ocean of blood. "No, they . . . they didn't.

They fumbled it. Didn't think—well, they're Weavers, aren't they? You don't hear about Weavers fumbling a mission like this. They're supposed to be like ghosts."

"They sent too many," I said. "They were fighting right here in—well, you can see that, I guess, you're in the aftermath up to your elbows—"

I had to pause while he threw up. It didn't make the floor any worse than it already was.

"Sorry," I said. "Anyway, they went in as a big group—they should have sent just two. One for Anfisa Zofiyat, one for me. Then they would have gotten away, but they sent too many and they weren't used to working together in so many numbers."

"I know," he said, wiping the back of his hand across his mouth. "We arrested them. Um. Most of them." He closed his eyes and gagged again, but managed to keep whatever was left in his stomach down this time.

Poor kid. He was about Ylfing's age but had nothing of Ylfing's coloring or manner. He had the broad, flat features of the west-country Nuryevens, limp dark hair, and rather fine and luminous hazel eyes. Ylfing probably would have looked him over at least twice.

"The blood ran into my cell," I said. "D'you have another spare rag? I can scrub up in here for you."

He had several tucked into his belt. He pulled one out, dunked it in the water, and handed it to me, moved the bucket over near the bars of my cell so I could reach it. With some difficulty, I lowered myself onto the floor and tucked the horse blanket under my knees so that I wouldn't be in *too* much pain the next day. "Never seen blood before, have you? Not like this."

He shook his head.

"You don't get used to it, so don't try. You're either born with the stomach for it or you're not, and there's no shame in not having it. Some people just can't learn to dance; some people just can't deal with blood."

"Can you stop talking about it?"

"Certainly. Sorry."

He wiped his sleeve across his nose. "They were going to kill you, you said?"

"Yes. No." I stopped scrubbing. "If they'd just wanted to kill me, they could have shot me through the bars." I swallowed. "If they'd gotten me out, I would have been as good as dead anyway. I mean, I'm as good as dead even now."

"I was told not to speak to you," he said, wiping his face on his upper sleeve.

"Said I was a blackwitch, didn't they?" He nodded. "I ain't." I picked up a stick and poked aside some of the twigs on the brazier. "*That's* a blackwitch." The head was blackened, the flesh sputtering. The foulness hadn't yet eased.

The kid gulped, but he didn't flinch or look away. "You should build the fire up more. Make sure that thing burns. You don't want it coming back again."

I don't think he could have said anything more effective. I scraped up every bit that I had, which wasn't much, and flung it all onto the heap, until the flames licked high and heat washed through the room.

I wrung the rag out into the bucket and kept scrubbing. It'd take a few days to get the stain out, if it ever came up entirely. It had already seeped into the mortar between the stones. That blood might mark this cell for the next hundred or thousand years.

"Vihra Kylliat was angry when she heard they'd come for you," he whispered, glancing over his shoulder down the corridor. "I don't know why. I'm just a slop boy."

"Why are you telling me?"

He shrugged. "You're helping me clean this up. I just thought I'd warn you. In case she moves your execution up, you know. So that you can write letters to your family or . . . or pray, I guess. Do black-witches pray?"

"No, but I do," I grumbled. "Seeing as how I'm not a blackwitch, or any other sort of witch for that matter. I don't have any family anyway."

"I thought they said you had visitors a while ago."

"My apprentice, his new lover, and my advocate. None of them have come to see me in ages. They've all abandoned me."

He glanced up at me and frowned. "I didn't think advocates were allowed to do that."

"What, run out on a case? She kept talking like she was going to. Said I had to convince her it was worth it for her to stick around. Not surprised that she lost her patience, to be honest."

"I thought they were just barred from the jail, the last couple weeks."

"Eh?"

"Because everyone's trials have been frozen until the mess with the Primes is sorted out. That takes precedence, obviously—at least, that's what my old mum told me. She's a court scribe, see."

"*Is* she? You should ask her if she knows this boy Ivo."

"Ivo who?"

"Okay, I don't know his last name or his 'nymics, but would you ask her? And if she does know him, could you ask her to ask Ivo to take care of Ylfing?"

He blinked. "Ask my mother to— Who is Ylfing?" He drew back. "I'm not supposed to carry messages out of the prison, actually. They're very clear about that in training. *Very* clear. So I'm sorry, but no, I can't do that."

"Of course you can't," I said soothingly. "Of course not. I shouldn't have asked you. I'm sorry. It's not really a message—Ivo is my apprentice's lover, you see, and since my stupid apprentice has decided to run off and *abandon me* as I always knew he would, I just wanted to make sure that—" It wasn't working, I could see that, so I fell silent just in time to hear the distant metallic rhythm of Vihra Kylliat's approach. "Well, never mind. You're going to need to change the water in that bucket," I said, tossing the rag towards him. "It's all full of gore."

He dropped the rags in and, stifling another dry heave, scrambled to his feet just as she rounded the corner. He jumped about a mile in the air when he turned and saw her. "Ma'am! Sorry, ma'am, I'm still working on the mess here, I just was going to go and—"

She seized the bucket from him and flung the bloody, grimy contents over me in one sharp movement. I gasped with the shock of the cold. "You," she snarled at the lad. "Get out of my sight. And *you*." She turned to me. "What have you to say about all this? Another pack of lies for me?"

"Nothing!" I cried. "Nothing! I told you she'd be up to something, I told you she'd try something, didn't I? Didn't I?"

"Clearly you know *something* of her secrets. They wanted to get you out before you spilled everything to me, didn't they?"

I struggled to my feet and started pulling off my wet rags. "No," I said miserably. "I expect they just wanted revenge for me telling you things that sent you haring off into Pattern's personal business."

"I don't believe you."

"You don't have to, I guess. You're only going to kill me anyway."

"Not," she hissed, "until you tell me everything you know. What was all that about that general? Some kind of hint?"

Nearly naked, I huddled up to the brazier and rubbed my skin, thinking that if I didn't have pneumonia before, I might by the end of the night. I was so dirty and smelly by that point that I wasn't sure if the water had lessened or added to it. The smell of blood likely would have attracted more lice and fleas, if the weather hadn't been so cold. "Hints," I said. "I guess it depends on what you think is a hint."

"Tell me what it meant!" she screamed.

"Nothing!" I snapped. "I was trying to butter you up so you'd maybe think about not killing me!"

"So you did make it up," she said, triumphant.

I pointed one finger at her. "No. That, I told the truth about. And about the blackwitch!" I pointed to the head in the fire and to the pile of rust and mangled parts that had once been the lock of my cell. It only occurred to me then that I could have run, I could have pushed open the door and escaped. I felt sick with terror just thinking about doing it.

"Guesses, weren't they. The strategic truth. To kiss ass."

I hid a flinch. "Yes, well, we all have to do it sometimes, I suppose, to save our lives."

"It hasn't saved yours. I'm having you moved to another part of the prison."

"Why?"

"Because I won't let Anfisa's little puppets dictate to me when I get to execute *my* prisoners. Their little gamble bought you some time, old man, because if I killed you tomorrow, they'd probably just be happy about it."

———◆·◆·◆———

So then I was dragged up to the new cell—it was cleaner, much more like the cell I'd been held in when I was first taken on accusations of witchcraft, before they'd buried me alive under a warren of stone tunnels. There was a window at the end of the hall, but it was *glazed*, and the temperature, while still chilly, was much more bearable than it had been down below. The walls weren't caked with mud and filth, the floor was swept, . . . The difference was that the bars below had been about a hand's width apart, and this area of the prison was all stone walls and tiny doors with no openings but a flap at the bottom where, I supposed, the food would be pushed through. The door had five locks on it, all of them shiny new—which wasn't much of a comfort. If the Weavers came again, maybe next time they wouldn't even need a blackwitch.

The guards shoved me in and slammed the door. There was the standard-issue bench, bolted to the floor. I looked around for somewhere to lay out my wet rags to dry—they already reeked of blood and I didn't have much hope that they'd be bearable to use anymore. My smelly horse blanket was just as sodden, and the wool had soaked up what felt like ten times its weight in water. It might go mildewy before it dried, but that wasn't too much more of a loss.

I heard footsteps in the hallway. They stopped just outside my door. I went and scratched at it. "Someone there?" I said softly. No answer. I got down on my hands and knees, then put my head to the ground and poked up the flap in the bottom of the door. I could see the heels of a pair of shoes directly in front of my face, and the butt of a crossbow, but that was about it. The boots' owner seemed to have settled in for the next few hours.

A captive audience who refused to speak. I love nothing more. "I'm bored," I said—bored, and frightened, and wanting comfort. "And you are too, probably, so I'll just talk to myself and you can listen if you like. If you want me to stop, I'll be needing some new clothes for the night and a blanket—Vihra Kylliat rather made the ones I have unusable."

No answer.

"Well, just let me know, then," I said. "I'd like to sleep at some point, and I'm sure you'd like to get some shut-eye on the job too. I won't tell anyone. Anyway, I'll keep you entertained until then. No tricks or witchcraft, don't worry about that."

THE ELEVENTH TALE:
Nerissineya and Adrossinar

A very long time ago and half the world away, there was a republic that had come together and called itself Illinleyelassalia, which means the Nation of a Thousand Towers at the Foot of the Great Mountains. That was a thousand years ago. Now they call themselves Elanriarissi.

There has always been a peculiar belief in this nation, going back as far as there are stories to tell about it, which is that the uncovered face renders one as bare and vulnerable as an uncovered body, or an uncovered soul. The Elanri, from the time they are named as babies, wear masks over their faces. They never take them off, even to sleep.

Adrossinar was a wealthy man in Illinleyelassalia. Some say he was a merchant or a noble. Some say he was a senator, or the consul himself. Whatever the truth, he was rich, he was respected, and he was extremely important. He was blessed with a family whom he loved dearly and whom he ruled with kind discipline—his wife, four sons, and a daughter.

When the girl was born, her parents saw that her face was stained by a dark birthmark blotching across her eyes and cheeks, like a mask itself. I imagine you are shocked, but see it how they saw it: a daughter who would always be masked, even when unmasked. Who would always be protected. It was a blessing from the gods, in their eyes, and they made no secret of it. They delayed naming her for a week, and then two, so that they could show their friends, and the friends of their friends, the great gift that they had been given.

But the time came, and Adrossinar and his wife took the child to the temple and paid the priestess for a name: Nerissineya, a good-luck name to match the good-luck mark across her face. The priestess gave the baby a mask as well, of red-purple velvet the exact color of her mark.

Nerissineya grew into a fine young woman: graceful, lovely, accomplished. Everything a man like Adrossinar could ever want in a daughter. He gave her the finest and most beautiful masks there were. She had a thousand of them, each one different and more beautiful than the last, but she had three that were particularly glorious. The first was a mask of the softest leather as white as a snowy mountaintop when the sun hits it at midday, with long wispy white feathers all around the edges that floated in the barest breath of breeze. The second was a mask of gold and silver, beaten with intricate patterns and inlaid with chips of dazzling jewels, a waterfall of silver-colored pearls falling in strands from the bottom edge. The third was a mask of purest black, so dark it seemed to draw the light into it, so dark it made her skin and eyes seem to glow like the faces of the moons, and it was wreathed in trailing veils of black silk.

Nerissineya hated each one of them, for she had a secret. All her life, she had looked into the mirror and seen a masked girl. The mark across her face was her greatest burden. A curse, not a blessing. "How," she would ask herself, "will I ever know who I am when I can't see my own bare face?" How, too, would anyone else ever really know her?

One day Adrossinar summoned his daughter into his presence and told her that the time had come for him to give her the very last gift a father gives his daughter: a wedding mask. He had already visited the finest mask makers in the city, and each of them had sent him their designs. "Choose," he told his daughter, "for I love you more than life itself and I would see you in the most beautiful mask the city has ever seen upon your wedding day."

Nerissineya looked at the drawings and said, "They are all so lovely. I could never choose."

"Come now," Adrossinar said. "You say that every time the mask maker visits."

"Your taste is so fine, Father," she said. "You'll pick out the best one. I like them all exactly equally." In fact, she despised them all equally.

"Hmph," said her father. "Well, my taste says that none of these is beautiful enough for my daughter. I shall send them back."

"Perhaps that is best after all," she said, and smiled behind her mask of shimmering blue feathers.

Adrossinar sent the drawings back. He began to talk about suitors and husbands and marriages almost every moment of the day—but the husband seemed less important to him than the mask he would have made for Nerissineya's wedding.

A week later he summoned his daughter again. The mask makers had come up with new designs, even more elaborate and fantastical than the first. Again, Nerissineya declined to choose, and again Adrossinar sent the drawings back.

Each week a new slew of designs would arrive, and each week Nerissineya hated them even more. The girl was deeply troubled. She donned her white mask, the mask with the floating feathers, and told her parents she was going to the temple to purify her soul for marriage.

On the way to the temple, she passed a troupe of actors from Faissal. Faissal is gone now, its land absorbed into the southern kingdoms of Girenthal and Borgalos and its people driven out and scattered over the wide world. But even in those days, they traveled too, performing great feats of skill all up and down the peninsula.

Nerissineya looked out and saw the players performing on their makeshift stage, scandalously unmasked. She envied them, but she passed them by and continued to the temple to pray and sit in contemplation, as a dutiful daughter ought.

She dreamed that night of the troupe of players, and she dreamed she was amongst them. One of them reached out to touch her face, and she realized she was unmasked. She awoke suddenly and it was morning.

That day, her father declared that he had chosen a mask—he had searched high and low and he had found a little-known mask maker of foreign origin, who had devised a mask unlike any that had ever been seen before. It was to be a marvel of velvety crimson suede, tooled and pierced in lacelike patterns and laid over a foundation of beaten gold, and it would have feathers of the rarest kind, and sparkling strands of crystals and opals draping across the forehead and hanging in long, delicate threads over her shoulders and down her back. Each of these crystals, the mask maker said, would be enchanted with the tiniest shard of starlight, and the mask would be a glory, a masterpiece, a treasure so unbearably beautiful that legends would be told of it for hundreds of years to come—and, as you see, so they have.

Adrossinar's eyes filled with tears when he looked upon the drawing the mask maker had provided him, for he didn't see a mask of legends. He saw, in his mind, his daughter wearing it, and smiling, and standing next to her betrothed as they were wed. He saw the mask hanging in his daughter's bedroom in her own house as his grandchildren played beneath it, just as Nerissineya had played when she was a child. He saw his granddaughter wearing it, his great-granddaughter, a whole legacy of daughters to come who would wear that mask in happiness, and his heart swelled and ached in his chest. He looked at the mask and he saw a symbol of joy, a blessing to be passed down through his line forever.

He gave the drawing to Nerissineya, and her eyes filled with tears, and she could not speak. She went to her room, and put on her golden mask, beautiful enough that no one would notice her weeping, and she went to the temple to pray for a divine intervention of one kind or another.

She saw the Faiss players again on her way home, and she remembered her dream so vividly that she stopped to watch from across the street, full of fire and want when she saw the men and women unmasked. When the performance ended and the players came around collecting money from the few people who watched, Nerissineya stepped forward and dropped a coin into the cap of a tall

boy with a wide face. He had pimples on his forehead.
Freckles across his nose. Blemishes on his cheeks. A scar
on his chin. She wished again to be rid of her mask so he
could see how the mark across her face grew darker with
blushing.

She dreamed of the players again that night, of the boy
watching her while someone else touched her face and
wiped away the mask stained into her skin.

The wedding mask arrived in the afternoon. It was
everything, and more, that the drawing had promised for
both father and daughter. Nerissineya hid her sorrow
behind her mask of swallowing black and slipped away
when her father was occupied with paying the craftsman.
She took her mask of pure white, and she took her mask of
bright gold, and she left her home.

She crossed a bridge and she flung the white mask into
the water. She passed a public latrine and flung the golden
mask into the pool of night soil. And finally, she approached
the circle of the Faiss players' wagons and their fires, and she
flung her black mask into a campfire that was unattended,
and then, with nothing on her face but her mark and the
shadows, she knocked on the door of one of the wagons.

I paused there, to see if the guard would speak, just as I always
pause when I tell this story. *What happened to her?* people ask. The
guard didn't, so I didn't finish it, but I'll tell *you* since I can see you
want to know: She begged the Faiss players to take her away with
them, and at first they refused, for she was clearly the daughter of
a noble house—they could tell by her dress and the softness of her
hands. But the freckly boy whose face she had seen bare, he spoke

up—he'd seen her at the performances. He'd seen her watching, seen her hunger. He'd listened to her plead for a place in the troupe, and he could recognize that the dearest desire of her heart was aligned with his own. So the players took her in and hid her, and left with her, and she learned the arts of the stage by sweeping up after them and cooking their dinners and listening as they rehearsed and performed until she knew all the lines, back to front and sideways.

The first night she ever went onstage as a player herself, the freckled boy blotted out the mark across her face with a thick paint that players use on their skin, and she saw herself in the mirror for the first time, unmasked by a mask of paint.

The boy became her lover, and *she* became the greatest player south of the Silver Mountains. She wrote forty plays and made the legendary theater of Elanriarissi what it is today, but all that is *history*, not *story*.

After I stopped talking, my eyes were heavy; I gave up on annoying the guard to death and curled up to sleep on my bench.

———————

Over the next few days, I ran through a chunk of my repertoire that was impressive even to me. The guard never spoke, so I hadn't the foggiest idea whether he or she was actually listening to me.

Vihra Kylliat came back on the fourth night. She opened the door and I shot up from my bunk—I'd wrapped my clothes around me for what little good they did me, but they'd dried crusty and stained. She staggered into the room, dragging a chair behind her, and placed it in the middle of the room. She didn't bother closing the door, but I suppose if I'd tried to make a dash for it, she would have had me pinned dead against the wall as soon as I twitched in that direction. She fell, unsteadily, into the chair—her face was beet red and she smelled strongly of drink.

"Good evening," I said.

"Why are you sitting around naked?"

"You dumped a bucket of filth on my clothes last week," I said. "They're ruined." I held up one wooden-stiff arm of a tunic. "I'm afraid it might snap off if I try to put it on."

"Private Vidar!" she bawled. "Vidar, send someone down to the debtors' ward and get some clothes for whosits. This guy." She squinted at me.

"Chant," I said.

"Stupid name."

"It's the only one I've got these days."

"Chant," she said. "Chant. Chant. You know what, Chant?"

"What, Your Majesty?"

"I killed Anfisa Zofiyat today." She slumped in her chair and waved one arm. "And I mean that. I killed her. Me. I mean, execution, yes, it was all official and everything, but I held the sword. Took her head right off."

My blood ran cold. "Her trial went badly, then."

"Trial, trial. Yes, badly. I probably would have had to let her out, but then her stupid puppets came and tried to break her out. Got her on conspiracy, then, and also conspiracy to commit murder—that was when they tried to kill you, of course—and trespassing on government property."

I raised my eyebrows. "You killed her for *trespassing?*"

"No, I killed her for conspiracy. And attempted murder. And *also* trespassing."

"She wasn't the one who trespassed, though. The Weavers did."

"Yeah, I know. Killed them, too. All of them. There were twelve of them that came to the prison. We killed seven in the fray the other night, including those two blackwitches. Arrested the other five, put 'em on trial, and executed them within six hours. Anyway, there won't be a Ministry of Pattern anymore."

"No?"

"No. I read the books on what I get to do, being the only active Prime and Zorya Miroslavat having already declared martial law for me. Convenient, really. Laws about it, you know. So I disbanded Pattern." She threw one side of her cloak back and fumbled a silver flask from a pocket of her trousers. She pinched it awkwardly between her artificial hand and her chest and used her other hand to work open the cap. She took a long swig from it, then closed her eyes, dropped her head back, and offered it to me. I took it slowly and dared a small sip. It was strong. Made me gasp for breath, made my eyes water. "Disbanded Pattern. No more of that nonsense. I reallocated all their property through the other four offices."

"So you thought there was merit in what I mentioned after all?"

"What?" she said thickly.

"When I thought that you might be interested in what would happen if you were the only Queen."

"Oh. That. No." She pointed at me sternly. "I'm not taking over. Not permanently. We're just in a crisis right now and we can't afford to be arguing about everything. I'm just going to fix it," she said loudly, "and then we'll have elections. And then it'll be fixed."

"What will you do about tiebreaks now that you've disbanded Pattern?"

"Ah, see, we didn't always have five," she said immediately. "We can manage with four, just like we used to back in the old days. Fewer than four, even. Anyway, Law is supposed to abstain. And Pattern was a waste of space and money no matter how you look at it. Most of what Pattern did should've belonged to Order anyway."

"Diplomacy and foreign affairs? Espionage?"

"Exactly. Sounds Orderly to me. We'll handle it now."

"If you say so," I said, though I disagreed—there had to have been a reason for Pattern in the first place, right? The area Pattern covered didn't seem to me like it could be so easily "reallocated," as she put it, but that was none of my concern.

"I do say so," she said. "War's a foreign affair. And war's always belonged to Order. So now we'll just look after all of it. Better this way. Loads more work, though." I handed her the flask, and she took another huge gulp of it without flinching. I admit, I was more than a little impressed. That stuff could have eaten through leather. "I was thinking," she said suddenly, "about that general."

"Oh?"

"The one you told me about the other day."

"Yes, I remember."

"When I was killing Anfisa Zofiyat, I was thinking about that general." I remained silent, and Vihra Kylliat soon continued. "She had to kill people in cold blood for the good of the empire, didn't she?"

"Yes."

"I thought of her. When I was doing that. I wondered how she felt about it."

"I don't think anyone feels good about killing in cold blood."

"Some people do. Some people are fucking crazy." She toyed with the cap of the flask. "We hire them as executioners. Only thing they're good for. Not good soldiers—too hungry for blood. They murder people on the street, they always want to go fuckin' pillaging . . . Can't control 'em, and it's like a plague, you know. One weird guy who gets hot over killing, he can fuck up a whole squad. So you make 'em executioners and you keep 'em on a short leash. At the front of the army, so they're the first to get killed if you're attacked, and so they're far away from the camp followers."

"You seem to have a good deal of experience."

"Years," she muttered. Another swig from the flask. "Killing in war, that's different. Your blood is up, everyone's in a mess together, the other folks are usually trying to kill you at the same time you're trying to kill them. It's not like execution. It's not like making a hand-cuffed woman kneel and lay her head on a block."

"Why didn't you have one of these short-leashed executioners do it?"

Vihra Kylliat was silent. "Because," she said slowly, "because of a lot of reasons. She was a Queen. She deserved the honor of a quick, clean death from a peer. And also, I don't think that . . ." She stopped herself and laughed. "Vidar!" she shouted. "Go down the hall, stand at the door." Vihra Kylliat lifted her head and whispered loudly, "They all try to eavesdrop when they can, you know. Don't blame them. Did the same thing when I was a kid like them." We listened to the steps recede down the hallway. "I was saying—I don't think that I could have had someone else do it, because I don't think that her charges should have"—her voice dropped to a whisper—"ended in a death sentence."

"Even with the conspiracy and murder and so forth? Not to mention the trespassing?"

"Even then. Should have had her stripped of her titles and exiled. Bound up and shipped off to somewhere far away, left with nothing but the clothes on her back and the boots on her feet."

"Why didn't you?"

"She's sneaky," Vihra Kylliat said immediately. "She would have come back. Like rats, you think you've gotten rid of them all, but they always come back." She stopped and shook her head. "No, that's not true. That's what I'll tell other people. I killed her because I wanted her dead. Because I was afraid of her." She fixed me with glassy, blood-shot eyes. "Because I thought she tried to kill me."

"When?"

"Few days ago."

I waited, but she didn't seem like she was planning to continue. "What happened?"

"Went home, and there was someone in my house. In the dark. No lamps lit. They'd gotten past all the guards and through all my locks and past my dogs. They were in my bedroom. Under the bed. They waited until I got in and then they—" She stopped and drained the flask, then threw it aside. She licked her lips. "But they didn't check the bed first," she said, almost giggling. "There's a dagger under my pillow and a club hidden as part of the bedpost, and I'd put my leg and my arm on the night table, and these both have sharp things hidden in them. Pretty heavy themselves, too."

"You clearly defended yourself well."

"Not well enough. They ran off, dove out a window. No tracks, no traces. *Must* have been a Weaver. No one but a Weaver could've done that."

"So it wasn't just conspiracy to murder *me* that you convicted her of."

"Couldn't bring up the assassin in court, though, because then I would have had to recuse m'self as a judge, and then I would've had to testify—too much trouble. Had blood on my knife, that was good enough for me." She rubbed a hand over her face. "I could've given Anfisa Zofiyat a different sentence. I didn't. So my ruling is blood on my hands, instead of on someone else's. It's only fair. And this way—this way I made *sure* she was dead."

"General Ger Zha killed the pretender, when the throne was retaken by the rightful emperor. I don't think she liked it either, but . . . It was necessary. And what you did was necessary."

"Was it?" She looked at me. "Or are you lying to me again, trying to save your own skin?" I was lying. There was no rightful emperor after all that, and Ger Zha died with the Eminent Prince and his mother.

"Does it matter? If you hadn't thought killing was necessary, you would have done what *was*. I know your reputation, madam. I know what kind of a woman you are."

She snorted. "If you say so. I suppose you're just trying to make me feel better about it."

"There's no way to feel better about it. You're trying to do what's right, aren't you? That is rarely an easy path, or a comfortable one. Take what consolation you can get, when you can get it. You'll live another day, and you'll keep trying to do the right thing. Maybe one right thing will include letting me appeal my death sentence, and maybe you'll send *me* far, far away instead of killing me. I live in hope."

"Hah! We'll see." Which was better than *go fuck yourself* or *keep dreaming, old man*, I supposed. From beneath her tunic, she pulled out that strange necklace of twisted metal I'd spotted before, and toyed with it. Not a necklace, she'd said. "The guards say you've been chattering away nonstop."

"Have they?"

"Through the flap in the door. Every moment you're awake, unless you're eating or shitting, they said."

I shrugged. "I'm bored and cold. My apprentice is vanished, or lost, or dead maybe. My advocate has left me to die."

"Has she? How do you know?"

"She hasn't been to see me."

"Because I've barred all visitors to the prison, stupid," she said.

Well, that's what the kid had said too, that guard who'd been scrubbing the floor, when I thought about it. My brain didn't seem to want to listen to reason. It was easier to conclude that I'd been abandoned, even if I knew better when I thought about it logically.

Vihra Kylliat was still speaking: "I thought something like the Weavers' raid might happen if I let visitors in. But there aren't any Weavers anymore, except psychopaths who might keep on keeping on out of odd loyalty to Anfisa Zofiyat, or some crusade to avenge her. You get lunatics everywhere. But she's dead now, and Casimir Vanyos is dead, and it's just me and Taishineya and Zorya Miroslavat."

"Zorya Miroslavat is still imprisoned?"

"In a nicer cell than this one," Vihra Kylliat snapped. "But yes."

"Oh. That's surprising."

"What's that supposed to mean?"

"I thought you would have freed her by now. The two of you seemed ... friendly."

"My personal regard for her is irrelevant. She *has* to have a fair trial. These are extraordinary circumstances, and we have to be lawful. I told you I wasn't going to be a traitor, didn't I? And besides that, it's for her own protection." I wasn't convinced, but Vihra was clearly doing an excellent job convincing herself. "The Weavers might have tried to kill her, too, you never know. We'll finish investigating Casimir Vanyos's death soon, and then we'll get this mess sorted out."

"So may I have visitors again?"

She waved one hand in a big wobbly gesture through the air. "Everyone else will be, as soon as word gets out that it's allowed, so I don't see why not. You'll have to speak through the door, though. No one's getting in or out of this room but me."

I relaxed. I'd been thinking of you again, you see, and I had come up with a plan—it seemed fanciful and improbable, and I really needed Ivo to be able to work it. Before anything, I needed information, and he was the only one who might be able to tell me what I needed to hear.

———◆———

And Consanza and Ylfing came soon after, as soon as they heard that visitors were permitted again. I saw their shoes coming down the corridor, lying as I was on my smelly, bloodstained horse blanket and chattering stories through the door flap again. I didn't cry. Obviously. I can't remember the last time I cried in my life. I've probably never cried ever, come to think of it. I was just relieved, is all. I was glad to feel not so alone in my little white plaster cell. Ylfing crouched down and clasped my hands when I reached them out to him. "Gods, Chant, are you all right? You got all the messages I left for you, didn't you?"

I couldn't speak for a moment, so I just squeezed his hands. "No," I said, after I'd swallowed a couple of times—I was just sick, you see, probably pneumonia. "No, I didn't get any messages."

"Why did they move you again?"

"Well," I said, "did you hear about the Weavers trying to break Anfisa Zofiyat out of prison?"

"Yes," Consanza said. "Was that to do with you?"

"Only because they tried to *kill me*," I said, too sharply. I was trying not to show how relieved I was to have them here. "They were going to take me away and kill me and dump my body in the harbor!"

"I can see why they'd want to," she mused. "I can't blame them." Of course the twit hadn't changed in the weeks we'd been apart.

I freed one hand from Ylfing's grip and wiped it over my face— sweat, you see. Just sweat.

"You're filthy, Chant. Haven't they let you wash at all?"

"No," I said. "And my clothes were ruined. I pile them on top of me at night to sleep, but I have nothing to wear except a tunic they took off one of the other prisoners, and it's almost as disgusting as my old clothes anyway."

"Well, at least it's not as cold here as it was below," Consanza said.

Ylfing pulled his hands back and I heard a clink of metal. He tried to shove his cloak through the flap in the door, but the flap was too small and the cloak too bulky.

"Oi, stop that," the guard said. "What are you doing?"

From Ylfing: "He said his clothes were ruined! How can you let an old man sit in a cold cell with only a tunic? He can have this—family members are allowed to bring things to people in prison, aren't they? Ivo said they were."

"I have to inspect it first," the guard said.

Consanza made some sort of shushing noise to Ylfing, and he must have allowed the guard to take it. "So, what news, Chant?" she said. "Anything I should know about, as your advocate?"

"No," I said slowly. I didn't think I had any sensitive information to tell *her*, but I hadn't realized the guard would keep standing there the whole time. It unsettled me. I closed my eyes and—well, I don't usually pray, as you know, it's not part of my personal attitude towards the world. There *are* gods, of that I'm sure, I just don't think that they have any call to be sticking their noses in my business, nor do I think they'd be interested in doing so anyway, except to fuck me over. Sadistic bastards, gods. But I sent up a little prayer anyway, hoping that one of the Hrefni folk heroes might be looking down favorably on Ylfing and thinking about sending some extra cleverness his way. He'd need it—as I've told you, he's a bumbling idiot of a child. "No, I'm sure you know the trials have all been frozen, so there's nothing to do but wait until the other Primes have been sorted out and either condemned or released."

Consanza made an assenting noise. "I'm not even allowed to do paperwork related to your case, you know. Or any cases. It's been a lean few weeks in my household."

"I'm sorry," I said.

"Oh, is it your fault?" she asked airily. "How convenient, I've been looking for someone to blame. Not surprised it turns out to be you of all people."

"Do you live to make me miserable?" I asked.

"All right, the cloak's fine. He can have it," the guard said. "Stand well back and I'll open the door. Prisoner, sit on your bench and don't move."

I scrambled back as far as I could—didn't bother getting up onto the bench, since it'd be difficult to get off the floor and I'd only have to get back down to keep talking to Ylfing and the twit. The guard opened the door six inches and flung the cloak in. I caught it—it was heavy wool with a thin fur collar and a lining of some soft fabric, and a simple metal clasp. I wrapped it around myself immediately and found it was still warm from Ylfing's own body heat. It was the loveliest thing, as lovely as that big chicken dinner that they'd brought in after my sentencing. I scooted back across the floor and lay down next to the flap. "Thank you, lad. You won't be too cold?"

"Don't you even think of me! I have mittens and boots, and I'll share Consanza's cloak if I have to. She's been taking me with her around the city, and I've been doing some assistant work for her for money, and—"

I groaned. "You're going to be apprenticed to an advocate now. You're fucking a Nuryeven court scribe and you're going to be an advocate's apprentice."

"No, I'm not, Chant, don't be like that. I can't keep borrowing money from Ivo forever. He's letting me stay with him, so I don't have to pay any rent, but I eat more than he does and—and I can't be a burden on his generosity."

"Even if you're fucking him?"

"Even then, Chant!" he squeaked. I could hear the blush in his voice and it made me smile.

I was dying to ask him about Ivo, to ask if he'd come clean to him about what he'd told me, but all I said was, "Do you have any spare money?"

"A little. I don't think I'm allowed to give it to you. . . . The guard is giving me a look. I'm definitely not allowed to give you any."

"I don't want the money, I just want some more clothes. And a new blanket, one that doesn't smell of horse and old blood." The other blankets, the ones I'd earned through trickery and deception, had been too sodden with blood to bother bringing with me—good for nothing but feeding the fire.

"Blood?! What happened? Did they hurt you?" I told them, and Ylfing made all the appropriate disgusted and sympathetic noises. He's a good lad. Dumb as a brick, but he's got a good heart. "Well. I'll bring you some. You don't mind if they're secondhand, do you?"

"Never have," I said. "As long as they're clean and they don't have bedbugs in them."

"I'll have them cleaned before I bring them. And I'll wrap them around a hot stone when I bring them over, so they're warm when you put them on."

My eyes pricked. Still not crying, just one of those odd things that happens when you get old. "Thank you. Will you be assisting Consanza, or . . . or do you want to continue your studies while we still have time? Perhaps Ivo could come along, I would like to see him again."

"Um . . . Hmm."

"I don't need you for much, Ylfing, you know that," she mur-mured. She sounded warmer when she spoke to him than when she spoke to me. Sort of motherly. But she'd mentioned she had a couple young boys, hadn't she? "Give me four days of the week, and Chant can have the other three?"

"Why do you get four?" I snapped. "He's my apprentice!"

"Because I need the *money*, Chant!" Ylfing said. "Clothes for you and—and maybe the guards would bring you a bucket of hot water and a cloth to wash off with, if we gave them a little present. Where's your brazier?"

"He can't have it in the cell," the guard said.

"Put it in front of the door, though, so it will warm the wood and he can lean against it. Or so he can stick his hands out through the flap and—have you felt his hands? They were freezing!" Ylfing made grabby motions, and I obligingly eased my hands back out. He chafed them gently for me and my eyes prickled again. "He's a very old man, you know. Don't you have a grandfather or an old uncle? How would you like them to be freezing in prison in the winter, with no clothes, with no heat? It's barbaric, is what it is!"

"Calm down, love," Consanza said.

"But feel his hands, and look how filthy they are."

"Is he filthy?" the guard asked. "I thought he was just brown nat-urally. Like her."

"Well, right at this moment, he is both," Ylfing snarled. "What a horrible thing to say about a person." Despite the venom of his tone, his hands hadn't gotten any less gentle. "Feel his hands, though, Consanza." He let go and Consanza's own nut-brown fingers wrapped around mine.

"Goodness. Ylfing's right, this isn't good for you. Guard, listen.

Have you had to do paperwork for documenting the death of a prisoner on your watch? I've never had to, not having your job, but I've *seen* the damn stuff before, and it's at least a hand span high. Now, you can take a gamble that he'll die on somebody else's watch, but you can't count on them looking in on him to check—or reporting his death even if they did. They might just figure some other sucker could take the credit for it and pretend like they never noticed. Or you could give this man a few creature comforts in the last weeks of his life, and severely lessen your chances of having to navigate all the red tape. Not to mention," she said in tones of dripping sarcasm, "I'm sure the gods would smile upon such generosity."

"I don't know where they put it."

"The brazier? Just bring him a pot of embers. Enough to warm his hands at the very least."

The guard sighed. "Karina Harnos," he called. "You'll watch them while I go downstairs, won't you?"

Karina Harnos, whoever that was, must have replied. The guard grumbled something and stomped off.

"Oh, well done," Ylfing said brightly. "Beautifully done."

"Heh. You only have to know how to manage them," Consanza said.

"That's what I keep telling him," I hissed. This assistant arrangement they'd worked out might not be so bad after all—he'd know more about Nuryevens than I did, by the end of it. And Consanza was a *good* Nuryeven to learn from, with a sneaky mind for figuring out people. "Listen, though, um . . . I need to ask you something," I whispered.

"Me?" Ylfing asked.

In Hrefni, I said, "You need to tell me—did you confess to Ivo about what you told me?"

After a long hesitation: "Yes," he mumbled.

"And?"

"He was upset. I'm not allowed to come with him to meet with his friends anymore."

Shit. "Could you bring him here?"

"What for?"

"I just want to talk to him." And then I realized—I *couldn't* talk to him. Even if he came, I couldn't. There was a guard standing right there in the hall. There would be one right by my door. "You said he'd been teaching you how to write beautifully like a scribe. Haven't you been teaching him anything?"

"Um . . . Stories and things. He likes stories." I made a note to find out which stories he liked, which his favorite was—that says a lot about a person, I think.

"Nothing else?"

"Like what?"

"Like Hrefni?" I said, ridiculously hopeful.

"Why would I teach him Hrefni?"

I swore and, finding the Hrefni oaths too vague and circuitous to really express the depth of my frustration, switched briefly to Tashaz. "Fine," I said, returning to Ylfing's native tongue. "Here is what you do. Ivo's a good scribe; teach him the Hrefni runes so he can read them, at least, and bring him here. Tell him I have something to talk to him about, and that we're going to pretend like I'm giving both of you language lessons. I can't talk freely in Nuryeven with the guards here."

"I don't know if he'll want to see you. . . ."

"Tell him that if he loves his country and he wants to make things better, he'll come."

I think Consanza was a little disgruntled to be left out of the conversation, but it wasn't anything *she* needed to know, and a few minutes into the discussion, I smelled her tobacco smoke and figured that she'd settled in to wait us out.

"That sounded awfully suspicious," she said when we were done. "Good job you waited until the guard was gone. Did I hear Ivo's name a few times?"

"I was only dictating my will to Ylfing for when I'm *dead*, since my *advocate* doesn't think she can save me from the noose. Gods above, I have to do all of the work around here, don't I?"

"Chant," Ylfing scolded. "She just got the guard to get some heat for you. Don't speak so rudely to her. You've hurt her feelings."

"He hasn't," Consanza said sharply. "I don't care whether he thinks I'm doing my job or not. I don't give a fuck either way."

"She really doesn't," I said. "I'm just some wandering beggar who has probably done *something* wrong, so why shouldn't I be drawn and quartered, or buried alive, or hacked to pieces with a wooden ax, or wrapped in sails and burned, or whatever barbarian punishment the courts decree will be my fate?"

"Exactly," Consanza said coldly. "Why not?"

"I wish you two wouldn't fight," said Ylfing. "I don't like it. It's upsetting."

"Just do as I asked and come back on your day off from being a *famous advocate's assistant*. Does she ask you to polish her boots, or was that your idea?" I pointed to Consanza's boots as I spoke. They were extremely shiny, and that was about all I could see of her.

"Her husband does it," Ylfing said. "He finds it relaxing."

"How would you know?"

"I met them the other day."

"Oh gods," I said. "You're going native."

"I know you're frustrated and lonely," he said, "but you needn't take it out on me like this. I've only been trying to help you."

There was a clank. "Here," the guard grunted. "Pot of coals, just like you said."

"And now some hot water," I said, enunciating carefully.

"Fat chance," said the guard.

"We're going," Consanza said, rising to her feet. "Come on, Ylfing." He got up slowly.

"Wait," I said, "why are you leaving?"

"Because I have things to do today, and because even though I don't give a fuck what you think of me, *Ylfing* gives one about what you think of him."

"Bye, Chant," he said. He sounded . . . gods, I don't even have a word for it, but it shot arrows into my heart. "I'll be back in a couple days, I guess. I'll . . . The thing you asked, I'll do it."

I should have said sorry right then. Found my tongue in knots, and by the time I untangled it, they were gone already. I didn't tell stories to the guards that day. I was too busy kicking myself.

Ylfing seemed to have forgotten it when he came back two days later. There was news, and that was all he wanted to talk about for the first half hour, alternating between yammering at me and to the guard, as if the guard had any desire to be invited into the conversation. He ignored Ylfing with fair success.

I had gotten no news since being isolated in this cell, beyond what Vihra Kylliat had told me—the guards in this area of the prison were rather more tight-lipped than the ones down below had been. Ylfing filled in the holes of what I had missed.

"And then yesterday the investigators presented evidence that it was Rostik Palos Taidalat Krekshin, the Duke of Law, *Casimir's second in command*, who killed him! He had been poisoning him for weeks, the doctors said! So he's been arrested, and Zorya Miroslavat was set free, and now Justice is back up and running, and people have been saying that they might start processing other trials before Taishineya Tarmos is sentenced. So—" His voice faltered here. "So that could be a good thing or a bad thing, you know. Depending on Consanza."

"Yes," I said. "Depending on Consanza."

He'd brought me a few more pieces of clothing—two shirts and a threadbare pair of trousers, and he said that was all he had, because Ivo had had a lean month, what with the trials being frozen, and had needed Ylfing to pay him back some of the money, and of course Ylfing had, and Ivo had been very sweet and apologetic about it, and—

Well, and then I had to listen to another ten minutes of improvised poetry about how simply wonderful Ivo was, and I grunted here and there and tried not to say anything that might hurt Ylfing's feelings like I had the other day.

"Did you talk to him?" I asked, when I could bear it no longer.

"I said I would."

"And?"

"He has a day off soon. We'll come then. I taught him the alphabet in an evening and he's already good at it."

Eventually the kid settled down and we got to work. I was a little heartened to see him more upbeat and energetic than he had been the other day, and by the end of our session, he was aggressively optimistic about Consanza's ability to win the appeal. I was less sure, but . . . Well, it doesn't matter either way, does it?

Towards the end of our session, Ylfing told me more of what had happened, sort of by accident.

"Oh, what time is it?" he asked the guard. It was about fifteen minutes past the fourth hour of the afternoon, the guard said, and Ylfing scrambled to his feet. "I'd better go. I need to be back at Ivo's flat by sundown, and it's getting dark so early these days, just like home, really—"

"What? Why do you need to be back?"

"Well," he said slowly, "it's not that safe on the streets at night, and there's the curfew to mind, you know, it wouldn't do to have both of us in jail, ha ha," as if he were trying to make a joke, but it fell flat on both our ears.

"It was safe a few weeks ago. You and Ivo and Consanza stayed quite late that one night."

"Yeees," Ylfing said. "Well. That was a few weeks ago, wasn't it?"

"Why isn't it safe now?"

"Um," he said, and I could almost hear him wringing his hands. "Well. You know. The riots."

"I knew they were rioting when—well, before, but I thought they would have stopped by now."

"Nope. Um. Nope. They have . . . gotten worse. What with Coin being in shambles, you know. Money's just a little tight right now, and people aren't very happy about it! And there were supposed to be some shipments of coal from the country, but they got mislaid. . . . Anyway, I always get home by sundown, and Ivo and I keep the windows covered and we double-check all the locks, and Ivo sometimes puts a chair in front of the door."

"Smart boy," the guard muttered.

"He's *so* smart," Ylfing said, but I cut him off before he could waste any time explaining Ivo's many charms to the guard.

"I didn't know things were that bad," I said.

"Yes. Very much."

"House down the street from mine was torn to the ground," the guard said. "I wouldn't be out at night if I could help it either."

"Does your shift go late?" Ylfing asked.

"Until nine."

Ylfing sucked air through his teeth in a disgusting Hrefni noise of sympathy and concern.

The guard must have understood what he meant. "There's a wagon that takes us all home when we work the shifts that end in the night," he said. "Since not everyone is too fond of an Order guard walking alone by themselves in the dark."

"Oh, good," Ylfing said. "I would have worried about you." I rolled my eyes. What did I tell you? The boy will go for any man who so much as blinks at him—all right, that was a little rude of me. Ylfing was smitten with Ivo; he only ever has eyes for one person at a time, but they come in such a *cascade* sometimes. You know when we were in Sharingol, he had a new crush twice a week? I'm not exaggerating. I kept a calendar and marked down all their names: Darsha, then Neric, then Tistin, then Ham, then Willet, then Pol. . . . The rest escape me. "Chant, I'll come back tomorrow, all right? I can't bring you any more clothes, but—sir, what's your name?"

"Private Vidar," said the guard. "Yours?"

"Call me Ylfing. I don't have any of those other names. Can you maybe get a few more coals for his firepot? Please? It'd be ever so kind, and I think it's going to be a little colder than usual tonight."

Vidar sighed. "All right."

"*Thank* you," Ylfing said, and for a moment I reconsidered whether or not the boy was flirting. Perhaps he was just pretending to flirt—which is a good skill if you can pull it off. I used to use it myself, back when I was a young man—

Excuse me, what was that look for? I'll have you know I used to turn heads every now and then. You know, back before my jawline started melting practically off my face. They used to say I was *chiseled*, and I used to keep my hair slicked back with fragrant oils when I was in the cities and had a whimsy for it. . . . Yes, I didn't do too badly for myself back in the day.

Hmph! I'm allowed a little nostalgic vanity.

Ylfing cleared out soon after that, and the guard put a few more coals into my little brass firepot and pushed it up close to the door. It made a nice warm spot that was quite soothing when I pressed myself up against it.

I didn't have long to enjoy it, because Vihra Kylliat came by within the hour, staggering drunk and dragging her chair again. The guards in the hall snapped to attention, and I had enough time to scuttle away from the lovely warm door and make myself as comfortable as possible—not very—on my cold, hard bench.

Her eyes were bloodshot and she all but collapsed into her chair. She had an entire large jug of some clear alcohol hooked on one finger by the little handle on the neck of the bottle. It was half-empty, and I assumed the missing half was what she had already consumed. "Chant," she said. "Good evening."

"Evening," I said.

"I set Zorya Miroslavat free today."

"So I heard."

"Guards been gossiping? How do you *do that*? They're trained never to speak to any of the prisoners. Ugh." She settled the jug of liquor in her lap. "Who do I have to fire now?"

"No, it was my apprentice. He visited today, told me the news."

"Oh." She wrestled with the cork for a moment and eventually worked it free. "Don't see what point there is in apprentices for your . . . alleged profession. Is he a spy too?"

"He's not, and neither am I," I said, which at that point wasn't strictly true anymore. Gave me a bit of a vindictive thrill to think about it—as long as I was being sentenced to death for a crime, why not go ahead and commit that crime? The only reason not to would be to take the moral high ground, and, frankly, fuck that.

"Hmm." She pulled a small cup out of one of her tunic pockets and poured herself a hefty tot of liquor.

"What is that?" I asked.

"Menovka. Local delicacy. It's made of potatoes and whatever grain is lying around. Flavored with tarberry. Aged in stone jars— granite, usually. Always, for the good stuff. This is the good stuff. Then it's whatsits. Distilled."

"Strong, is it?"

"Could topple an ox." She offered me the cup and I took a tiny sip of it. It burned four times as badly as the stuff she'd offered me a few days before, and I couldn't feel my lips or tongue for a few minutes afterwards. Strangely, it didn't much taste of anything, but when it was done burning it left a cold feeling in my mouth, though the actual liquor itself was room temperature. Needless to say, I didn't have any more of it. I think she was amused by the coughing and choking, though. *She* drank it as if it were beer.

"I was thinking about my general," she said suddenly. She plonked the bottle and the cup on the ground beside her, pulled her artificial leg up to rest across her other knee, and started fumbling at the button of her collar.

"*Your* general?"

"The one. You know. That you were telling me about before. I keep thinking about her. I almost didn't let Zorya Miroslavat out. I could have kept her in custody—'cause of the assassins, and the riots, I could have done that. Martial law and all, that was her idea too, she knew I could do it if I'd wanted to. But I thought about the general, and I thought about what she would have done in my position, and then I did that. Dunno why that was important. Just was." She finally got the button undone and pulled the chain of her not-a-necklace over her head and peered at it.

"Why don't you tell *me* something?"

"Tell you what?"

"What is that if it isn't a necklace?"

"Key. To wind up my leg, not that it's any of your business." She turned it over and scratched at part of the calf of the leg until a little panel popped open. She fit the key into it, after two or three tries, and . . . wound it up. Just like a child might wind up a clockwork toy.

"It's a beautiful piece of work," I said. "The artificer must have been a real master."

"Aye, it came very dear, and from very far away. But it's better than a peg." She clicked the panel closed, looped the chain around her neck, and picked up the menovka again. "And worse in some ways."

I wasn't quite sure whether she wanted me to inquire or leave off entirely, so I just made a thoughtful humming noise and fussed with my blankets.

"I spend a lot of time counting," she said suddenly. I hadn't expected her to say anything else. "The clockwork, see. I can take about a thousand steps before I absolutely need to wind it again. Around eight hundred, it starts jamming or seizing up at random, and then sometimes I stumble. So I count, all the time I count. Sometimes I find myself counting even when I'm not walking." She picked up her cup, gulped menovka, and stared hard at the floor. "That's why it's worse. All things have a price. I miss the peg because I didn't have to count for that, I didn't have to be *aware* in the same way, but then it didn't let me do as much as this thing does. I couldn't fight with the peg, couldn't run. So I endure, and I count and count and count. If I forget to count, I embarrass myself at best, hurt myself at worst. So it's better than the peg, and it's worse."

When she volunteered no further information, I said, "Tell me something else. Anything. One of your campaigns? Something funny or sad that happened during a siege?"

"Never done a siege," she mused. "I heard other people do it. We don't fight that way. I've always wanted to try."

"How do you do it?"

"The commander of one army, or battalion if you're all broken up over a distance, writes insulting letters to the enemy commander, and their messengers run them back and forth, and then they say, 'Well, let's meet in two days on the hill with the big rock that looks like a nose.' And then they get their troops to polish all their boots and armor, and everyone trots out in the morning two days later, and then they have a fight, and someone goes home, and someone doesn't. I mean, I've read lots of foreign books about how to do war differently, but I don't see why you would, unless you were a dirty cheat. This way has rules, and everyone knows how to play it, and you know who wins fair and square."

"As long as you can count on the other person playing by the rules too. They don't, always."

"Dirty cheats," she said again. "I might not win that battle, but they'd lose everyone's respect."

"Not everyone's, not always. If you're on the side of righteousness—or whatever people have decided is the side of righteousness, rather—you can get away with all sorts of shady things. Not that I'm recommending you *should*," I added hurriedly, in the face of her stony glare. "I'm just saying, people do. Other people might, even if you don't. *Other* people might have popular opinion behind them, and know it, and decide that they have a little bit of leeway to work with. Not with ethics, but with what people will forgive."

"I don't want to believe that people are like that," she said. She added another slosh of menovka to her cup, even though she hadn't yet drained it. "I have to believe that people are basically ethical and won't forgive a duplicitous leader."

"Surely you've seen it happen."

She waved dismissively. "Might have looked like that was what was happening, but I think it was something else."

"Tell me about what it was."

She paused. She wavered. I held myself in readiness. And then she said, "No."

THE TWELFTH TALE:
Memory
I'll tell you about something else.

There was once . . . I was just a kid, hadn't even learned to ride a horse yet, and we went off to settle up with Enc over whether or not they owned Lake Yuskaren. Not for any *reason*, really, just because it was something to bicker about and the King of Order at that time felt like it had been too long since we'd had a good lively fistfight with Enc. It's just a lake. It doesn't matter.

So they packed us off in carts and we met up with the Enc and it was all fine. Heigh-ho, just your typical slap-fight with live steel. Saw people around me dying. Saw people on the other side dying. Probably killed some of 'em myself, that said. I don't think I managed to strike a single fatal blow actually there on the field, 'cause after all I was still brand-new to this thing and didn't really have any idea what I was doing. I know I got a couple good limb shots in. If I killed anyone, it wasn't on the field, but later, when they'd been taken bleeding back to their medics.

Anyhow.

Maybe I've been in too many battles. Maybe that one was worse than I recall. Remembering it, it's like looking at something through a dirty window. I can see what's happening, for the most part, but it's blurry and grimy and it doesn't make me feel anything. Sort of makes me . . . *not-feel.*

I suppose you're expecting me to say something about the horrors of war. Yeah. There's only two types of weather in which battles happen: it's always either beating down sun so you're dying of heat before you even get your helmet on, or it's raining so hard you're slodging through the mud and then all the blood on the ground makes it worse. Too inconvenient to fight in the snow, so at least there's that.

There is a spot on the grimy window that's clean, though. One bit that stands out clear. Don't know why. We were marching home, and we'd stopped for the night. There was a little brook near my camp, and a friend and I took off our boots and socks and soaked our feet in the water and refilled our canteens. Just sitting there in silence. We didn't have anything to talk about. And he just started crying out of nowhere. That's what I remember clear—the biting cold of the brook over my feet and the tears on his face. Still didn't say anything, we just sat there while he took these wrenching, gasping sobs, and I was ... embarrassed, I suppose. I must have asked him eventually what was wrong, and he—war does funny things to your brain, you know. He was devastated, apparently, because he'd torn a hole in his pack.

That's what he said. Clear as crystal I remember that. Happens to soldiers a lot; I know that now. It's called battle-fatigue. Affects everyone differently. Some, they wake up with nightmares and cold sweats for years. Some go to the drink. Some fall into anger over and over, as suddenly as a landslide. And some cry over torn holes in their packs, inconsequential things, because they feel like ... like the hole is there because they've failed, maybe, or like they don't have any control, even over something very small and simple. I don't rightly know.

And I suppose for some people, it means they let the windows of their memory get grimy so they don't have to look through anymore.

"So that was that," she said. She had turned her chair around and straddled it so she could rest her elbows on the back. She refilled her cup again—offered it to me, but I declined. We sat in silence for a few minutes while she drank. "Zorya Miroslavat told me she's going to get Taishineya out of office while we have the opportunity," she whispered.

"Didn't you just say something about the people's opinion of a duplicitous leader?"

She nodded. "I've only ever seen Zorya Miroslavat build the law strong and solid, but she's kicking dents in it now, and I'm afraid the people won't forgive her." She was quiet, then snorted. "I'm lying again: I'm afraid she'll do something that *I* won't forgive her for."

"Is she more popular than Taishineya Tarmos?"

Vihra Kylliat shrugged. "I think the common folk don't much care about either of them. Taishineya's popular amongst the upper crust: merchants and foreign nobles and rich folk and so forth. Zorya Miroslavat is in charge of the Ministry that sends people to jail, but that also gets justice for wrongs done. She's half and half with public opinion."

"And you?"

"Oh, everyone hates me," she said immediately. "Unless there's a war, which . . . well, we haven't been at war in a few years, Anfisa Zofiyat's predecessor took good care of that before he went crazy and threw himself out of the Tower."

"Figuratively threw, or . . . ?"

"No, literally. Out a window. It was probably suicide. We checked. The room was locked from the inside, and he'd tacked strips of cloth across the door too, from frame to frame. There's no way someone could have murdered him and then done that *and* gotten out. And of course, the note he left, even though it was mostly incoherent. Definitely suicide." She took a sip and looked speculative. "Or a black-witch, now that I think about it. We didn't think of that before."

"Perhaps it's better that Pattern has been unmade, then. I've heard that none of their Primes ended well in . . . How long? Decades, at least."

"Something like that."

"But you were saying that everyone hates you?"

"They do. Unless there's a war."

"What about the skirmishes with the Umakh?"

"Pffht. That's nothing. They raid a few border towns once a year, usually in the spring, and they kill people, they steal livestock, they attack the tax caravans. That's all the trouble they give us.

They're nothing, anyway; we outnumber them, and we have better weapons. . . . And cities, you know, with walls to keep them out."

"And if they lay siege?"

"Not their style either. They don't have the patience for it. They're idiots and savages with a pack of wild horses. They'd camp out for two or three days and get bored." She shook her head. "They pillage a few towns just to ease the boredom. Capture sheep and husbands and wives."

"Surely you must get some public goodwill from chasing them off?"

She shrugged. "Maybe a few hours, when the troops come home triumphant. By the end of the day, though, someone's been arrested for disorderly behavior or public drunkenness, or for brawling in the streets, and then it's back to general complaints about the great unfairness of the Ministry of Order. There's no way to win—we're the big mean grouches, the wet blanket, the people who ruin everyone's fun. And now Zorya Miroslavat might turn the people against her too, if she ends up exiling Taishineya. She might be a frivolous idiot, but she's got a good public face and people feel good about Coin in general. People *like* the post office, and the mint, and being able to buy interesting things from far away. And banks. People *love* banks. Jails and armies, not so much." She let her cup dangle by its rim from her fingertips. "Casimir Vanyos is dead, and Rostik Palos— that's the Duke of Law—is going to be killed, so we'll have to have an election for Law, which wasn't due for another ten years. Pattern is disbanded, but we still have to sort out the transition and reallocation of jurisdiction, which will be a huge fucking mess from beginning to end. I can already see it happening. And, *and*, we'll have to investigate Taishineya's entire office for embezzlement if she's found guilty, which she will be because Zorya Miroslavat's already said as much. So once that's sorted out, we'll have to elect Coin anew as well, but we were expecting an election for that next year, so there's already been a few interested candidates putting themselves forward. Two elections at once. Can you imagine? That's only supposed to happen once every forty years. Chaos. I don't *like* chaos."

"I somehow suspect you vastly prefer Order," I said.

She barked a laugh, then sobered. "Some of them have already started campaigning."

"The candidates?"

Vihra Kylliat nodded. "Vultures, all of them. Fighting over who gets to peck out the eyes from the carcass. It's your fault, you know."

"I don't see how that could possibly be true!" I still don't see how it could have been true—not at *that* point, anyway. Regarding what came later, all right—I'll own that. But at the point I'm telling you about, I was still playing short-term games: things that would keep my neck intact a week or a month out, that's as far as I was thinking, and usually it was shorter—keep myself from freezing to death each night, for example. And I suppose that's why everything I'd been doing had been so ineffective, had only dug myself in deeper. If I had just stopped battering myself against the bars of my cage, I might have saved myself sooner.

"You threw everything out of balance and you know it. You spoiled the system."

"It wasn't a very good system, then, if one harmless old man could cause so much trouble. You're probably better off this way—build a new one. A better one." You see? I was already testing the lines I was planning on presenting to Ivo.

"Who the fuck are you to tell us whether our system is any good or not?" she asked sharply. "There's no such thing as a perfect government. Ours was working well enough. We were muddling along. Then you come in with your fucking wonder-tales, you tattle on everybody to anyone who will listen to you, you watch everything fall to pieces, and then you sit here as prim as anything and tell me it's not your fault at all."

"Muddling along!" I scoffed. "Your Duke of Law was poisoning your King of Law! And, may I point out, he started long before I ever got here. You call that muddling along?"

She shrugged. "If you hadn't been here, we would have fallen for it. He was *extremely* old, after all. But since you *were* here, spies and treachery were on everyone's mind already, and so—investigation. And what do you know, we found the bloody dagger. Figuratively. He died in his sleep, very calmly; I think they said his heart gave out from the poisoning. We would have fallen for it, and it would have been very sad, but we would have just kept muddling along without much of a fuss. But you? You secrete fuss from your pores."

I crossed my arms. "You can't blame me for the death throes of a country I only stepped foot into a few months ago."

"I don't know about that. I somehow think you're the type to leave destruction and ruin in your wake." Which is patently ridiculous, of course. She didn't know anything about me and she never cared to learn. "Anyway, some of the potential candidates for Coin want you killed. Executed. Done away with. A sacrificial goat, as it were. So they can point to it and say that the government ought to obey the will of the people, and so on and so forth. And so they can say that they were the ones who pushed your death sentence through and got justice for the people of the realm, and so on and so forth, you get the picture."

I said nothing, except, "And will you?"

"Will I?"

"Have me killed?"

"Not yet," she said, with unusual candor for the topic. "You haven't told me the rest about my general. You never finished the story about her and the Ten Noble Heroes."

"So when those stories are done, you'll kill me?"

"I don't know yet. I can't trust you an inch with anything where the truth might be important. But I can sit here"—she gestured expansively with her artificial hand—"and drink menovka. And make you tell me things that might be lies, or might not. Doesn't matter if they are, I guess."

"No," I said, "it doesn't matter if they are."

THE TENTH TALE (CONTINUED):
The Sergeant of Yew and Silk

Where did I leave off? She was standing in the banquet hall and telling her story, talking about how she'd carried General Ano out of the mountains, though he was ancient and gravely injured and sick with fever.

"Does he live still?" asked Empress En Bai.

"Yes," answered Ger Zha. "He has been taken to the healers."

"Thank you," said the Empress, and this caused a stir of wonder through the hall, for the emperors and Empresses of Genzhu do not *thank* mere lieutenants. They do not thank their archpriests or high chamberlains either. "He is a great man and the ancestors smile on him. We must honor him for his work on the campaign, even in noble defeat. He will have the finest healers and physicians, and when he is well again, he will lead the second campaign. A mind like that must not be wasted."

If you ever doubted that Ger Zha was an extraordinary woman, you may lay your doubts to rest, because she laughed. She laughed in the middle of the banquet hall, amongst all the glittering nobles and lavish feast dishes. She laughed while the Empress stared at her. "Imperial Majesty," she said, "Reflected Brilliance of the Mirror of Heaven, a mind like that has had its time. It is not wastage to let it rest. It may well waste another mind that could have had its chance to do the thing properly. General Ano is no longer *fit*."

"How dare you," the Empress said. "How dare you speak such treason?"

"I carried him through the mountains, Your Majesty!" Ger Zha cried, all mirth lost. "I carried him across half of Genzhu! Through forests, over hills and rivers, through valleys and the karst peaks. I know better than anyone that he is no longer fit! He is an old man, a tired man, a man near death even now, a man who has laid down his life for the empire's glory for *multiple* generations now, and he is no longer fit. I'll call it a miracle if he ever rides a horse again, and that's if the healers can pull his mind back from the fevers that ravage it.

"And you think his defeat noble, Majesty? You think it merely a fine and tragic story, the prelude to a second story where General Ano leads the empire's troops to crush the mountain tribes? That story has already happened, madam! That was the Second Battle of Sie Jeu, sixty years ago, and you may recall that General Ano was *not* the one who led the first battle. Honor him now by letting him be remembered in his days of glory! Honor him by allowing him some grace in his twilight years! If you send him out again, he will lose again, and thousands more Genzhun soldiers will die, and the treasury will be reduced by millions, all for naught."

The Empress called for her to be silent, called for her to be arrested, and the court was cycling towards chaos, but Ger Zha held something bright in the air and screamed, "You will *not*! You will not take me! You will not touch me! I am sworn directly to General Ano, I am under the wing of his personal protection, and my words are his words!"

The bright thing she held was Ano's own signet, still on its chain, which he had worn around his neck for decades. The sigil was stained carnelian from the hundreds of thousands of wax seals it had pressed. The hall stumbled to a halt again.

"He demands no honor, Majesty," Ger Zha said. "He expects a trial. He expects death for what he's done. *He* knows himself a fool and a failure, even if you do not. My words are his words, and I have sworn to bear them to you. As a messenger-in-fealty, I *cannot* be punished for speaking for him."

She could, of course—the Empress could have done whatever she wished with Ger Zha. But it would have been a dishonorable thing, and it would have gained nothing for the Empress but personal satisfaction.

And so—General Ano was put on trial a little time later, a frail old man, his mind further muddled though his fevers had broken, and Empress En Bai found him guilty of negligence in the pursuit of his duty, and she requested his resignation as general, which he gave with a quavering, weak voice. The Empress proclaimed he would spend the rest of his days under house arrest—which is what they called it when frail old generals were sent to live in quiet, peaceful houses in the country with every comfort they could possibly require. And when she had said her piece, the general cleared his throat and blinked his eyes like a tortoise, and said, "I have served faithfully for more than half a century, Majesty, and I would beg a boon of you."

And that is how Ger Zha was promoted to sergeant. And a year or two later when Ano passed away, she found that he had left her a generous portion of his estate, and a message—that no one but they two could ever really know those mountains, because they two were the ones who had passed through them like thieves in the night. That there was glory to be won, if she reached out her hand. That honor, not strength, had carried them both out to safety, and that honor would carry her as far as she ever wished to go.

Which was almost true, as it turned out. It carried her all but the last step.

———◆———

Ylfing and Ivo came the next day as promised, and I immediately sent Ylfing back out for monk's-puffs, wheedling and sighing until he went. Ivo and I were left alone. I cleared my throat. "Hello, Ivo," I said. "I hear Ylfing has been teaching you some Hrefni."

"Yes, sir," he said. "I know my letters."

"Runes," I corrected. "How nice. I thought I could help teach you. Did you bring paper? We'll have to write most of it down."

"No paper," Ivo said, "but I have a slate and chalk."

"Even better," I said, trying to sound as jolly and unsuspicious as

I could. "We can wipe it all away when we're done. Pass it through the slot, lad."

I clutched it to my chest when I had it in my grasp, and I prayed to any god that was listening. I even prayed a little to Shuggwa, old Shuggwa, though I doubted his Eye would be turned towards this wretched corner of the world, and I didn't particularly expect any kind of special treatment just for being a Chant.

I set the chalk to the cool, blue-gray surface, and I transliterated Nuryeven sounds into Hrefni runes. "I'll say it aloud to help with the pronunciation, and then you can copy it down again for practice: *Ēow maga ic áhilpe. Ic ēow áhelpan ályste.*"

I saw Ivo's fingers as he picked up the slate and read what I'd written: *I can help you. I want to help you.* A moment later, I heard Ivo's chalk scratching on the slate, and he pushed it back through. *Why?*

We made all sorts of little scraps of conversation as we passed messages back and forth, but they were so inane and irrelevant that I'll leave them out, so as not to bore you to death. Here are the important things we said, all written in scraps on the slate:

You told me about how bad things are. I have an idea.

We've thought of everything.

Not this, I wrote. *And even if you had, you wouldn't have had the resources to make it happen.* It was a pretty small slate. We couldn't fit much on it.

Go ahead, he replied.

"By the way," I said aloud. "Vihra Kylliat came to speak to me recently and she said something—you're from the west, aren't you, Ivo?"

"Yes," he said. "By the mountains."

"Mm. She told me about the Umakha raiders, how they come over the mountains in the spring."

"Yes," Ivo said. His voice was as flat as the door in front of my face.

"I was just wondering if you'd ever seen one of the raids," I said, chalk poised above the slate. "They sound fearsome."

"Yes," he said again, solemnly. "I have. I'm lucky to be alive."

You're lying, I wrote, grinning from ear to ear. *Because if you've really seen them, then you know.*

Yes, I am, he wrote back. *What of it?*

You know they don't care about killing people who aren't offering a fight; they want money. And some livestock just for the fun of it.

Yes, I know.

If you like, I can open the door for them, I can invite them in. And I can ensure they succeed.

How?

Chants have their ways.

Why haven't you done this already?

Because the price of inviting them to rid you of your corruption is that the country will be theirs. They come in, they take over, they stay.

"Can you explain that one again?" Ivo said, handing the slate back almost immediately.

"Yes, of course." *This is how they have done it before, in Mwit and Bhoshnu and so on. They install an overseer and collect taxes and tribute, but for the rest, they leave you to your business.*

Footsteps hurried down the hall. "I'm back," Ylfing announced breathlessly. "I hope they haven't gone too cold." They had, but it wasn't his fault—the temperatures had plummeted and would have whisked away their warmth in a minute no matter where he'd carried them from.

"I suppose I've given you a lot to think about," I said to Ivo. "Perhaps we could finish the lesson another time." I hadn't, at that time, decided not to tell Ylfing; it's just that you can't *untell* something, and I didn't know if I'd need him to be innocent, as blank as a slate wiped clean.

"I'll see what my schedule is like." He scratched something on the slate and pushed it through the door and got to his feet. "Sorry to leave, Ylfing, but I'm supposed to meet someone for lunch."

"Oh," he said, sounding a little sad.

"I'll see you at home later? I might be late."

"All right. Yes."

I was busy reading the slate: *I need to think about it.* Which was exactly what I expected. "Well," I said, when Ivo had left. "Shall we get to work?"

"I suppose so," he sighed. The brown paper wrapping around the monk's-puffs rustled, and he pushed the parcel halfway through the slot so we could both reach them.

I told Ylfing about the visits from Vihra Kylliat to distract him from wisting about Ivo, and he said that he'd heard that there was some tension growing between her and Zorya Miroslavat. I nodded, and belatedly realized that there was still a solid door between us. "Some people think they might have a falling-out," Ylfing said around a mouthful of pastry. "Ivo doesn't know, but I think he isn't really all that interested in politics." He switched to Hrefni. "Not these politics, anyway. He just wants things to be different, and he thinks all this is useless and tiresome."

"How do you feel about that?"

"I don't think it's tiresome, if that's what you mean. Politics are people fighting about things they believe in—I think it's a good way to find out about the Way People Are. It's just them telling stories to one another."

I took another monk's-puff from where he'd laid it out right in front of the door's flap. "An unusual stroke of insight, apprentice," I said.

"I don't think it's that insightful. It seems obvious to me. It's just something that makes sense."

"Well, you've had some training in seeing the stories in things, and most people haven't. Tell me more about the tension."

"Ivo told me about it after he went back to work last week—*finally*. There's so many things piled up from the courts being frozen that he's been at the scribes' offices for ten or eleven hours a day, and he comes home almost too tired to eat, but I've been making him. He's being paid again now. I'm still paying him back what he lent me, of course." I felt a little bad then about making him buy monk's-puffs for me, but what's done was done. "Ivo heard that Zorya Miroslavat and Vihra Kylliat have been having screaming arguments in the Justice offices, and he said he's never heard of that happening before, and I'm going to ask Consanza what she thinks about it when I see her tomorrow, and then I'll come back the day after, probably. Unless she wants to come see you tomorrow. I don't know if she will. And, um . . . I thought we should talk about what happens if you . . . you know. If they kill you. Because everyone thinks Vihra Kylliat should have scheduled your execution ages ago."

I grunted. "What happens is up to you, isn't it? I won't be around to care about it."

"I know," he said, his voice a little unsteady, "but I thought you might have something that you wanted done? Or messages carried? Like . . . Well, when you found out Xing Fe Hua had been killed here, it was surprising, wasn't it? Isn't there anyone you want me to tell, if you die?"

I thought about it. I've walked back and forth all across this wide world, and there are friends in every corner of it, but few so great that they would have particularly mourned for me. Pashafi would have poured some water on the sand somewhere in the Sea of Sun, maybe. I suppose Azar and Heba would have lit candles for me, and Aimenta. And Ciossa in Elanriarissi, if she still lived. And you, of course. But I didn't want Ylfing to spend half his life tracking down people who might themselves have already died. I didn't want to bring unnecessary grief to people for whom it would do no good. Ylfing was young, and he had better things to do than the errands of a dead old man. "No," I said. "But if you think someone in particular should know, you may go to them if you choose."

"You don't want *anyone* to know?" he asked.

"*You* will know. Will you go home?"

He paused. "I haven't decided," he said softly. "I think I might, at least for a little while. Two or three years, maybe. I miss my family sometimes." This he said as if he was dragging it out of himself, as if he was ashamed to admit it. "I dreamed about the little boat that Finne and I used to row out on the lake in the spring before dawn, when there was just a little shimmering veil of fog across the water, and it seemed like the pines on the opposite shore were rising out of nothing. I dreamed we were fishing, and he said I should come back, and he took my hand, and it was so warm that it startled me and I woke up. I don't miss them *always*," he hastened to assure me. "And I hadn't even thought of Finne in . . . years."

"It's not a bad thing," I said. "It doesn't make you a poor Chant, to miss the ones you love. It makes you human, and you can't be a Chant without being decidedly, stubbornly, gloriously human. It's the only way to really have the slightest hope of even beginning to comprehend the things we're trying to understand."

He drew a shaking breath. "I thought it must be very bad to miss them like that," he said. "Because the Chants have to sink their homeland beneath the waves. Give them up forever, isn't that the point?"

"Sort of?" I waved my hands—maybe gesturing could be heard

in the voice even if it wasn't seen. "It's an oath, not a literal thing. A ritual, symbolic. Once we got to that point, where we were thinking of you taking that step, we would have gone back to Hrefnesholt and seen your family and—"

"*Oh*," Ylfing said, and began to cry. I sat frozen and silent. If watching him cry through the bars had been awkward, this was twice as bad.

"What are you doing? Why?"

"You told me before we left that—you told me about sinking my homeland beneath the waves," he gasped out between sobs, "and at first I thought you meant the *whole thing*, but then you explained that it was saying some words and throwing a rock or something into a lake or a river, so I . . ." His voice got very small. "I brought a rock from home with me because I thought we were never going back ever."

Something shattered in my chest, and I leaned my head against the door. He's a very stupid boy sometimes. "Sorry." I cleared my throat and tried again. "Sorry, I suppose I didn't explain it very well. You brought a rock with you? You still have it? It's been years."

"Yes," he said in an even smaller voice. "I thought I'd lost it once, remember? When we were in Ondor-Urt and I tripped and dropped my bag over the rail of Pashafi's house, and it spilled open across the sand, and I almost jumped down to get it because the huts weren't even walking that fast, and—"

"And you would have been eaten in seconds if your feet had touched the ground, yes, I remember. I wondered why you cared so much about a spare set of clothes."

"It was the rock, is why. I thought . . . if you asked me to sink my homeland beneath the waves, I thought I was supposed to be ready to do it at *any second*. I thought if I didn't have it, you'd send me home and I'd never get another chance. And sometimes I thought about how maybe if you asked me to, I could just pretend that I'd lost it, because . . . because once in a while, I thought maybe it wouldn't be so bad to be sent home. I've seen more of the world than anyone I know. Or knew." His voice was still thick and sniffly, but the tears already seemed to be easing up—Ylfing's tears are ever as brief as summer rain showers.

"You were prepared to sink your homeland beneath the waves at *any second?*"

"Yes. I thought I was supposed to be. I thought the whole apprenticeship was a test."

I wanted to laugh at him, I really did. "You already know you're not my first apprentice. I don't talk much about the others, but I've had fifteen or sixteen of them, Ylfing. It's not . . . Well, it is sort of a test, but it's a test that you're giving *yourself*, and you get to figure out whether you passed it or not. It's not *me* that tells you if you did. Of the sixteen or so, I took seven of them back home to sink it beneath the waves, and . . . Hell, Ylfing, when we got there, only three of them came away with me again. They came with me as journeymen for a little while—journeywomen, actually, all three of them were women—but then the time came for us to part, and I don't know what happened to them after that. Don't know if any of them ever kept on as Chants in their own right. It's been years. I don't go back to their homes, because I don't want to know if they gave up, and because if they *didn't* give up, then there might still be someone who carries a grudge against me for taking them away."

"Only three of them?"

"Only three. For some people, a few years of apprenticeship is enough to scratch their itching feet. Some people don't have the knack for it, and they figure that out on their own. And sometimes they think it's what they want to do until they go home, and then . . ." I shrugged. "There's nothing wrong with that. Sometimes you forget what home is like, and what it's like to be around so many people who know you and love you. Sometimes they've changed for the better; sometimes *you* have. That might still happen to you, and there's *nothing wrong with it*. If I get out of here and we go back to Hrefnesholt one day, and you decide to stay in your village instead of leaving again as a journeyman, that's fine. You won't have disappointed me. It's your choice, do you understand? Every day with me is your choice."

He sniffled. I don't know if he nodded or shook his head in addition to that, but he didn't answer.

"We might go back, and you might decide to stay. Or you might find that they've changed, and you've changed—because you *will* find that you've changed, that you're not the same person who left—and that you *can't* go home, not really, because home doesn't exist anymore in the way that it used to be. The houses will still be there, some or most of the people will still be there. . . . The fjord and the pine trees and the mist on the water in the morning, those will all be there. But *home* might not be. So you might leave. Or you might stay, and it'll be a different *home* one day, even though it's in the same place." I paused. "Were you in love with Finne?"

"Sort of," he said.

I rolled my eyes a little. Of course he was—like I said before, he'll fall in love three times a week if he's given the opportunity. "So you might go back and find that the two of you still have feelings for each other, and that he missed you and waited for you. Don't get your hopes up about this," I added. "I'm just saying that is one of a hundred thousand possibilities. There are more possible endings where you go home than possible endings where you become a master-Chant. That's only one ending in thousands. And it's important to consider the idea that others might arise instead. As we have established already with Taishineya Tarmos, neither of us can tell the future unless we're faking it. But if we consider several threads of fate rather than just one, we can be more prepared when the path twists away under our feet and takes us somewhere other than where we first thought we were going."

"I love traveling with you," he said. "I don't want to stop."

Poor kid. "Do you love traveling with *me*," I asked as gently as I could, "or do you love traveling? Because execution or not, I won't be in this world forever."

I sat back and looked down at the opening in the bottom of the door. He was toying with one of the monk's-puffs, tearing it to tiny pieces. "Well, I've never traveled without you," he said, "so I don't know. Other than going to the Jarlsmoot when I was a kid. I loved that, too, but . . ."

"But it was the Jarlsmoot, and you were a kid. It was exciting in and of itself, and every child would have loved to go."

"Yes."

"Your life is your own, Ylfing. You have taken no vows, you have made no promises. Not even to me, you understand? I told you when we first started out that you could stay as long as you liked, unless you proved to be more annoying than you were worth, because *I* get to stay with you as long as I like too."

"Do you like it? Having me with you?" he whispered.

I spent a moment rearranging my cloak.

"It's just that I sometimes think you don't like it," he said. The monk's-puff he was shredding was looking more like a powder.

"It's fine," I muttered. "As apprentices go, you're not the worst I've ever had." I didn't realize until after it had come out of my mouth how that would sound to a Hrefni. I hadn't meant it as a compliment, not *really*, but that's what it was to him. They have this odd thing about wanting to know where they are on a spectrum of worst to best.

Not-worst would be a wonderful place for Ylfing to stand, in his own estimation.

I heard him take a deep breath. "Oh," he said. "Thank you."

———◆———

I vo came back, very, very late that night—I don't know if it was some privilege of being a court scribe, or if he simply knew which palms to grease. "Are you awake?" he said, tapping on the door. "I forgot my slate here. I came to collect it."

I rolled off my bench and tottered over to the door. The only light was what little came from the torches in the hallway, shining through the slot in the bottom of the door. "Yes, sorry, let me find it for you. Did you have a nice day?" I was casting around, trying to find a way to ask him what he thought of my offer without revealing anything to the guards.

"Yes. I'm in a rush, though, I can't stay to chat."

"Oh . . ." I was disappointed. Perhaps the slate was all he'd come for after all.

"Next time, you'll have to tell me another story. The one earlier, I liked that one. I had to think about it, but I liked it."

My breath caught in my throat. "That's kind of you to say, lad," I said carefully. "If you liked that, you'd probably like the tune that goes with it. Ylfing could sing it for you—ask him if he remembers the 'Song of the Two Firesides.'"

"I will," he said.

"It's a song I often sing when I'm crossing a border into somewhere new." This was, of course, a lie for the benefit of the guards. "It brings luck and protection to travelers. Perhaps one day you'll go abroad and remember it."

"Perhaps."

"Ylfing can teach you," I said again, trying not to sound too much like I was stressing it.

"I'll ask him. But do you have my slate? It's past curfew and I need to get home."

I patted around in the dark and found it, found the chalk, scribbled a line or two the same way we had done earlier—Nuryeven transliterated to Hrefni runes: *Cross the Tegey Pass. Find the city of tents and sing. Go soon.*

It was the fastest trial I've ever seen," Consanza said, a few days later. That day they brought me a cushion and a blanket (carefully inspected by my guard, as usual). The blanket was woven in stripes of scarlet and maroon, and had been washed so often that the wool had turned almost to felt and had begun to wear thin in places. There were a few stains, too, but it didn't smell of horse and blood, so that was something. I had the guard take away my old horse blanket and the last of my old clothes, and folded the new blanket to lie under the cushion in front of the door. There were crunchy rolls of dark bread today, but that was about all. "Pastry vendors out sick?" I asked, picking one up.

"No, they've all shut down. Enjoy these; they were all we could get. Wouldn't have gone to such trouble, but Ylfing insisted. I hope you appreciate him like you ought to. He's a good assistant."

"You can't have him," I snapped. "Tell me about the trial. Fastest ever?"

"Yes. Six hours, start to finish. Taishineya Tarmos had one of the most prestigious advocates in Vsila, obviously—it was Brina Sekos Lankat Mestyrin. Ylfing, has Ivo told you about her? He's worked with her a few times." Ylfing mumbled something around a mouthful of bread, and Consanza continued. "Zorya Miroslavat barely let either of them speak. She's extremely good at what she does, and she's good at twisting mostly innocuous evidence into something that *looks* gruesome and monstrous, at least. The worst thing Taishineya Tarmos did was to use treasury funds for a gala in honor of the trade agreement with the Cormerran merchants, which . . . It's not outside the bounds of what's allowable, but the gala was more frivolous and excessive than necessary—which is not surprising; considering it was hosted by *Taishineya Tarmos*, no one should be shocked—and Zorya Miroslavat was able to scrape together a case for gross laxity and neglect in the pursuit of duty to a public office. That usually carries only a fine, but Taishineya Tarmos's lackadaisical attitude towards the running of her offices and financial policy in general infected the rest of her Ministry, and several serious errors were found in her books, including a few instances of actual embezzlement, even if Zorya Miroslavat couldn't prove that Taishineya Tarmos did any herself. Anyway, start to finish, six hours, and most of it was monologuing by Zorya Miroslavat. And now Taishineya Tarmos has been officially exiled. She was shoved on a boat that was sailing out on the afternoon tide, so she's already gone out of the city. I believe it was bound for Tornasse in Ezozza. It's south of here. About two weeks' voyage."

"Yes, I know where it is," I said. "I've been there."

"So they're scrubbing out all the corrupt clerks from Coin, and then they're going to hold the Coin election early. Speaking of elections—you've heard all the candidates want you dead?"

"So I'm told."

"Have you been saying something to Vihra Kylliat? She's publicly resisting them."

"She says you're still useful," Ylfing added.

"She comes in drunk every few nights and we just talk. We trade stories."

"Drunk? Vihra Kylliat?" Consanza said. "Seriously?"

"Yes. You're surprised?"

"She always seemed as sober as steel. Being regularly drunk enough to talk to *you* . . . doesn't seem her style."

I could have told them about the visits at that point, but sometimes people tell things to Chants that should be kept in confidence. I can tell *you* now, of course, because . . . well. We'll get there. "Ylfing said she and Zorya Miroslavat have been arguing?"

"Yes. About you. About whether or not to kill you. Miroslavat is all for it. She's in great support of some of these new candidates for the Primes. . . . Why do you think there's this guard right outside your door every moment of the day and night? And another down the hall?"

"Guarding this cell block, I thought."

"Guarding *you*. Vihra Kylliat can't have another raid to . . . kidnap you or assassinate you, whatever that was. She obviously thinks there's some advantage to keeping you alive. She doesn't want to give that up—not when eliminating your game piece from the board might be exactly what her enemies wanted."

"Hmm," I said. I didn't think it was about advantages for her. She had seemed lonely. Why else would she stumble drunk into my cell a few times a week and do nothing but talk to me? It was precisely because I didn't matter at all that she wanted to keep me, no other reason. I didn't fool myself about that.

"They've been the closest of friends and allies since Vihra Kylliat took office. Since before that, even," Consanza said. "And you've somehow driven a wedge between them. What *have* you been saying to her?"

"It's none of your business," I said, because it wasn't. "How's your family?"

"Worried. Frightened. Stressed. The riots, you know. We live in a fairly good part of the city, but there are houses burning only a few streets away. And now the banks are only open for a few hours a day, until Coin gets their whole mess sorted out. I'd take us away to the countryside for a few weeks, if only this were summer, but travel in winter with small children is too difficult to bother with. Especially with Helena pregnant too."

"You could have left on the same ship that Taishineya Tarmos went on," I said.

"I'm Nuryeven. I belong here. And if I had put my family on a boat by themselves, then I wouldn't have anything to come home to. And the sea is dangerous in winter."

"I'm not criticizing you."

The only reply was a soft muttering and the eventual snap and flare of a flick match, and the faint smell of her tobacco. "So," she said, "now that Taishineya Tarmos is done, I expect we'll be called in for your appeal one of these days. And then I'll know whether I can wash my hands of you or not," she added, more viciously than was strictly necessary, I thought.

It wound down into our usual bickering, while Ylfing made a few small noises trying to convince us to back off from each other—it was about as ineffective as usual. I could tell she was about to storm off in a huff again when Ylfing suddenly said, "Oh. Consanza, it's—"

"Am I interrupting?" I heard Vihra Kylliat ask, her voice uncharacteristically (for my recent experiences of her) sober and cold.

I watched Ylfing and Consanza's feet as they scrambled up. "No, Your Majesty," Consanza said, instantly slick and polite. "Not at all. We were just about finished here."

"Good day, then," Vihra Kylliat said, then banged on my door. "Chant, are you paying attention?"

"Aye," I said. She didn't bother having the guards open the door.

I could just see Consanza's shoes still—she was lingering all she could. Horrible woman, but a decent advocate, I suppose.

"Your execution—five weeks from today."

"Five *weeks?*"

"That is how long it will take for Zorya Miroslavat and I to run the election for Prime of Coin. We desperately need one, ideally one who isn't planning on being an incompetent, criminal idiot. Since all the candidates support your execution anyway, we've concluded that whichever of them is eventually elected would continue to support that, so I've agreed to schedule your execution. And if they are elected and they change their mind, then we'll cancel it. But they won't."

I had to remind myself to keep breathing. I watched Consanza's shoes as she finally drifted off down the corridor—she'd heard. She'd undoubtedly heard. Five weeks was . . . well, it wasn't enough time, but it was something. Ylfing hadn't mentioned that Ivo had left town, and that seemed like the kind of thing that would be immediately on his lips. And whenever the message arrived to you, you'd need time to arrange things, even if you'd had everyone ready to go. Supplies must be gathered, riders raised, weapons sharpened, and then everything packed, and unpacked, and repacked. These things take time, and it's difficult to buy time if no one is selling. "Five weeks more of life is very generous," I said, after swallowing several times to find my voice. "I appreciate it." Perhaps Consanza's appeal would buy us a few more weeks—just a few more, that's all I needed.

"I didn't do it for you," she said.

"No, of course. I apologize. The election, of course."

"The election, yes." She ground the heel of her artificial foot into the floor. "If you had been more useful," she snapped, "I might have been able to convince Zorya Miroslavat to make some other ruling."

"But I haven't been."

"You haven't been. You've been the opposite of useful. You're bad luck."

"I wouldn't have pegged you as the superstitious type, Your Majesty."

"All soldiers are superstitious. My general would have been."

I paused and considered this. "Yes, I guess you're right. Ger Zha had her little good luck charms too."

"How blessed she must have been to not have been saddled with *you*."

"Have I angered you?"

"No," Vihra Kylliat snapped, and turned sharply. Stormed off up the hall until I couldn't hear her steps anymore.

I sighed and rearranged my cushion and blanket beneath me. "Zdena?" I called to the guard. I had spent enough time staring at their shoes and hearing the occasional brief exchange between them that I could match each name to the scuffs on their toes and heels. "I know it's you. I thought I'd tell you another story today." Zdena never answered. None of them ever did. I squinted at the ceiling and wondered whether they'd fall for some amateurish trick like telling a story wrong—like telling them about Vanya and the Four Iron Swans, where Vanya sells them to the villagers immediately because he's greedy, and gets so much money he can buy the biggest anvil anyone has ever seen. Maybe then they'd speak. If they spoke, then I could begin to turn their hearts towards me. Anything to buy just a little more time.

Five weeks to live, a little voice in my head reminded me. Five weeks to live. And I had to make that into eight, at least, if I had any hope of living to see you ride over the horizon. That was assuming you were where I thought you would be this time of year, and that your horses were well rested and your saddlebags full of grain. I want to apologize now, because I know I was asking you to cross the mountains in the coldest, stormiest part of winter. You're not the type to shy away from a little blizzard, but I know it must have been hard going, regardless.

You must have ridden your horses as if they had wings. One day I'll make it into a story for you. I'll tell the Great Khar that your wizards made the horses' steps so light that they danced down the avalanches, and that you sang off the storms until you'd safely passed the mountains.

So there I was, imprisoned, with five weeks to live. I had at my disposal a useless advocate, a nigh-useless apprentice, an inexperienced would-be revolutionary, a Queen who had condemned me, a Queen who wanted to keep me alive for some reason, though she had made her career of killing, and an exiled Queen. . . . Taishineya Tarmos, I thought, might have done me a favor or two if she'd still been around. There would be no new Prime until it was too late to turn them to my side. And so, I thought, if I couldn't turn them to *my* side, it was time for me to turn to someone else's side again. Order had exhausted its usefulness for me, Justice was unassailable, Law was unreachable, and Pattern had evaporated like mist in the sun. I turned my attentions, then, to the exiled Queen. She, of all of them, was the only place where any gamble I took had a chance of paying off—and she would know about paying off on gambles. She was, after all, the rightful Queen of Coin, and I intended to let her know that I thought so. I hadn't a clue what she might do or how she might help, but . . . She had power. She had money. She had resources. And she might be persuaded to help me if she thought I could give her something big in return.

ALEXANDRA ROWLAND

t was done the same way: by pretending to practice languages with Ivo and Ylfing. The guards were so bored with me by then that they never suspected. Ivo had taught the song to a friend and sent her off to cross the mountains, which I wasn't terribly happy with. I'd thought he would do it himself. He seemed a sensible, competent sort.

When I explained to him that we had to write to Taishineya Tarmos and bring her back to Nuryevet, Ivo scowled and Ylfing clapped his hands over his mouth.

"Stop that," I hissed in Nuryeven, loud enough for the guard to hear. "It's not that shocking of a word. You've heard worse." And then, in Hrefni: "Ylfing, for gods' sake, *act better*."

"Sorry," he replied in the same language. "Ivo really hates her."

I huffed. "I figured he would, but we don't have time to be fussy about these things."

Ivo shoved the slate through the slot. *Good riddance to her. I'm glad she's gone and I won't help her come back.*

I rolled my eyes and wrote back: *The next Prime of Coin will be newer, stronger. They'll have public opinion on their side. Taishineya has power now and I know how to get her to use it.* He didn't reply, only wiped the slate clean and shoved it back through. *Trust me. You'll only have to endure her for a little longer, and then it'll all be over.*

Fine, he wrote.

I thought for a long time. *Do you have another friend to carry the letter? Someone from the Stonecutters' Guild, for preference. Or the Carpenters'.*

"The . . . the *what?*" Ylfing said. He must have been reading over Ivo's shoulder. "Why?"

"Because I said so, boy, and because I know how stories work," I snapped. "Now, attend, this is too long to relay on the slate, so here is what you'll have Ivo write later. . . ." And I told him in detail. And

284

I told Ylfing the secret sign the stonecutter or whoever should give Taishineya Tarmos that would make her do whatever I told her to.

<hr />

And that was that. Five weeks while the weather got colder, five weeks with just enough warmth to keep me from freezing to death. I don't know how the prisoners in the lower cells survived. At least my little isolated chamber didn't have the airflow to keep it terribly cold, and the cloak and clothing that Ylfing had brought me, not to mention the cushion and the ratty old threadbare blanket, made all the difference in the world. There was a tiny window—even an arrow slit would have been wide and expansive by comparison, and it was covered in wire mesh pasted over with paper, so only a thin, feeble light could get through. I was cold, but not unbearably so, and in the daytime I sat with my back against the wall so I could be warmed by the firepot. I think the guards went out of their way to keep it topped up with fuel—it kept them warm too, after all.

I spent those five weeks talking through the flap at the bottom of the door to whoever was standing outside. Zdena, with the heel of her right boot worn thinner towards the back than the left one (I noticed her scuffing her right heel against the floor when she was bored); Durko, with the boots that were never polished at all, and probably had never been polished since the day he had been issued them; Vidar, with the deep scratch across the outside of his left ankle, which couldn't be hidden even with polish; Anysia, with her custom-cobbled shoes that were just *barely* within regulation, but somehow far more stylish and attractive than her peers'; Vasileva, with her flawlessly polished boots that never had a scuff or a scratch on them; Mihalei, with the threads beginning to pick loose on the back of both his heel seams . . . I knew their boots like the lines on the palms of my hands, and I had never seen their faces, that I knew of. I talked to them, called them by name, and never once in five weeks did they speak to me. To Ylfing and to one another? Yes, sometimes. That's how I learned their names one by one. I don't know if they ever guessed how I knew, or if they were puzzled and bewildered the whole time. Perhaps they, too, thought I was a blackwitch.

I tell you, though, five weeks is a long time to be telling stories. I was combing through the dregs of my repertoire by the end, telling stories that weren't very good, stories that I had never found interesting, stories that didn't generally get a warm reception, although they were excellent in their own right. . . . I was telling stories that I hadn't told in sixty-odd years, if I'd ever retold them at all. Somewhere in Vsila, or elsewhere in Nuryevet if they've fled the city by now— somewhere there are six guards who have, between them, heard the better part of a century's worth of stories. Who could, between them, be a damn good Chant. And they, like Vanya with his thirty iron swans, have no idea of the wealth they're carrying with them. Isn't that sad? Isn't it funny?

I told them one of yours, one of the ones you told me. Actually, it's been so many years since you told it to me, I'd like to make sure that I remember it correctly.

THE THIRTEENTH TALE:
How the First Woman Tamed the Horse
Woman woke in the snow at the beginning of the world.
She sat up, she looked around, and for miles and miles,
all she saw was empty steppe billowing off to the horizon.
She wandered for the day until the sun went down and she
began to grow hungry. She ate the snow and it melted on

her tongue, and she dug through it and found earth below, and a sharp rock. She cut into the frozen dirt with the rock and scraped it up, and rolled it between her fingers and on her tongue until it melted too, and from this she shaped Rabbit.

Rabbit wiggled his nose at her and twitched his whiskers and leaped all about, and then he sat down and tucked himself up into a little ball and said, "Yes, this is good. Is there anything to eat?"

"There is snow," said Woman.

Rabbit ate a little, but soon he asked, "Is there anything to eat?"

Woman said, "There is dirt."

Rabbit ate a little, but soon he asked, "Is there anything to eat?"

"I don't know," Woman said sharply. "Why don't you look around and find something?"

Rabbit nodded. "A good idea," he said, and he looked all around, and kicked the snow drifts with his heels until the sun set and the moons rose. "Aha," he said. "Why don't we eat those?"

"You can try," said the Woman. "I'm tired from walking all today. I will rest."

"You do that," said Rabbit, and he kicked his heels and dashed off to see if the moons could be eaten. He came back in a little while, with a bowl of cheese curds and a bowl of brown rice. "Here," he said.

"Where did you get those?"

"From the moons," said Rabbit. "You may have them. They are not to my taste."

Woman ate with her fingers until all that was left were three grains of rice in the one bowl and the milky scum of the cheese curds in the second bowl. Woman took the three grains of rice and turned them into a bow, a fine hat, and a clay pot. Then she scraped out the milky scum with her fingernail and flicked it into the clay pot, which became full of milk. "Oh," said Rabbit, "What is that?"

"You may drink some, but I will have the rest in the morning when I wake up."

Woman went to sleep and when she woke up in the morning, the clay pot was empty but for two drops of milk in the very bottom. "That Rabbit!" she said, and stomped her foot, and the print of her shoe filled up with water and that became Lake Qoyora. "Now I will be hungry all day until he comes back, and then I will shake him by the scruff of his neck." But she thought that Rabbit was very fast and she might not be able to catch him, so she scraped up more earth and mixed in a little lake water and the two drops of milk, and made Dog, who was brown with milk-white spots. Dog was very serious, and sniffed the bowl and sniffed all around where Woman had slept. "Yes, this is good," she said. Then Dog said, "I can smell that Rabbit, and lots of other things too. I'll watch the milk while you sleep."

"Good," said Woman. "And if he steals it again, I shall shoot him with my bow."

"And I shall rend and tear his flesh with my teeth until he asks me nicely to stop," said Dog.

Woman walked along the shore of the lake, and she picked up pebbles here and there and flung them into the water, and they became fishes, and she flung pebbles into the air and they became birds. And in the evening, she came back to the camp and found Dog with Rabbit hanging from her jaws by the scruff of his neck.

"What's the meaning of this?" Rabbit demanded. "What have I done, and who is this rude creature?"

"That is Dog," said Woman, "and she is a better friend than you are. You drank all the milk!"

"I didn't either!" said Rabbit. "I only stepped away behind a snow drift to attend to some personal business, and when I came back, it was gone."

"Because you drank it! And now I have nothing to eat."

"I will go back to the moons and get you more if that's what you want," said Rabbit, "only tell this Dog creature to let me go."

Woman nodded and Dog dropped Rabbit, who scampered off to the moons right away and came back with two more bowls, one of rice and one of cheese curds. Woman gave Dog a few cheese curds, and Dog went loping off to snap at fish in the lake. Woman scraped the cheese scum into the clay pot and it filled with milk, and then she fashioned her three leftover grains into a tent and a fine pair of boots. When she went to sleep, she told Dog to guard the milk from Rabbit, and Dog agreed.

In the morning, Woman woke up and found that Dog was asleep and the milk was gone, and she kicked at the ground and cried, "That Rabbit!" The earth and snow she kicked up fell in a great pile to the east and became the Tegey Mountains. Dog was very embarrassed when she woke up and saw that Woman's clay pot was empty again, and she went slinking off into the snow to feel sorry for herself.

"I shall have to make something smarter than Dog and less deceitful than Rabbit," Woman said, and she thought to herself for a long while. At noon, she gathered reeds from the waterside and fashioned them into a skeleton, and then she packed mud around it until it was almost the same shape as she was, and the two drops of milk left over in the pot went into his eyes, and then she had made Man. And Man counted all his fingers and toes and rolled his shoulders and looked at Woman's tent and fine hat and fine shoes, and said, "Yes, this is good."

"I have a problem," Woman said. "And if you help me, I'll let you sleep inside my tent where it is warm, instead of out here in the snow."

"That sounds fair," said Man.

Woman told him about Rabbit, and the bowls of rice and cheese, and the clay pot full of milk that Rabbit drank every night. And Man nodded and cursed Rabbit's name with Woman, and promised to sit up and guard the milk that night. He hid in the tent when Dog caught Rabbit that evening so that Rabbit wouldn't see him, and Woman shouted at Rabbit until he scampered off to bring her bowls of rice and cheese. There wasn't much to eat that night, for Woman had to share the two bowls between herself and Man and Dog, but they assured one another that they would drink their fill of rich, fatty milk in the morning.

Man sat outside the tent with Dog, and Woman went to sleep, but no sooner had she drifted off than Man came charging into the tent, shouting and crying and carrying on. She jumped out of bed and would have smacked him, but she saw he was trembling with fright. "What's wrong?" she said.

"It's Rabbit! Why didn't you tell me he was so big?"

"He isn't! He's small enough for Dog to pick up and carry in her teeth!"

"Then he must be able to change shape!" Man cried. "This was huge, as tall at the shoulder as I am, and its head even taller, with enormous ears and fearsome teeth!"

Woman grabbed her bow and ran outside. She saw that the clay pot was empty of milk, and in the light of the two moons, she saw something very large indeed disappearing over a swell of the steppe.

"That can't be Rabbit," she said to Man. "I shall have to apologize to him. A wicked beast has come to steal from us, and Rabbit has been most sorely mistreated through no fault of his own."

But Man was still trembling with fright, and the thought of a wicked beast did nothing to soothe him, so Woman took him into the tent and made him lie down beside her, and showed him a little of her magic, so that he would have nothing to fear from wicked beasts, and showed him a little of what two people can do alone in a tent at night, so that he would forget about beasts entirely and go to sleep, which he promptly did when they were finished. Woman got up and put on her fine boots and her fine hat, and took her bow. She looked in the bowls and found three grains of rice that they hadn't eaten. She made one into a long, stout rope, which she looped over one arm, and she put the other two grains of rice in her pocket.

She went outside and made Dog lie down in front of the door to guard Man while he slept, and she told her, "If I am not back when the sun rises, take Man down to the lake and see if the two of you can find something else to eat. And be very polite to Rabbit if you see him."

Then Woman strode off into the darkness and found the tracks that the wicked beast had left, and she followed them across the steppe while the stars swung above her and the moons rolled down the other side of the sky and set.

When the sky was just turning green in the east, Woman saw a big shape, and she began whistling to herself as if she hadn't noticed. The wicked beast looked up and watched her approach curiously. When she got closer, she saw he was dark gray, like deeply tarnished silver, and the whole lower half of his face was suspiciously white, as if he had dipped it in milk.

"Hello," she said, "I'm Woman."

"Hello," said the wicked beast. "I'm Horse."

"What a fine color you are!" she said.

Horse arched his neck a little. "I am a very fine color, yes."

"And what muscles you have!"

Horse pranced in place. "They are quite strong, yes."

"And what a beautiful tail you have!"

Horse flicked his tail. "It is very beautiful, isn't it?"

"Very! You are clearly a mighty and noble beast—is there any other in the world like you?"

"None," Horse whinnied, extremely pleased with himself, and added, "I know magic things too," because he didn't want Woman to miss an opportunity to admire that as well.

"Truly? How did you come by those?"

"There is a magic lake with red banks and frothy white

water, and every night I drink it dry, and every day it fills up again. It was after I first drank from it that I got my magic."

"I don't believe you. Anyone could say that they've found a magic lake with red banks and white water," she said, lofty. "So I don't think you can do magic at all."

"I can, though!" said Horse.

"Can you? Show me, then."

"Fine," Horse harrumphed. "I will." He flicked his tail and clouds filled the sky, and then he stomped a hoof and a bolt of lightning struck the ground in the distance.

"Is that all?" Woman scoffed. "Why, I can do the same." And she clapped her hands together and a roll of thunder roared across the steppe, and she shook out her hair and the clouds cleared from the sky.

Horse snorted and shook his head and droplets of sweat flew into the air and became butterflies and shiny beetles. Woman spat on the ground, and the spittle turned into jerboas and mice, which hopped and scampered off into the snow and burrowed below the ground to keep themselves warm.

Horse reared and stomped both hooves into the ground, and burning embers scattered across the grass between them. Woman took one of the grains of rice from her pocket and made an iron box, which the embers flew into. She put the box in her pocket. "We could be at this all day," she said. "How about a different game?"

"What is it?" Horse asked.

"I have here a magic rope. Nothing can escape from it."

"I doubt it!" Horse said. "Have you seen my muscles? They are very strong!"

"Let me put it around your neck, then, and I will climb onto your back. If you can get away from me, then I will admit that you are the more powerful magician."

Horse flicked his ears one way and another as he thought about it. "Well, all right," he said. "That sounds easy."

So he stood still while Woman tied the rope into a halter and put it around his neck and head, and draped the end of it over his withers as reins. The Horse was busy looking at the butterflies and beetles that his sweat had turned into, and so Woman, while Horse was distracted, took the last grain of rice out of her pocket and turned it into a very fine saddle, carved with designs and decorated with malachite beads and gold leaf, and she cinched the girth strap tight and leaped into it before Horse noticed.

"That feels very strange," Horse said, arching his back and twisting one way and another. "Have we started the game?"

Woman picked up the reins and said, "Yes." And Horse whirled round and round, and bucked and reared, and then he began running as hard as he could across the steppe so that the wind blew his tail and Woman's hair out behind them like war banners. He kicked and shied and he leaped high into the air, but Woman would not be unseated.

"Is this all you can do?" she asked Horse, as if she were bored. Horse bared his teeth and ran her to the horizon, so close that the sun nearly burned them, and then he turned and ran the other way until the night wind almost froze them both to the bone, and still Woman would not be unseated.

At long last, Horse fell still and dropped his head, his sides heaving and flecked with froth and his legs trembling a little. "I give up," he said. "You are the greater magician, and I am bested."

"That is because it was *my* pot of milk you were drinking every night, foolish Horse! Are you ashamed? A kind Rabbit took the blame for you, and you will come and apologize to him."

"All right," said the Horse, who was far too tired to argue anymore.

Woman twitched the reins and guided Horse back in the direction of her tent at the pace of a slow walk. The froth dripped off Horse's sides onto the ground, where it melted the snow and sprouted into grasses and flowers.

When they reached the tent, they saw Man and Dog and Rabbit sitting together, looking very forlorn, and Rabbit's whiskers were singed. "What's the matter?" Woman asked.

"We explained to Rabbit what happened," said Man, "and he was very generous and forgave us our mistake, and he helped Dog and me catch a lot of fish from the lake, because we thought we could eat them, but they are cold and slimy and not at all good."

"So Rabbit thought that perhaps they would be better if they were less wet, and he went to get some embers from the sun to cook the fish over," Dog said.

"I had nothing to carry them in, and I burned my tongue when I tried to pick them up," Rabbit finished, lisping a little. "So we have a pile of fish, which will begin to stink, and nothing to eat. What is that you're riding?"

"This is Horse," said Woman, "and he has been drinking the milk."

The three of them kicked and stamped their feet in shock and cried out, "The wicked beast!"

"Horse has something to say to Rabbit," Woman said. "Hush, and attend."

"I drank the milk, and you took the blame for it," said Horse. "I am very sorry, and I would like to make it up to you. Ask any gift of me."

"Hmmm," said Rabbit, looking Horse up and down. "I shall have your beautiful long ears."

"Wouldn't you rather have something else? They're not very good ears at all, you know," said Horse nervously, because *he* thought they were beautiful too and didn't want to give them up.

"They look fine to me, and mine are terribly stubby." So Rabbit got Horse's long, soft ears, and Horse had to make do with Rabbit's old ones.

Woman got off Horse's back and gave the rope to Man so that Horse could not run away, and she took the iron box out of her pocket. She instructed Dog to help her dig a shallow hole, and they piled in grasses and dry animal droppings, and she poured the embers in and blew on them, and soon there was a comfortable fire. Man and Dog roasted the fish, and Rabbit ran off to the moons for cheese and rice. Woman made the iron box into an iron spike and drove it into the ground, and tied Horse's rope to it. "You'll have to stay here," she said. "I don't want you drinking any more milk, but here you can graze." Horse was too tired to argue.

They all ate well, and at the end of dinner, Woman scraped the cheese scum into the clay pot and it filled with milk, and she took the last three grains of rice and made another very fine saddle and two exquisite bridles. Finally Woman took the little bones from the fishes and some mud, and she made a beautiful Mare, which she painted pure white with the milk and the last patch of melting snow. Mare tossed her mane and shied at a stick on the ground and pushed her soft nose into Woman's hand and said, "Yes, this is good."

"This is Mare," said Woman to Man. "And she is kind and gentle, and so she will be yours to ride."

Then she took Mare to Horse, and she spoke to Mare. "This is Horse. He will be your mate, as Man is mine, but Horse is wild and he knows magic, so you must be wise and clever, and you mustn't fall for his tricks, and you must help him learn that if he is less wild, then he will be fed until he's fat, and brushed until he gleams like water."

"What a very fine color you are," said Horse, eying Mare's milk-white coat. "You look rather like a magical lake I once drank from."

So Mare and Woman tamed Horse, and Man and Dog learned to fish and to cook, and Woman made all the animals in the world, and bore children until the earth was filled with them, and then she and Man struck down their camp. When everything was packed, Woman flung her clay pot into the sky, where it got stuck, and she sent Rabbit up to keep watch over it, since Rabbit had proved so respectable and trustworthy. Rabbit was very honored and promised to guard it well, and he walked in circles around and around the pot until the milk in it became a whirlpool.

The last thing Woman did was to fashion a sled using four hairs from Horse's tail, and then she and Man and Horse and Mare and Dog moved away and no one ever saw them again. But you can still find the Tegey Mountains, which Woman kicked up in her anger, to the east of the steppes, and you will still find Lake Qoyora, where Woman stamped her foot, and you can still find a huge hollow in the ground near the lake where she built the first campfire, and if you look into the sky on a clear night, you can still see the whirlpool of milk in the Woman's Clay Pot. And that is how you know this story is true.

———————

Four weeks and six days later, I was lying in my cell that night, alternating between staring at the ceiling and counting the stones in the wall. I had pried a splinter of wood out of my bench towards the beginning of those five weeks, and I had kept track of the passage of time by scratching marks into the plaster of the wall. At that moment, I was contemplating marking the very last day. The last day of my life, I thought. I had almost convinced myself that I had accepted my impending death. Ylfing had come by briefly, early that morning, but he was too upset and afraid to linger for very long—those last days leading up to the supposed date of my execution were hard on him. He did what he could, drank down all the information I could give him, just in case. Consanza came too, less frequently, particularly after my appeal was flatly dismissed. And Ivo, even less frequently than that.

But there was a new national crisis brewing, and everyone was about to be far too busy to think about the wretched little spy in

Vihra's prison. The crisis was that Taishineya Tarmos had flung together a company of about fifty mercenaries somewhere in Ezozza and had hired the fastest possible ship to carry them back. Luck smiled upon her, which only increased her fervor for the cause . . . a cause that had been bolstered by a secret sign, presented brilliantly by the stonecutter who had carried the message to her.

Fifty might not seem like much, and they wouldn't have been much at all, if Taishineya hadn't begun to show her cunning. It was a simple merchant ship from Tash, that's all the port authorities thought that it was, and that's how they marked it down in their records. A merchant ship carrying twenty-five passengers, all allegedly family members of the Captain, who wanted to explore the city and make some investigations into mercantile opportunities in Vsila.

In point of fact, the twenty-*six* passengers and twenty-five of the thirty-odd crew made their way in ones and twos towards the bank: the hub of finances and commerce in the city and the home of the mint, where all the legitimate money in the realm came from.

Fifty men and women walked into the building and calmly, methodically began killing people. In the chaos, they drove out the crowds, they locked the door, they swung the bars down. The bank had a walled forecourt with a fountain, as it had once been the domicile of a prince or someone, years and years ago when Vsila was one town in a nation of warring city-states. It was well fortified. They locked the gates, they locked the doors, they killed all the Order representatives in the building who had stayed to fight, and Taishineya Tarmos unveiled herself before the rest. She pointed out the officers of Coin who she recognized, ones who had been mostly loyal to her, and sweetly offered them their lives to live if they'd swear fealty to her as the true and only Queen of Nuryevet.

Unsurprisingly, they did so without hesitation. I mean, I would have done the same, do you doubt me? Would you have done any differently, offered the choice between death and fealty?

She was called the Queen of Thieves in the street, when the rest of the city realized what had happened—not just the sardonic epithet they gave her during tax season now, but something sharper and . . . well, more literal. Vihra Kylliat sent Order guards to storm the bank, but Taishineya's Fifty Thieves, as they were soon called, picked them off with crossbows and slingshots. Vihra had that siege she'd always wanted to try. I don't think she found it to her taste.

Of course, no one bothered to tell me any of this.

———— ◆ ————

The next morning I waited to be taken to my death. I waited through the afternoon. I waited through the evening.

Perhaps, I thought, they meant to kill me in the dark, so I would never see the sun again, so that no one would be around to make a fuss about me.

I waited and waited, and then I heard Vihra Kylliat coming down the hall.

The cell door opened. She dragged her chair in. The door closed. She sat down.

I stared at her—what was this? What was happening? Did she want to have a *chat* before she killed me?

She looked fucking miserable, and also fucking drunk. She reeked of menovka.

"So," she said. "You may notice that you're still alive."

I just sat there, trembling like a rabbit.

"I suppose," she said, with an exhausted kind of sarcasm, "that you've already heard all the news."

I cleared my throat. "News?"

She leveled her gaze at me. We looked at each other. "Hmm," she said. "Shocking."

"I haven't heard any news."

"That's what's shocking." She let her breath out long and slow. "Suppose we skip all the pleasantries and you just tell me about my general."

"Pleasantries like . . . why I'm not dead? Or what the shocking-I-haven't-heard-it news is?" I was more interested in the latter than the former, I must admit: you can lead a Chant to the gallows, but you can't make him stop gossiping.

"Yes, exactly like those," she said flatly. "Get on with it."

"It seems to me like something happened and it's bothering you," I said carefully. "There are lots of stories about the General of Jade and Iron. She had a very long career. Perhaps if I knew what was going on, I could tell you something about her that you'd find helpful—"

"Taishineya came back with mercenaries and took over the bank," she said flatly. "You're not dead because we've all been distracted today."

"I beg your pardon," I choked out. "She what?"

"Don't get your hopes up. This means nothing for you. She'll be dead by morning. We'll pry her out of there like . . ." She clenched her fist. "Like cracking opening a clam and scraping out the meat. You'd be dead by now, but we've all been too busy with *that* mess to even remember you were here, and I didn't feel much like reminding anybody about executing you." She smirked. "Wasn't my idea to go ahead with it, so why should I make sure other people keep their appointments?"

"I see," I said, and babbled something about Ger Zha that would illustrate the benefits of patience and prudence and avoiding impulsive action. *Slow*, I willed at her. *Go slow. Give Taishineya time. All she needs is a few days.* I hoped, anyway. She needed me, however briefly, if she wanted to win.

If I hadn't been so shaken, if I hadn't spent the day sick with fear, I would have had to struggle to hide my delight—she'd come back. She'd *listened*. My relief could not be quenched even when Vihra mentioned that the prison would be closed to visitors again—all spare personnel were assigned to resolving "Taishineya's little stunt," as Vihra called it, and no one was going to be available for nursemaiding folks about the place.

———◆◆———

Taishineya Tarmos had already broken the rules of fair combat, so no one would think any less of Vihra Kylliat if she did too. Not that she *was* breaking any, of course, because a woman and fifty mercenaries hardly count as an *army*, do they? Vihra Kylliat just had to make sure that no one could get in or out of the bank, because without food or water, how long would they last?

Well, that was a problem. The bank had a kitchen for its staff, with a significant amount of food in it, because no one had been allowed to leave the building during business hours. They'd had to either bring their own lunch or eat what was provided by the bank. Made it harder for thieves.

So they had food, and they had the fountain in the courtyard *and* a pump, not to mention a reliable supply of snow. Water aplenty, and enough food for several days at least.

Vihra could have ended things quickly if she'd been willing to do what was necessary—swarming the bank with overwhelming numbers or tearing it down to its foundations, but there were problems: The streets were cramped, so it didn't matter how many soldiers Vihra Kylliat sent, because only about a hundred of them could be useful at any given time. There wasn't room to maneuver a battering ram, and with the ground frozen, it was nearly impossible to tear up the cobblestones and undermine the walls.

Order's whole approach to this was a sort of incredulous, "It's fifty people in a bank, how hard can it possibly be to take it?"

Surprisingly hard, as Vihra Kylliat soon found out—the siege mentality was not one that her soldiers were accustomed to, and no one liked having to stand the night shift, particularly in the hardest part of winter, which was what we were coming up to.

During the daytime, they stood a solid guard. But the night shift? Well, soldiers are lazy, and the Bank District had something like two dozen coffeehouses.

The rank and file worked out that as long as a senior officer wasn't around (and you can bet that senior officers were *never* around past ten o'clock at night), and as long as the infantry on watch made sure no one came out of the bank, they could go on break in shifts of fifteen minutes—half of them would trot off for a cup of coffee or a bite at one of the coffeehouses, thaw their fingers and toes out, and then off they'd go and shake hands as they passed the other half, who would take their turn. Never have you met a more caffeinated group of bright-eyed young soldiers, nor ones who stayed so warm in the coldest winter in living memory.

And yes, the coffeehouses stayed open all night. They were legally required to close their doors at nine, because of the curfew, you know, but the people who would have arrested anyone for violating curfew were Order, and Order was the only clientele that they were actually serving, so there you have it. I believe the coffeehouse owners made a damn mint off those boys and girls, but that was before everything really started going to shit.

And it went to shit because, you see, Nuryevens have these wonderful *coins*, and the great thing about coins is that they're imaginary.

You laugh, but it's true. If I take out some bit of silver and I say,

"This is worth one good horse," then you have to, you know, consent to be part of my hallucination. And then we have to get a bunch of other people on board with it, until we are all collectively hallucinating that this little bit of metal is worth one good horse, or three goats, or a really terrible horse and a decent pig, or however many bushels of wheat.... You get the picture? Coins are imaginary. The metal that makes them up is real, but the magic that makes them *coins* instead of metal with pictures on? That's all in our heads.

And it's a damn painful thing to wake up to, you know. It's damn painful to have your illusions shattered. No one actually realized it at the time, but while Vihra was besieging the bank? The bank was besieging the *entire city*.

No one gave Taishineya Tarmos enough credit, I say. I couldn't stand her then and I can't stand her now, but I tell you what—that woman had more cunning in her littlest fingernail than an entire basket of snakes.

She drew all the attention she could to the bank, drew Order's forces away from the prison, and so there was very little resistance when the kidnappers came for me.

———◦•◦•◦———

It was a very swift operation, much more smoothly executed than the botched affair that Anfisa's agents had attempted some weeks prior. But what did I tell you? A small group, late at night, one target, in and out and away. Done.

My cell was pitch dark when they opened the door, and I was lying awake, wrapped in my threadbare clothes and shivering so hard I thought my bones would break from it. I couldn't even see the door open, just heard the squeak, and I froze. I thought it was Vihra Kylliat, come to be drunk at me again, but then I saw that there was no light. She would have brought a light with her, I thought, so perhaps it was someone come to kill me.

The door creaked open. Four figures came in, as silent as cats, and—do you remember being a very small child, and lying awake at night? Do you remember staring so hard into the darkness that you swore you saw something move, that your mind *screamed* at you that something had moved? I saw these figures, and my mind screamed, *Blackwitches! Blackwitches!* I thought the ones we'd killed must have risen and returned to finish me off.

They were nearly impossible to see in the dark. And it's *not* my eyes, by the way. My eyes are as good as ever they were. I didn't even have time to shout for help—they pounced on me, muffled me, gagged me, tied me up, and dragged me out, and I thought, *This is it. This is where it ends.* And at the same instant, I thought to myself, *Unless they're from Taishineya. Are they? Are they?*

There was a lamp at the end of the corridor—the single low flame gave just enough light to see the bodies of two guards lying on the floor, but we passed by too quickly for me to tell whether they were dead or simply unconscious.

What I did see, however, was that the people holding me wore knee-length charcoal-gray coats, with scarves wound around their heads and over the bottom half of their faces.

Weavers. Just like before. My heart stopped in my chest. Pattern might have been disbanded, but the Weavers were still about.

Their faces were darkened with ash, to blend in with their scarves and the shadows. There was nothing shiny or reflective anywhere on them—even the dull luster of their fingernails had been buffed off. You know why they wear gray instead of black? It's because sometimes, if there's a tiny bit of light, black is darker than the dark.

One of them stayed to lock my cell door behind us, and I saw that they had to replace the padlock. They took the old one off the door and pocketed it, but not before I saw that it was broken in pieces, covered in a hundred years' worth of rust.

Blackwitch. I could feel that foulness now that I was paying attention, but it was faint—not distant, but weak, like tea before it's finished brewing. It was just enough to make me feel queasy, to prickle at the back of my neck. I think now that that blackwitch must have been . . . younger? Newer? I hear it's supposed to get worse as time goes on. At the beginning, I'm told, they're almost like normal people.

These Weavers were clearly more experienced than the previous ones had been, and they must have been trained in a group. They spoke only in hand signs to one another, and even then we barely hesitated. I was bound too tight to move anything but my feet. There was a Weaver holding each of my arms, and one several yards ahead of us, and one several yards behind. My ears strained and strained to hear which one of them was breathing with a death's-rattle in their chest.

We saw no one. I didn't even hear prisoners at that point. Grey Ward was as silent as an abandoned mine. I only knew that we had made it outside when the cold smacked me in the face. I hadn't realized how warm my cell had been by comparison—the insulation of the walls and the heat from other bodies had made the difference. My feet, wrapped only in rags to protect them from the cold stone floors, crunched now across crisp-topped snow. The snow was cold enough to be dry, a small mercy, but the rags were no protection at all, and my feet were stabbing with pain in moments. Within another minute or two, they were numb, and the Weavers had to haul me along bodily so that I didn't trip and fall on my face.

There was a wagon waiting in a back alley, and I was shoved into it with the two Weavers holding on to me. The third jumped into the driver's seat and flicked the reins, and we began to move. The fourth Weaver, the one at our backs, had vanished. Melted away into the snow and shadows.

I couldn't move even to curl up within my cloak, so I lay on my back, between the two Weavers (also lying flat), and stared up at the sky.

I hadn't seen it in months, not since the first time that Pattern came to take me away. It was a crystal-clear night, not a cloud in all the sky. The moon you call Aghton-qer was the tiniest slipper of a crescent, and Tem-qer, I think, was new. The only light was starlight.

I thought, honestly, that I was going to die. Weavers and black-witches? I thought it must be another attempt to avenge Anfisa Zofiyat. This, at least, was far more competent than the last. I looked up at the stars and accepted it. Heh. I saw the Broken Wagon at its zenith, and I thought it was funny I should die with those stars watching over me, as they've always sent me a little bit of luck in the past. And then a bag was shoved over my head and I was trapped in the dark again. At some point, they pulled me out and dragged me again.

Turns out the Broken Wagon was sending me a bit of luck that night too. The Weavers took me to Taishineya Tarmos. See, when Pattern had been disbanded, the Weavers were at loose ends, angrier at Vihra Kylliat than they were at anyone else. And when Taishineya came and took the bank? Well! She took them, too. *Paid* them.

With the bag over my head, I had no idea how we got into the bank. For all I know, we may have just walked right in the front doors. Sometimes you have a sense of things, even when you can't see—you notice that the echoes change depending on how the walls surround you, or you feel a shift in the movement and quality of the air. The Weavers were so quiet, and the night was so cold and still, that I honestly could not get any clues—for all I know, they could have taken me through tunnels or flown me over the walls.

Then, *warmth*. A breath later, the bag came off and my eyes were dazzled with light. They untied me and took the gag out of my mouth, and someone pushed me towards a beautiful velvet couch.

I can't tell you what it was like to sink down onto those cushions, to run my hands over the fabric. I couldn't quite seem to grasp that it was real—the softness of the velvet, the give of the cushions, even the color. That rich purple was almost *edible*, ripe summer blackberries bursting with sweet juice.

Do you know that your eyes hunger for beautiful things? You can, as it turns out, actually starve yourself of it. Try it. Spend months locked in dim, dingy plaster cells and then look at a purple velvet couch with gilt trimmings.

I almost cried, I'm not too proud to admit it. I was entranced with that damn couch for so long that I didn't notice that someone else had come into the room until she cleared her throat. I looked up, and there was Taishineya Tarmos, resplendent and dripping with jewels, diamonds dazzling at her throat and her wrists, pearls gleaming in her hair and on her fingers, purple sapphires hanging from her ears.

"Surprised to see me?" she said. She must have thought that's what my gawping was. I wasn't attracted to her, mind you—she was young enough to be my granddaughter or great-granddaughter, for gods' sake, and I thought she was an unbearable twit, even if she was a cunning fox of an unbearable twit.

But you remember what I just said about your eyes being starved for beautiful things? You know how wonderful it is to be really hungry and have a piece of soft fresh bread, still warm, with sweet butter and a bit of honey? Or a bowl of thick stew? It's *satisfying*; it hits you where you need it. That's what looking at that fucking velvet couch was like.

Looking at Taishineya Tarmos was like . . . like drinking an entire jar of honey in two gulps. She should have been lovely, but it was too much all at once and it *hurt* to look at her, somehow, and when I flinched and closed my eyes, I felt faintly ill. That's how I think a mortal would feel if they looked at a goddess—like she was beautiful, but it was too much to bear without feeling sick and disgusting. Oversweet. A cake made entirely of frosting.

"Are you going to kill me?" I asked. I wasn't sure anymore. I'd figured out on the way that the Weavers were working for someone, and by their rough treatment of me I'd guessed it was someone who didn't particularly care if I arrived in one piece. Perhaps I had miscalculated once again. "It's just that I'd like to write a letter to Ylfing first, if it's not too much trouble."

"What? No, of course not. *Kill* you?" There was that godforsaken tinkling laugh again. I'd forgotten she did that. I glanced around the room, careful not to look at her lest I actually vomit on the floor, but I didn't see that fluffy little animal she'd been carrying around everywhere. "No, you're going to *work* for me."

Well, that was a better option than death in a back alley and being dumped in the harbor, at least. At that point, I still didn't have any hopes of walking out of Nuryevet alive, and I was still waiting to hear of any signal from you. "Work for you," I said. "How so?" In my letter, I'd only given her the idea to come back and take what was rightfully hers, to use Coin as a weapon. I had implied that the will of the people was behind her. I'd told her this was the moment of her destiny. And I'd said that if she could rescue me from prison, I'd give her the keys to the country.

She sat on a chair facing the couch and folded her hands on her knees. "You've given me such excellent advice all this time. And you can see the future! You were right about what I needed to do, both in the prophecy and when you told me to come back. So I'd like you to do further work for me."

That wasn't exactly what I'd pictured—I'd had an idea that I'd feed her some bullshit and then she'd let me go free, and Ylfing and I would run off west to meet you, and I'd tell you how to sweep all the game pieces off the board, and then we'd be done and I'd be left to my own devices.

And instead she wanted to keep me. Annoying, not part of the plan, but that was when I knew I had her. Do you remember what I told her when I read her fortune?

When we'd sent the message to her in exile, we told the stonecutter who had carried it to take his chisel with him, and to "accidentally" drop it at Taishineya's feet when he handed her the letter from me. *Pick up the chisel*, you see. That's what I'd said—originally, it had been just a whimsy, meant only as a suggestion that she should pay more attention to the working class instead of wasting all her time on silly parties, but as it turned out, it gave me a tidy little back door into her brain. Success at last. At last.

"And," she continued, "because I remembered what you said about most people being fools, and about how politics is really just telling the right story. And you seem to be a man who knows what the right story is, and how to tell it. So you're going to do that, and I'm going to finish crushing Vihra Kylliat. And then I'll be the only Queen."

"There's still the others," I said. My mouth was dry, but this was a woman who wanted something. Something that I could sell to her! Something that would keep me alive until you arrived in a terrifying horde from over the mountains. "Zorya Miroslavat—"

"Oh, she won't be a problem after tonight," Taishineya said airily.

"They're off killing her as we speak, I expect. I have such excellent helpers now. Powerful ones."

I thought of that blackwitch, the signs of them—that rusted lock. The creeping feeling of unease. The way one of the Weavers had vanished into the darkness. I suppressed a whimper. "And—and you've heard they disbanded Pattern? And elected a new Queen of Coin?"

"That's nothing. She'll be dead soon too. No one will even remember her name by Midsummer. You'll ensure that—you'll come up with the stories we'll tell them."

"This isn't my country. I've given you what advice I have, and I was thinking I might just . . . go. It's not my revolution. It's not my problem."

"It's your problem now," she said. "Because I say so. Because your *Queen* says so." She wasn't *my* Queen. I hadn't voted for her. "You can come up with stories that will make me popular and powerful, or you can come up with a new way to breathe water. Either way, I'll make *sure* you get to see your inventions tested—maybe that apprentice of yours will help with the water-breathing project?"

"Oh, come on! Don't go dragging him into this!"

"I certainly will drag him into this if you don't cooperate. You needn't whine about it so. It's not like you won't be compensated for your work, anyway. I'm not an unfair employer—you'll get your own room, and a desk, and things to write with, and three hot meals a day."

"Visitors?"

"What do you need visitors for?"

"Because I'm human! I need to talk to other people!"

She waved one hand dismissively. "I'll think about it."

"Will I be allowed to go outside? Will I be allowed to speak to anyone?"

"Outside!" she cried. "On the street? Heavens, no."

ALEXANDRA ROWLAND

"In the courtyard, then! A morning constitutional around the fountain."

"Under supervision, or alone?"

"With my visitors."

"They wouldn't count as supervision. You'll have someone to guard you at all times, but you may go anywhere in the bank that you please. But remember—I have Weavers working for me now. If you try to escape, they will be able to track you. I don't know if I'd order them to bring you back alive or not. I suppose it depends on how I'm feeling that day."

Having my run of the bank building seemed like riches in comparison to the tiny cells I'd been confined to since late fall. A man could rest a little here. It wasn't what I'd planned, and I didn't hold out too much hope for what *three meals a day* meant. I thought it was safe to assume I'd be given the same variety of plain slop that I was fed in Grey Ward. But it was a step away from the gallows, and so I took it.

"All right," I said, "fine. I'll work for you, for now. Do I get to leave at the end of it? After you're the Queen of all Nuryevet?"

"That remains to be seen. I suppose it depends on how well you do." She paused and turned one of the glittering diamond bracelets around her wrist. "I might be more convinced to set you free one day if . . ." She wanted me to say *if what*, but I didn't feel like giving her the satisfaction. We sat in silence (stony on my part, expectant and then frustrated on hers) until she said, "If you tell me another prophecy as good as the one you gave me before. It seems to have been quite accurate. Or you could tell me several. The more I know of my future and how to guide it, the more likely I am to not need *your* guidance around to help me. You can be sure that I will repay my gratitude with a substantial reward."

I muttered something about how the ways of the gods were

as unclear to me as thick fog, how I could not always just call for a prophecy on command, as if I were ordering wine at a brothel. But in this muttering was also the implication that one might come to me at any moment, and that that event was not entirely out of the realm of possibility. I saw my fate well enough, and I still had a few weeks before I had any hope of hearing from you. A few weeks at the minimum.

Taishineya seemed satisfied and she left soon after, having brushed off another request for a message to be sent to Ylfing. I was thereafter introduced to my guard for that night. I can't remember his name, just that he had a jaw like a cliff face and a nose that had been broken so many times it was almost squashed flat. We'll call him Flat-Nose.

The room that Flat-Nose took me up to had been an office, once. There were four desks of sleek wood with a satin-soft polish, chairs, what seemed like a thousand filing cabinets. . . . But it was not an unlovely room, certainly not in comparison to a prison cell. The desks and chairs had been moved against one wall, and there was a long couch against the other wall, near the windows, with some plain blankets laid over it. A tiny iron stove, its pipe running up and out through the wall, provided just enough heat to blunt the sharp corners off the wintry chill and no more. Flat-Nose poked into all the corners and places where someone might hide, and peered out each of the windows in turn, looking both up and down.

He dragged one of the chairs in front of the door, and I saw there was a chain on its seat. He hadn't spoken a word to me this entire time, but he locked the chain around the door handle and looped it through the arm of the chair. He sat down in it, crossed his arms, tucked his chin into his chest, and promptly went to sleep.

I looked at the desks and thought about rummaging through them to find what treasures they held for me, but . . . there would be time for that in the morning, and better light for it too, so I took off my cloak and my snow-sodden trousers, hung them on a chair in front of the stove to dry, and nestled into that couch. It seemed the softest thing that I had ever slept in—that anyone had ever slept in. A feather mattress could not have been more blissful at that moment. The blankets smelled musty, and the couch was old enough that it had developed a dip running down the middle of the cushions, but I sank into them and was asleep the moment I got the blankets tucked up to my chin.

————◆————

Flat-Nose and I ate breakfast together in silence the next morning—eggs boiled in their shells, with a piece of toast and one thin piece of some kind of salty meat. I devoured all of it in moments, and eyed Flat-Nose's, too, but he didn't look like a man I dared to beg food from. I spent a little time going through the desks, as I had thought to do the night before. Plenty of blank paper, twenty or thirty different blank forms, ink and pens in great quantity and variety . . . A few personal effects of the desks' owners, here and there. A pair of green-and-white knit mittens with a lacy stitch around the cuffs, a calendar with a lot of dates and memos written into it, a pocket-size notebook containing what seemed to be a list of ideas for stage plays or operas . . .

Flat-Nose abandoned me after breakfast. He left the door open.

The next twenty minutes were very strange—I fixated on that open door. I wanted to run straight through it, but somehow I couldn't.

I paced around the room.

I looked at the door from the corner of my eye.

I pretended not to notice it.

I pretended to walk past it as if crossing to the other side of the room, and then suddenly changed my mind and veered towards it, but every time I got to the threshold, I froze, my heart pounding and my mouth dry.

No, I see what you're thinking, and it wasn't wizardry. I had simply forgotten how to exit a room without being bodily dragged from it. Being imprisoned does odd things to your mind.

At last, by sheer force of will, I flattened my back against the wall, squeezed my eyes shut, and sidled out step by step, squeezing against the jamb. Once I got into the hallway, I had to lean on my knees and catch my breath, but that was the worst of it. I looked down the long, long length of the corridor and my head spun at the sheer *space*.

The hall was floored with marble tile and thick red-patterned rugs; the walls were paneled wood, painted with fantastic murals of forest scenes—creatures gamboling amongst a profusion of flowers, amorous mythical creatures pursuing attractive young men and women, that kind of thing.

I know, I know, it *is* sort of odd, and I hadn't thought it would at *all* be in the Nuryeven style. But a bank is a bank, I guess, and pointless luxury always seems to grow out of the walls like mold. The wall sconces were all decorated with tasteful accents of gold leaf, the staircases were wider than usual, the ceilings were vaulted. There weren't any lamps lit; all the light came from the wide windows at either end of the corridor, and through the open doors into the various rooms and offices along either side, but it was more than there had been last night, and more than enough light to work by. The office I'd been stuck in was more drab and bleak than the hallway—I deduced that it must have been remodeled more recently, while the hallway had been preserved in its original function as a passageway of the palace.

How lovely it was to stretch my legs! I spent all the morning exploring the bank, running up to the top floor and poking my nose in corners and cabinets and under tables, fiddling with things that invited fiddling, peeking out of windows and around corners and behind paintings. I found stern-looking men and women in some of the rooms—Taishineya's Fifty Thieves, though they didn't call themselves that, of course. Most of them didn't speak to me; a few of them ran me off like a feral cat. I heard some of them complaining about cabin fever, and I laughed! How I laughed! Those young bucks didn't know shit about cabin fever. I had five floors to wander through completely at liberty. It was only when I tried to go outside that I was stopped and turned back. Had to have my keeper with me, they says. *Queen's orders.*

I asked where she was, and they directed me to what must have been the master suite of the building when it was still a residential palace. When it was a bank, it was the chairperson's office; now it functioned as Taishineya Tarmos's receiving room and seat of power. I knocked on the doors—vast oaken things, with polished fittings and fixtures of hammered brass. They were certainly imported from the south—I hadn't seen trees big enough to make doors like that the entire time we'd been in this godforsaken country.

Someone opened one of the doors for me, and I poked my head in. Taishineya lounged on a couch, a book hanging from her hand. "Oh, Chant," she said, in a tone of exquisite boredom. "What do you want?"

"Can we get letters out of here? I mean, clearly *you* can, with your Weavers. I suppose you'll be moving against Vihra Kylliat next."

"Within these walls," she yawned, "I prefer her and the other one to be referred to only as 'the Pretenders.'" It did not escape my attention that the *other one* was now a singular, not a plural. Ice trickled through my stomach, and I decided not to ask how things with Zorya Miroslavat and Taishineya's other Weavers had gone the night before.

The *Pretenders*, though. Vain bitch, but when you're standing in someone's palace surrounded by fifty-odd people who are apparently willing to kill for her, you say *yes, ma'am*.

"Yes, ma'am," I said.

"You mentioned who you wanted to write to last night," she drawled. She seemed absent, like she was thinking of something else. Or maybe nothing at all. "Who was it? Your servant, was he?"

"My apprentice," I said. "The one you met."

"Of course. Apprentice. What was his name?"

"Ylfing."

"Ill-thing, yes. Foreign boy, wasn't he?"

"As foreign as I am. If I write a letter to him—I'd like to bring him here, you see. To help with my work for you. Teaching him as I'm telling your stories—it'd be a valuable addition to his education."

"I'm not here to provide 'valuable additions' to the education of strange foreign children. I don't see how making up nice things to say about me needs an assistant or apprentice or valet, whatever he is."

I cleared my throat. "And then there's the prophecies, madam, as I'm sure you recall. Unless you'd like me to spend four or five years training one of your other staff to Ylfing's level?"

"He didn't do much last time. Surely it can't be that complicated."

"He is trained in perfect memorization—if I were to have a fit, he would be able to remember every word and twitch I made, whether they were nonsensical or not."

"Ugh. Fine, I don't care. Write whatever you like, take it down to the kitchen, and ask for someone to deal with it. I have *such* a headache from all this."

I went back up to my room—I was going to be so sick of all those stairs by the end of it, let me tell you, but at the time I was thrilled with the novelty of having to walk a distance. I had some trouble going back through the door into my room, particularly standing outside and looking in, seeing how bare and unlovely it was compared to the rest of the building. I didn't quite have to squeeze myself through against the wall the way I had before, but it was a close thing, and once I was inside I found that I couldn't close the door without my heart seizing up.

Once the note was written, I forced myself back out of the door. Every time I passed through, it got little easier, and I hadn't had such trouble with the doorways that weren't mine. It was just when I was going into or out of the space that was intended to keep me in one place, you see.

Took the letter down to the kitchen, and then there was a bit of confusion about where it was supposed to be taken—I didn't know Ivo's address, or Consanza's. There was an almighty row between me and two of the Thieves, but I bullied them and browbeat them into finding out where Consanza lived and taking it to her, and I gave them all the information I had ever gleaned about her—that she lived in a more well-to-do area of the city, that there had been houses burning a few streets away from her, that she was a famous advocate and surely anyone would know where she lived if only they asked around a little bit.

I was rather at loose ends for the rest of the day, and I thought about coming up with some propaganda for Taishineya Tarmos, but it was necessary to consult with Ylfing and find out some news about the outside world before I started that. No one in here seemed to be in any particular hurry.

That's the thing about a siege—they're very expensive for the people outside. As long as no one tries to dig under the walls, or climb over them, then the people inside just have to sit and wait. That is, they wait either for the siege to pack up and leave or for the food and water to run out, whichever comes first. Taishineya Tarmos seemed to have a solid supply of food and water, and she held the majority of the currency in the city via the bank and the mint that it housed, so it was only a matter of time before first wages and then patriotism ran out permanently.

———◆———

It was apparently easy enough to get a letter out and delivered, and to get a teenage boy back inside, because Ylfing was there at breakfast four or five days later.

This time I really did hobble across the room and catch that fool boy up in my arms, since there was no one stopping me from doing otherwise. He was freezing cold and a little damp all over—he'd clearly just come in from outside, and it was snowing then. He seemed taller, too, and he was strong enough to hug me hard enough to hurt my bones a little.

"Thank goodness, thank goodness, I was so worried! Chant, I was so worried! We thought Vihra Kylliat had just vanished you in the night and killed you in secret!"

"Pull yourself together," I said gruffly. "Sit down. Do you want to eat?" Of course he did; he was a seventeen-year-old boy.

That was a nice day. After he ate, I showed him all around the bank, and he goggled at the gilt wall sconces and was driven to distraction by the murals of the amorous mythical creatures, which is no less than I expect of him. It was unspeakably pleasant to be walking with him at my side again. At length, we drifted into a disused storage room on the upper floors and told each other everything that had happened. I saw then a glimpse of the Chant that he'll become one day—he seemed more grounded and serious than he had been, a little more grown-up. I supposed he'd been getting some sobering life experience in the past few months; either that or Consanza was a good influence on him, which is a conclusion I refuse to consider.

"You look better," he said. "Better than the last time I saw you." It had only been a week or so, but I didn't doubt him.

"They let me bathe here, but I have to haul all the water myself," I grumbled. "Taishineya Tarmos wants me to compose propaganda for her. Help with public opinion, you know, so that when she takes over the rest of the government, the people will be on her side." I switched over into Hrefni. "She's taken rather well to the prophecy thing we fed her before. Really took it to heart. She's *all* about the common working folk now, or so she claims." It wouldn't have lasted. People like Taishineya care only about the things that will advance their agendas. If you hadn't come, she would have been back to grinding those common working folk into the dirt within . . . weeks? Probably too generous to say months.

He nodded slowly. "Do you need help with the propaganda?"

"Why? Do you have some brilliant plan?"

"I can think about it."

"There's more. She wants prophecies from me. With me under her thumb like this . . . She has too much access to me. She has me by the throat, Ylfing, so I can't just bullshit something, I can't just leave it to chance. I have to tell her something will happen, something really *specific*, and then I have to have it come true. She said if I could tell her a good deal about her future, so that she didn't need me around, she'd let me go."

"So have you thought of what to do?" he said.

"Yes," I said. "But I can't do it yet." I was waiting to hear that you'd come over the mountains. I had only the barest skin of a plan— originally I'd had the idea that I'd just summon you here and you'd sweep across the country, raid Vsila, break me out, and then we'd all vanish into the snow and live happily ever after. But then I was worrying, and I was having second thoughts about how well that would actually work—what if you could only raise a small band of riders? What if all your wizards had come down with colds and couldn't sing? What if the message had never reached you and you didn't come at all?

So I had to wait for a sign.

"I've been watching things," Ylfing said later, as I was wrapping an extra cloak around him and preparing to send him on his way. "In the city, as I go around. I've been paying attention to people, like you taught me."

I grunted. Did he expect a pat on the head and a cookie for doing the bare minimum required of the job?

He asked, "Have you been outside?"

"They don't let me outside," I said.

"You should look. Go up top and look at the front of the bank. Watch for a while."

"Or you could just tell me what I'm supposed to be seeing."

"It's the Order guards," he said earnestly. "I've noticed them."

I groaned so loud it was almost a scream. "Gods and *fishes*, Ylfing! I really thought we were going to get through a whole conversation without you mentioning some new cute boy you saw! What the fuck happened to Ivo? Beautiful handwriting not doing it for you anymore?"

"I noticed what they were *doing*," he said, rolling his eyes.

I paused and squinted at him. "What are they doing, pray tell?"

"Buying coffee."

"So fucking what? The ones standing outside in the snow, pretending that we're having a siege? They're cold! Of course they're drinking coffee."

"Yes, those. This is the business district; there's something like eleven coffeehouses within three streets of here—at night, after all the senior officers go home, the rank and file has this system." He was getting very excited then. "There's only half of them on post at any given time, because the other half are down at the coffeehouses warming up. They go in fifteen-minute shifts."

I put my head a little on one side, considering. "Huh," I said. "That's interesting. That could be useful knowledge."

"It's just . . . I was thinking . . . Taishineya has all the money here, right? All the money in the city?"

"That was the point of taking the bank, yes. Well done."

"So . . . they're spending all their money on coffee."

"Sure. Idiots."

"What happens when they don't get paid?"

"They walk off and we win. This isn't news to me, kid."

"Yes, I know, but that's not what I meant—they're drinking coffee all night long to stay warm and stay awake, and when they run out of money, they'll stop buying coffee."

"I really am blessed to have such an insightful apprentice," I said wearily.

"Chant! They're going to go through withdrawal." His eyes were shining with his joy.

"Hmm," I said. "Hmm. They go in shifts now, and they'll have the shakes later, if their livers don't give out under the onslaught first. All right. Good. I'll . . . keep that in mind."

"It's *interesting*, don't you think?"

I shoved him towards the guard who was to show him out. "Come back in a few days."

<hr />

Two weeks passed. I watched the Order guards out front, as Ylfing had suggested. There were a few rooms on the top floor at the front of the building where I could easily see them milling about, their bright red coats targets against the snow. They stayed well back, out of crossbow range. There were stains on the snow, as bright red as their coats, which suggested that not everyone had been so wise at first.

The rate at which they were pouring coffee down their throats got a little slower in the few days before payday, when everyone was scrimping. The first payday had been fine; everyone got their money on time, no one thought anything of it. But I suspected (correctly) that those were the last of Order's available funds, and things were about to get interesting.

It had been eight weeks since Vihra Kylliat told me I would die in five weeks, and nine weeks since I'd sent you the message, so we would have been somewhere in the vicinity of midwinter by then, with snowdrifts as high as your eyebrows in some places. Every day I listened for word of you and waited for a sign. Ylfing visited from time to time; I would have tried to get him to stay in the bank, but I needed him out there in the city, being my eyes and ears, scraping together the sort of information that I needed.

I'd begun to write Taishineya's propaganda pamphlets, and Ylfing helped me. I've never been much good at coming up with stories myself; I just repeat what other people have told me. Ylfing, though, he's got the knack for it. I think I mentioned before that story he came up with about Nerelen, the god of wine, and his romance with a beautiful shepherd boy? That's not the only example. It's something of a Hrefni thing, you see—the Hrefni have a collection of folk heroes, and it is a great pastime amongst their storytellers to come up with new tales about those shared figures. It's not as disorganized as you might expect—they put a great deal of emphasis on accuracy in their depiction of these heroes.

So Ylfing was an excellent resource in the propaganda venture. Together we invented all sorts of stories. At the beginning, we were trying to come up with things that were true, but garden-variety truth is so dull. It just doesn't catch the heart and mind the way Truth does, and to tell the Truth, oftentimes you must lie. So we lied: we wrote about how Brave Taishineya was trying to liberate Nuryevet from the tyranny of the Primes, how bureaucracy was a devilish thing and would contribute to the downfall of the country. In Taishineya's name we exhorted the citizens of Nuryevet to rise up against their oppressors. We made wild promises about what Noble Taishineya could do for the country once the corrupt Vihra Kylliat was knocked down from her place of power. We said things about how Enc would give up Lake Yuskaren for good, how we'd force them to pay reparations for the damages they'd caused us in all these little wars. We offered the Nuryevens a dream.

Most stories begin with an invocation of some sort, like *a very long time ago and half the world away*. It doesn't matter exactly when it happened, or exactly where it happened. The invocation tells us that it's set in the Age of Stories, the Time of Dreams, which is beyond any calendar's date and outside any mortal reckoning. The invocation invites us into the dream.

The Age of Stories is also the time that people invoke when they talk about the so-called good old days. "The youth nowadays, hah!" they say. "They have it so easy." Or perhaps: "Things have really gone downhill lately; when I was young, it was better." But it wasn't. Not really. It's all a trick of perspective.

Ylfing and I, we're like artists. An artist can fool your eye into seeing depth in her painting by the use of vanishing points and scale and so forth. Chants can do the same. We invoke the Age of Stories, we convince folk that it was real, but more than that, we convince folk that it's attainable again. It's a time that they could get back to, even though they were never there in the first place.

Or, more accurately, it's a time that Taishineya Tarmos could take them to. We wrote promises into her mouth on those pages. Through our pens, she swore she would change things when she took her rightful place as Queen of All. She'd make Nuryevet a strong country, unified again under one ruler, a country where the men were beautiful and the women were powerful and the children were healthy and bright-eyed.

All nonsense. Words are cheap. Emotions, though, emotions can buy you anything.

When we'd drafted the pamphlets, I bullied a couple of the Thieves into helping us, and we all trekked down into the basement, where the mint was, to figure out how to use the printing presses. There were barrels of ink, rolls of paper, sheets of blank copper, and no type. Of course. Why would a mint have any need of type? They etched the designs of their bills onto the copper sheets; no typesetting necessary.

This caused us only a brief delay in our proceedings, because Ylfing instantly, instantly concluded that we could have Ivo (with his beautiful handwriting) copy out the pamphlets onto the copper for etching. Ivo objected most strenuously, I think, at being recruited to the proceedings, but Ylfing brought him in the next day. I watched him work, not having anything particularly better to do with my time—Ylfing fluttered around him like a sparrow, making admiring noises all the while and asking intelligent questions, fetching materials as Ivo needed them, and so on.

Ivo did not seem particularly impressed with this. I sensed a little bit of distance there, a vagueness. Ylfing spoke to him and he didn't quite listen, and I should know—I've spent my whole life watching people to make sure they're listening to me. Ylfing hasn't learned that yet. I don't think he noticed, or if he did, he must have ascribed it to tiredness on Ivo's part.

But he did a beautiful job copying the pamphlets. He has a lovely fair hand, does Ivo.

We printed a couple of thousand copies of each type that we had, and then we went to work on the next batch.

I had a moment alone with Ivo when everyone else was hauling bundles of pamphlets upstairs. "An opportunity to talk freely," I said quietly, coming up to stand beside him at the press. "You seem upset."

"I'm helping my worst enemy," he said back. "I'm helping the person responsible for starving my family. I'd rather just kill her."

"Have you ever played chess, lad?"

"Never heard of it."

An Araşti invention, which had spread at least as far as Genzhu, and all around the Sea of Serpents—and to you, of course! I remember now; you know how to play, don't you! But you're much more civilized than the Nuryevens, so of course you'd know. "It's a game," I sait to Ivo. "And it's like politics: Sometimes you sacrifice a battle so you can win the war."

"I hate that," he said.

I patted his arm. "Trust me. Be patient."

He gritted his teeth and pulled away a little—he didn't want to be touched, so I took my hand away. "If I'm patient, the whole thing comes down, right? It comes down and we start from scratch with the—with your friends."

"Yes," I said. "Just as you wanted."

<hr />

Two more weeks passed. Order did not get paid. Taishineya held the wealth of the city in the palm of her hand, and under her management there would be no withdrawals.

Heh, except the withdrawal that Order's night shift went through a few days after that. They'd run out of pocket money, and as Ylfing had predicted, the result was not comfortable.

But the Order guards weren't the only ones suffering. Four weeks, it had been, without access to the bank, four weeks without *money*. Do you have any idea what that does to a city? Taishineya Tarmos had them by the short and curlies. People had left en masse to go to the country, where they could still buy and sell things. Where the lifeblood of the community wasn't paralyzed.

There were riots again, worse than before. Mobs of people with torches and any weaponlike thing they could lay their hands on stormed the city granaries and stole every bit of food they could lay their hands on. I don't know if I can impress upon you how bad it was, because you're hearing it thirdhand. All I saw of it were the shadows under Ylfing and Ivo's eyes, the way they practically inhaled food whenever they came to work on the pamphlets. Ylfing got thinner, too. He'd lost some of the baby-softness in his face, and his bones stood out sharper now. He hadn't shaved in several days, not that a boy of seventeen has much call to be shaving—his would-be beard was all patchy and scraggly. And his eyes seemed suddenly too big for his face.

We paid them, of course, for helping out, but it didn't do much.

Taishineya Tarmos. More cunning in her littlest fingernail than a basket of snakes, I tell you. She may have been called the Queen of Thieves, but she was the quintessence of a Queen of Coin.

Taishineya's Fifty Thieves didn't even speak to anyone outside, not publicly. They made no demands, they said nothing for that month beyond the boxes and boxes of pamphlets they smuggled out.

Order was where you went if you had a natural inclination towards following and a good pile of patriotism, and so it took another week before they started actually deserting their posts, throwing off their uniforms, and joining the mob. The remaining ones ... Well, the mob left them mostly alone—what would the point of it have been? Order had no money, had hardly any food. So they got taunted, they got some mud thrown at them, but I think that served only to motivate them to actually make a raid on the bank.

Have you ever tried to get a squad of hungry soldiers going through caffeine withdrawal to successfully take a fortified building?

I didn't think so.

* * *

It was a pathetic thing. I watched it all from my little eyrie in that top-floor storage room. About sixty Order guards, sluggish and weak and chilled to the bone, but damn it if they didn't do their best. They had crossbows, but their hands were shaking too hard with hunger, cold, and caffeine withdrawal to aim true. The worst injuries our side took were scratches. But they shot a lot of free quarrels into the courtyard, and the Thieves went around gathering them up and then cheerfully climbed up to the top of the wall and shot them back. Killed probably twenty or so before the rest finally, finally decided that they'd had enough and turned tail. The snow in front of the bank was dark with blood again.

At least I could see *something*. I held on to that every day, no matter how frustrated I was. History was happening there, right outside those walls, history enough to wade through up to my balls, and the only feet I had on the ground out there were an inexperienced seventeen-year-old and his boyfriend. And my former advocate, if I cared to reach out to her.

Taishineya Tarmos's first official proclamation came just after that—it fell in line with the propaganda we'd been writing already. She declared herself Queen of All, and I wrote up something that used her victory as evidence of her righteousness, which is a classic piece of bullshit, but reliable as hell. Vihra Kylliat we called only the Pretender. She was the only one left. The new Queen of Coin had, as Taishineya had promised me, faded into nothingness. I don't know whether she was killed or if she left for the countryside like so many others in the city.

The other part of Taishineya's proclamation was to declare that she would award a duchy to whoever brought her Vihra Kylliat's head. (The implication was that said duchy would be awarded *after* Taishineya Tarmos was safely installed in supreme rightful power over all Nuryevet.)

The city was already tearing itself apart in the riots, and if the propaganda had fueled the fire, then the proclamation did it five times over.

But there wasn't much time for philosophy. People were hungry by then, and they were still clinging to their hallucination about the value of coins and bills, though that dream had long since shattered. I tell you, the thing to do would have been for everyone to collectively shift over to bartering—a few loaves of bread in exchange for your wheel of cheese, a fine cart for a decent horse. . . . But these people had grown up with the coins, and although bartering did happen, there was a kind of *compulsion* when it came to these little bits of metal and paper with pictures on them.

Ylfing told me all about it—how surreal it was for him, because of course he comes from a place without that particular hallucination. He and Ivo went out on the streets, begging and trying to sell whatever little skills they could think of—at least, ones they didn't need an official license to practice. Ylfing told me about a man who offered them either the heel of a loaf of bread or a single copper penny in exchange for Ivo writing out a note to the man's sister in the country. Now, in a time like that, you'd expect that the sensible thing to do would be to take the bread, because it's clearly more valuable, right? You can eat it. At that time, you couldn't buy *anything* for a copper penny.

And yet, Ylfing told me, Ivo pounced on that coin like it was made of gold. Didn't even look at the bread. Even though the boy *knew* that it was worthless, even though I'd explained as much to him. Well, he should have known, but everyone was hoarding everything by that point, and the very scarcity of the coins had made them all the more precious, at the same time that it had made them all the more worthless.

This is the behavior of *delusional* people. This is the behavior of people who have forgotten that something they made up can be just as easily unmade. This is the behavior of lunatics.

As I said before, money is imaginary. Coins are just a story that some people came up with and told to one another, so they are within my purview and I feel like I can speak confidently about them.

After that first proclamation from Taishineya Tarmos, Queen of Thieves, she began courting the guilds of the city, the third most powerful institutions after the offices of the Primes and the bank itself. I believe she offered the usual sort of deal sweeteners—lighter taxes for guild members, limits on the importation of foreign goods the guilds were in competition with, and so forth. Maybe another duchy or two.

She started with the Stonecutters' Guild, which bewildered everyone but me and Ylfing. *Pick up the chisel* again, you see.

Because, as she knew, as I had told her, that was the thing she needed to do to ensure that she would remain in power. She picked up the entire Stonecutters' Guild, the Leatherworkers' Guild, the Shipbuilders' Guild . . . Safeguarding all the possibilities, you see: anyone who used a chisel. Well, this turned out to be a wonderful move on her part, because there were a *lot* of stonecutters in Vsila, and when you're staging a coup, it's always a good idea to have the working class enthusiastically backing you up. But she was holding their money hostage, so they didn't really have a choice but to support her—politically at least, if not outright.

———◆———

The Thieves had always been suspicious of Ylfing coming in and out of the bank so much, and at the beginning the Thieves had wanted Taishineya's permission every time they brought him in or let him out. After a few rounds, and a few almighty rows wherein I made a nuisance of myself about Ylfing being my personal scout and collecting the information I needed to do my *job*, they relented. Oddly, Ivo was less of a concern for them; perhaps it was because he was Nuryeven, perhaps it was because they'd already lost the battle about Ylfing. They never let either of them discover how to get in or out. Every time, they were escorted through with bags over their heads. They had as little clue as I did.

Secret tunnels sound more and more romantic, but I can't be sure, and you know I would only ever tell you the truth with no decoration and nothing added for the sake of smoothing out the story. That will come later. That's for other people, who weren't there, who didn't ride a few hundred horses down a mountainside, their hooves light enough to dance on top of the avalanches. For you, the truth. And the truth is, to this day neither of us knows how they did it.

Ylfing visited two or three times a week, and I made sure he got a hot meal every time. Even then, when it was getting harder and harder to buy food, even for us in the bank.

"How are things out there?" I said during one of his visits, before he'd even finished scarfing down the bland meal of fish and boiled potatoes that was all I'd been able to provide him.

"Bad," he said. He paused, looking down at his plate in strange silence. "Ivo got thrown out of his apartment. We're living at Consanza's house now. We all sleep in one room, because they've sold all the furniture and it conserves fuel. Only have to heat one room, you see. Drives Ivo crazy, drives Consanza and the others crazy. I don't mind it—it's just like home, everyone sleeping in one room in the winter." He bit his lip. "I shouldn't have eaten all this. I should have packed it up and taken it back with me."

"Of course you should eat it! Finish!"

He shook his head and pushed the plate away.

"You look like a sack of wet trash, if I'm being honest." I'm always honest, as you know. His clothes were in tatters, his shoes had holes in them. Even the cloak I'd returned to him was gone, replaced by a worn felt one that only reached his mid-thigh. "You haven't been eating much, have you?"

"Look, Consanza and two of her spouses can go out and work, but work is thin as it is, so they don't have money for the nurse, and all the schools are shut down besides, so Helena has to stay home and take care of *four children*—"

"Ah. That's why you wanted to take your food home." I wasn't even angry, but he must have thought I was. "You've been giving yours to them."

"Of course I was. I've been hungry before. Those kids haven't." He sat back and crossed his arms at me. I didn't know how to tell him that it was fine. His eyes dropped to his plate, and I could see his stern look waver to longing for a moment, but then he looked away from the food. "There's no more merchants in the harbors."

"I thought the winter sea was too rough for shipments."

He shrugged. "People take risks when they think there's a chance they might profit. But now they know there isn't. They had their holds full of goods, but almost no one had the money to buy things, so they all just went away again. To Cormerra, probably; that's what everyone said."

I patted his hand. "It won't be too much longer. We'll be out of here by spring, if not sooner."

He laughed sharply, and I was a little taken aback. I'd never heard a sound like that come out of Ylfing before. "If we even survive until then," he said.

"Of course we will. Why wouldn't we?"

"People are starving. We're starving."

Ah—he and I had been using "we" to mean two different things. His we meant Consanza and her family and Ivo. His we was much wider than mine—mine was just him and me.

"It's not going to be as bad as all that," I said.

He sniffled a little and wiped his nose—that was more comfortable. That was familiar. Ylfing crying was much less shocking than that steely, moody, stony thing he'd been doing a moment before. "I heard someone talking about some trouble out on the western marches."

I was suddenly all attention. The western marches, he said. The feet of the Tegey mountain range, in other words. "Trouble. What kind of trouble?"

He bit his lip, uncertain. "No one's really sure. There hasn't been much travel into the city. Just people leaving. And with the storms lately, all the snow . . . Anyway, I didn't hear much, just something about fighting. Raiders, maybe, that's what Ivo thinks. Consanza says they wouldn't come until spring."

I let out all my breath, long and slow. It felt like a sign. It felt like it. "All right. All right. I need you to go find out."

"I've been asking around already. I tried to find out if anyone knew anything, and they don't. Just impressions and allusions."

"No, I mean I need you to ride out west and see what's going on. And take a message for me." Things had, of course, changed since the last news you'd had from me, and I had clarified my plans by then.

"By myself?" he cried.

"You can ride," I said. "I'll give you money. You can go buy proper clothing and food—and there's garrisons and outposts on the road, and villages. You'll be all right."

"Oh gods," he said, and looked completely wretched. "What about Consanza and the kids? What about Ivo?"

"You won't be gone that long, boy!" I huffed. "Two or three weeks, that's all. You'll be fine." There wasn't anything else to do about it! And even if I got killed sometime in those three weeks, at least he would have gotten out of the city, and he would have been somewhere safer, somewhere closer to the border, where he could just keep running. And of course ... Well, if he found you, then he'd be safer still.

Look, he's a very stupid boy, and I wasn't sure that he'd be able to do it without tripping over his own feet and falling down into a ditch and breaking his neck, or running off and marrying some smelly tinker he met on the road—you know what he's like.

"Consanza's family relies on me," he insisted miserably.

"I'll think of something, all right? I will. Give me a few days—I'll get you money, enough to give to them, enough that they'll be able to buy some food."

"There isn't any food to buy."

"There's a harbor full of fish," I said, which was true—it's what most everyone in Vsila was eating, if they were eating anything.

He looked, if anything, even more wretched. "I'll go," he said. "But I thought you said you'd never been to Nuryevet before."

"I haven't."

"Then who is the message for?"

I smiled then. I couldn't help it. "Surely you remember the time we spent with my oathsworn-family on the steppes."

He froze. "Syrenen's family?" Of course he'd landmark his memories with which cute boy they featured. "You want me to go *all the way there*? And *back*?"

"No. I think they're the ones causing trouble on the western marches. I just want you to go see if it's them, and if so, say hello. And tell them a few things for me."

"You only *think* it's them? Ivo said the raids don't happen until spring. He said that's when the tax caravans come."

I rolled my eyes. "I know it's them."

"How?"

I cleared my throat. "Well," I said. "Because I already sent them a message inviting them to come."

He boggled at me. "You sent—*how*?"

"Ivo helped. And," I added quickly, seeing his surprise, "so did you! You taught Ivo the song, and he taught one of his friends and sent them off."

"That was weeks ago."

"So it was."

"But . . . but why didn't you tell me?"

"It was just something between Ivo and me," I said, trying to be soothing. I didn't want to send him away into the snow and wilderness with hurt feelings, after all.

"No," he said, "it was between you and Ivo and Ivo's friend. Probably all of Ivo's friends, right? The ones who don't like me because I told you about them. What did you call them? Revolutionaries?"

I honestly hadn't expected him to be so upset about it, but there it was. The color was high in his cheeks, and his expression was tight and closed off. "I'm sorry," I said carefully. "If that's what you want to hear, then I'm sorry. I did what I had to do, and I didn't want to worry you. It's just a little thing. Ivo asked me for help."

"*When?*" he cried.

"It doesn't matter!"

"I've been right there next to him every time he was near you. I don't remember him ever saying anything about wanting help. What kind of help? When was it?"

"It was the time that the two of you visited me. He brought the slate, remember? And I sent you out for monk's-puffs. So you weren't right there next to him every time." I was losing my temper then, getting frustrated. "And after he thought about things, he came back on his own."

"So neither of you told me."

"I guess not. I said I was sorry." He was going to start crying in a moment if I didn't divert him quickly. "Listen," I said, pitching my voice low and a little pleading. "You trust me, don't you?"

After a long pause: "Yes."

"There are things about being a Chant that you're not ready for, and there's no point in being upset about that. You've still got seven years left of apprenticeship at a minimum, by my guess—do you think you've learned everything? Do you think," I said, invoking Hrefni mores, language that would make sense to him, "that you're perfect at the Chant skills?"

"No," he said immediately. "Of course not."

"Of course not," I agreed. "No one would expect you to be. If we were cabinetmakers, you'd trust me to know whether you were ready to learn about working with ironwood or mahogany, wouldn't you? So you must trust me on this, too. You'll get better with practice, and next time you might be skilled enough to learn the tricky, difficult thing."

"You're right. I'm sorry."

"Quite all right, my lad. Just a bit of a miscommunication. Are we all forgiven?"

"Yes. Yes." He shook himself to clear out the fog of emotion. "Let me know where I should go and what I should say, and I will."

He'll be a good Chant one day if he can learn to keep asking questions—notice that he was so distracted with his own reactions that he entirely forgot to ask what exactly Ivo had wanted or why in the world you, of all people, were coming to help with it.

And yet I thank any gods that were watching over me the day that the hands of Fate assigned Ylfing, of all people, to be my apprentice. He's a Hrefni, you know, he has snow in his blood. He understands winter travel as well as anyone can. Even more than you, maybe. No offense, of course, but the steppes just don't get as much snow as Nuryevet and Hrefnesholt. He knew how to survive out there, and if he'd had any other upbringing, I wouldn't have sent him. You have to be born into it, I think.

I gave him another cloak, which I bullied off one of the guards, and I made him promise not to sell it. He tried to argue—he could have gotten food for Consanza's kids with it. We bickered about it for a while, and I agreed he could let them use it as a blanket the next couple of days, but I told him not to be stupid. Cross-country travel in the middle of winter? Without a cloak? He's a very foolish boy, as I've told you before.

I hugged that stupid boy again and I sent him off with another cloak, my own one, and I tried to pretend I wasn't colder for not having it with me.

I needed information. I needed money.

The thing about camping out in a bank for a couple of months is that it twists your hallucination about coins just as much as suddenly not having access to coins. Gold was worthless in here. They must have broken into the vaults and safe-boxes within five heartbeats of stepping foot across the threshold, I swear to all the gods.

There were gold coins everywhere. The Thieves used them as game pieces or as small-wager stakes, the way you and I would use pebbles. Taishineya Tarmos walked around dripping with diamonds and jewels because she'd been looting the safe-boxes too—all the Thieves had bits of dazzling jewelry on them: signet rings, gold bracelets, diamond earrings.... They were as ubiquitous amongst the Fifty Thieves as shoes and smallclothes. They couldn't spend them on anything, except when someone snuck out to buy supplies, and Taishineya Tarmos had strictly forbidden them to take any of the jewelry or large-denomination coins out of the bank, for fear that someone would be able to trace the supply purchases back to them and strike a blow to their comfort and security during the siege.

So. We were swimming in wealth that was essentially worthless in here, and I had at my disposal a set of tools. The Thieves had cabin fever? I started making friends with them, told them what I knew of what had been happening outside. That didn't work too well, since they had a route out and they all got to sneak off every now and then.

I don't know how Taishineya Tarmos kept them on such a tight leash. The promise of more money than they could ever dream of, I suppose. Estates, titles, riches beyond their wildest imaginations ... And a certain essential laziness amongst the Thieves, I suppose. They were fed, they were sheltered, they were filling their pockets with gold ... it was almost like a holiday in the countryside for them, I suppose.

If the purpose had been just to pick up enough to fund Ylfing on a pell-mell ride across the country in the middle of winter, I could have done that in an afternoon. But the boy was going to give most of whatever I gave him to Consanza and her family, because he had *morals* or a *conscience* or something like that.

So it took me an afternoon and an evening instead. I played a few card games with the Thieves. I've never been any good at cheating at cards, but it didn't matter—I'm telling the truth! Would I lie to you? It didn't matter in the end, because after I'd made a meager showing at cards, I asked them where they'd gotten all the coins, and they were only too happy to trot me down into the treasury room, which I had not found before. The door looked like that of a broom closet and led into a long, twisty, cobwebby hall. At the end of it was a thick door, which had been dismantled and now leaned against the wall several feet away. I saw that a few of its several locks had been smashed, but a few others had been rotted into rusted rubble. Beyond was the vault.

I paused at the threshold, my heart beating very fast. Something like this happened almost every time I came up to a doorway I had to pass through, though it helped if the doors were wide open and had something set against them so that they couldn't slam closed and trap me. It helped too if someone was leading (dragging) me through; that just seemed the natural order of things. I couldn't stand to shut doors behind me, and opening them took minutes of preparation and left me sick and weak in the joints. So for a moment I just stood on the threshold there and peered into the vault.

"Aha," says I. It was a small room, with shelves on every wall, stuffed with cloth bags. "And you just walk in when you've rolled all your game pieces under the couch, and you get another bag?"

"Pretty much," said the Thief who'd brought me down—we'll call her Nine-Fingers.

So, a bag of coins, which clinked terribly. I took one. "I'm just going to borrow this," I says, and Nine-Fingers shrugged like she couldn't give less of a fuck what I did with these stupid bags of useless metal they had lying around.

There were some maps up in that storage room I used as a look-out, but after rifling through them, I realized that they weren't what I needed. Maps are useful when you already have some context, and I knew nothing of Nuryevet's western marches. But one of the Thieves did: Flat-Nose, my occasional bodyguard. He'd grown up in Nuryevet before he had left to seek his fortune in fairer climes.

"I was hoping to write a few letters," I said to him brightly.

He groaned. They were thoroughly fed up with me, and I'm sure they wondered how many more people I'd need to write letters to. "Fuck off," said Flat-Nose.

"Don't be rude, young man. *You* don't have to carry it anywhere for me."

"What the fuck do you want, then? You've got paper, and I don't much care whether you use it to write letters or wipe your arse."

"I've traveled around so much that I've gotten the names of places all mixed up. There was one little village, towards the west end of the country. . . . Not all the way out in the country, but not very near a big city either. . . . Do you know of anywhere like that? I'm sure I'd remember the name of it if I heard it. So that I know where to send my letter. A sort of smallish hamlet."

He grunted. "Menova? Seneb? Semynsk?"

"Semynsk! That sounds right. There was another place, a fairly large town? Again, out in the western marches, quite near the mountains? A mining town, I think it was?"

"Probably Derisovet."

"Possibly . . . And one more, it was a middlish town on a river? Sort of in the middle of the country, I think? There was a mill with a large waterwheel and a—"

"Czersdo," he said instantly, and then peered closely at me. "I grew up there."

"Oh, did you?" I chuckled, trying to disguise my nervousness, hoping that he wouldn't ask me about who I knew from Czersdo, because of course I knew no one. I had never heard of the place in my life, nor either of the others. "How nice. It seemed a pleasant town, there on the river."

"Sure, if you like boring," he said.

"My lad, after the last few months, I would take to boring like a farmer takes to his bed after a long day."

I left him alone after that and wrote down the names he'd given me. And then I wrote you that letter, the one with all those instructions about which of those towns you should terrorize and in what order.

After all, I had some prophecies to give Taishineya Tarmos, didn't I? It's easiest to tell the future when you already know what's coming.

———◆◆◆———

I would have been all set to dump the bag of coins on Ylfing. We weren't allowed to take large amounts of coins out of the bank, but I could have had him swallow them or smuggle them somehow, or fill his boots with them. I was all ready. I had the coins, I had a letter for you—except that the next day, he brought Consanza with him.

Damn fool child.

He was in trouble with the guards, of course, because he'd taken her to the place where he met with them whenever he wanted to come into the bank, the same place they released him whenever they brought him back out, and he hadn't told them he was going to be bringing her. So they had no choice but to bring her in to see if Taishineya wanted her killed or imprisoned or what.

Of course, I got dragged into that mess too, even though none of it was my fault, because she'd been *my* advocate, and therefore was somehow my responsibility.

Consanza came over all simpering at Taishineya Tarmos when we were dumped in front of her, and she immediately went on and *on* about how much she believed in Taishineya Tarmos's cause, how much she had always supported her when she had been the Queen of Coin, how Vihra Kylliat was running the country down into the mud. . . . I stared at the floor hard so that I wouldn't roll my eyes and ruin whatever damn game Consanza thought she had going.

Ylfing had caved. He'd told Consanza he had to go on an errand out of town, and she'd instantly and logically concluded that he'd seen me somewhere and that I was the one who had assigned him the errand in the first place.

Gods know why Ylfing thought it was a secret at all. *I* didn't care whether he told her where I was, but somehow he'd gotten it into his damn fool head that he wasn't supposed to say anything about it. And Consanza? She was one of the finest advocates in Nuryevet, and he was but a seventeen-year-old boy. To boot, she was a *mother*. Of course he had no chance of keeping a secret from her. I believe she had it out of him in less than five minutes of sustained interrogation. Once he told her about me, well. The dam had broken, and all the rest came spilling out too.

Specifically, he'd told her about the food. Things were dire enough that Consanza was clearly willing to throw her lot in with the person who would keep her children fed, which I supposed was understandable. It's just that, as usual, I had objections as to *how* she went about it. The woman only ever had dignity when it was inconvenient for me, you know!

Taishineya Tarmos kept shooting me these suspicious looks,

like it was my fault that Consanza was here. I just kept spreading my hands as if to say, *What do you want me to do about it?* until finally she asked outright if I'd sent Ylfing to bring her.

"You wanted me to come up with propaganda for you, right?" I asked blandly. "I had to test it on someone."

Consanza's skin was too dark for her to go purple with rage like Ylfing might have, if he'd ever been that angry. She breathed sharply through that awful ax-like nose of hers. "So it was a trick? A lie?"

"No," said Taishineya. "I wasn't expecting you to take to your work with such . . . *enthusiasm*, Chant."

"What can I say? It's a tactic for the new draft I'm working on. I hope," I said, looking at Ylfing, "that my apprentice didn't tell anyone else."

"Um," Ylfing said. "No, of course not."

"See? No harm done, Your Majesty. And it's clearly effective," I said, waving towards Consanza. "She's infuriating, but she's willing to take your side, so accept the help. That was what you wanted me to do, wasn't it? Have everyone willing to take your side, offering to help your cause?"

"Hmm," Taishineya Tarmos said flatly. "Fine. Welcome. I'm so grateful for your support. So very grateful."

"I need protection," Consanza said in a rush. "And my family. It's still dangerous out there for—for your loyal supporters."

"You can be sure that those who take the path of righteousness will persevere," she said, which rather surprised and flattered me— that was a line from one of my little pamphlets, almost verbatim! "And mine is the cause that is just and true."

"Yes, ma'am," said Consanza promptly. "But I was hoping to really get *involved* in what you've got going on here. You know, volunteer work. Because I'm so devoted to, ah, the cause. I can be useful,

Your Majesty. I'm sure you've heard of me; I studied at the House of Justice, and I received my preliminary certification from, ah, Judge Liezanska Liezanskat, and then I received my secondary certification from Ivan Vetos only a year later. I've never lost a case, Your Majesty. I could be very useful in whatever legal situations you may find yourself in."

"Legal situations?" Taishineya said dubiously.

"Yes. You know. All the paperwork. There's quite a lot of paperwork, being Queen—particularly if you're Queen of All. Five times as much paperwork as you're used to, I imagine."

We could both see how uncomfortably that struck Taishineya. She was the sort of person for whom paperwork was abhorrent.

"It'd be so much more convenient if you had an advocate of some kind to keep track of everything for you, don't you think?"

"And you're offering to do that as *volunteer* work," Taishineya said slowly. "You're offering to work for free?"

"Well," said Consanza, drawing it out into six or seven syllables. "Free-ish, at least for now, until we've triumphed over our enemy, the Pretender Vihra Kylliat. For now, I would love a roof over my head and some food. You have room here, don't you?" she said. "Allow me to move some of my things here. I'm at your service, madam, any hour of the night or day."

"All right," Taishineya said, still somewhat disgruntled by the mere mention of paperwork. "I'll have someone show you a room."

"Although, madam, I would be worried sick about my family. They are all enthusiastic supporters of your cause as well, and perfectly willing to put themselves to work however they can. My husband Velizar, for example, an accountant! Surely you'll need a, um, secretary of some kind to attend to the financial matters of the realm. Nothing as powerful as a Prime of Coin, of course, but just an overseer. And then there's my wife Miriana, a very shrewd businesswoman—much like your own mother, I'm told, ma'am! My whole family is willing and able to advance your cause and secure your power."

"How many are there in your family?" Taishineya Tarmos growled.

"My three spouses, and our four children," Consanza said promptly. "Soon to be five."

"And your personal secretary," I said, clearing my throat pointedly. "Ivo what's-his-name, right? Her Majesty may have met him in passing recently."

"A copyist! A trained court scribe. He'd make a wonderful assistant for you," Consanza said fervently. "He has lovely handwriting."

"Three spouses, five children, and your secretary?" she said, blinking. "That's all? That's your whole family?" She relaxed. "Well, that's fine. The way you were asking, I thought you had a big one."

Nuryevens. I tell you.

So Consanza's family was smuggled into the bank and given two nice rooms on the floor above mine. I met Miriana and Velizar in passing, but I didn't think that we would get along very well, so I kept out of their way—they were very much like Consanza, and I could see why the three of them had been friends since their youth. They all three had that same wryness to them, the same dry humor, the same sharp attention. The three of them in a room together moved like a pack of rangy hunting dogs—or wolves, perhaps.

It seemed like I kept running into Helena every five minutes, though, no matter where I went in the bank. She's a nice girl. Soft face, soft eyes, looked like she'd been soft and plump all over before food got so hard to come by. She was huge-bellied with child, and I remembered Consanza said it was due in late winter or early spring.

She spent much of her time playing with the children, reading books to the older ones and making paper dolls with the younger. She was nothing like the other three. If anything, she reminded me of Ylfing.

I n the tension and minor chaos of moving Consanza's family in, I managed to slip a handful of coins and the fateful slip of paper into Ylfing's pockets. It was just our luck that Ivo walked in right as we were whispering together.

He looked Ylfing up and down, took in the cloak and the satchel at his feet. "Are you going out?"

"Actually, I . . ." Ylfing glanced at me, and I shrugged.

"I'm sending him off for a little while. The whole nation needs to hear about the evils of the Pretender. It won't work if it's the city folk against the country folk. So he'll be taking the pamphlets with him and spreading them about in some of the smaller towns. And he's sending some more through the post."

"Oh," said Ivo. "How long?"

"A couple weeks. Two or three."

Ivo nodded mildly. "All right." He did not seem to be much bothered about this, and then he turned away.

Ylfing went to him and took his hand. "Aren't you going to say good-bye?"

"Oh, you're leaving now?" He still did not seem much bothered. "Good-bye, then."

Ylfing beamed and leaned forward to kiss him.

Ivo didn't kiss him back. I couldn't help but notice. I busied myself and my attention with some things on the other side of the room and held my tongue.

Off Ylfing went, and I went back to waiting. At least this time I had something to do—lots of things to do. I wrote articles and essays about how Taishineya Tarmos would . . . I don't remember what I said, exactly. Something about *free the people of Nuryevet from the tyranny that has too long oppressed them*, more of that kind of thing. It was all pretty standard stuff, as revolutionary propaganda goes. With every passing day, there were fewer Order guards standing siege outside. They tried to storm the bank a couple more times, and bless their stubborn little hearts for trying. In general, we were left well enough alone. A severe blizzard all but crippled the city—more than it already was, of course. I know many people left for the country. I wrote speeches about how Taishineya Tarmos would bring stability and serenity back to Vsila, and I sipped tea and ate a hot dinner every night while the city struggled to survive. This part is all a little muddy and vague for me because, obviously, I'd sent my primary source off into the backcountry.

One day Taishineya looked out the window and said, "I'm sick of all the snow in the courtyard. I want to go for a walk. Don't we have anyone to clear all this away?"

There were exactly three Order guards on duty outside. At that point, we could have overtaken them, but then what? We couldn't take the city with fifty people, no matter how weak it was. And Taishineya felt it wasn't dignified, and I rather agreed. We would be handed the city on a silver platter, and we would wait smug and patient in our fortress until such time as that happened.

But because Order was so light then, Thieves floundered through the snow out to the gates and, so I hear, found a few city kids trying to break into the shops across the street. Even with Order standing right there! But of course the guards didn't give a shit—to do a job, you either get paid in money or in passion and personal satisfaction. The ones who were left were the ones who really, really believed that *some-one* had to guard the bank. The siege was an ideological thing for them. The kids on the street, though? Fuck it. That wasn't part of the ideology.

"How would you like to earn a little money?" said the Thieves to the kids.

"Doing what?" said the kids, rightfully suspicious.

"Shoveling snow. We'll pay you."

Pay! Pay! People came out of the woodwork to shovel our court-yard, to Order's frustration and chagrin, but the Thieves just kept a cheerful crossbow trained on every soldier they could see and they had to stay out of range or step up to their deaths.

The courtyard was clear in an hour, and we paid the thirty people who had gathered a penny apiece, and sent them away singing the Queen's praises.

———————◆◇◆———————

Taishineya lost her patience from time to time. She'd decide suddenly that dignity was not at all important to her, and that she wanted to take the city right now, immediately, as soon as possible. So what that she had only fifty people? The city supported her, she said. Everyone in the city supported her tremendously.

I held her back. "It's not time yet. It's not time," I said.

Thing was, hardly anyone was coming into the city in those days—no one was clearing the roads, and there wasn't a great system of information. It was pure chance that we heard that a band of riders had ransacked Seneb—Nine-Fingers heard about it one night when she snuck out, I think. There was some brothel that she liked to go to, somewhere on the other side of town.

I didn't know if it was you. I hoped it was. I took a chance.

I was lucky that I overheard the Thieves talking about it amongst themselves—Nine-Fingers had just gotten back, and she was emptying the snow out of her boots in the kitchen. Off I whirled to Taishineya Tarmos and banged on the door as loud as I could. She opened it, and I fell at her feet as if in a dead faint. "Gods above! What's the matter with you?"

I groaned and rolled onto my back. "It's happening," I gasped. "It's time!"

"Time?" she said, and fell to her knees next to me. "Time for what?" she gasped. "Is it a prophecy? Tell me!"

"The enemy bites at our flanks!" I wheezed, clutching at her hands. "You must rise up and repel them! The furious wind comes from the west!" I garbled a bit after that and rolled my eyes back in my skull, frothed at the mouth for dramatic effect, and pretended to fall senseless.

I heard Taishineya Tarmos's skirts rustle as she got to her feet. "Ugh," I heard her whisper to herself. "If he dies in here, I'll have to move to a different room." She pushed the door farther open and called for the Thieves. I kept moaning and lolling my head about as they picked me up and dragged me into the kitchen, propped me up next to the stove.

"Where . . . am I?" I creaked after a few more minutes of this. "What happened?"

"You fainted on Her Majesty, apparently," Nine-Fingers said.

"F-fainted?" I accepted a cup of weak broth. "Did I say anything?"

"Hell if I know, we're only the ones who dragged you in here. Someone go tell her he's awake, would you?"

Obviously Taishineya Tarmos would never step foot in a kitchen—gods forfend!—so there was a bit of foolish back-and-forth that I had to endure in subdued silence until someone decided to just carry me back to her room so she could question me herself.

I remained obstinately vague and pathetic, despite her increasingly frustrated queries, even after she called Consanza in to help her, supposing (I suppose) that Consanza knew me best out of anyone in the building and might be able to get me to be more useful. She wasn't able to, of course, and she seemed deeply disturbed by my pathetic, feeble-old-man act.

"But what did I say? I don't remember what I said! Where's Ylfing? I want Ylfing," I quavered.

"Oh stop," Consanza said. "He's out on that *errand* you sent him on." Ivo might not have particularly cared that Ylfing was absent, but Consanza? Oh, she was furious. I'd explained to her in simpering tones that it was all for Taishineya's glory, because weren't we all servants of the Queen now?

"Chant, focus!" Taishineya Tarmos hissed. "What ferocious wind from the west? What enemy?"

"Eh, what's that?" Nine-Fingers said, and I would have kissed her right then, if only I'd been able to reach. She was extremely tall even when I wasn't sitting down, you see. Quite broad in the shoulders, too, and heavyset. "Enemy in the west? Have you already heard about it, then?"

"Heard what?" Taishineya Tarmos asked.

"Oh—Umakha riders pillaged a border town. Burned the Order garrison to the ground, killed every soldier there, kidnapped some folk and some livestock, looted everything that wasn't nailed down. The usual shit, they do that every year in these parts. That's what the boys at the whorehouse said, anyway. I dunno if it's true."

"That's strange. I've never heard of them coming so early in the winter. It's always been closer to spring, after the worst of the snows." She sat down slowly at the vast desk that dominated the room. "Huh. I suppose you were right, Chant."

I sniffled and tried to look pathetic. "The Umakh. They are well known?"

"Yes, but they're mostly an annoyance in the capital—we hear about them, but they never come this far. Wretched thieves, they are. They're a scourge in the west—no matter how many Order soldiers we send with the Coin caravans . . ." She shook her head bitterly. "They cost us a lot of money."

"People are afraid of them," I said. "Use the fear. Ask Order to break from Vihra Kylliat and come to your side. Send them out on campaign to fight off the raiders."

"You want me to declare *war* in the *middle of winter*?"

"You hold the coin," I said. "Loosen your fist a little. Let it trickle out and they'll come running, like dogs in a drought."

"It will take some time," Consanza said. "Getting the troops in order, fitting them out, supplies, horses. With the city like it is now, it might be months."

"It will recover," I snapped. "Order is powerless, the city is crippled. Declare yourself Queen *now*, and announce that you'll defend the realm from the western devils. Nothing like a war to stimulate the economy."

"Or to drain it dry," Consanza muttered.

"No," Taishineya Tarmos said. "If Chant says we go now, we go now. He was right about picking up the chisel." Consanza didn't know what Taishineya Tarmos was talking about—she gave the Queen a rather odd look and walked out of the room without another word. Taishineya Tarmos turned to me and said, "So how do we do it?"

"Renew the offer of a duchy for the person who brings you the Pretender's head. Add a thousand-mark bounty and a hot meal on top of it." I sipped the broth a little and eased back my playacting. "No one really believes in duchies at a time like this, but money and a steak dinner? They'll deliver her by tomorrow morning, tied up with a bow. Just in time for Long Night."

———◆———

Taishineya Tarmos did all I advised her to do. I wrote another essay, lambasting the "former" government as a hotbed of greed and corruption, and I called for a return to the old days, when there was one person in charge and that person could be relied on to know what was best for the realm. We used huge amounts of the paper in our stores printing pamphlets and sent out crates of the things. We could have let them snow down on the city like drifts; we could have flung them into the sky from the rooftops and let the wind carry them.

Vihra Kylliat tried to rally Order with appeals to their patriotism, but it was all for nothing. When the dam finally burst, when Order tore off their colors and turned against her, Vihra Kylliat holed herself up in the former Tower of Pattern—the best defensible structure in the city besides the bank. It was almost purpose-built for protecting a Prime who was under threat of assassination at any moment, regardless of whether that threat was real or a paranoid fantasy. And then *she* was under siege, with none of the advantages and amenities that we had enjoyed. She and her few bodyguards, like us, had access to clean water from the drifts of snow that collected on Pattern's flat roof. But they had no way of smuggling in food—or at least, they had no knowledge of the ways they might do such a thing. We'd cornered her, then. It was only a matter of time.

People came to Taishineya Tarmos's side, and then other people went to Vihra Kylliat's side. And then things happened as they always do in these sorts of situations: debates got heated and turned into arguments, and then into brawls. And once the bloodshed starts, it's difficult to stop it. People died for one or the other of them. There were streets, I heard, where you couldn't see a speck of white snow; it was all crimson until the next snowfall, and then it was pink. The ground was frozen too hard to dig graves, and no one was willing to spare the wood to burn them, but they had rocks aplenty and a nice harbor right outside their doorsteps. Burial at sea, it was. I suppose that must have helped the city recover too—the rotting bodies in the bay brought in schools of fish to eat them, and the fishermen brought in several impressive catches. Taishineya Tarmos bought up every fish that was brought in and made it known on Long Night's Day that anyone willing to follow her banner could come collect the fish for free. A midwinter gift, a gesture of goodwill to the people.

There were a few moments, in the endless monotony of printing those blizzards of propaganda, when Ivo and I were alone in the room together. I spared a pitying thought for poor Ylfing, who had to miss the admittedly wondrous sight of Ivo, in the overwarm, stuffy mint, working the presses with his coat and kirtle off. He cranked the heavy press down, cranked it back up, peeled the page off. . . . All shining with sweat like that, he reminded me of a young man I had once known, but I don't much like to talk about my personal business.

"It was kind of you," I said, "to look after Ylfing for all that time."

He looked at me, his expression flickering, and then deliberately looked away, as if the press crank required his whole attention, as if he hadn't done it two hundred times already. "It was nothing," he said, in a pleasant, neutral tone that I found highly suspicious. He was angry. He resented me for working for Taishineya, for talking him into doing it too. He probably wondered whether I could really keep the promises I'd made him; news of raiders didn't mean anything. He knew well, because I had explained to him, what my plans were—to let Vihra and Taishineya fight each other until one was victorious, with a weak and ragged force behind her, so that things would be as easy as possible for you.

Ivo didn't know me like Ylfing did, like Consanza did. He wasn't looking at me, so he couldn't see how I stared holes into the side of his head. I was in the process of deciding that I actually didn't like Ivo at all, beautiful handwriting be damned, revolutionary tendencies be damned. "He's a nice boy, isn't he?"

"Yes," said Ivo.

"I miss him a lot, don't you?"

A split-second pause. "Of course," said Ivo.

It was at that point that I decided that Ivo didn't deserve to have me play fair, so I stopped. "You know, young man," I said, letting my tone be colored with a suggestion of sternness, "that Ylfing is my apprentice, but what you may not know is that he is like a nephew to me."

"Okay," said Ivo. He lifted the press and picked at the corner of the page.

"And I don't know how you do things in these parts, but if you're planning on asking him to marry you, you'd better ask my permission first, in the absence of his actual parents."

Ivo choked, and the ink on the page that he was peeling off smeared horrifically. "I . . . ," he said.

Now, that's not how they do it in Nuryevet, but it's also not how they do it in Hrefnesholt or, for that matter, Kaskinen. It's got nothing to do with Chanting, either. "I'm not going to push you into anything, lad," I said, holding my hands up. "Don't get me wrong. I just thought it'd be all to the good if you and I had an understanding."

Ivo cleared his throat loudly and crumpled up the ruined page.

He turned to look at me, all prim and businesslike. "You needn't worry. Ylfing and I aren't like that."

"Oh," I said, feigning surprise. "Aren't you?"

"No," he said firmly.

"I don't understand. What are you saying, lad?"

"Just that."

"Is there something *wrong* with him, that the two of you aren't 'like that'?" This was all purely to fuck with him. I may complain about Ylfing's *taste*, but his decisions are his own.

"No," Ivo lied. "We just aren't like that."

"Hmm," I said. "I see."

And I did see. I saw that this was not going to end well.

———

I took a gamble one evening. I collapsed in a fit in front of a few of the Thieves and babbled another so-called prophecy for them. The furious west wind would crash down on the village of Semynsk and leave it in ruins.

They couldn't fetch Taishineya quick enough for her to witness my performance herself, which was my own slight error. Fortunately, the Thieves had heard my babble clearly enough and relayed it to her while I lay there wheezing on the ground, completely unattended.

"Semynsk?" Taishineya said. "The furious wind—the Umakha raiders again?" She frowned. "They're still on the move? That's . . . unlike them." There was a general murmur of agreement, more sincere than the garden-variety ass kissing one might expect. Of course, we all knew your habits—come over the mountains sometime in the late winter or early spring, steal a few sheep, knock over some tax caravans and tragically slaughter the soldiers, and ride home soon after. Clean and simple. No reason to linger.

The Nuryevens were always so focused on the Order soldiers that died defending the caravans that they never thought to wonder why the Coin ministers generally survived to make it home with the horrible story—and it's because they never tried to fight you, wasn't it? They were all soft, boring men and women with good heads for numbers and a comfortable plumpness from spending most of their careers behind desks. It would be *beneath* you to kill someone cowering in a cart, trying to hide.

Neither did these city folk know what you did with the money. Even I didn't know until Ivo told me about all the times a raiding party would amble into his town with their saddlebags full of freshly stolen gold from the caravans that had just stolen it themselves from the peasants. He said they'd buy the good horses, if there were any, for bafflingly exorbitant prices, and no one quite knew why, when you had no qualms about taking sheep and goats.

Oh, yes, I should apologize—I did end up explaining that to Ivo. Don't be upset with me, though, I only told him the bare minimum—just that horses are sacred and can't be stolen. Just that they must be bought honorably, and that you wouldn't want to insult the horse by haggling. That's all I told him, I swear it.

"Should we send word to Semynsk?" Taishineya mused absently. "A warning, of sorts, so they're ready to fight? Or do you imagine it's too late for all that?" She finally took notice of me. "Chant, is it too late?"

I only moaned a little in reply.

"Oh, for heaven's sake, someone take him up and put him to bed," she snapped. "And—I don't know, find me Consanza and Miriana and send them to my chamber to discuss this." Taishineya was fed up with the Thieves. They were a rough, crass sort, and none of them made any kind of competent adviser.

I was hauled off to that squashy couch in what served as my room. Under the warm cover of a thick cloak, I took the opportunity to have a brief nap.

I woke to a soft touch across my forehead and pried my eyelids open.

Helena leaned over me, concerned. "Sorry to wake you, Chant," she whispered. "I heard something happened—you took ill?"

I pondered my options. "A little," I said weakly. "I have some gift of prophecy that comes on me in odd moments. It takes a lot out of me."

"How frustrating that must be. Can I get you anything? There's fish-bone broth in the kitchen."

I had no use for fish broth, but the offer softened me right up. I extricated one arm from the piles of wool and patted her hand. "I'm all right, girl. You're too kind."

She smiled, and her smile was a comfortable afternoon by a cool, shaded forest brook in the heat of summer. "Anything else you need? Some company for a little while? Or would you prefer to be left alone?"

More and more charming by the minute. I said before that Consanza and I are quite similar people, and in that moment I could completely understand why Helena had turned her head so. "I wouldn't mind company, if you're free."

She laughed and perched on the edge of the sofa by my knees. "If *I'm* free! Grandfather, I've hardly exchanged three words with you these last weeks. You're always running about up and down the stairs and into the basement, or hunched over a desk to scribble. *You're* the busy one, grandfather."

I pushed myself up a little, and she immediately helped tuck a few cushions under my back and shoulders. Her face was intense with concern. "Important work to do, girl," I said demurely.

"Of course. But you should take care of yourself. If the fits of prophecy take such a toll on you, you must be sure to rest and recover your strength."

I decided she was a very nice young lady. "Consanza said you were a schoolteacher."

"Oh, yes." A light came into her eyes at the mention of Consanza. "I love children. But you're something of a teacher yourself, aren't you?"

"Bah, Ylfing's just an apprentice, that's not really—"

"No, I meant in what you do. Consanza was having one of her little mutters about it—oh, months ago. Right when they gave her your case. It must have been after the first time she met with you in the prison."

"What did she say, exactly?"

"Well, she told us about her cases, and she told us a little about you—not very much, because of course there are things she has to keep secret. But she said you were like a storyteller, and like an advocate, and like a teacher, and like a merchant. Velizar pouted all through dinner that he'd gotten left out—but you're not much like an accountant, are you?"

I decided not to lecture her about the uselessness of money and how it wasn't real at all. "No, I'm not much like an accountant." I paused. "Those other things, though, they're ... part correct, all of them."

"So tell me about the parts that are like a teacher." She gave me a brilliant smile, and I decided that I liked her.

———

We heard, not too long afterwards, that Semynsk was in ruins—and yes, I know now that that was an accident. I take responsibility. I did tell you to lay waste to every Order garrison you could get your hands on. Temay Batai explained the whole thing, about setting the fire and how the wind shifted unexpectedly and carried burning embers to the thatch roofs a few streets away.

Even when I first heard the news, I was a little bewildered, and I assumed something odd must have happened. Besides that, I felt a great rush of relief just to hear of your movements again, but tempered it immediately—it could have been a coincidence, and I still had no way of knowing for sure if Ylfing and my message had reached you. Semynsk was a town near the border, as Flat-Nose had told me.

I decided to be reasonable, and so I had to totter back up those infernal flights of stairs once again, up to my quiet little storage room, where I found a map to mull over.

It took ages to find Semynsk on it. The light in that room wasn't very good, you see. North-facing windows. Nothing to do with my eyes. They're as good as ever they were.

Here, I'll draw it out so you can see it as I did.

According to the map, Nuryevet is shaped like this, sort of a squashed monk's-puff. All the way east, right on the coast where the Osered River meets the Grey Sea: Vsila. Over here in the far west, the Tegey Mountains. On the far northern end of those, the Tegey Pass.

Now, Ylfing's message instructed you to come across the pass and attack three key towns on three specific days: First, Semynsk; three days later, Derisovet; five days after that, Czersdo. As I mentioned, you were free to do as you liked and plunder any other towns that struck your fancy, but I needed those three towns left smoldering on those three precise days.

But when I looked at the map, I saw something that alarmed me. Look as I draw it: Semynsk? *Here.* South of an Osered tributary, alarmingly far south of the Tegey Pass. I looked at that and I said to myself, *Oh gods, what in the world?* I should have double-checked with Flat-Nose. I should have made sure that I was giving you a workable, practical schedule. Not to offend you, but I had concern for your horses. I had horrible visions of them ridden lame for the sake of my stupid scheme.

Derisovet was . . . distressingly far from Semynsk, all the way up near the north coast, and Czersdo was off in the corner of nowhere, with no landmarks other than Lake Yuskaren—Nuryevet is so small, particularly compared to your lands, but the map showed these towns days and days' rides apart, and that would be in amicable weather, not the middle of winter. I cursed my foolishness thrice and thrice again. I'd gotten lucky with the prophecy about Semynsk—luckier than I should have been. Luckier than I deserved. But there was no way you could keep to the schedule I'd given you, and so there was no way for me to guess when you might reach the towns, if you were even able to find them at all.

My plan was in ruins, and it was my own damn fault.

Flat-Nose found me there some time later. I was standing next to the window with my forehead against the glass, trying to convince myself that the cold would wake me up and shake some new idea loose, some new plot to get myself out of this awful mess.

He didn't bother with preamble: "She wants to see you," he grunted. None of them ever specified who *she* was, but they didn't need to.

I sighed heavily and didn't move away from the window. Snow was falling lightly. I pressed my forehead more firmly against the windowpane and concentrated on the burning cold.

"You hear me? I said she wants to see you. Now."

So I went to see her.

L et's just go now!" she said, petulant as a child. "Vihra's in her stupid Tower, and we have her surrounded—"

"There's still people in the city who are against you, madam," I said for the thousandth time. I was sitting at the table in her chambers and watching while she paced about the room. The table was scattered with papers, many of which were my propaganda pieces. Consanza stood at the back of the room, her arms crossed. She'd had no time for me; she'd barely said a dozen words to me since she and her family had arrived. Hadn't even introduced her spouses to me. I suppose it wasn't a surprise. Her attention and energy were fully occupied with brownnosing Taishineya, sometimes so ardently that I thought it might have approached flirting. "The streets aren't safe; there's fighting all over the city. Vihra—er, the Pretender still has supporters in the city, and it's not safe yet for us to leave."

She scoffed.

"It's not *dignified*," I insisted. "You wanted them to hand you the city on a silver platter, didn't you? You wanted there to be no question. You need the consent and mandate of the people, or you'll be off the throne again within the year." Or the season. Or the month. But that was not for her to know. All I needed was for her to stay in power just a little longer; better to put you up against an incompetent and easily led ruler than someone with experience. Even so, the tides were shifting with her.

"Nonsense."

"We're building our power with words," I said, gesturing to the pamphlets across the table. "And with total economic control. But neither of those are *real*. Swords are real. Arrows are real. The knife in your back from some former Order guard who thinks you a thief and a usurper? That's real."

"The people will give me their mandate when they see me *crush her*."

"Patience! The time is not yet come." I still felt as scattered as a spilled bowl of grain over what I'd discovered on the map, and I was nervous of her—she'd been coming into her power lately, realizing that she didn't have to listen to me, or to Consanza, or to anyone else who told her something she didn't want to hear. She was not yet a sinking ship, but she was scraping against the rocks, and I was just the rat in the hold with a dream of dying dry. I had to hold on to my way out.

I wanted to stay alive, so I needed to remain useful to Taishineya, and that meant advancing her interests. And yet, I had a growing certainty of what would happen if I made myself *too* useful—when she ascended to power, she'd keep me. She would hold me as long as she could. What reason did she have to let me go, to free me? What sensible person would give up a tool as useful as me? And then, when you inevitably arrived on our doorstep and brought the fight to her, who knows what might have happened? I certainly didn't want to be in the middle of a mess like that. It's a good way to get killed, you know. But I tried not to think of all that.

"I'm sick and tired of this place," she snarled. She wasn't the only one. I longed for freedom so keenly that I trembled with it sometimes. "The city is nine-tenths mine. You said 'pick up the chisel.' Why not pick up the city?"

"Wait," I said. "Just wait. Just a little longer. You lose nothing by waiting."

She dismissed me soon after that, and I went to the door, and shut my eyes tight, and forced myself through it so I wouldn't trouble her with my hand-wringing. I had to lean against the wall outside for a minute afterwards, my skin clammy with sweat, and I must have jumped out of my skin when she slammed the door closed behind me.

If I had been thinking clearly, I might have made some different choices. I might have realized that escaping before Ylfing returned likely would have separated us permanently. But I was panicking, flustered, scattered. I didn't think ahead. I didn't plan for that. I could only think that I needed to leave quickly and quietly, as soon as possible, and my idea for finding Ylfing afterwards was simply, *find Ylfing afterwards*. It was a problem for another day.

I had to do *something*. As relatively comfortable as the bank was, I could not bear confinement an instant longer. I have spent my entire life wandering wherever my two feet have taken me, even when they have taken me straight into prison, treacherous things.

The guards had gotten bored and lazy. No one paid any attention to anything! I could just walk right out the front door, if I wanted! Even Flat-Nose had stopped chaining himself to my doorknob at night. What had been stopping me before? Just Taishineya's threats, I suppose, and my newfound difficulty with doors.

That night I took a pair of boots from one of the guards as they slept. They were much too large for me, but that was fine—all the rags I wrapped around my feet would just keep them warmer. I poured gold and silver into the boots too. I know, I know, glaring hypocrisy. They're imaginary and I don't like carrying them, but if someone gives you an illusion that they believe in, you might as well take advantage of it.

I wrapped up dried fish and cheese in a cloth too, and wrapped my blanket around my shoulders for a cloak. I longed to take more than that, but I'd be weighed down enough as it was.

Part of me wanted to stomp down the stairs, boots jingling with coin, and make no effort whatsoever to conceal myself, just to *show* them. Just to *spite* them. Someone would say, "Oi, Chant, what are you doing up at this hour?"

And in reply, I'd trill, "Going for a walk! Stretching my legs! Taking in the fresh night air! Lovely evening for a stroll!"

I still didn't have much of a plan beyond *get out, get out, get out now*, and then *don't freeze to death once I'm out* and then *don't starve once I avoid freezing long enough to worry about that* and then *find Ylfing afterwards*. But even that thin excuse for a plan required me to set aside my spite and sneak *quietly*.

It would have been easier if it wasn't for my issue with the doors. The sneaking, apparently, made it worse: they were all doors I knew I wasn't allowed to pass through. That night was the worst it had been since the first time. I stood frozen on the threshold of my room for a few long minutes, and I broke out in a sweat again. When I finally managed to get across, I stumbled into the other wall, caught myself, and leaned there until I caught my breath and blotted my forehead dry.

The long, dark halls of the bank rang with silence. I felt my way along, one hand against the wall to guide me. Even with the windows, there wasn't enough light to see by. It was a cloudy night, and it had begun to snow a few hours previously.

I placed my feet carefully, breathed slowly and deliberately, winced every time the coins clinked against one another. I brushed my fingers along the wall as I crept down the corridor, feeling the rough texture of the brushstrokes of the painting on the wall—it was the mural of the mythical creatures and nubile virgins that had so distracted Ylfing. At length, I felt the edge of the corner and then just empty air. That would be the staircase.

Down two floors and around another corner and there was finally a bit of light. A door was open, and a few of the Thieves were inside, still awake and playing a sedate game of cards, from the sounds of it. I averted my eyes, not wanting to spoil my night vision, and drifted past.

A coin fell out of my boot and bounced on the polished wood floor, ringing bright and loud in the quiet.

The intermittent conversation in the room ceased entirely, and I froze. There was nowhere to hide, no furniture to duck behind, no convenient alcoves. I heard the scrape of a chair against the floor and just managed to flatten myself against the wall as one of the Thieves (we'll call him Troll) stuck his head out into the hall. He was facing away from me.

I slumped in relief.

And then he turned.

Came face-to-face with me, and we both nearly died of fright.

Three other chairs scraped back instantly, but Troll gestured to his fellows. "Belay, belay," he said. "It's just her pet skulking around in the dark."

"Why?" I heard Nine-Fingers say. "Old man, what's your business?" Sounded right suspicious, she did.

I drew myself up and stuck out my chin. Troll's night vision was blunted by the light, and he must not have seen how hard I was shaking. "Just visiting the kitchen," I said. I was a little surprised at how difficult it was to steady my voice. "When you get old, you'll find it becomes more difficult to get to sleep. Young people like you just don't understand."

Troll grunted. "Bring something up for us, would you?" he said. "Pickings were mighty slim for dinner, for those of us who'd rather eat rocks than fish broth."

"Of course," I said, and he turned back into the room. I steadied myself against the wall again and gasped for breath.

I made it down to the main floor with no other mishaps. Then the choice: front door or kitchen door? Prudence won out—even if there was anyone in the kitchen at this hour, I could use the same excuse I had for Troll, unless they noticed my boots.

The kitchen was empty; the fire in the heavy iron stove was

banked. Thin, weak light limned the high barred windows, doing nothing more than indicating that they were there.

I went to the alley door—locked, of course. There was a key somewhere around here, but it wasn't on its hook. Now, the kitchen door key was a regular and major point of contention amongst the Thieves, and I had witnessed several instances of sniping regarding the Protocol of the Key and almost everyone's inability to adhere to it and return the key to its proper place. It was missing from that hook more often than it was there.

I spent a frantic few minutes patting down all the counters and cabinet shelves, stumbling in the dark and sometimes spilling another coin or two from my boots, before I concluded that locating the key would have to be someone else's problem.

There was still the front door . . . and the secret entrance, somewhere. Nothing was brought through the kitchen door except buckets of snow to melt. All the bundles and bundles of supplies to feed more than fifty people came in as I had, somewhere mysterious and probably underground.

The front door, then.

I breathed for a moment, gathering my strength, standing there in the dim light, and then off I tottered, past Taishineya's door, past the Thief asleep in front of it, into the cavernous main hall with the tellers' desks around the edges, a border to the massive mosaic covering the floor—the crest, I suppose, of the family who used to own the palace.

The huge double doors at the front had no locks, but they were barred from the inside. It was a piece of work, I tell you, wrestling down that slab of wood by myself without making a noise. Such a piece of work, in fact, that I failed at it. The bar was heavier than I expected, and it slipped out of my fingers just as I got it free of its rest.

It *slammed* onto the stones of the threshold with a crack like a bolt of lightning hitting a tree. My heart leaped into my throat and I stood just long enough for the echoes to fade . . . and the growing-thunder sound of approaching footsteps to reach my ears.

It took all my remaining strength to heave one of the doors open the scant few inches to allow me to pass, and I shut my eyes and flung myself bodily across the threshold, fighting back a wave of nausea. Snow was falling lightly still, piled in drifts where it had been shoveled aside, and the first breath of cold was a sharp punch to my lungs. I scuttled down the front steps and halfway across the courtyard. The new snow was already inches deep, and glancing behind me, my heart fell into my feet—my tracks could not have been clearer.

If I had been a younger man, I might have made it away even so. I found my way into *and* out of many youthful scrapes back in the day—many marital beds I found myself sprinting from, many an intimate tête-à-tête I was required to fly from with great haste . . . I have scaled my allotment of walls and fences in my time. I've even done my fair share of self-defenestration.

That was many, many years ago, when my knees were still my allies.

Those days are long past. It was a stupid thing, trying to run. A very stupid thing. I think in my panic, I'd forgotten that absconding at midnight is very much a young Chant's game.

Heartbeats later, the Thieves came pouring out of the front doors, and they found me doddering in circles around the fountain, mumbling to myself and smacking my lips together with satisfaction.

"Oi!" they shouted, and surrounded me as quick as thought. "*You!*"

"Going to the kitchen, you said!" said Troll. "And we find you—"

"Good!" I cried. "Nice night for a walkabout, young man, good to see you youthful sorts have vim and vigor in your blood."

ALEXANDRA ROWLAND

They were never quite sure what to do with me, the Thieves. They were rough and hard men and women. No trouble giving their employer the respect and deference she was due, but me? I was just her pet, as they'd called me earlier. A prisoner, and yet a prisoner with the ear of the Queen. And they were young, and the young are never quite sure what to do with the aged when they misbehave.

"Come, come!" I said. "Walk with me!"

Nine-Fingers bent down and picked something out of the snow. "Gold," she said, and held it closer to their lantern. "A ten-mark piece. There were some on the floor inside, too." They all looked at me harder.

"Carrying a lot of cash for a midnight walkabout, aren't you, old man?" said Troll.

"Eh?" I said innocently.

I squawked when they started patting me down, but my protestations only seemed to encourage them. They wrestled me into the snow and pulled off my boots, spilling two fortunes onto the ground.

"Looks like his *walkabout* was going to walk him right out the front gates," Troll snarled. "Take him inside."

I was dragged back through the door, which of course didn't nauseate me at all, and then we paused in front of Taishineya's quarters. "Wait," said Flat-Nose. "We were about to bang on her door and report this, weren't we?"

There was a soft murmur—of agreement, of hesitation, of dawning dismay.

"Aye," said Flat-Nose. "I can see by your faces that we've all got the right of it now."

"Up to his room, then," said Nine-Fingers.

My room. I was unceremoniously dumped on the couch that served as my bed, and my ankle was shackled to the leg of it, with

Flat-Nose chaining himself and his chair to the doorknob, without breaking eye contact.

"Now," he said, "you and I need to have a heart-to-heart. All civilized."

"I don't know what you mean," I quavered. My blanket was damp with melted snow, and I'd hung it in front of the barely warm stove to dry. I had to chafe my hands together to warm them.

"Don't play stupid with me, old man," Flat-Nose said. "You were making a run for it."

"Just a bit of a walk to clear my head."

"With thousands of marks hidden in your shoes? I very much doubt it." He sat back and tapped his fingertips against the arm of the chair. "You may be wondering to yourself why we didn't drag you in front of Her Ladyship."

"Majesty."

"Whatever. Are you wondering this?"

"I expect you didn't want to bother her for something so trifling as an old man stretching his legs."

His eyes narrowed. "You seem to think that I'm an idiot. Well, that's all right; it doesn't hurt me any. See, I like this job. I fill my pockets with more coin than I've ever seen in my life, and Taishineya doesn't give a flying fuck about it. I get regular meals, I've got a roof over my head. It's a good deal. So I'm not going to let you spoil that for all of us—how would it look, eh? Us carrying you in by the scruff of your neck, telling Her Ladyship that you nearly escaped because we thought you had a regard for your personal comfort and security that matched our own, so we let you alone. Eh? How would that look to her? Not great." He tapped his fingers on the chair again, and the shackle on his left wrist clinked. "So you're not going to mention your *little walkabout* to her, and we're not going to mention it either. But now we know that you're not the loyal servant, and we'll keep a *very* close eye on you."

"I was just getting a bit of fresh air."

"And the freshest air, I suppose, is ten miles out into the country-side." He drew a dagger from the sheath at his hip and pointed it at me. "Look at this. Your death, if you try that shit again, hangs from the tip of this knife. Are we clear? On the tip of this knife or . . . This building's dangerous for an old man walking in the dark. Too many stairs. One wrong step and—" He circumscribed a series of descending spirals in the air with the point of the dagger. "Found the next morning, neck broken, cracked skull. Tragedy. Are we clear?"

We were clear.

To my frustration, I now found myself with a permanent guard. The Thieves took shifts with me, one of them following me silently from room to room no matter where I wandered. I spent days trying to bore them into leaving me in peace, then trying to annoy them—I had an effect on them, certainly. They were no saints, after all. Nine-Fingers once was infuriated enough to shove me against a wall and raise her hand to strike me, but went no further. And none of them, no matter how angry or bored they were, ever left my side.

Eventually I stopped caring and returned to my usual habits.

I spent a little time with Helena and the children, after a humble request from her to help teach them a little geography. That sounded to me like a prime opportunity to do some Chanting—*proper* Chanting, not this tedious propaganda manufacturing, nor the vain attempts to plan and plan and plan.

We all sat down in the schoolroom (another empty office that had been appropriated for our purposes), and I told them stories of far-off lands and wondrous things: the enormous heat in the Sea of Sun and the way the sun blazes off the dunes; the round-walled theaters of Avaris and their acting troupes, who performed a different play every day of the week and held as many stories in their heads as the Chants do; the sleepy, humid river towns of Map Sut, all broken up into a hundred little family compounds, each with its own spiring pagoda to their house gods; the sprawling imperial splendor of Genzhu and its precision-engineered city streets, each as straight as an arrowshot. I told them about the Straits of Kel-Badur, the temple-wagons of Arjuneh, and the magnificent merchant-princes of Araşt. And they watched my every movement, rapt and agog, and Helena sat towards the back of the little group, with the youngest cuddled beside her lap, and listened with shining eyes.

Children are some of my favorite audiences. When they ask questions, they ask good ones in good ways. They never, ever ask, "But why should I care about this?" They know what some adults have forgotten: a hunger for the world, to understand, to absorb every piece of it.

"That wasn't exactly what I imagined I'd get when I asked," Helena said to me afterwards.

———————

The geography lesson had put me in a glowing mood, and interestingly, it even survived after I ran into Consanza in the corridor. She was reading a messy sheaf of papers and nearly walked right past without looking at me, saying only, "Helena was looking for you earlier, Chant."

"She found me," I said.

"Oh, good," she said absently, still drifting down the corridor.

"She wanted me to teach geography to your children."

Consanza stopped dead in her tracks and turned around. She was intensely puzzled. "Geography? You? Oh. Actually, I suppose that makes sense. If Helena wants you to do something, you'd better do it."

"I already did."

Consanza nodded. "How was it?"

"Helena said it wasn't what she was expecting."

She rolled her eyes. "Why am I not surprised? You can't cooperate with anyone, can you?"

"I'll have you know," I said, drawing myself up as tall as I could, which was nowhere close to as tall as Consanza, "that she and the children all enjoyed what I had to say, and I got the impression she was expecting it to be much drier and more boring than what I gave her."

Consanza raised her eyebrow at me and my tone but shrugged. "All right, then. As long as Helena is happy with it."

"She is."

She turned to walk away, then paused and turned back again. "What exactly did you tell them?" She didn't sound quite suspicious, just . . . cautious.

"Just interesting things about all the places I've been. Geography things. Things to give them an awareness of the world beyond the horizon."

"Places like what?"

"Everywhere," I said, rolling my eyes.

"You hadn't been to Nuryevet before this," she replied sharply. "So maybe you haven't been everywhere."

"Everywhere that *matters*," I couldn't help but reply. But she was too intent on me to take offense. "All around the Sea of Serpents and the Gulf of Dagua, up and down the coast of the Amethyst Sea, from the Sea of Sun to the Ganmu River. And more."

She hesitated again, and then she said, "Arjuneh?"

Silence, while we both considered how much of her hand she'd just revealed in this card game I hadn't realized we were playing. "Yes," I said at length. "In fact."

"Did you tell them about it?" She was using her advocate voice now, and her advocate posture. Guarded, arm's length, perfectly neutral.

"A little," I said, using my own approximation of the advocate voice. We were at an impasse.

"Did you like speaking to the children?"

"I always like speaking to children."

Another long silence.

"Inga," she said. "Inga is mine."

"I know." Inga stood out from the other children—Consanza's only daughter of her own body, about seven years old, beautiful and brown. She had Consanza's black eyes and dark hair, though the texture of it was a little softer, and it curled on her shoulders.

"You could tell her more about Arjuneh, if you wanted."

That wasn't at all where I thought the conversation had been going. I blinked. "Oh. All right."

"If she's interested," Consanza said.

"I'll ask her. Have you told her anything?"

"No," Consanza said quickly. "That is, not much." There was another long silence, but I could tell she was trying to find words, or perhaps trying to weigh the scales to determine whether she should say anything else. "I told her a story once. A story from Arjuneh."

"Which one?"

"You mentioned it once. Priya, Majnun, and the Wondrous Blue Panther."

"Oh. Yes. I know it." I paused, thought back as far as I could.

I'd heard her matronymic exactly once, as far as I could recall. "Your mother was named Priya, wasn't she?"

Another pause to weigh the scales. "Yes."

"Was that on purpose?"

"Yes."

"Your grandmother must have been a romantic."

"Yes," and then, unexpectedly: "Both of them were."

"Mm," I said. I was dying to ask another question, but I was in too much of a good mood to ruin it by picking a fight. "I think that's lovely," I said. "The way your grandparents carried Arjuneh with them in the name they gave their daughter."

She had no idea what to do with that. I'm not sure *I* knew what to do with that. I can't recall if I'd ever given her any kind of compliment up to this point. "Yes," she said, for lack of anything else to say.

I decided to risk the fight and ask the question. "You just said that both of your grandmothers were romantics."

"Yes."

"Was your father's name Majnun?"

A very, very long silence. She was bowstring-taut. "Yes."

And suddenly I felt like I could fill in a lot of blanks—maybe not with perfect accuracy. They were just guesses, after all. . . . But you only need two points of information to draw a line, and a line is a story: two women and their husbands leaving Arjuneh for the far, bleak north. Two women, probably close friends, bearing children around the same time: a son and a daughter, named for a love story and a land left behind. "It's none of my business, but I've wondered. . . . Why did they leave Arjuneh?"

"You're right, it really isn't any of your business."

I held up my hands and took a step back. "No offense meant, advocate. Curiosity is a hard habit to break. It was only an idle fancy."

"Fine."

"Are you glad they did?"

"What?"

"That they came to Nuryevet."

She was trapped between confusion and anger. I wonder if such a question had ever occurred to her. "How should I know?" she snapped. "I've lived here all my life. I've never known anything else."

I nodded. That made sense. "If they hadn't, you wouldn't have met Helena," I offered.

She took an unsteady breath. "Then yes, I guess I'm glad they did."

"Did Inga know her grandparents?"

"No."

I nodded again.

"I just thought she might want to know, someday. About Arjuneh. I thought she might be interested. Since they . . . didn't live long enough to tell her."

"I could tell *you*," I said. "And then you'd have something to tell her if that someday comes."

"No," Consanza said quickly. "That's all right. I'm fine as I am. But what she wants might be different."

"It's very wise of you to say so. Most parents assume their children are going to want the same things they do."

"Thank you," she said, in a way that meant, *Let's stop talking about this, back off.*

I nodded and . . . backed off. Walked away, my guard following a few yards behind as usual, and left her there in the hallway.

Sometimes as a Chant you can sense the shape of the things that people are carrying around in their hearts. A Chant spends so much of their life learning about how groups of people are in one place or another that they naturally come into a familiarity with the way individual people are. And the way that Consanza was? There was something big and tangled and complicated under her surface, something to do with Arjuneh, and her grandparents, and her daughter.

There are many stories that aren't mine to tell. And, more important, there are some that aren't even mine to hear. Consanza carried a story in her heart that I would never have a hope of reaching, or even understanding if I did reach it, not in the way it deserved to be understood. But it was there and I could see the outlines of it, like the shadow of whale below a boat. If she wanted me to talk to Inga, then I would. And I did. But I can't tell you about what we said. That's not a story for you to hear.

Regardless of the glowing mood I'd been in earlier, the downswing happened as it inevitably does, and by evening I was miserable again, even worse than before. Flat-Nose would not be shaken from my heels, and I longed for a moment to myself.

I went up to the top floor to punish him, because I knew he'd have to follow me up all those fucking stairs, and I got the map out of its hiding spot and spread it out on a table, because it didn't goddamn matter anymore. I didn't know why I'd even bothered to try.

"Did you make that?" Flat-Nose asked.

"No, of course not," I snapped at him. "I'm no cartographer."

"Neither was the person who made that," he said, snickering to himself like the uncivilized fool that he was.

I harrumphed at him and concerned myself with staring glumly at the map, imagining all the different paths you could have gone, hoping that Semynsk hadn't been a coincidence, hoping that Ylfing had found you and was returning to me.

A thought itched at me. I brushed it away.

It itched more insistently.

I huffed and sat back from the map. "What do you mean?" I demanded, irritated more at the thought tugging so intently on my sleeve than I was at Flat-Nose.

"I mean it's a shitty damn map," he said, which was not at all helpful.

"It looks like a perfectly fine map to me," I said, gesturing across it. It was in good condition—old parchment, but the edges weren't torn or frayed, and all the lines were neat and clear.

"*Looks*, sure. *Is*, no."

I counted to ten and managed to ask calmly, "Would you care to elaborate?"

He jabbed a finger at the Osered River. "Look, it's wrong. That big bend there, it doesn't exist."

"Rivers change course all the time," I said primly. "This map was likely made before that."

"The Osered hasn't changed course in four hundred years." I squinted at the parchment. It certainly wasn't four hundred years old. Flat-Nose slid his finger to the key in the upper right-hand corner. "Drawn in 1132 for the King of Coin Evitsen Perholat. Fifty years old."

"So he got a little imaginative with the river's course."

"And Vsila is too far inland. Nearly eighty miles too far. We're to the *east* of that little river draining into the bay. And—look, look at that!" he said, scornful, indicating a hamlet in the middle of the country. "They've put Kovazska in the Ninth Ward, and it's in the Third."

"Where's the Third Ward?"

I watched his finger track from the center of the country to the far northeastern corner of Nuryevet, several inches above Vsila, where a stubby peninsula jutted into the ocean. He circled the area with his finger. "Third Ward." I glanced up at him and watched his eyes move across the paper. He leaned on the table. "And here. Zlavoi: drawn in the Fifth Ward, belongs in the Seventh. And Promuk—it's in the right ward, at least, but everyone knows it's a day's ride away from Lake Mira, not right on the banks." He stood up and snorted. "Shittiest map I've ever seen, if I'm being honest with you."

Hope glimmered within me like the first rays of dawn over the mountains. If the map was wrong, perhaps all was not lost. Perhaps I hadn't set you an impossible task.

I rummaged through the shelves—there were a few other maps in here, older ones, more worn. Worn from use, by my guess, and perhaps the near-pristine condition of the other one I'd been using should have been a clue. I brought a few of them over to Flat-Nose and shoved the long, rolled-up sheaves of parchment into his arms. "Show me. Show me one that's right."

He shoved them back. "Fuck off."

"Please. I'll put in a good word for you with Her Majesty. And I'll behave. I promise."

He grumbled and grunted, but at last he picked through them, unrolling them one by one and giving each fair scrutiny. On the third or fourth, he said, "This one's not bad."

I very carefully resisted the urge to snatch it from his hands and let him lay it out on the table. I looked back and forth between the two—indeed, the Osered River was a dramatically different shape in this other map. "Not too bad, you say?"

He shrugged. "It's a hundred years old. The borders of the wards have changed a little, but the landmarks are there."

"Is Vsila placed correctly?" I said, tapping the miniature of Vsila's distinctively bland city walls and squat, squarish buildings.

"Aye."

My finger traced west, up the Bay of Vsila and along the Osered. "And Uzlovaya?"

"Aye," he said.

"And, ah, Tova?" I said, picking a minor-looking town at random from the Athakosa Plain, north of Vsila.

He leaned in. "As far as I know. Never been there myself."

"Thank you," I said with the greatest sincerity. "This has been extremely enlightening. I owe you one."

He grunted at me. I returned my attention to the map, found what I was looking for, and breathed a silent sigh of relief. The towns I'd named for you were perfectly placed; I couldn't have chosen better if I'd tried. With a little luck, we'd probably be all right.

———◆———

And then came the day that we heard about the raid on Czersdo, and then I knew for sure that Ylfing and my message had reached you safely and that my plans were in motion. I burned that damn fucking map in celebration—and kept the other one as safe as a King's treasure, of course.

That night, I had a very public, very noisy attack of the prophetic vapors in the main hall not far from Taishineya Tarmos's chambers. I writhed around, screaming and carrying on until everyone in earshot was crowded around me, arguing about what to do, and Taishineya Tarmos stood at my head, shouting at all of them to shut up in case I said anything important.

"In Derisovet! Three days after the new year!" I gasped, and pretended to faint.

Silence, and then an uproar—what did that mean? Where was Derisovet? There was an argument—Consanza's husband Velizar kept trying to say that it was a little ways in from the western marches and the Tegey Mountains, but no one was listening to him then, of course.

Before I "recovered," they'd sent for a map, and Flat-Nose, remembering our conversation from a few days before, had fetched down the nice, correct one from where I'd stashed it in the storage room. They located the little town, as I had known they would. It *was* a little farther in from the western marches, but . . . well, everyone knows prophecies are uncertain creatures: The previous one had clearly been about the Umakh; was this the same or was it some new and unrelated catastrophe? If it was the raiders, would they continue on their path eastward? This possibility was met with great concern, arguing, shouting. Of the Thieves, only Flat-Nose was Nuryeven, but I found out then that Taishineya Tarmos had promised them various estates and holdings in the western parts of the country (which, she had claimed, were very valuable—draw your own conclusions, since you laid waste to the vast majority of those little hovel towns). They were primarily concerned with whether they would be able to sell their holdings profitably if everything on them had been razed to the ground.

Taishineya Tarmos eventually shouted them all down—she'd gotten rougher in the months with these ruffians, less polished, less *calculated*. She was still a cunning bitch, and I didn't like her any better, but she wasn't the sickly-sweet piece of fruit candy that she'd been when she visited me in the prison. There was steel in her. I mean, I suppose there had been steel in her before—there would have to be at least some, to be elected to office in Nuryevet, but it had been harder to see before, behind the tinkling laugh and the coy smiles. She still hadn't given those up entirely, but I'd heard her laugh like a real person at least once. No, I didn't like her any more than I did before, but it was easier to respect her when she was authentically ferocious instead of disingenuously girlish.

So, as you well know, because you were there, Derisovet fell, and the messengers that Taishineya Tarmos had sent out brought the news back to the city that it had happened exactly as her oracle had said it would. Dozens of soldiers dead, we heard, but no one ever seemed to ask how many civilians. Two or three, I'd expect, right?

Taishineya came to me all in a snit about it, saying that they would surely believe her now and so forth, and she fairly shook me until my teeth rattled in my skull, trying to get me to give her another prophecy about the next village that would come under attack. I begged and pleaded and professed myself to be just a feeble old man, already weakened by the toll that the prophecy had taken. These things could not be rushed, I reminded her, so rarely could things be told on command. "But you did it before," she said, as petulant as a child. "The first time I asked, you just did it! And you were in a repulsive little *cell* then." And in turn, I reminded her that I'd had supplies, incantations, my apprentice. . . .

So she sent out to find the supplies I asked for—I requested a lot of useless extra things, just because I was terrifically put out about having been shaken to bits, and because I thought it would make some starving alchemist in the city happy and perhaps keep him or her alive for another day or two.

I held off on actually doing the damn show for her, pretending to come down suddenly ill with a winter cold.

Taishineya Tarmos had no army; she had fifty-odd people who were pretty enthusiastic about doing what she said, since she'd brought them to a nice warm building and filled their pockets with literally more gold than they could carry. Even though they couldn't eat it, even though it was as useless to gamble with amongst themselves as pebbles would have been. Even though there was nothing to spend it on except when one or two of them snuck out to see the city at night, and even then they couldn't spend more than pennies and the occasional liriya.

Vihra Kylliat also had no army; she had a bunch of men and women who wouldn't work for her anymore because she couldn't pay them. Not through any particular lack of loyalty, but because almost all these people had families they needed to provide for. And even if they didn't, they had their own stomachs to fill.

There was some bloodshed, yes, that happens, and certain neighborhoods barricaded themselves off from the others.... Look, I'm telling you all I know, but I was locked in one room or another for the entirety of the interesting events, and I heard about them all secondhand, so you're hearing about them all thirdhand. I'm doing my best here. If you wanted more gory details, you should have asked Ylfing about it; but then Ylfing was with you for the worst bits of the revolution, so there you are. Take your thirdhand stories and be grateful for them.

I had no more prophecies to give Taishineya then: you'd attacked Semynsk, you'd attacked Czersdo, you'd attacked Derisovet, close enough to the schedule I'd given you that I could have worked with it, if I hadn't been catastrophizing like a spooked horse.

But it didn't matter, because Taishineya Tarmos drafted a decree that she was ready to hire professional soldiers to go forth and meet the invading barbarians as they came west. Order came to her side in a steady trickle, threes and fours.

Within the day, Vihra Kylliat surrendered herself at last. She did it with dignity, too. Some people would have locked themselves in the Tower of Pattern until they starved to death. She only did it until they ran out of food, and then she admitted defeat with as much grace as could possibly be expected in a situation like this.

The Thieves standing siege at the Tower of Pattern took her straight to us at the bank. She was locked in a windowless room on the same floor as mine, the closest thing we had to a cell.

I went to see her as soon as I could. I wasn't sure whether she wanted to see me—in fact, I was more certain she wouldn't want to. But . . . I needed to. For the sake of my soul, I needed to.

Her door stood open, flanked by guards, but they didn't seem to care if I went in.

There was a surreal feeling to it, this mirroring. I could have dragged in a chair and a bottle of menovka, could have done it up right and proper, but that would have felt like petty mockery.

I edged through the door. She looked worse than the last time I'd seen her. She had huge dark bags under her eyes, and she'd gone thin, like most everyone else in the city. Roughly shaped wooden limbs had replaced her fine and elegantly crafted artificial ones—I expect that she sold them for money to feed herself.

The ravages of broken hallucinations touch even the highest of the high, in times of trouble.

She looked up at once when I came in. It was like she didn't recognize me. I don't know—she didn't react, is what I mean. She just sat there and stared at me with dull, glassy eyes. She had resigned herself to death at that point, and she knew it would come for her in its own time, not on her schedule. She wore Order's red, still, the cloth old and faded. And though her clothes were threadbare and shabby, the boot on her good foot was polished to within an inch of its life. A soldier's habits never completely leave her, I supposed.

"Well, hello," I said to the woman who had shut me in a miserable, damp, filthy cell for weeks. Who had denied me heat and personal cleanliness. Who fed me slop. Who, in anger, had poured that bucket of filthy water on me and left me in the dark to freeze. Who would not have cared if I had taken sick and died. Whose so-called kindnesses had been incidental and self-serving at best. Who had taken clothing away from another prisoner to clothe me, likely leaving them as helpless and naked as I had been—but they weren't as important, were they? They were just a debtor.

Two people can have a connection, as we did, but a connection doesn't require caring. When she was extending mercy to me, when she was delaying my execution, it wasn't because of her own good intentions. It was because I influenced her. And before I'd done that, she was very equitable—she treated me the same as she treated all her prisoners: filth, misery, abuse. She did not deserve mercy. She didn't deserve kindness.

"So you were on her side all along, then?" Her voice was crackling-dry, her lips pale and chapped.

I shrugged. "No. She took me from the prison, fed me, clothed me. Offered me that and a job, or death."

"You're the worst person alive. I kept you safe as long as I could. I would have set you free eventually. I tried to help you. It was all stupid. I see that now."

Words are cheap; I know that better than anyone in the world. She could have just been bullshitting to disquiet me. It was probably what I would have done. Maybe she had learned something of storytelling in all those drunken nights she visited my cell.

Despite everything, I felt sorry for her. Taishineya Tarmos seizing control of the bank had been a fatal blow, but a slow one—the moment that Taishineya had crossed the threshold, Vihra Kylliat's fate had been sealed. She would have ended up here in this room one way or another, eventually. I think she knew it. I think she may have known it when everything started going wrong. Who knows? She's not around for anyone to ask now.

She had tremors in her hand. I wondered how long she'd been able to keep herself supplied with menovka after I'd been kidnapped. We didn't have anything that strong in regular supply. Taishineya Tarmos had some kind of prejudice against hard liquor. Velizar, Consanza's husband, had taken over duties as quartermaster, and he had a prejudice too, except his was the straightforward belief that it wasn't an essential supply and that we had no call to be spending money on it, particularly when we didn't need beer as a source of clean drink, free from pestilence. We had the well pumps in the alley and the courtyard, he said, and all the snow we could want besides.

She didn't seem willing to talk, and I was overcome with a fit of shyness—sort of like when Ylfing or someone starts crying. Sometimes I just don't know what to do with people. Can't help it. I understand why people do it, and it's not that I can't identify their emotions. It's just that other people's feelings are as uncomfortable to have shoved in my face as their privates would be. For one thing, I'm too old for that nonsense, no matter how much of a hound I may have been in my youth. I like to decide for myself whether I want to deal with someone else's business or not.

After a long, long silence, I left, and I wandered, and I wondered if any of the Fifty Thieves had a liking for menovka, if any of them might have smuggled some back into the bank, and if a measure or so of it could be poured off for me to share with her. I felt sorry for her, and even if her kindnesses had been incidental, there they were: she'd offered me drink once or twice, though it was too rough for me to stomach, and she'd let me keep the clothes and comforts that Ylfing and Consanza had brought me, had allowed the brazier in my low cell and the firepot outside my isolation cell. Trivial, meaningless gestures that cost her nothing. She didn't deserve kindness.

But she did deserve understanding, and that's what a Chant can offer. That's the only thing a Chant can offer.

There was menovka, of course—I mean, have you met men and women like the Fifty Thieves? There's always drink around them, sooner or later, regardless of the prejudices of their commanders. It's just that they wouldn't give me any, so I had to plead with my current guard to bring back some for me when next they went out. Seems there had been some unspoken agreement that if someone wanted drink, they went to get their own and no one else's. Independent lot, these people. I had a nation's worth of gold just a flight downstairs that I could have bribed them with, if only they'd cared a whit about it, so I had to barter with something else.

Fortunately, I carry a lot of tradable material with me in my head. Also fortunate, the Thieves were *ridiculously* bored by then.

THE FOURTEENTH TALE:

Skukua and the Twelve Travelers

A band of twelve was walking through a forest one day when they met Skukua, the trickster. He stopped them and asked them what they were doing, and they said they were mercenaries, on their way to the sea to find a boat that would carry them off to seek their fortunes.

"Fortunes!" Skukua said, howling a great bellowing laugh and slapping his thighs. "Your fortunes are written on your faces plain as day. Why do you need to seek for them?"

"A person without an occupation might as well lie down in the street and die," said one of the twelve.

Skukua jabbed his finger at her. "Your fortune lies behind you, stupid woman, not ahead." He pointed at another of the mercenaries. "Yours, stupid man, lies three weeks hence at the bottom of too many pints of ale, and in the glint of your coin on the table and in the eyes of the men who saw it and thought some thoughts to themselves, and in a dark alley where you stop to piss."

"Who are you, to say such things?" said the leader of the mercenaries.

("*Damn right,*" *said Nine-Fingers.* "*I'd punch him.*")

"A fellow traveler," said Skukua, "from a land I left long ago and half the world away."

"A sorcerer, too, to know our fortunes," said one of the twelve. "Or else a fool yapping into the wind."

"Why not both?" said Skukua. "Take me with you."

The twelve were all unsettled, but it was terrible bad luck to turn away another traveler met by chance on the road. "You may join us if you wish," said the leader. "But we travel at our own speed, and we will not slow down for you."

"Fine with me," Skukua said. "I can match anyone's pace!" And indeed it seemed that he could, for he bounded up and down the pack train with an unflagging energy, speaking to everyone, never staying still for long.

There was a young person who had more patience than the others, a woman by the name of Hesera, and she managed to tie up Skukua's attention and draw him away from the others for a time, to give them a rest. "And where does my fortune lie, stranger?" she said, when they had talked and boasted for a time.

"In the arms of someone called Nge Olutenyo," Skukua said immediately.

"Ha, I know no one by that name."

"You will," he said. "In N'gaka."

"N'gaka, you say? That's a ways off."

"Closer with every step we take," he said, cackling. "As are all fortunes. With every step and with every heartbeat."

"And what if I tried to escape my fortune? What if I didn't go to N'gaka?"

He looked up at her with his oddly luminous eyes and said, "Then N'gaka would come to you. Or bring you to it. You cannot escape fortune."

"I disagree," she said. "The rope of the future frays into many strands."

"No," said Skukua with a smile. "It doesn't."

"Nge Olutenyo, then," she said. "In N'gaka."

"In N'gaka," he agreed.

When they stopped to make camp for the night, Hesera could not keep Skukua occupied, and he got into a conversation with one of the other mercenaries that almost ended in a fistfight. Skukua taunted him until his temper snapped, and then danced back, shaking a finger at the young man and warning him off with reminders of Skukua's sorcery. "Touch me not, for you are as a snail to me and I could crush you beneath my foot if I so desired."

(*"Are any of them going to punch him?" Nine-Fingers asked, incredulous. "Never known a soldier with the patience these ones have."*)

"The pointless babble of a fool," said the man, whose name was Perun. "If you will not fight me fairly, then still your tongue! We are all sick to death of you."

Skukua's eyes glittered strangely then, like the glow of molten gold. "No," he said, "but that is *your* fortune."

"Peace," said Hesera, pulling Skukua back by his shoulder. "As travelers, we owed you safety in our company when you asked for it, but as our companion, you owe us something too."

"Do I indeed?" said Skukua.

"Courtesy," said Hesera, "and an attempt to make yourself as little of a burden as possible. There are miles to go yet before we reach the sea and part company. Let us strive to make them at least reasonably tolerable."

"I'm not yet satisfied," said Perun, his hand on the hilt of his knife. "I'll have it out with him here and now, or I'll have an apology from him."

(*"Good man, Perun," Nine-Fingers said. "Forget punching him—cut his throat."*)

Skukua's eyes glittered again, like emeralds at the bottom of a cup of wine, and then smiled. "I take back my offensive remarks. Consider them unsaid, with my regrets for saying them at all."

Perun nodded and cleared his throat. "Fine then," he said. Then he turned and stomped through the camp, calling for something stronger than water to ease his parched tongue and hoarse throat.

In the morning, he had a fever. He moved as if half-

drunk, staggering through camp only by steadying himself
against the trees. They could not stop to nurse him, and
they had no horses or wagons to let him ride. He lagged
behind, trailing at the end of the company as they collected
themselves and pressed onward.

By noon, there were blisters rising on his skin, tight
white-yellow pustules inflamed with a halo of scarlet. He
coughed incessantly and gasped for breath, and groaned or
whimpered with every step he took. Some of the blisters
beneath his clothes ruptured, dribbling blood and pus in
streams down his tunic and trousers.

*("This wouldn't be happening to him," Nine-Fingers said, "if Perun had
cut his throat when I said so. Men!")*

Skukua took no notice. He was as unburdensome as a
traveling companion could be. He kept himself to himself,
he spoke to no one unless he was spoken to, and he didn't
even whistle but restrained himself to a soft and near-
tuneless humming.

("There's that, at least," said Nine-Fingers.)

Perun stumbled and fell before the sun was halfway
down the sky, and the other eleven travelers and Skukua
stood well back and watched him shuddering on the
ground. "Can anything be done for him?" someone asked.
"It's too late for medicine, I suppose."

"Much too late," said Skukua.

Not since the first blisters started rising on him that

morning had anyone willingly come within fifteen feet of
him, out of fear and disgust, and they wouldn't get any closer
now. While Perun sobbed and begged and coughed up blood,
they stood back and argued, and then at long last they drew
straws, and a woman named Maliye was chosen to raise her
bow and shoot Perun, to put him out of his misery. Skukua
grinned from ear to ear and clapped his hands.

("Holy shit," Nine-Fingers said flatly.)

His pleasure did not go unnoticed.

("Damn right it didn't!")

That night when the travelers set up camp on the banks
of the Black River, they welcomed him to the fireside and
plied him with every ounce of hard liquor they had with
them—a not insignificant amount!

("Damn right it wasn't," Nine-Fingers said, and took a healthy draft of
her own hard liquor.)

They let him drink until he was giggling and flushed,
and then they waited until he rolled onto his back and
began to snore as loud as earthquakes and avalanches.

They had to do something, they agreed. He'd killed
Perun right in front of their eyes, and he'd do the same to
any of them that crossed him next. And him so capricious
and changeable? It was only a matter of time.

Perhaps others would have fumbled about in the woods,

trying this trick and that until Skukua killed them off one by one, except for the man whose fortune lay in a dark alley two weeks thence, and for Hesera, whose fortune waited for her in N'gaka. But these men and women were *clever*, and they had little reason to spare Skukua any mercy. So they attacked him while he slept, dead-drunk, and they garroted him with their shoestrings, and chopped him to pieces with their knives and hatchets, and threw all the parts into a river. But as they did this, they noticed that wherever they cut him, Skukua did not bleed. They could see the blood; if they touched a cut, their hands came away bloody. But it didn't run out into pools on the ground or flow like clouds in the river water.

In the morning, they woke up, and they found Skukua sitting by the campfire, poking sticks into it and rubbing his head.

("Gods damn it," Nine-Fingers said.)

"I have the worst hangover today," he said to them. "It feels like I've been beaten to pieces and drowned."

So they set upon him again and immediately hacked him to pieces.

("Yep," said Nine-Fingers. "Good.")

He laughed all the while, and even his head continued laughing after they'd dragged his hands and feet and arms and legs off to the river. They threw his head into the fire and it sang:

On a log in the forest old Skukua sat,
He chewed on roots and he chewed on fat,
He ran six times round the sun and back.
Twelve fortunes he saw, twelve sets of dice.
They killed him once and they killed him twice.
They drowned their sins in the River Black.
They burned his eyes and made him lame,
And still they could not burn his name,
You cannot burn a thing you lack.

So they fished the head out of the fire and carved
S K U K U A into what skin was left across his forehead,
and tossed it back in. The head sat in the fire all morning,
the flesh burning and cracking and finally flaking off the
bones, the eyes shriveling in their sockets until the only
thing left was the skull clattering around, laughing and
singing. The mercenaries argued about what to do with it,
and finally they quenched the skull in the river and stuck
it in a bag and smashed it against a tree until it fell to
pieces and went silent.

Just as they were ready to stop for the evening, they
saw a glint of firelight in the wood, and one of them—
Hesera—went to scout ahead.

In a little clearing just the right size for their band,
Skukua crouched next to a fire, singing to himself.

'Twas long ago and far away,
and half again the world away.
A flower grew in golden sprays
in a hollow, hidden place.

And shen they called it, meaning sweetness;
they took it when they went away.
And now it grows in farmer's fields,
and fevered wounds it swiftly heals,
and brewed as tea, small pains it shields,
its roots distilled, weak poison yields,
and skem it's called now, meaning nothing,
the true name was long since concealed.

'Twas long ago and far away,
and half again the world away.
Fat tasty birds flew o'er the bay
so thick one arrow felled a brace.
And ggeb were fashioned from their bones,
sweet simple flutes for children's play.
Alas, the birds of here and now
have bones too brittle to allow
such sturdy instruments; yet now
the humble ggeb still has its place,
with bone or antler made; somehow
the flute, these days, is called by kep.
The piping's just the same, I'll vow.

'Twas long ago and far away,
and half again the world away.
A mythic hero in his sleigh
amongst the winter stars was placed.
His name was Dwera then; his deeds
were sung by hearth for feasting day.
And when the oceans frothing came,

o'er land and made their deathly claim,
the people took the boats and blame.
They followed Dwera's northward race—
and Tueha now lives on instead,
and still they cannot burn my name.

Hesera crept back to the band of mercenaries and related to them what Skukua was singing, and they puzzled over what it could mean, until someone thought, "If it is a song about names that changed, perhaps Skukua is a changed name too." Then from each verse they took the sounds and, like a wizard's knot-spell, unraveled the threads of centuries. And when this was done, they looked at the name they had scratched into the dirt.

So they dashed into the clearing and set upon him again like wolves, and tore him to pieces while he laughed. He grinned at Hesera while she carved the first letter into his flesh, but his smile flickered a little when she got to the second letter. The third. The fourth. "Another fortune I'll see for you!" he sang. "If I see it, it will certainly come to pass! A chest of gold, robes of purple and silver! A child, a husband, a fine white horse!" But she finished the name: S H U G G W A, in deep cuts across his face.

And a trickle of blood ran out of those cuts.

("Thank fuck," Nine-Fingers said.)

And they threw the head in the fire, and Skukua shouted curses at them and fell silent.

The mercenaries trekked on through the forest, and they

came to the port, where they parted ways.

Your fortune lies behind you, stupid woman, not ahead, Skukua had said to one of the mercenaries. She remembered just as she was about to set foot on the boat, and she hesitated, and glanced over her shoulder, just in time to see a young woman with beautiful dark eyes looking back at her.

Another mercenary continued on, and three weeks thence stopped at a tavern, and drank too many pints of ale, and laid his glittering coins on the table, with no heed for the eyes of the men who might see them and think some thoughts to themselves, and when he left the tavern and stopped in a dark alley to piss, his fortune came out of the shadows.

("*He was fucking murdered,*" Nine-Fingers said.)

It was an old man, who could see what the mercenary's trade was, and hired him as a guard for a rich man's household, where he was fed and clothed, well paid, warm in winter, and pensioned.

("*Oh,*" said Nine-Fingers.)

And Hesera went to N'gaka to find her fortune in the arms of a man named Nge Olutenyo. She swore herself to his service, and saved his life too many times to count, and he saved hers, and she never married, and never had a child, and never had a chest of gold or a fine white horse or robes of purple and silver. But when she died, it was in the service of an honorable man, and he held her in his arms and wept on her face while she went, and that's the best that any of us could ask for.

And it seemed that Nine-Fingers agreed. She handed me a small flask. I opened it, sniffed it—menovka, of course, but more vile and astringent than the stuff Vihra Kylliat had brought before. I didn't think she would mind. Nine-Fingers and the others were quiet and reflective, so I left, and took the flask to Vihra, tucked it in her one good hand, and left her there.

———◆———

Taishineya wanted to leave the bank, but the Tower of Pattern had to be ransacked first. I suppose she had a few of those former Weavers doing it for her.

Ylfing came back a few days later, cheerfully reporting to anyone who would listen that his mission to distribute the propaganda amongst the outlying cities and villages had been a great success. He was even smart enough to assure them that the peasantry was in full support of Taishineya's cause. (When he saw Ivo, he leaped into his arms, and though I did not appreciate Ivo's cool initial reaction, I couldn't help but notice he seemed to warm up a little as Ylfing kissed him ardently and told him how desperately he had been missed. For a moment, I thought perhaps Ivo had just had a bit of cabin fever; perhaps he'd just needed some time apart. And then Ylfing broke off kissing him to start chattering about all the little adventures he'd had on the road, and Ivo's expression . . . flattened. That is the only way I can describe it.)

We'd already heard that Taishineya's forces had rousted the Umakha riders, and Ylfing's account supported this, though he gave

me a significant look that promised a different story for me, which
I had later on that evening—the greetings you'd sent with him, the
knowledge that you had only melted into the hills and mountains
and were nothing close to being routed as you'd led the Nuryevens to
believe, and that you were going to strike the town of Asoth next and
then hide and wait for further instructions.

Taishineya's army began to assemble. She paid them in advance
and fitted them out in mostly repurposed and secondhand uniforms and boots, with barely sharpened weapons, and they all spent
a significant chunk of their pay on food and whores and new socks
(and some of them on coffee, which was worth its weight in gold by
then).

Very soon after that, we reopened the bank, and the city gasped
with life like a drowning wretch pulled out of the dark water. The
price of bread dropped. People went back to work. Consanza and her
family moved back into their own home, as did Ivo, though they all
turned up at the bank every day to work.

Some semblance of normalcy crept back into certain areas of
the city—although there were pockets that denounced Taishineya as
the Queen of Thieves, who should be exiled again or, better yet, executed for her treason. Most of those rabble-rousers were dismissed as
hysterics and shouted down by the people who were happy to have
bread on their tables again. The more tenacious were silenced in other
ways—Grey Ward Prison acquired a few new tenants.

Most people don't really care about who is in power—no, that's
a lie. They do care, but it's not as high of a priority as simpler things,
like making sure they have enough food to eat, or enough fuel to keep
themselves warm over the winter. The citizens of Vsila may have been
willing to tolerate Taishineya Tarmos's sole rule until spring, possibly even until Midsummer. She had relaxed her fist from around

the throat of the country, and even this little mercy was a relief. But to keep her as sole ruler in a proper monarchy, when they had been electing their Primes for centuries? I doubt it—but then again, it's not my job to tell you how things would have gone. My job is only to tell you how things already went.

I had my usual fit of prophecy and spoke the name of Asoth. Taishineya's map showed that it was significantly farther east from the border, and there was a general outcry of dismay.

We had almost a proper war on our hands! If there's one thing war is good for, it's giving the economy a short, sharp jab of the spurs to the ribs. Taishineya Tarmos let the bank fairly hemorrhage money as she organized a vast muster for the army.

Around this time, we heard some belated news—all the other border towns you'd been overrunning, besides the ones I'd picked for you. All those government buildings destroyed, the Order outposts, the minor branch offices of Coin and Justice. It was excellent timing, the arrival of that news: added some tension, you know, when Taishineya found out and realized that I couldn't predict everything for her. She was angry about it; almost slapped me, in fact. I gave her some bullshit line about how the gods wouldn't send me a prophecy unless it was of paramount significance.

I brought drink to Vihra Kylliat a time or two. I don't think she was eating much, and she barely spoke to me. She wasn't really living anymore. Not even surviving. Just . . . waiting for a death that Taishineya was too busy and distracted to schedule. I thought that was cruel of her. The waiting, as I know from my own experience, is the worst part.

There was only one more time that Vihra Kylliat and I had any kind of conversation as significant as the ones we'd had when I was her prisoner.

There had been another blizzard, and the snow had fallen so thick that everything was muffled and quiet. Alcohol was the only consumable that she would reliably accept. I'm not a softhearted sort, as you know, but I have some basic compassion, and I remembered how much being isolated had broken me down. I went to sit in Vihra Kylliat's room almost every single day—I did my work in there some days, I took my meals in there more than anywhere else. It's just that we didn't talk, and she barely ever looked at me.

But then that night, I was standing at the windowsill, wrapped in a blanket to keep out the chill. I looked out on the snow that covered the whole city and softened all its planes and angles and corners, gleaming blue and white in the moonlight. Pinpricks of warm yellow fire lit windows here and there. It was another of those crystal clear nights, and being so high up in the bank, I had a clear view over most of the rooftops and across to the southeastern quadrant of the sky, where Hatun's Gate was just peeking over the horizon—the whirlpool of milk in the Woman's Clay Pot, as your people call it.

"Vihra Kylliat, what do you call that?" I asked her. Sometimes I did that—asked her questions. Most of the time, she ignored me.

This time, though, she lifted her head off the couch where she was curled up. "Call what?" Her voice was rough and crackly. She sounded ill.

"On the horizon, the big bright cloud of stars that looks like a whirlpool."

"It's just stars," she said. "Some people name them. I don't know the names."

"You have names for the moons?"

"The Boat and the Runner."

Not the worst names, I supposed. Not as uncreative as I was expecting; the Xerec call them the White One and the Stately One, which is worse, but I cut them some slack because they're not aggressively boring like the Nuryevens. "That thing is just as significant in the night sky, so long as it's clear." I guess she must have decided to ignore me. "You know," I said, quietly so that no one else would hear, "the Chants don't pass much knowledge of ourselves down. Our histories, certainly, and each apprentice learns a little of their lineage: their master-Chant, and their grandmaster, and their great-grandmaster and so on. And we have very, very few rituals—if I have an apprentice when I die, and if I see my death coming, I'll tell them my true name then. The last person in the world to hear it. For the most part, the job is about learning *other* people, not learning Chants. We don't have many traditions." I suppose I was telling her all that because I knew as well as she did that she was going to die soon. I'm only telling *you* this because I trust you more than almost anyone else in this world—and deservedly so, I might add, not to flatter you overmuch. "But that— those stars, that's something we remember. Thousands of years ago, the ancient Chants called those stars the Eye of Shuggwa. General Ger Zha would have called it the Mirror of Heaven, the door to the afterlife."

"We don't have one."

I yawned. "One what?"

"An afterlife."

I almost started banging my head against the wall, I swear it to you. These damn Nuryevens and their complete lack of imagination. If I never set foot in this country again, I'll die happy. "So when you die, you just . . . end?" I said. I tried to keep my voice even and calm—I was fully aware that afterlives and death must have been on her mind more than usual. "And here I thought you were all terrifically superstitious."

"Things can happen to you at the moment of death—a blackwitch can capture your breath, or you can become a blackwitch yourself. But all those things foreigners have, about a beautiful place that's comfortable and soft and where nothing hurts and everyone lives happily and is reunited with all their other dead loved ones? No, that doesn't happen. When you're dead, you're either gone or you're a bad thing."

"How do you become a blackwitch?"

"Nobody knows. It's just a thing that happens sometimes," she said tensely. "Though . . . if nothing's done with your body . . . it makes it more likely. People who get lost in mines, or up on the mountains. Or who drown. Or die of sickness with no one around." She swallowed. "Violent deaths too. Nobody becomes a blackwitch by dying peacefully of old age in their own bed."

"What ought to be done?"

"A funeral. Prayers. Burning the body, if you want to be really sure."

I went over to her couch and perched on the chair that I'd pulled in front of it days before. "I want to talk about something. I want to be forthright." She gazed at me with glassy, dull eyes. "You're going to die soon."

"Yes."

"Is there anything that I can do for you?"

"No. You can't help me."

"I can't stop your death from coming to you when it is your time, no. But if you tell me what you'd like done with your body afterwards, I can try to see that it happens. I can speak for you after your death if you give me the words you want spoken. And I can try to ease your fear and pain until that day comes."

"Stories aren't going to help anything now, Chant."

A long time ago and half the world away . . . , my brain whispered, but it wasn't the time. If she didn't want to hear it, this was one time to respect that. Most of the time people don't know when it's good for them to listen, when they really need to hear something. Most people only want to listen when it's easy and convenient for them, and sometimes it's important to *make* them listen, to speak even when there's no one willing to hear.

But a woman's last days? A person gets a better idea, in times like that, about what she needs, about what's important. I could provide comfort in the moment if she wanted it, but if she didn't want it, then she wouldn't be around long enough for it to make a difference.

So I sat in silence with her, and stared towards the window, where I could just see a few stars above the rooftops, and the edge of one moon. "Is there anyone who should hear about your passing?" I asked eventually.

"Anyone who needs to hear will hear. Her Majesty will make it known. I don't think she's got the stomach to parade my head through the city on a pike, but she'll make it known."

"I think I'll tell a story about you one day," I said half-absently. I was only thinking about some of the things she had told me when she was drunk. I was thinking that there might be another Vihra Kylliat one day, in some other place, in some other city, and if I ever met her, she might need to hear these stories, the same way that this Vihra Kylliat had needed to hear about Ger Zha, the General of Jade and Iron, and the way that Ger Zha had probably once heard stories about a brave and honorable woman before her. And perhaps the next one wouldn't be destined to die like this.

That's something I never told Vihra Kylliat—how Ger Zha died. It was eerily similar to this, in fact. She fought hard for her faction of the empire to prevail, to preserve the status quo and behave with honor and charity, though she was as hard and unbending as steel. And in the end, she lost, and she was imprisoned by the new Empress, and

ALEXANDRA ROWLAND

then she was quietly killed, with all the other high-profile supporters of the opposition's faction. She died with honor, and I knew Vihra Kylliat would die with honor too. "I'll tell someone, someday, about you."

"If you must," she said. "I won't be around to care."

"I will, though."

"I know you've never felt much of a need to stick to the truth, so just . . . don't tell them about this." She flopped her hand weakly. "Tell them I was brave, when I was taken in. Tell them I didn't break. Tell them I didn't waver."

"There's truth and there's truth," I told her. "Some things are true even if they didn't happen that way in real life." She didn't react. "That means I'll tell them you were brave, that you didn't waver."

"Good." She turned over, away from me, and pulled the blanket up under her chin. I left soon after that, when it was clear that the conversation was over.

That was the last time I ever saw her or spoke to her. She was taken away early the next morning and killed.

She was brave.

She didn't waver.

When I found out, I asked Taishineya Tarmos to ensure that the proper rites were spoken over Vihra Kylliat's body, but she said that they'd already dumped the corpse in the bay. Any words she'd had said over her had been spoken in passing, casually, by whoever dragged the wheelbarrow down to the quay and dumped her into a dinghy to be rowed out to the deep part of the water.

I never got a chance to speak words over the bay like I wanted to, after I heard. But a few days after that, we moved from the bank to the Tower of Pattern (it was more defensible, and the bank had to function as a bank now), and I climbed the endless stairs to the very top of the Tower, and I stood on the parapet, up to my knees in snow and shivering. There was the slightest sliver of water visible between the buildings, and I didn't even know if that was the bay or the ocean, but I whispered words for her, and wished her peace, and freedom from blackwitches who would twist her into a monstrous thing, and I said that I would tell stories of her so she would be remembered as she was—and so I have.

———◆———

It was soon afterwards that I decided that it was time, again, to attempt my escape. I knew that events were, by this point, well under your control, and so all that was left for me to do was to find a way to get myself and Ylfing out of the city alive.

I had to make an appointment to see the Queen, she was so busy these days. As it turns out, being the sole ruler of a warring nation recovering from the near implosion of its economy takes up a lot of time in one's schedule. So I went to her personal secretary.

I found Ivo standing in the corridor outside Taishineya's chamber, right at the base of the godforsaken spiral staircase that formed the central spine of the Tower. He was speaking to Ylfing in a low voice and stroking Ylfing's arm in that way people have when they're trying to comfort and dismiss someone at the same time.

"We can talk later, all right?" Ivo said.

"Sure." Ylfing was smiling, but with only about eight-tenths of his usual cheer. "Yes, that would be nice. I'd like that. But—"

"I'm just busy for the day."

"I could keep you company." Ivo couldn't quite suppress his wince, and—gods, even Ylfing couldn't miss that. "What was that for?"

"Nothing," Ivo said, shaking his head. "Honestly, nothing. Her Majesty needs my full attention today, that's all. I can't waste my time on—that came out wrong. I just meant that I'll be very boring today."

"You're never boring," Ylfing said, all sparkling smiles once again.

Ivo forced a fairly convincing smile and kissed Ylfing's forehead. "We can spend time together later, I promise."

"Sorry to interrupt," I said loudly. "I need to talk to Her Majesty today. I'd like an appointment with her, if she has any time available."

Ivo opened the messenger bag hanging at his hip, took out a booklet, and flicked through it; Ylfing slunk away up the stairs while he was occupied. His shoulders were hunched in a way I didn't like. "She's only available during lunch. She's having the rest of her household moved here to the Tower later today." He snapped the book closed. "Will that do?"

I snorted. Of course it would. "Lunch would be fine," I said.

"And I'd like a word now, if you don't mind."

I sighed heavily. "What else do you want from me? I'm doing all I can. Just be patient."

"We could be doing more," he hissed. He glanced around and leaned in close, his voice low. "We could just get rid of her now. Why wait?"

I glared hard at him—my guard was about twenty feet back down the corridor, and even if she was occupied with cleaning her fingernails, Ivo had no call to be acting so obviously suspicious. "Well," I said, pasting on my sunniest smile, "that sounds like a fine notion. I'll leave all that to you, eh? Since it was your idea." He stilled and got pale. I snorted and went after Ylfing, steeling my soul and my knees as I always did when I had to go up those damn stairs.

I caught up with him after a floor or two, and I took him by the arm and turned him— "Oh, Chant," he said, wiping his face and pretending like he hadn't. "Hi."

"Hi. So what was all that about?"

"What?"

"Just now, between the two of you. What's Ivo's problem?"

"Problem? Nothing."

"Tell a better story, if you're going to lie."

He cringed. "He's busy."

"Uh-huh. I heard. What is it really?"

Ylfing couldn't meet my eyes. He reached out and picked at the edge of a stone in the wall. "I'm not used to people who won't tell me what they really think of me."

"That's because everyone likes you," I said, which is obnoxiously true. "Everyone has always liked you."

"Yeah," he said in a small voice. "Do you think being liked is a skill?" The Hrefni and their attention to skills, I tell you.

My first instinct was to say *well, yes, obviously*. I thought about it then, thought about it hard. Ylfing deserved a careful answer in this moment. "No," I said slowly. "I don't think it is. Because being liked is more about other people than it is about you. Liking people is a skill, though, one that you're . . . very good at. But being liked, no. Why? Are you worried Ivo doesn't like you?"

"I don't know," Ylfing whispered. "He liked me before. He liked me a lot before. Now, I don't know."

"Well, that's his business," I said brusquely. Comforting people— now there's a skill. I'm terrible at it. "You can't control him or what he thinks or what choices he makes, so tell him to go fuck himself."

"It's not his fault he's busy."

"It *is* his fault if he thinks you're a waste of time," I said, and Ylfing flinched again. "That's what he was about to say."

"I just . . . He has things to do, and I don't. Not really. I've been talking to all the Thieves and Consanza's family, trying to get them to tell me stories." It's Chant practice, essentially. Whenever we stop somewhere, he goes and makes friends, and looks, and listens, and gathers all the raw material he can find, and then we talk about it—sometimes every day, sometimes once or twice a week, depending on how fruitful his scavenging has been. He tells me all the stories and rumors and gossip he's heard, and together we separate the wheat from the chaff, and I ask him questions until I feel like he's been made to think about things sufficiently. "But I think they're tired of me too. They keep saying they're not in the mood, or that they don't have anything else to tell. So I'm bored, a little bit, and I want to spend time with Ivo, and he . . ." Ylfing shrugged, still picking at the wall. "I'm always around when he wants to be with me, but . . ."

"But the reverse is not always true."

He nodded and swallowed hard.

"So does that say something about him or about you?"

Ylfing chanced an uncertain look at me out of the corner of his eye. "Him?"

I shrugged. "Figure it out yourself. Now, unfortunately for Ivo, I have assignments for you for the rest of the day and probably most of the evening. So you won't be available at all." I waited and watched to see if he'd protest. If he did, I would have dropped the issue immediately. It's not like I was about to keep him from Ivo against his will.

He sniffled, and wiped his face, and nodded. "All right," he said, and managed a wan whisper of a smile.

———————◆————————

I took him to my meeting with Taishineya. He stood quietly at the door and said nothing, and while Taishineya prodded unenthusiastically at a dish of baked fish with lemon, I offered my life in exchange for my freedom.

"I have had a dream," I told her. "And the gods have offered me a choice. And so I offer you a choice. Will you hear me?"

"When are you going to tell me another prophecy?" she demanded, as if she hadn't heard. "The raiders are laying waste to the western marches. I need information. They're coming east."

"My dream concerned my prophecies, Your Majesty."

"Dream? What about a dream?"

"In the dream, I stood on the edge of a great cliff, looking down into an abyss. At the bottom, a storm was raging. Behind me, a desert. Above me, the sky was black, and the sun burned cold. I heard a voice from out of the abyss, and it said that there were only two paths in my life. I could accept the gift of the gods one last time, and do some good in the world, or I could turn back into the barren wasteland, from which I could never return."

Taishineya Tarmos furrowed her brows at me. "You just get to *pick?*"

"Yes, but it comes with a price. If I choose to take the gift, it will destroy me. It will leave me shattered. This is what the dream told me."

She narrowed her eyes at me. "You don't want to do it, then."

"I want to offer you a choice, so that I can make my own—I want my freedom, my liberty. I am a very old man, and I want to live out what little of my life is left to me somewhere safe and quiet. I want to return to my homeland. If you allow me to leave, I will give myself to the gods for you, one last time. They said my sacrifice would change the world, but I believe that the price is that it will burn everything out of me—my mind, my wits. . . . I will be nothing but a doddering, drooling husk. I might not even be aware of myself or my surroundings after that, but I want to know that I'll be taken care of, that I'll be living where no one will trouble me." I nodded towards Ylfing. "My apprentice knows, and he is a good lad; he will stay with me until the end. I don't imagine that I will last very long in that state, afterwards. I may not even make it home."

"So all you want from me is your freedom?"

"And passage to the border. Perhaps a few coins for Ylfing, to help him get us the rest of the way, if Your Majesty feels inclined to generosity."

"And in exchange, I get . . . ?"

"As I said—a great prophecy, one that will change the world, one that will shake the foundations of destiny. One that will empower you to carve whatever you wish into the tablets of fate with the chisel you've picked up."

She sat back and tapped her fingers against the arm of her chair. She had done away with many of the jewels that she had been wearing during our stay in the bank. She now wore only a diamond pendant around her neck and a few simple rings. Her clothes were still finely cut and finely woven, with secret subtle glimmering in the extravagant folds and masses of cloth. My eyes had become accustomed to beautiful things as one's eyes do to bright light when one first wakes in the morning, and it was no longer searingly painful to look upon her.

I thought she might be getting a few tiny traces of wrinkles across her forehead and around her mouth. But perhaps that was simply wishful thinking. "Do you need time to think about it?" I asked her.

"No, of course not, why would I? You will accept the gift. That is not a question. You will give me everything I need to know."

"And after that?"

"If you are correct about what will happen to you, you'll be used up. Useless. As you say, a doddering husk. Why would I care where you and your apprentice go after that?"

I nodded. "I would rather live as an imbecile in freedom, than live another day in possession of my wits, yet in bondage."

She shrugged. "When will you tell me this great prophecy?"

"It will likely come to me during the night, while I sleep. The gods prefer to speak in dreams; they are easier to move than creatures or signs in the real world. Will you stand vigil to witness it, or will you trust my apprentice to transcribe it accurately for you?"

"Of course I'll stand witness," she snapped. There was a light in her eyes—the dreams of power were reawakening in her, and it was dawning on her that this was what she had been waiting for, truly.

"That was scary," Ylfing whispered to me in the hallway afterwards. "It sounded real."

I stopped. I looked at him. And then I said, "Lad, it was real."

He frowned. "But you said you didn't have any magic. You said—you said none of the Kaskeen have it, that it's not in your blood."

"Some people say that it's not about your blood, lad. There's stories here and there—people move somewhere else, and live there for a long time, and sometimes they get the magic of that place. Look at Consanza—can you imagine her ever having Arjuni magic?"

"No," he said slowly.

"No," I agreed. "The land sinks into your bones, and she's lived in this land all her life. If she had any magic, it'd be the Nuryeven kind."

"And you?" He was confused, poor lad. Bewildered more than brokenhearted, but I knew that'd come too. I'd resigned myself to it.

"Who knows? I've been so many places. Who knows where my dream came from?"

"It really happened?"

"Yes," I said.

He was confused, deeply so. "You're going to die?" he whispered.

"Something like it." He began to cry; I steeled my heart and held firm. He's not a good liar yet. I couldn't tell him the truth. "You'll stay with me, won't you?" I said. "You won't leave me to rot?"

He cried harder, big hitching sobs, and shook his head. "Of course I won't, of course not."

I patted his arm. "Do me one favor, lad. I don't imagine I'll care much where we go afterwards. I leave it up to you. You'll know what's best. But do me one favor and take me out of this city. Anywhere but Vsila, all right? Maybe you can convince Ivo to leave too, and the two of you could set up and make-home together, eh? Just not in Vsila." All I needed was for him to take me out of the city. I could handle the rest if he just got me *out*.

Taishineya wouldn't allow anyone but Ylfing in with us—she set me up in her very own rooms that night, in fact, up high in the Tower of Pattern—gave me a pile of cushions and blankets on the floor of her sitting room, which was fine with me. More comfortable than the cot I'd been sleeping on, relegated to my former cell *once again*, though this time I was allowed to wander. It was an unsettling place to be, even so. It made my skin crawl, and I kept seeing ghosts around every corner, or Weavers, or blackwitches.

As far as Ylfing knew, I was really giving up everything for our freedom. He spent most of that day begging me not to do it, swearing that we could find another way, but I was resolute. He cried for a few hours, and when we went down into Taishineya's chambers that evening, his eyes were still red and swollen. He kept saying that he just didn't understand how it could happen, and I kept shrugging and saying, "No one understands magic, lad, not really." Again and again, ever more desperate, he asked if I was sure about this. Again and again, I told him what I'd told Taishineya: I'd rather be witless and free.

He fussed over me as we settled down—I to sleep, and he and Taishineya Tarmos to sit vigil. Tried to tuck me in as if I was a child, until I snapped at him and batted his hands away, but I saw his eyes fill up with tears again. *I* knew this was all a scam, and that no one was saying good-bye to anyone tonight, but Ylfing, poor lad, thought this was the last time that we were ever going to speak to each other before my soul was burned out of me.

Now, I don't know if you've ever had to stay awake for hours while pretending to be asleep, but it is tricky. I couldn't sneak coffee beforehand, because then I would have been jittery and twitchy the whole time. It would have spoiled the, you know, dramatic tension. I made do with flexing my hands and feet under the blankets when I thought Ylfing and Taishineya Tarmos weren't looking, and I pinched my arms hard when I really started to drift off.

"This is taking too long," Taishineya Tarmos grumbled after a while.

"He's giving up everything for you," Ylfing replied, more bitterly than I thought wise. "The least you can do is show some patience." Some *fucking* patience, that's what it sounded like he'd wanted to say. "A man is making a sacrifice tonight—a great man, and a great sacrifice. Be respectful."

I half expected Taishineya Tarmos to throw him out of the room, or call off our deal entirely, but I think she must have been too surprised to realize she could. She wasn't a woman who had to face down adolescent impertinence in her everyday life.

My foot cramped. I gritted my teeth through it and supposed that this, at least, would keep me awake.

I waited, and I waited, and I waited. Ylfing and Taishineya Tarmos said nothing more to each other.

So then I started screaming. They jumped about a mile in the air, both of them, and Ylfing was at my side immediately. I flailed and struggled in the covers, tore at my hair, screaming all the while. Pissed myself too, because why the hell not? No one would do that if he were faking it. At least, no one would *accuse* someone of faking it if he did.

You've either got to be dead fucking serious about your ruse to do something disgusting like that, or it's got to be real.

I babbled in a language neither Ylfing nor Taishineya knew—some obscure tribal dialect of Perland. Sounds hellish the first time you come across it, all guttural throat-scraping consonants. In fact, it's a really beautiful language in its content, with some very elegant and subtle ways of expressing emotional nuance. But when you don't know what it means? Gods, you'd think that the speaker had just sucked off an entire pack of demons not an hour previously.

So I recited delicate springtime love poetry at them in this Errachkhak Valley dialect of Perlish for a few minutes, until Ylfing was near crying, and Taishineya Tarmos was frozen by the wall next to the door. Don't know what she thought I would do, but I could see that she regretted not letting any of the guards in to stand by.

I wheezed in a huge gasp of air and arched my back, and I let my eyes roll up in my head. "Five battles. Five battles until glory. Tova and Vsino, you will lose. Do not try to win them. Send your men and women and let them die. Kasardat and Tishero you will win, as if you wield a sword from the hand of a mighty god. But let Tova and Vsino be lost, and take your troops to the Athakosa Plain near Byerdor and have them wait in the ravine there. The enemy will break upon your shields like water upon the rocks. Glory. Glory. Glory. Long live the Queen."

And then I fell silent.

Ylfing's sobs were the only sound in the room. He gathered my head to his chest and cradled me. "There," he sobbed. His tears were falling hot on my face, but I was feigning unconsciousness and couldn't wipe them away. "There. Are you happy? It's done. You know how to win now. Are we free?"

"You're free," Taishineya Tarmos said. "Your debts are all paid."

I almost swore then. Debts. *Debts.* I had all but forgotten that I had promised Consanza, months ago, that I would owe her a favor.

Now, you well know that I never got along with her, and probably never would have, even given a hundred years to try . . . but damn it, a Chant has got to have some honor. I had promised her a favor in return for the ink and paper she'd brought me once, and that had to be repaid before I stepped foot out of this godforsaken country.

So I stirred a little bit and whispered. Ylfing gasped and stroked the hair out of my face, wiped his tears off my skin. "Chant, Chant, are you all right? Can you speak?"

"The woman," I rasped. "The woman of dark robes and dark skin. She must be sent away."

"What?" Ylfing said. "*Consanza?*"

"She will secure your glory, O Queen," I whispered, faintly now. "You may win the battles, but to ensure your realm's prosperity . . ." Another feeble, whistling, shuddering breath. "Send her to the south. Send her to carry your words. She is destined to serve you, O Queen."

"What is he saying?" Taishineya Tarmos demanded.

"Ambassador . . . ," I said. "To . . . the land of endless forest."

"Echaree! You have to send Consanza to Echaree as the Nuryeven ambassador," Ylfing said, voice shaking. "To secure the prosperity of your realm."

"Lose two battles, hide my army in a ravine . . . and send that woman away as ambassador. And this will be the key to winning?"

"That's what he said." Ylfing sniffled and started pulling the befouled blankets off me. Strong boy, he didn't even flinch or gag in the slightest. No sign whatsoever of distaste, just swift businesslike movements.

Taishineya Tarmos, on the other hand, clapped her hand over her mouth and almost threw up. "Disgusting!"

"Like I'm going to let him lie in his own filth!" Ylfing snapped. "His heart may be beating still, his lungs may be working, but he is *dead*. Because of you."

Hush, Ylfing, I thought. *Hush.* Not the time. But then, when have I ever taken the time to curb myself from running my mouth? And nothing bad had ever come to me—I'd lived this many decades, and I probably have at least a couple left in me. It's a system that hasn't done me too much harm. I mean, they only *nearly* executed me for witchcraft, espionage, and brazen impertinence.

I would not be roused, or so they thought, so Ylfing stripped me bare, and Taishineya Tarmos threw some towels at him, carefully not looking lest she choke again. Ylfing wrapped me up tenderly and called for some of the servants to help carry me up to my cell so that Taishineya's floor could be scrubbed and she could have her room back.

I think she must have left; I don't think she could stomach setting foot in that room again.

Ylfing had a brazier brought to my cell, and it was piled high with sticks and twigs until the room was toasty warm, and he bathed me carefully—he truly is a jewel amongst apprentices. My heart was moved, I tell you. I knew he was going to be angry at me later, but what could I do? He's not a good actor; he's far too honest. He would have given the whole game away. He wouldn't have cried over me, if he'd known.

He kept crying, actually, as he wiped me down with warm water and dressed me in a new long tunic and smallclothes. "I guess it's good I have practice," he murmured to me at one point, and I nearly jumped out of my skin—thought he'd seen through my act, but no. It was something else: "When I was very young, my grandmother . . . Well, she lost her wits too, after she took sick one summer. Couldn't move or feed herself, couldn't clean herself. Couldn't speak, and her face went droopy on one side. We all took turns with her. I hated it then. Hated it. Not—not because it was disgusting, but because she had been so wonderful before she went sick. She used to be soft and clean-smelling, like hay and meadow flowers in the springtime, and her hands were always warm, even in winter. I used to go play out in the cold and the snow, and then I'd run into her house, and she'd lay her hands on my cheeks when they were wind-chapped, and it was just like the sunshine on my face. I hated it because I lost her even though she was sitting right there. I hate this, too," he whispered. That same tone of guilt and abegnation as when he'd confessed about being homesick. "I know it's stupid, but I hope you'll get better, and I also hope that if you don't get better, you'll die quickly. I wish you'd told me more of what to do. How to be a Chant. I wish you'd told me whether . . ." He sniffled. "Whether you'd want to suffer or not, trapped in your mind." He tried to look into my eyes then. It was rather difficult to make them go unfocused, so I added some drool. Poor boy. I put him through a lot.

Only a few days, I thought at him. *Only until we cross the border and we're safely away.*

He bundled me into my cot, and he sat on the floor next to it, stroking my hair and leaning his head on the mattress next to me. He sang a few Hrefni songs—lullabies, they must have been, and he told me a sweet, familiar story that I'd heard a hundred times before.

THE FIFTEENTH TALE:
How the Jarlsmoot Came to Be

You know, a long time ago when there were still stonemen living up in the mountains, there was a fog-spirit who got into all sorts of mischief. He was little all over, with little hands and a little face, and little, little feet. And he lived in a little burrow in the side of the mountain with a view of the land tumbling down to the fjord and the big, big sea. He was so high up he could see almost all the way to the ice fields in the north, where it's so cold that the snow never melts.

The little fog-spirit was out gathering berries one day when a stoneman came stomping down the mountain—*thump, thump, thump! Crash* went his right foot, straight through the berry bushes, and *smash* went his left foot, straight through the roof of the fog-spirit's burrow, and *crash* went his right foot again, and so on. The fog-spirit cried out in dismay, but he was so little and the stoneman was so big that his voice was quite lost in all the crashing and smashing.

The fog-spirit picked through the ruins of his little house. It was quite a mess. The only thing he could rescue from the rubble was his little belt pouch, where he kept spare scraps of fog. He stomped his little foot, and he crossed his little arms, and he pouted his little mouth. "That stoneman!" he said. "Someone should teach him to look where he's going!"

The little fog-spirit sat down in the ruins of his house and had a good cry, and then he dried his face and he tied his belt pouch around his little waist, and he went flying off to find someone who could help him. But the stonemen were bigger than anything else on the mountain, and stronger, too, and none of the other spirits would help him, and none of the animals, either.

Finally, the fog-spirit had asked everyone on the mountain for help, and he'd gone down into the green valley and asked there, too, and then out to the rocky shore—not even the scuttling crabs wanted anything to do with the stonemen. So the fog-spirit sat on a pebble by the water and had another good cry, until one of the sea-women heard him and came to see what was the matter.

She was terribly beautiful, with long, wet, twisty green curls woven with seaweed and shells, and she was chubby all over like a seal, the better to keep the cold out when she swam in the dark, cold parts of the sea, and she had big, big eyes like a seal too, and a seal's tail instead of legs. All the sea-women look like this, you know.

The fog-spirit thought she had a very kindly face, and so he told her all his troubles, from the beginning to the end.

"Well!" said the sea-woman. "I've never seen one of these stonemen before, but I can't say I think much of them, if they're all like that. What are you going to do about it?"

"I don't know," said the fog-spirit. "No one will help me, and all I have to my name is this purse of scraps."

"Well!" said the sea-woman. "You could go build another home."

"Only to have it crushed by the stonemen!" cried the fog-spirit.

"Well!" said the sea-woman. "You could go somewhere they don't go."

"There is nowhere!" cried the fog-spirit.

"Well!" said the sea-woman, getting a little testy. "You could go talk to the stonemen and ask them nicely to leave your house alone."

"Do you think that would work?" asked the fog-spirit.

"I don't see why not," said the sea-woman, and slipped

beneath the waves. Remember, though, the sea-woman had never seen a stoneman, and she didn't know anything about them.

The fog-spirit wandered up the mountain to where his house had been, and he followed the stoneman's footprints for miles and miles until he came to the stoneman's big, big house. The fog-spirit crawled through the crack under the door and found himself in a big, big room, with a big, big fire in a big, big hearth, and a big, big stonewoman sitting at a big, big table. "Excuse me!" said the fog-spirit. "I'm sorry for barging in like this, but—well, I suppose it's fair, considering what happened to my house!"

But he was so little and the stonewoman was so big that she didn't hear him. She was sucking the roast marrow out of some bones. So the fog-spirit took out the scraps of fog from his pouch and braided them together into a little sail, and he held it above his head and blew into it and *whoosh!* Off he went, just like a puff from a dandelion! He floated up onto the table by the stonewoman's plate and he jumped up and down and shouted to get her attention until she noticed him.

"What on earth are you?" she said, much surprised.

"I am the fog-spirit!" said the fog-spirit. "And your husband—or whoever—stomped my little house flat!"

"I see," she said. "So what are you here for? Oughtn't you be building another house?"

"Not if he's going to come along and stomp it flat again! People should watch where they're going! He could have killed me! Squished me flat, just like my little house!"

"He only walks on the land we own," she said, cracking

another bone and sucking the marrow. "So it's your own fault, really, for trespassing."

"Fine," said the fog-spirit, crossing his little arms. "Where does your land end?"

"We own all the mountain, and all the valley, and the rocky shore, and the mountain across the water, and the mountain on the other side of the valley. A very modest homestead."

"Modest!" said the fog-spirit. "That's practically the entire world!"

"Really, you should have been paying us rent if you've been living on our land all these years," said the stonewoman. But then she looked the fog-spirit up and down and laughed. "I suppose for a homestead your size, you'd pay us a single grain of wheat once a year and we'd consider that great wealth."

The fog-spirit was hopping mad by now. He didn't like being laughed at, and *he* wasn't unusually little, it was the stonewoman who was unusually big! So he said, "I will buy it from you, my little plot of land, and I will pile up stones all around the border, and all your husband or whoever has to do is step *over* the little plot."

"And how little is this plot?" She spread out her napkin on the table and gestured to it. "How many napkins, little fog-spirit?"

He paced around the cloth and measured it out with his footsteps, and finally he looked up and said, "Four of these."

The stonewoman laughed and laughed, loud enough that the fog-spirit had to clap his hands over his little ears, loud enough that the rafters shook and dust came trickling down. "What madness! Expecting my husband to go out of his way to avoid a scrap of land that small? Madness! What could you possibly give us that would be worth the inconvenience?"

"I'll find something," said the little fog-spirit. "I haven't anywhere else to go."

"You have nothing we would want," said the stonewoman.

"Fine!" shouted the little spirit. "Then I'll win it from you!"

"Will you, now?" said the stonewoman. "In what kind of contest?"

"Whatever you like. Whatever your husband likes," said the little fog-spirit, stomping his little foot. "Name anything!"

The stonewoman rolled her eyes. "If you insist," she said, "but what if you lose?"

"I won't!" said the fog-spirit. "But if I do . . . If I do, then I'll just have to build my house somewhere else. Maybe in a briar thicket."

"You'll have to pay us rent, if you live on our land," said the stonewoman. "And you haven't anything of value anyway."

"I—I have a pearl!" said the fog-spirit. "A pearl from the sea-woman! It's as big as my head, and it's kept in a very safe secret place. I use it as a looking glass, it's so fine. If I lose, you can have it."

"I have pearls aplenty," said the stonewoman, yawning.

"But this one is magical!" said the fog-spirit. "Let it be three matches, and if your husband wins, he can have my pearl as the first rent payment."

"I'll discuss it with him," said the stonewoman. "Come back in a few days."

Now, what the fog-spirit didn't know was that the stonewoman was terribly interested in this so-called magical pearl from the sea-woman. They owned the mountain across the fjord, but they had a terrible rough time getting to it, because the sea-people's enchantments would call up a storm whenever the stoneman set his foot into his boat. The stonewoman suspected that the sea-woman's enchanted pearl would be able to tame the waves, you see.

But of course the fog-spirit didn't have such a pearl. So he went down to the edge of the water again, and he cried and cried until the sea-woman came back to see what was the matter with him, and he told her all his troubles. She was quite surprised that he'd taken her advice after all and had gone to see the stoneman, and she laughed in his face when he told her about how he'd blurted out that lie about the pearl.

"Foolish little spirit, you can't enchant pearls, everyone knows this."

"Then whatever will I do?" the fog-spirit wailed. "I shall have to live in a briar thicket, and they may squish me flat when they find out I don't have the pearl for them!"

"Only if you lose," said the sea-woman. "But look, I'll do something for you if you go away from the shore and stop weeping and carrying on so." And she poked through the pebbles on the rocky beach until she found one that was just about the size of the fog-spirit's head, and she rubbed it between the palms of her hands until it was quite shiny and nearly round. Then she kissed it, and winked at it, and she rubbed a little earwax onto it and then washed it clean again. "There," she said, and gave it to the fog-spirit. "Put that out in the moonlight for a couple of nights and that should be enough of a magical pearl to please anyone."

The fog-spirit thanked her sweetly and carried the pebble back to a little hollow between the roots of a great oak tree, and he used some leaves to build a little tent for himself, and he put the pebble just outside, where the moonlight was sure to fall on it. The next day, the pebble seemed to have gotten a little lighter, and it gleamed a little if you squinted at it. Then the day after that, the pebble was as white as milk, so white that when the sun shone on it, the whiteness hurt to look at. Then the day after that, the pebble was a beautiful silvery color, and it glowed faintly, just like the moons. The fog-spirit covered it up with leaves and hid it under the root of the oak tree, just in case.

Then he went to meet with the stoneman and his wife.

"We will have a contest," said the stoneman to the fog-spirit. "And it will be in three parts."

"Yes," said the fog-spirit.

"Running," said the stoneman. "Whoever can get from the top of the mountain to the water quicker."

"I see," said the fog-spirit. "And weaving! Whoever can weave the finer cloth in a day."

"Naturally," said the stoneman. "And for the third, we will have our judge decide, so it is impartial." The stoneman liked to fancy himself a very fair-minded sort of person.

"Nothing to it," said the fog-spirit. "Shall we start tomorrow?"

"If you like," said the stoneman. "Good-bye."

The fog-spirit left in a tizzy, but he was so shaken up and nervous that he stopped outside the door of their house and rested against the wall. His little heart was going so fast!

That was when he heard what the stoneman was saying to his wife: "Once we have the pearl, we can calm the waters whenever we like and row across the fjord. I rather think we could put in some nets and scoop out all the sea folk—if we own the land on either side, then the fjord is naturally ours as well, and the sea-people aren't paying rent."

"A wise insight, my husband!" said the stonewoman. "I don't like the idea of those layabouts in our waters, eating our fish."

"Just so," said the stoneman.

Well, the fog-spirit knew something about what it was like to have one's home wrenched away, so he flew down to the water and shouted for the sea-woman and heaved pebbles into the water until she came and asked him what was wrong *now*.

And he told her all he had heard, and she got very solemn and nodded. "Well, if you say so, then I believe you. I wouldn't like to be made to leave. Well! I suppose I'll have to help you after all, then."

"You needn't," said the fog-spirit. "But you helped me with the pearl, so I wanted to help you in return, somehow, by warning you."

"You can help us best by winning your contests," said the sea-woman. "That pearl isn't magical at all, but it won't stop these people once they've gotten an idea like that in their heads. What will you do about running?"

"Lose!" cried the fog-spirit. "How can I win when his legs are so much longer than mine?"

"Well, can you be sure of winning the other two?"

The fog-spirit thought and thought about this—he was a good weaver, but perhaps the stoneman was better. And who knows what the third contest would be? The sea-woman sank down into the water until only her eyes and forehead were above the surface, and she waited.

"I don't know," said the fog-spirit.

She bobbed back up to speak. "Here is what you should do, then. Suggest a fishing contest. The stoneman loves to fish, but we will drive all the fish to your nets and you will win. As for the weaving, surely you must weave beautifully. I have seen the fogs you've laid out over the bay in autumn."

"Perhaps," said the fog-spirit.

"Then all is not yet lost. And, well, if you lose, there are other fjords and other mountains."

"And other stonemen who own the other mountains," grumbled the fog-spirit.

"Perhaps," said the sea-woman, and vanished with a splash.

The next day the fog-spirit stuffed the pearl into his pouch with all the little scraps of fog he'd been able to find, and he went to meet with the stoneman. The stoneman brought them to a very old tree and said that the tree was to be the judge of their contests.

"Hrmmmmmmmmm," said the tree.

"I won't have it be said that I didn't choose a fair judge," said the stoneman, very proud. "I chose fairly, you see, because I am not at all afraid of you."

"Yes, I see," said the fog-spirit.

"First, show me the pearl, so I can be sure that you are playing fairly too."

The fog-spirit lifted the flap of his little bag and showed the pearl, and the stoneman nodded.

"We will go to the top of the mountain and run down to the tree. Agreed?"

"I suppose," said the fog-spirit. The stoneman laughed and sprinted away up the mountain, and the fog-spirit took his little scraps of fog and blew into them again, so he flew—*whoosh!*—up after the stoneman, just like a dandelion puff.

The stoneman had been waiting for a long while by the time the fog-spirit made it to the peak. "Are you ready?" he said.

"I suppose," said the fog-spirit.

The stoneman dashed away down the mountain, and the fog-spirit followed, trying not to cry.

By the time he made it back down to the tree, the stoneman was agog. "You're so slow! It took you ages!"

"I didn't need to rush," said the fog-spirit, hiding a sniffle.

"Very wise," said the tree. "Rushing grows weak roots."

"The next contest, the next contest!" said the stoneman.

"First," said the tree, "a rest. The sun is pleasant today, and the shade is cool. And the fog-spirit hasn't caught his breath yet."

The stoneman grumbled, but he sat in the shade by the tree's roots and uncorked a bottle of something.

"Hrrrmmmm?" said the tree. "What's that? It smells wonderful."

"Mead," said the stoneman. "Would you like some?"

The tree agreed, and the stoneman poured a little out on the tree's roots. "Don't be impolite," said the tree. "Oughtn't you offer some to the fog-spirit?"

"I—yes, of course!" the stoneman stammered, a little taken aback. "I'll give him a whole bottle if he wants, my best vintage, too!"

The fog-spirit blushed and fidgeted his hands and shook his head. "A mere thimbleful would suffice," he said, after he'd taken a few minutes to collect himself. "It seems right we should all have a drink."

"Yes, of course, yes," said the stoneman, who was not collected at all. He took a hearty swig from the bottle, and splashed a little more on the roots of the tree, and then looked down at the fog-spirit and frowned. The fog-spirit whisked out his little pouch and weaved a scrap of fog into a cup, and the stoneman carefully trickled mead into it.

"A fine vintage indeed," said the fog-spirit. "Come, let's drink again." And they did.

"A very fine vintage, hrmmmmmmmmm," said the tree. "Perhaps just one more round." And so it was.

The fog-spirit and the stoneman were both a little wobbly by the time the tree said, "Hrrrrmmmmm, the next challenge. You must weave. Whoever's cloth is the finest shall be the winner."

Well, the fog-spirit had been planning on weaving a cloth of fog scraps, but when he settled down at his loom, he found that his little pouch of scraps was entirely empty.

He cried out in horror and dismay, but neither the tree
nor the stoneman could hear him over the sound of the
stoneman's shuttle already clicking back and forth and the
beater thumping down and the heddles rattling as they rose
and fell.

The fog-spirit cast about frantically and cursed his
senses for being so drowsy and slow with the mead—ah!
His eyes landed on the bottle. With a huge effort he tipped
it over, and it sloshed into a deep-gold puddle by his little
loom.

He pulled the heady vapors into a long strand, and he
made it into something much *like* fog, though it was slicker
and silkier and the color of sunlight glistening in stagnant
brown forest ponds, and he began to weave it into cloth.
The mead-fog was slippery and difficult to work, and it
twisted and squirmed, nothing like the friendly, downy
softness of his usual fog.

When the tree called time, the fog-spirit removed his
cloth from his loom, a length of shimmering pale gold that
ran through his hands like water when he touched it, but
floated in the air when he let it billow.

The stoneman had woven a piece of linen, fine though
it was, sheer enough for a bride's wedding sleeves and soft
enough to swaddle a baby. It was an excellent piece of cloth,
but when the fog-spirit unrolled his mead-fog cloth over
the roots of the tree, they all fell silent until the only sound
was the chirping of the birds in the tree's branches.

"Hrmmmmmmm," said the tree, marveling. "As
uncontested as your victory in the race, stoneman, the
weaving contest is an uncontested victory for the fog-spirit."

"Yes," said the stoneman, staring wide-eyed at the mead-cloth. "What will our third contest be?"

"Perhaps fishing," squeaked the fog-spirit.

"Hrrmmmmmm," said the tree. "I will decide. Tomorrow morning. We mustn't rush this kind of decision."

The next morning the tree said, "I have been thinking about the contest, hrrrrrm, and I have pondered that fishing is not very fair. The fog-spirit is very small, no bigger than a fish himself, and the stoneman is very large, as large as I am, hrrrrmm. It is not a fair contest. I have decided we will do something else."

The fog-spirit was very alarmed, and he thought of the sea-woman, but then he saw that the stoneman was also alarmed, and that helped a little.

"I will ask you riddles," said the tree. The stoneman and the fog-spirit both fidgeted, for neither of them was particularly good at riddling. The tree said:

> *"A veil in the morning,*
> *it creeps along at gloaming."*

("Usually," Ylfing said, dropping his storyteller voice, "when you're telling this story to children, you pause here and let them try to guess the answer, and whatever they say, you reply, 'Which is just what the stoneman said' or 'Just what the fog-spirit guessed,' and if it's right you continue on, and if it's wrong you say that the tree said no, and you let them keep guessing until they get it right, and you give them hints if they can't think of it, and you keep track secretly of how many riddles you have awarded to which character, because of course the fog-spirit has to win in the end. But um. Well. I'll just have to tell you the answers.")

"Fog," said the fog-spirit.

"Yes. Next:

> Turns the sword, turns the spear.
> Does not see and cannot hear.
> Falls unharmed, lands unbroken,
> Holds its secrets all unspoken."

"Stone," said the stoneman.

"Yes. Next: *A dozen arms, a hundred hands, a thousand fingers, hidden feet.*"

The two were silent for a long time, until the fog-spirit tentatively offered, "Tree?"

> "Runs fast and forever until it lies still
> One mouthful could save; one mouthful could kill."

"Water," said the stoneman.

"*A magic bowl of many colors, dry and wet by turns.*"

"Sky," said the fog-spirit.

> "Fair lady of flowers stepping fresh from the thaw,
> Pointed ahead and gasped when she saw,
> 'The end! My end!' But she could not retreat.
> 'Why must you end me each time that we meet?'"

"Summer," said the stoneman.

"*Ancient men, white-haired, garbed in green, and silent, the ocean laps at their feet.*"

"Mountains," said the fog-spirit.

"*The beast untamed ravages village and wilderness. At home, it curls tame in its bed, it eats from your hand, it fends off the wolves of winter.*"

"Fire," said the stoneman.

> "*A box, a cave, a house, a field*
> *The cool smell of dirt that's freshly been tilled.*
> *Hands, voice, smells, and heart*
> *Without these it dies, but remains when we part.*"

"Home," said the fog-spirit.

("*Of course you can go on as long as you like,*" Ylfing said. "*Or cut it shorter if the children get bored, or if they're very small. And it doesn't have to be these riddles. Any will do.*")

"Hrmmmm," said the tree. "It seems the fog-spirit has won."

The stoneman harrumphed, but it was beneath his dignity to be a poor loser, and the fog-spirit *had* shown himself the finer riddle-guesser. "I will grant you your homestead," he said.

"And no rent!" cried the fog-spirit. "The tree must witness."

The stoneman grumbled again. "No rent for this year," he said. "And next year, we will compete again."

"Every year?" said the tree. "Hrmmmm, surely you can afford to be kinder than that. The fog-spirit is quite busy with his work, and you have your own business to attend to. Let it be every other year."

And so they agreed, and every other year, the fog-spirit and the stoneman met by the tree and exchanged gifts and measured their skills against each other. And some years the fog-spirit lost, but the stoneman, with his big stone brain, had very little time to bother with small things, and he never remembered to collect his rent.

Over time, other stonemen and other spirits joined in. When humans came to that place, the stonemen left for the far northern ice fields. But those humans were the Hrefni, and they maintained the contests every other year to honor the spirits of the land. In time, the contest became the manner of choosing the leader of all the villages, the jarl. And that is how the Jarlsmoot came to be.

I just lay there as he talked, obviously, and didn't say anything. It was fine. I was fine.

———◆———

Ylfing cared for me constantly for the next few days while he and Consanza's family packed and prepared to set out—he fed me soup and gruel and soft-boiled eggs with new bread smeared with butter. I stayed as catatonic as I could—the damn child was with me almost every moment of the day, and he simply would *not* leave me be! I'd been thinking that I would be left to my own devices in isolation, as I had been for months, but no. Apparently, when you're a severe invalid, you get company for every waking moment.

He brought visitors to me from time to time, and talked like he could fill up my silence with words and bring me back to myself. Nine-Fingers deigned to play cards with him a few times, and he yammered on at great length about the games he used to play as a child in Hrefnesholt. Taishineya Tarmos did not visit.

He brought Consanza to see me. That was the worst. The two of them sat there gossiping, as they must have done when they were alone by themselves, before everything happened. Except that Consanza kept shooting me these looks out of the corner of her eye. "Does he know where he is?" she asked. "Does he know who he is?"

Ylfing's aggressively chipper mask slipped a little, and I caught a glimpse of a haunting sorrow before he yanked the wall back up. "I don't know," he said airily.

"Chant?" Consanza said, leaning forward and resting her elbows on her knees. "You in there, grandfather?" Nothing, obviously. She had a very strange look on her face, and she straightened her back and rummaged through her pockets—a new pipe, I saw, and a new tobacco pouch, and what I assumed was new tobacco, too. I thought her hands might be trembling a little as she packed in the leaf and lit it. "That's *disturbing*," she said, quiet and intense. "The way his eyes are so dead. The way he looks at you but he's not looking at you." She shivered and cradled the pipe close to her mouth with both hands, as if she was shielding herself. "Is he going to get any better?"

Ylfing's mask flagged again, briefly. "I don't know."

"Where are you going to take him?"

Another flicker, this one longer. "I don't know."

"But you're leaving with us, aren't you?"

He nodded, sniffled.

"Ylfing . . ."

And I had to watch as he buried his face in his hands and wept. Consanza got up, set her pipe on her chair, and wrapped her arms around him. She had proper robes again, with sleeves so voluminous they engulfed Ylfing like wings. He put his head on her shoulder and sobbed, and she hushed him, and stroked his hair, and rocked him a little back and forth. "Sweet boy, sweet boy," she called him. "You're so young for this."

"It all happened so fast," Ylfing gasped, between wrenching, racking sobs. "He was fine one day, and then I had to watch him choose to *die*, I had to watch him burn himself out just so that we'd be able to leave, and now—now I have to stay with him."

She tucked his head under her chin and tightened her arms around him. "Sweet boy. He's family, isn't he?" Ylfing nodded, sniffled wetly. "You have to take care of yourself, too, sweet boy. Remember that, all right? It's okay to get out for a while and have time to yourself. It doesn't make you a bad person. It makes you a *good* person, actually, because then you won't run out of energy and you'll be able to continue taking good care of him. Right?"

Ylfing gulped a few breaths, nodded again.

"Now, I hear I'm being appointed the Nuryeven ambassador to Echaree, which isn't really what I planned for my life. Some glamour, I suppose, but too much actual work."

"You're going to be really good at it," Ylfing said, as if his heart was breaking. "It's an appointment from the gods, and you're going to be amazing at it. I'm going to miss you—*so much*."

"Well, that's the thing," she said. "I'm taking my whole household with me to Echaree, and if you're going to be traveling a ways with us anyway . . . I was going to ask you if you'd like to stay on as my assistant." *What?* I thought, and had to stomp down any visible reaction on my face. That presumptuous bitch. I always knew she was going to try to steal him from me. "You can stay as long as you want—you've been a good help, and I daresay there's going to be a disgusting amount of paperwork in Echaree." She sighed. "And you know the language, don't you?"

"Some," said Ylfing. "I'm not that great at it." He wasn't being modest. The Hrefni are always exactly accurate and honest in their assessment of their skills.

"And you have some training in . . . how did Chant describe it? The way people are?"

"I'm just an apprentice," he said quietly. He hadn't unburied his face from her shoulder.

"But it would give you something to do while you're waiting to see if he improves. And then I could pay you, so you'd have a little money when you left."

"Chant never needed money when we were traveling."

"Chant might not have, but Ylfing might. It's a useful thing to have." I mentally rolled my eyes. Look at that woman trying to foist the hallucination off on my apprentice. "You can come as part of my household. And . . . Would you like me to invite Ivo? He's an excellent scribe, and I might be able to persuade Taishineya Tarmos to let me add him to the payroll. She can find another secretary, and he doesn't seem like he enjoys working with her very much."

Ylfing paused. *Don't do it*, I thought at him hard. *Don't do it. I'm going to make a miraculous recovery the second we step over the border.* "No. He loves Nuryevet. He wouldn't leave. And his whole family is here, his friends. . . ." He didn't say the rest. He knew Ivo wouldn't have come away if he'd asked. Ivo was not at all the Chanting sort.

"I thought he might be a comfort to you," Consanza said. "But . . . I noticed you haven't seen him in a while."

"Busy," Ylfing said. "That's all. Just busy."

Consanza stroked the boy's hair once more and guided him off her shoulder and into one of the chairs. I stared at the wall and drooled down my front. "The invitation for you and Chant stands. You have your freedom. You can leave whenever you like. But I'd love to have you with me, and so would my spouses and the children."

Ylfing nodded. "Can I think about it?"

"Certainly. Her Majesty wants me on my way in the next couple days."

"I can decide by then. There's nothing to pack."

She leaned down and kissed the top of his head. "Take some time for yourself before then, all right?"

"I just don't want to leave him on his own. . . ."

No! I cried out mentally. *Leave me on my own! Listen to the uppity twit!*

"Helena seems to like him, for some inexplicable reason. I could ask her if she'd be willing to sit with him for a few hours."

Helena wasn't the worst option. But damn it, Ylfing, not every moment had to be supervised. I longed to stretch my legs, but I didn't dare to show that much strength and initiative yet. If Ylfing helped me to my feet, I would stand, and if he led me I would shuffle along after him. But show enough impetus to do it myself? Not yet. Far too soon.

———

Ylfing accepted Consanza's invitation, as you already know. I didn't mind—meant he didn't have to do any of the planning, or lay in supplies and rations. All he had to do was gather up a bundle of some things we needed for ourselves, and show up with me at the carriage. Did more than that, as it turned out—he ended up leaving me alone for a few hours with Helena, who sat quietly with me and read a book aloud. I didn't listen to her. Ylfing came back in the evening, his eyes puffy and red, carrying several paper parcels—woolen hats and mittens, thick socks, secondhand cloaks, and a pair of new fur-lined boots for me. These ones I'm wearing now, in fact. They're the second-best pair of shoes I've ever owned, wonderfully soft. It's like walking on morning fog, the kind that seeps up from the ground right when spring is beginning to stir within the earth. Second-best shoes ever. Maybe these won't get nicked off me by street urchins, like those wonderful turn-toe boots I had in Map Sut.

Ylfing sniffled as he was unwrapping all the things. Would have asked him about it but . . . well, I had the act to keep up. He told me anyway, as I knew he would.

"I went to Ivo's apartment," he whispered. "I was going to—to pay him back the rest of the money I'd borrowed." Ylfing swallowed hard and scrubbed the tears off his face. "I was going to say good-bye. I didn't think he'd care that I was going, but I wanted to say it for me. He, um . . ." He took a huge breath, let it out in a long, slow stream. "There was, um." He couldn't get the words out. "There was someone else there with him. A, um. A gentleman caller. He was just leaving when I got there. It was . . . really early this morning." Another long, shaky breath. "I was just across the street when Ivo was show-ing him out, and they were holding hands and . . . they . . . um. They looked cozy." He bit his lip. "Then Ivo saw me across the street and he was . . . Well, you could tell he hadn't thought I'd see that. I went over, and he introduced me to the man, but I forgot his name. He left. Ivo and I had a fight right there on his doorstep, and I gave him his money, and I left. And that's all." A desperately sad little laugh. "That's it. It's all over."

Poor little mite, he's terribly young. Hasn't had his heart broken too often, you know. Hasn't learned how to love someone at arm's length, like a Chant has to. Regular folk, they'd wonder if you can really ever love someone like that. There's plenty who do—monks, nuns, mothers. It's not about keeping them out of your heart. It's knowing that you can't keep them, and they can't keep you. You love them like their heart is a bird in your hand. You hold it so gently, and

you cherish it while you have it, you are filled with the wonder of it—
and then they flutter their wings, and you open your hands and let
them fly. And you don't begrudge them their flight, because you held
them for a few warm moments, and how often is it that that happens?

Anyway, he sobbed for a while, and I drooled, and he fed me
dinner, and I let most of it dribble out of my mouth, and he never lost
his patience with me once. Ylfing has a heart as big as the world, you
know. And I have walked back and forth all my life, from one end of
this world to the other, so I know exactly how big it is, better than
most anyone else.

We were to head southwest over land; the late-winter storms
were coming up by then and the harbor was locked in ice. We had
a small caravan of carriages, with their wheels locked and mounted
onto sleds so they could skim over the snow and frozen ground, and
we had horses to pull them, a motley set of the most mismatched
beasts you've ever seen. Well, I suppose you have seen them, actually,
come to think of it. You know horses better than I do—they're not
very good, are they? No, I didn't think so. They're built for a purpose,
though, which is pulling things over snow and through drifts. Heavy,
ugly things, I thought. Nothing like yours. *Those* horses couldn't
dance down an avalanche like yours did.

The ride down was so boring that there were several times
I almost forgot myself and spoke. And I think I wasn't dribbling
enough, because Ylfing started talking to me less like I was a complete
imbecile. It was just so cold, the drool on my face froze into my beard
every time someone opened a door. So I gave up on that right quick,
as you can imagine.

There were two carriages for Consanza and her family, and two
more for the retinue and staff that were naturally required by the
ambassador's office, and a *fifth* carriage, which was exclusively for

hauling the paperwork they'd need along the way. Damn Nuryevens can't take a piss without filing a form in triplicate.

It was a dead quiet journey, as I just said, for the first three days. Utterly nothing happened.

And then one afternoon, we came upon three blackwitches.

———————

The whole caravan came to a halt, and the Nuryevens clustered all the wagons as close as they could and then wandered around between them, muttering or peeking out to look at those three still figures standing off in the middle of the field. People came to tell Consanza everything, of course, since she was the most important person present. We were all frozen in fear, unwilling to move any closer to the blackwitches in order to pass them.

But we stood there in the snow for an hour, then two, with the Nuryevens muttering more and more darkly, and Consanza and Helena holding each other ever more tightly. Velizar ran up from the other carriage to check on us; Consanza snarled at him to go back and take more of the guards with him to protect the carriage that held the children. I sat there and tried to look neutral, tried not to shake myself right out of my boots. I couldn't do anything or say anything. I just had to sit there and drool.

But Ylfing had never seen the blackwitches like I had. I think he still thought they were half fairy tale. His curiosity was piqued, so he bundled his scarf around his head and neck, and pulled his cloak around him, and went out.

"Wait," Consanza said, and looked him up and down. She made him open his cloak, and then she pursed her lips. "Keep it closed tight. *Tight*, you hear?" And then she snatched away his mittens and gave him a pair of her own.

"Um?" said Ylfing. "Yes, I was planning to. The snow and everything."

Consanza grabbed his chin in her hands and looked fiercely into his eyes. "Do *not* open your cloak. And stay well back from them. *Well* back."

Ylfing nodded solemnly and hopped out of the carriage, wading through the thigh-deep snow to the front of the caravan. I tried not to fidget, but he returned soon enough. He climbed back in, shaking off the snow, and settled himself again beside me. He was trembling and pale.

"Did you see them?" Consanza demanded.

"What? I . . . I saw *something*," Ylfing said. "I don't know what a blackwitch looks like, but . . . they were certainly people, and they were certainly wearing black. I think I—" He cut himself off, shook his head.

"Mmmm," Consanza said, brows knotted, and pulled out her pipe. She packed the bowl with a tiny amount of leaf, just enough for a puff or two, and lit it.

"The guards seem very concerned," Ylfing said.

"Good," said Helena, who was riding with us.

After a long pause, Ylfing said, "Why'd you take my mittens?"

Consanza sucked her pipe at him and breathed out a slow, thin stream of smoke. "They were green."

Ylfing looked down at the ones she'd given him in return. They were made of undyed yarn, naturally charcoal gray. "Is that bad, if you see a blackwitch?"

"Only sometimes," said Consanza. "They don't like color, or so it's said. Dark hues, or dull, muddy ones—those just irritate them. Make them itchy, like someone who gets sick on shellfish. Bright ones . . . Depends on the blackwitch. A lot depends on the blackwitch."

"Some people become blackwitches when they die," said Helena. "They creep around, curse people, steal things, frighten livestock. As time goes on, it's like they lose their minds. Growing up, I had a friend whose father was a farmer, and one day he went into the barn to milk the cow and there was a blackwitch just standing there. Just standing there in the middle of the barn with its hands at its sides. And he froze, because it wasn't looking at him, and of course he didn't want it to. And it didn't move at all, except it opened its mouth and sort of . . . made this soft noise in its throat, like a creaking door or a yowling cat. Made the hair stand up on the back of his neck, and he ran back to the house and got a shovel out of the garden shed and came back to kill it, but it was gone by then, and the cow never gave milk again."

Started thinking again about what got me into this whole mess— it's been so long, I hardly remember the details. Let's just say there was a sick goat that I saw somewhere, and I happened to have some herbs, and there might have been a woman who was a little startled to see me.

And, come to think of it, I believe I remember I was wearing clothes that were likely pretty grimy and grayish by then. It had been quite a while between towns, and there's not much point in paying for a launderer when you can just do it yourself in a river. But all the rivers we'd passed were slow and silty.

Helena went on, heedless: "I guess the one my friend's father saw must not have been one that was quite so bad. Or maybe it just wasn't as far gone—they get worse the more magic they use, that's what everyone says, but no one knows for sure. Some of them are like animals—they tear open rabbits and mice with their teeth and eat them raw, and they'd tear you open too if you angered them, or if your clothes were too bright. And some of them—some of them look just like real people. They can even talk. Those are the ones that come up in stories."

"No one ever bothered to tell us any stories about blackwitches," Ylfing said.

"Well, no," Helena said, uncomfortably. "You wouldn't want to talk about them, would you?"

Like drawing Shuggwa's Eye, I thought at Ylfing, as hard as I could.

"They might come for you if you did?" Ylfing said.

Helena shrugged and tilted just a little bit closer to Consanza, who blew out her second stream of smoke and laced her fingers with Helena's. "They might," Helena said tightly. "Best not to risk it."

Ylfing nodded and glanced at the carriage door. "You know," he said softly. "There already are blackwitches outside. And we know they're the . . . the kind to stand in one place and make that noise. So they're not as bad as they could be, and they're just off in the snow by themselves, off to one side of the road." He paused. "So . . . would now be an all right time to tell me one of the stories? They don't seem . . . feral."

Helena and Consanza shared a look, and Consanza squeezed her hand. Helena took a deep breath.

THE SIXTEENTH TALE:
The Blackwitch and the Farmer
You will know the blackwitch by the drabness of its garb (because it cannot stand to touch color or see it), and by its black cat-skin boots (because it has no heart, and so it lusts to kill soft things), and by its broad-brimmed hat (because it will not abide the touch of sun or moonlight).

Once, a blackwitch came to a farm on a cold, crisp autumn night with no moons. When it knocked, the farmer opened the door, and the blackwitch raised its eyes and said, "I am a traveler all alone, and I beg leave to sleep in your hayloft tonight, and in return I will give you a magic

token that you can bury in your field, and all your crops
will grow as huge as your wife's belly is now."

*(Here Helena paused and bit her lip and looked as if she wanted to unsay
it, to twist the metaphor. She rubbed her own huge belly; Consanza's knotted brows tightened still further and she squeezed Helena's hand.)*

The farmer was frightened out of his wits, and he
wondered how the blackwitch knew about his wife, for
her pregnancy had been difficult and the midwife had
prescribed her strict bed-rest for several weeks now; she
had not stepped foot outside the house. But the farmer
thought that the only thing worse than allowing the
blackwitch to stay in the hayloft would be to refuse.

The blackwitch bowed, and the next morning the
hayloft had nothing in it but hay, and there was a little
wooden disk lying on the front step, with strange markings
burned into it. The farmer picked it up, and put it with the
seeds for spring, and poured a little milk into the cup before
the icon of Brevo in their kitchen, and prayed that no
blackwitch would ever darken their doorstep again.

A week later the blackwitch came back, and it was pale,
and it had grave dirt beneath its fingernails, and its breath
rattled in its throat like someone dying of sickness, and it
begged leave to sleep in the stable with the horses, and it
promised a token that, hung with the cows, would make
them give rivers of milk, and the farmer thought that the
only thing worse than allowing this would be to refuse. And
in the morning, there was a little wooden disk with strange
markings on the doorstep. He hung it in his barn, as he'd

been instructed, and the cows' udders did indeed give rivers and rivers of milk.

A week later the blackwitch came back, and its eyes were glassy and reflected the firelight oddly, and its black clothes looked wet and sticky, and its teeth were yellowed. And it asked to sleep by the fireside in the kitchen, and in return it would give the farmer a token that his wife could wear around her neck, which would protect her in childbirth, and each baby could wear when it was born and be protected from illness until it could walk—and if the blackwitch had offered this two weeks before, the farmer might have allowed it. But his wife was cheerful and energetic lately, not sickly at all, and she had already borne three children safely. . . .

So the farmer said that the blackwitch was welcome to sleep with the animals again, no payment needed.

And in the morning the midwife came to visit, and the farm was silent, and there were rivers of blood running out of the barn door, and blood running out from under the threshold of the house, and when she ran inside, she found the whole family torn to pieces, and the blackwitch crouched over the farmer's wife's belly, and—

Helena stopped quite abruptly, as pale as death herself, and I don't think anyone really wanted her to continue.

Well.

Well!

If I hadn't been pretending to be catatonic, I would have caught her up in my arms and kissed both her cheeks. Every last rock in this godforsaken country can go straight to hell—but Helena, though! A garland of blessings for Helena. What a story! What a delight, to hear such a story told so well, and a story I've never heard before, to boot!

I'll stop myself now, otherwise I'll sit here crowing about the wonder of Helena until the sun falls from the sky and the moons crack in half.

The guards eventually gathered enough of their courage to stop wringing their hands—or possibly they'd been worrying themselves ragged, finally ran out of patience for their own terror, and decided that the options were as follows: that they could die standing still when the blackwitches inevitably turned on them, that they could have a staring contest with the damn things and see who froze to death first, or that they could at least *try* to slink past them and hope that they didn't take notice.

I got just a glimpse of them as we went by—I said before that the Kaskeen don't have magic, and that's true. But because we don't have it, we can feel it when it's about. You know how a cook can grab a hot pan without flinching, when anyone else would drop it, howling? It's like that. Or like a tanner who stops smelling the filth a year or two into his apprenticeship. Nuryevens have lived with their land's particular flavor of magic all their lives; their senses are dulled to it. But me, I can feel the heat when I grab the pan, and I can smell the filth—but magic usually doesn't feel that vile.

The blackwitches did, though. They must have been thirty or forty feet off the road, but when I saw them, my teeth itched and my fingernails felt sore and it felt like there was just one single fly crawling around the inside of my eyelids. It was like what I'd sensed that night the blackwitch and the Weavers came to my cell to kidnap me, but so much worse. Ten times worse. Vile magic, and no good could possibly come of it.

I was glad to be past them. We all were.

The whole caravan was on edge the rest of that day, and the next, and we were just starting to unwind the day after *that* when, to everyone's surprise, we were overtaken by that marauding party of your riders, led by Temay Batai. Your niece, isn't she?

I'm surprised that there were only three deaths, to be honest. Fortunately, most of the Nuryevens fell into the snow and started begging for their lives, because a ferocious band of horse demons was just too much to bear after the ordeal of getting past the blackwitches. Consanza and her spouses all went ashen and tried to hide the children. Helena, though! Again, Helena! What a champion she was—she must have taken her own story to heart, because she was armed to the teeth! She was full ready to fling herself out a door and start hamstringing any horse or rider in reach, pregnant or no. If I were riding through hostile territory again, she's the first person I'd want with me.

What a jewel. Another heart as big as the world, I think. I can cast aspersions on Consanza all day and well into the night, just as I have been doing, but by the stars and moons above us, I simply cannot find fault with her taste in women.

Of course, the second I saw that it was who it was, I flung myself out of the carriage and started singing the "Song of the Two Firesides," just as loud as I could. My voice croaked and creaked with disuse, and I nearly got skewered by a couple javelins before the riders near me heard and came to a blundering halt. It took a second or two for them to get their wits about them and collect their jaws from the ground where they'd dropped them, and then they cried out in loud voices and sang the descant back to me just like I was long-lost family, and it rang along the caravan and brought tears to my eyes, I'm not too proud to admit.

"Honored elder!" someone bawled at me, tumbling off her horse and catching me up in her arms. I hadn't the foggiest idea who she was, but she kissed my hands, so I patted her beautiful brown cheeks and clucked at her for getting all wind-chapped, which made her beam with joy, and then there were others crowding around too, just as if I were their own grandfather back from a long journey.

I explained what had happened, then, and exactly who I was, and they explained they were a scouting party and they'd been nearly as startled to see us as we were to see them, and we all agreed that the thing to do would be to rejoin you as quick as we could, me and Ylfing and as many of the Nuryevens as would like to come along.

I grabbed Temay Batai's hands when she came riding up—I could tell she didn't recognize me, because she called me *honored elder* instead of *oathsworn-uncle*, but I wasn't at all offended. I suppose the last time I saw her, she was about knee-high to a jerboa and still had to be strapped onto her horse. But I introduced myself again properly, and I scolded her for the scuffs on her stirrups, which pleased her deeply.

We yammered away for a while about this and that, and made plans for the journey back to the main camp, and I was so thrilled that it took me a while to get around to turning back to the carriage.

And then I did.

And there was Ylfing, sobbing his eyes out, crying so hard that the tears didn't even have time to freeze on his cheeks. He'd shot out of the carriage after me and promptly tripped on his own feet. Don't know what he thought his poor invalid master was doing, but as soon as I started singing . . .

Well, it was a big emotional mess, the next few hours. Ylfing couldn't even stand up, he just curled up in the snow where he'd fallen and *bawled*, and I tried to explain myself to him, in between trying to explain to Consanza and the Nuryevens what had happened and why we didn't have to worry about being slaughtered unless someone did something stupid like leap at one of the Umakh with drawn steel.

You know, your people have this funny way about them. I suppose it's obvious to you, but I don't know if you've ever realized what an interesting thing it is—as soon as they know you're a sworn kinsmen, it's as if they had never even considered killing you. One minute there was this storm of ferocious riders, weapons bloody, horses like war demons; the next moment the meekest, gentlest ponies you ever saw, and the riders—well, they're still holding bloody weapons, but it's with this natural, careless air, as if a bloody spear is as harmless as a bowl of milk. As if they had been caught with it by mistake, or they were just holding it for a friend. A complete transformation, in seconds! And you know, you people don't ever say, *Ah, sorry for the mistake, I didn't know you were kin.* It's as if the fact that they were about to kill us became *untrue* the moment they knew who we were. It's as if it never happened at all, as if it weren't even something that a person could consider possible. It's a sheerly delightful thing, and I quite love it.

Nuryevens are nothing like this—you can show them that you're a friend, but they still think you might stick a knife in their back if you get the chance. Took so long to calm this particular flock down that your people all dismounted and started setting up half-camp, lighting a bit of a fire and brewing tea from melted snow and mare's milk.

Ylfing wouldn't be comforted at all. Every time he caught a glimpse of me, he was wrecked again and went right back to sobbing. "Listen, you can stop," I said to him, a good dozen times. "I'm fine, see? It was all a story." But it was no good.

I gave up on him after a while. I know you people are a little dubious of men together, but I found the cutest boy rider of the lot and bullied him into taking tea and hot milk to Ylfing. Figured that'd cheer him up if nothing else would. That boy could fall in love with a *rock* if it had eyelashes to bat at him.

So then I had to explain to Consanza why the Umakh had ridden so far into the heart of the country, told her everything. You're supposed to tell your advocate everything, aren't you? She was furious with me, obviously, especially when I told her that I was going to tell you people to ride straight across the country, pretend to lose two battles, and then massacre the Nuryeven army at the ravine on the Athakosa Plain near Byerdor, the extremely, *extremely* poor tactical position I had talked the Nuryeven army into taking. I mean, hiding in the bottom of a ravine? Against an army on horseback with short-bows and magicians? This is my gift to you: you saved my life, and I hand you a country on a silver platter for you to do with as you please.

Consanza was upset with me about that, even after I had explained about Ivo and his friends, about how it had been their idea as much as it was mine—but of course she would be furious. She wasn't one of the people who had suffered, who had grown up suffering. She's lived in the city her whole life, she has an education that she didn't have to walk twenty or thirty or forty miles to get, she has a good job and so do all her spouses. There were things going wrong, and she knew about them. She'd had a chance to do something about the way things were, and she had been in a position where she *could* have done something about it . . . and she didn't. Because there was no glory in that, no glamour. Because it was too much like real work.

She shouted at me and stomped back and forth through the snow, and I told her that all the prophecies had been a lie, that she wasn't meant to be ambassador. I'd just said that so she and her family would be sent out of the city. I owed her a favor, you see, so I made her and her family safe. Debt paid.

Some of the Nuryevens ran off in the night, of course. They

know nothing about the plan. All they will say is that we were taken by raiders, and that there was a spy in our midst. I mean, if they're going to convict me of it, I might as well commit the crime.

And then the rest of it is what you already know. Your niece brought us here to you, escorted us for the rest of the journey. Consanza saw sense, once she'd cooled down a bit, particularly when I convinced her that you'd be needing an ambassador and a Nuryeven translator in the next few days. When she saw the size of your army, I think she was convinced then. How could a force like that lose against Taishineya Tarmos and her half-starved mongrels *lurking at the bottom of a ravine?* She's a horrible twit of a woman, but she's fairly savvy, I'll credit her that. Knows which way the wind's blowing. Knows how to pick her battles.

Ylfing cried and cried, and then he was just . . . *broken* for a few days. Followed me around like a lost puppy, all big sad eyes, like the miracle was about to end and I was about to collapse back into doddering imbecility at any moment. Then there was a day or two where he was angry at me—really angry, angry like I've never seen him before. I thought he was about to stomp off and leave me for good. I think he's forgiven me now. Just a story, I told him. Just a tall tale that I'd spun to save our skins, and if he had swallowed it the same as Taishineya Tarmos and the others, then what was there to be angry about? It meant it was a good story, didn't it? That it was truer than truth? It wasn't that I'd lied to him, it was just that . . . Well, a Chant looks at a story and can see the shape of it entire. It's not the same for us as it is for other folk—we don't get lost in the woods, because we have maps. I needed Ylfing lost. He couldn't know that he was part of it while it was happening. He said he felt like he'd been duped, said he felt like a fool. Said he'd thought that I trusted him. I *do* trust him, inasmuch as you can trust any seventeen-year-old boy. Wouldn't have kept him around as my apprentice if I didn't trust him. It's just that he *needed* to be lost in the woods with the rest of them to get that particular forest to work properly. Maybe there was another way out. I only did what I felt I had to.

And here we are. So that's that.

I don't know what you plan to do next. Nuryevet is weak and hungry and ready to fall—it could be yours if you want it. Smash their army at the Athakosa Plain ravine: stand at either end, line your archers up along the edges, and just shoot and shoot until they're all dead. Simple. Easy. You won't lose more than five or ten on your side, if you lose anyone at all.

Take the army's banners and ride southeast as hard as you can, and you'll come to Vsila. You'll know it when you see it. It's the biggest thing you'll have ever seen—as big as the winter Gathering of the Clans, or bigger. There's a city wall you'll have to get past, but that will be simple. Perhaps one of your wizards has a song to make it even more simple—otherwise, send word ahead to Ivo, and I daresay he and his friends will throw open the gates for you. Ylfing can tell you where to find him. Go into the city, and do whatever you feel you must. I daresay you know more about conquest than I do.

From there, you have options. You could go to the bank and fill your saddlebags with gold and silver and copper and ride home as rich as gods. Melt it down, make useful things out of it. Little silver bells for your horses and wizards, golden wind chimes to hang by the door of your tents . . .

Or you could go south to Enc and Cormerra, to Echaree and beyond. You're past the mountains that protected them. You could be rich in gold or you could be rich in land. Vsila has a very passable harbor, and they get trade. Keep a presence here and you could have the finest horses brought to you from anywhere your coin can reach—from Vinte, from Bramandon, from Calabog. I leave it up to you. I can see you're having some thoughts.

But you must excuse me now. I've been talking for *ages*, and my throat is as dry as the Sea of Sun. I'm going to go find one of your camp brewers, and I'm going to—oh, hell, I don't have anything to trade but stories. I guess I'll go talk someone *else's* ear off until they give me a drink or five. Surely I've got enough left in me for a fair deal.

Oh, and by the way—as soon as my hangover eases enough for me to walk in a straight line tomorrow, I'm grabbing Ylfing and we are getting out of this goddamn country with all speed.

May the Woman and the Horse protect you and grant you cunning, wisdom, knowledge, and all that. Now I'm off to drown myself in milk-beer.

Acknowledgments

A very long time ago and half the world away, there was a little girl who felt a story in her fingers.

Hello. Here we are, at last. I've been looking forward to meeting you here. Before we go any further, I want to say thank you. My whole life, since I felt that first story in my fingers, *you're* the one who has been at the center of things. You were never far from my mind when I was writing this book or the others. You, right there—yes, you, holding the book—you've always been the one who matters most.

Think of me reaching out and pressing your hands between mine when I say: Thank you. Thank you for letting me tell you this story.

I'm *so happy* we both made it this far.

There are, of course, dozens, if not hundreds, of people who helped me get here. I couldn't possibly recognize them all, but there are a particular few who have especially distinguished themselves. So thank you, also . . .

To Vihra's namesake, Veera Mäkelä, one of the softest and kindest and most full-of-thoughts people I know, whose friendship is summed up by our Facebook relationship status: "in cahoots."

To Ryan Boyd, my favorite swamp goblin and a dearly cherished treasure of my heart.

To Amie Kinch, a creature of pure fire—a hearth-flame and an inferno by turns—who read this book in one sitting and *believed*.

To Jennifer Mace and Freya Marske, both innocent flowers and the serpents under them.

To Grace Slater, who arrived at the dawn of all things and will be here at the end of them, though she may wander in the interim.

To DongWon Song, my brilliant, rock-steady agent, who always seems to know exactly the story I mean to tell, even when I'm stumbling around in the woods trying to find it myself. One day I will manage to surprise him, and I consider that aspiration a very worthy one.

To Navah Wolfe, the perfect editor for this book, who didn't let me get away with bullshitting anything, who is *so* intimidatingly cool, and whose vision and wisdom made the book better by several orders of magnitude. I might have forged the sword, but she and her whetstone put the edge on it. She made it from a pretty object into a beautiful weapon.

To every other person who laid hands on this story on its journey to being a Real Book out in the world. The incredible team at Saga and their care and expertise, precision, and talent has been nothing less than mindblowing. Jeannie Ng, the managing editor; Elizabeth Blake-Linn, the production manager; and Nicholas Sciacca, the jacket designer: Your work on this book awes and humbles me every day.

To every colleague and professional acquaintance who opened a door and invited me in from the cold, who introduced me to someone who then turned around and introduced me to someone else, in the long chain of serendipity that led me here, to this spot, to this moment, writing these words.

To every friend and family member and professor and bank teller and grocery cashier and stranger on the Internet who smiled and nodded and said, "Yes, you are," when I told them I was going to be an author one day, beginning at age thirteen until the present. "Yes," they said, as if they were agreeing that the sky was blue. "Yes. You are. Of course." Sometimes they believed even when I had lost faith.

And lastly . . . to my father, who raised me on stories and who would have *loved* this book. He was a storyteller himself, one of the best I've ever known, although I don't know that he would have thought of himself that way.

It takes a village to raise a child—or to write a book. I've had an incredible village, better than I sometimes think I deserve. I've gotten so lucky at every step of this journey, and there is no way I can adequately thank the people who need to be thanked . . . except by going out and telling another story, and striving, always striving, to make it even better than this one.

This book belongs to all of you. It belongs a little bit to everyone who loves it.

Thank you, thank you, thank you.

Turn the page for a sneak peek at

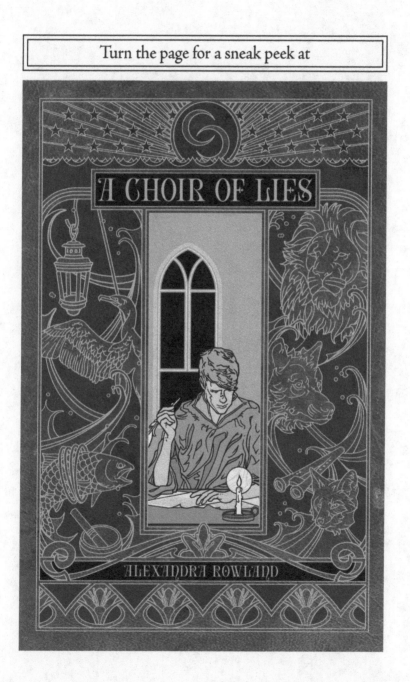

A CHOIR OF LIES

ALEXANDRA ROWLAND

All right . . . I suppose things like this usually start with an apology of some sort.

ONE

My former master-Chant thought we shouldn't write down the things we know. I don't know if he was right. I don't know if I agree. Rather, I don't agree entirely, but I don't disagree entirely either. I'm still exploring all my options. But one option must be to write a little down, because here I am, writing, even though I'm not really supposed to. The argument he gave was that mere ink and paper can be lost or destroyed or *taken* from you.

These won't get taken from me. These are mine, and I'll burn them up once I'm done with them. And anyway, if he cared so much about what I do, he shouldn't have—

I won't write it. I can't. ("Can't" here meaning both "I don't want to. I refuse to. I won't face it," and "If I *were* to face it, there would still be no language in the world with strong enough words to make myself understood. Whatever I wrote would be a work in translation, and it's just not linguistically possible.")

There's a kind of magic in writing down the things you know. It makes mere ink and paper into weapons. It makes them a mind, in a way: A paper copy of a mind with some of the mental abilities that its writer possessed—persuasion, or charm, or insidious destruction.

But paper can't think and ink can't adapt—they are an arrow shot into a foggy night by a blind man. At least this way, I know that there's no one in front of me, no one to be struck and killed by a stray bolt carelessly shot, and no witnesses. And even though there's no one to hear my words, no one to see what I'm doing, no one to care at all ... Sometimes, I'm going to lie, even here, when I'm all alone: I'm a Chant now myself, after all, and Chants are liars.[1]

But first, something true.

---

1   You little shit. I'd argue with you, but you've already proven your own point, haven't you? And not just a liar, but an oathbreaker (and in regards to that: Fuck you very much, thanks). Why am I even bothering with this? Why even waste the ink to call you a shit and an oathbreaker? You've already run off—at least you know how to abscond in the night like a proper Chant. It's not like you'll ever read anything I write here. It's not like you'd particularly care about it even if I did catch you. But ... Dammit, I'll have the last word, even if you aren't around to witness me getting it. The last word and the satisfaction of yelling at you the way I want to, and what does it matter that you won't ever hear me? You never heard me before, so it's really no different.

TWO

A truth: I wonder if it was right for me to become a Chant.

Another: I think it changed me. I think I'm different than I used to be.

Another: When I was becoming a Chant, finishing my apprenticeship officially, my master-Chant led me through the rites to sink my homeland beneath the waves and unname myself.[2] But I'm afraid, now, that I must not have meant it hard enough,[3] because I still feel like I have my name. I whisper it into the dark sometimes, and it feels like I'm breaking a tenet, though the tenets of the Chants are few and vague and abstract.[4]

Chants are—

They—

This is difficult.

Chants are storytellers, right? That's what I'm supposed to be doing. I'm supposed to be a collector and a curator.[5] The things humans make up are delicate when they're out in the wild. Stories

---

2   I don't even want to think about what that man told you were "the rites." It was horrific enough the first time I heard it. Can you really even use the word "led"?

3   Gods and fishes, every time you mention that man and what he did to you, I want to tear something apart. Of course you didn't mean it! How could you have meant it in those circumstances? You were *coerced*.

4   I rest my case. He didn't teach you anything. I *did* keep telling you.

5   NO!

and languages and secrets, they have a lifespan. If no one passes them on, then they die with the last living person to remember them. A Chant tries to—

They go around—

They learn stories, and they tell them to other people. And when an apprentice becomes a master-Chant in their own right, they give up their name and their homeland. They have to. There's no other option; they have to do it.[6] I think this is because . . .

Why, why is this so hard?

It's because you need to put yourself aside, if you're going to be a Chant. You have to be humble. You can't put too much of yourself into the stories you're telling; that's what my master told me. Because they're not *your* stories. You're just an empty vessel. So you have to keep yourself separate. I think that's why we unname ourselves.[7]

But people call me Chant now and I still think they're talking to *him*. My master-Chant. Chant isn't *me*.

This is a mess, isn't it? Everything in my head is a big tangled knot. I'm not doing a good job of this so far.

I always do this. It's my weakness—that's what my master-Chant used to say. I talk too much about things that aren't important, I babble, and I get sidetracked.

———◆◆◆———

There's no translation for what I'm thinking and feeling. Why can't I stop talking about him? Why do I have to keep carrying him around with me? Why can't I just *forget*? I don't want any of this anymore, I—*why aren't there words?* Why can't I just excise it like a surgeon

---

6   Your bias is showing.

7   Sort of? But not really. Why are you bothering to chatter about this? If this is your idea of explaining yourself, my patience is already wearing thin.

cutting out a tumor? Or exorcise it, more accurately—naming the evil thing to gain power over it and casting it into salt water to burn it away. Why can't I name it? Why isn't there a word that means the same thing as . . . I don't even have a metaphor to lay hands on.

"My heart scrubbed raw with steel wool." There, that will do. "Drowning on dry land, feeling like the water is about to close over my head at any moment, frantic and panicked and scared." Or even, "Lying down in the middle of a deserted road and crying and screaming until my throat bleeds." Or, "So much anger and hurt and anger and fear (and anger, and anger, and anger) that it chokes me, that it paralyzes me, that I fall down crying again because I *just—can't—do anything* with it, and there's nowhere to put it down, so I have to hold it in my heart, and there's no one to turn it against except myself—so settle in, self, and hang on."

<hr>

But all right. I have to get it out somehow, excised or exorcised. I have to put it somewhere besides my own heart, or it really will choke me. Sooner or later it's going to start getting literal. I can put it here on paper, and later maybe I'll throw the paper in the sea—good clean salt water to unmake my hurts from the world.

Let's see if I can pick all these knots apart and weave them into something shaped like a story. And I'm going to lie, because Chants are liars. I won't be able to help it. I'm going to lie on purpose, and I'm going to lie by accident, and it's going to feel better than the truth, sometimes, and I'm so, so tired of not feeling better.

I'm going to write down my real name here,[8] because it strains to burst from my lips and the tip of my pen like a flooding river of snowmelt in spring, and I want more than anything to take it back, to take *me* back, to go back to the way things were when I was . . . him. And I can't. It's done. It's over. It's lost to me, just like the ancient Chants lost their homeland and couldn't ever reclaim it. My name, too, has been erased from the world. That's the whole point of the rites, isn't it? It's to remember what they lost. It's supposed to feel like this.

Whenever I introduce myself now, I say, "Call me Chant."

But my name used to be ~~Ylfing~~.[9]

---

9   How *dare* you. What the hell are you *doing*? I won't stand for this. There—
I've scratched it out. One little thing I can do to save you from your folly.

SIX [19]

19   This section was also summarily thrown into the fire—you wouldn't mind that, though, would you? You were going to burn them yourself. It needed to be burnt, anyway; it was too depressing for words. That passage about how you woke up, a lone Chant for the first time, and began walking until you came to the first crossroads, whereupon you sat down and sobbed for an hour because you couldn't decide which way to go? Unbearable. I couldn't bear it. Might as well have slapped a title like "Nobody Loves Me" on it, you pathetic wretch. And by the pillars of the world, boy, it was like you didn't even notice that cart driver that passed was trying to help you—you could have hitched a ride and had company. But no, you take the other path to avoid the one person you met on the road and you mutter stories to the wind to make *yourself* feel better, as if writing them down wasn't bad enough. What other heresies are you going to confess to?

A PRINCE AND A PRINCESS MUST
WORK TOGETHER TO SAVE THEIR
KINGDOM FROM INVADERS . . .
AND FROM DANGERS WITHIN.

THE
MOUNTAIN
OF
KEPT
MEMORY

RACHEL
NEUMEIER

A GORGEOUS FANTASY IN THE SPIRIT OF
GUY GAVRIEL KAY AND ROBIN McKINLEY

PRINT AND EBOOK EDITIONS AVAILABLE
SAGAPRESS.COM

Step into a gorgeous new anthology of cross-genre fairy-tale retellings...

The Starlit Wood transforms eighteen stories you thought you knew and takes you on a journey at once unexpected and familiar across time, space, and amazing new worlds.

Featuring all new stories by
CHARLIE JANE ANDERS
ALIETTE DE BODARD
AMAL EL-MOHTAR
JEFFREY FORD
MAX GLADSTONE
THEODORA GOSS
DARYL GREGORY
KAT HOWARD
STEPHEN GRAHAM JONES
MARGO LANAGAN
MARJORIE LIU
SEANAN MCGUIRE
GARTH NIX
NAOMI NOVIK
SOFIA SAMATAR
KARIN TIDBECK
CATHERYNNE M. VALENTE
and GENEVIEVE VALENTINE

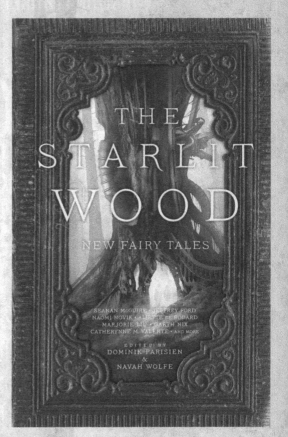

"A classy, smart, and entertaining volume of stories put together with consummate care— and featuring the best and most exciting fantasy writers working in the field today."

—JEFF VANDERMEER, *New York Times* bestselling author of the Southern Reach trilogy

"Lots of strange and wonderful goings-on in *The Starlit Wood*. Fairy tales you thought you'd left behind in childhood are back in some very poignant, sly, and original versions that will touch the Wow in most readers."

—JONATHAN CARROLL, World Fantasy Award–winning author

PRINT AND EBOOK EDITIONS AVAILABLE
SAGAPRESS.COM

STARRING:

Mary Jekyll, Diana Hyde, Catherine Moreau, Beatrice Rappaccini, and Justine Frankenstein!

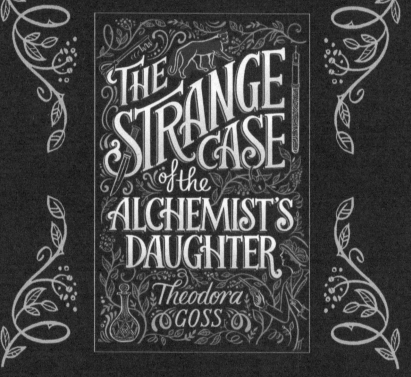

The daughters of literature's most famous mad scientists must come together to stop a murderer—and solve the mystery of their own creation.

PRINT AND EBOOK EDITIONS AVAILABLE
SAGAPRESS.COM

A GORGEOUS FANTASY IN THE SPIRIT OF PAN'S LABYRINTH AND NEIL GAIMAN'S THE GRAVEYARD BOOK.

PRINT AND EBOOK EDITIONS AVAILABLE
SAGAPRESS.COM

Printed in the USA
CPSIA information can be obtained
at www.ICGtesting.com
CBHW021128280524
9185CB00004B/235